ADVENTURE TIME ™

PRESENTS

MARCELINE
AND THE SCREAM QUEENS

ROSS RICHIE CEO & Founder • MATT GAGNON Editor-in-Chief • FILIP SABLIK President of Publishing & Marketing • STEPHEN CHRISTY President of Development • LANCE KREITER VP of Licensing & Merchandising
PHIL BARBARO VP of Finance • BRYCE CARLSON Managing Editor • MEL CAYLO Marketing Manager • SCOTT NEWMAN Production Design Manager • IRENE BRADISH Operations Manager
CHRISTINE DINH Brand Communications Manager • SIERRA HAHN Senior Editor • DAFNA PLEBAN Editor • SHANNON WATTERS Editor • ERIC HARBURN Editor • WHITNEY LEOPARD Associate Editor
JASMINE AMIRI Associate Editor • CHRIS ROSA Associate Editor • ALEX GALER Assistant Editor • CAMERON CHITTOCK Assistant Editor • MARY GUMPORT Assistant Editor • KELSEY DIETERICH Production Designer
JILLIAN CRAB Production Designer • MICHELLE ANKLEY Production Design Assistant • AARON FERRARA Operations Coordinator • ELIZABETH LOUGHRIDGE Accounting Coordinator
JOSÉ MEZA Sales Assistant • JAMES ARRIOLA Mailroom Assistant • STEPHANIE HOCUTT Marketing Assistant • SAM KUSEK Direct Market Representative • HILLARY LEVI Executive Assistant

ADVENTURE TIME: MARCELINE AND THE SCREAM QUEENS, March 2016. Published by KaBOOM!, a division of Boom Entertainment, Inc. ADVENTURE TIME, CARTOON NETWORK, the logos, and all related characters and elements are trademarks of and © Cartoon Network. (S16) Originally published in single magazine form as ADVENTURE TIME: MARCELINE AND THE SCREAM QUEENS No. 1-6. © Cartoon Network. (S12) All rights reserved. KaBOOM!™ and the KaBOOM! logo are trademarks of Boom Entertainment, Inc., registered in various countries and categories. All characters, events, and institutions depicted herein are fictional. Any similarity between any of the names, characters, persons, events, and/or institutions in this publication to actual names, characters, and persons, whether living or dead, events, and/or institutions is unintended and purely coincidental. KaBOOM! does not read or accept unsolicited submissions of ideas, stories, or artwork.

BOOM! Studios, 5670 Wilshire Boulevard, Suite 450, Los Angeles, CA 90036-5679. Printed in China. Third Printing.

ISBN: 978-1-60886-313-6, eISBN: 978-1-61398-036-1

★ ★ ★ ADVENTURE TIME™ CREATED BY
PENDLETON WARD

★ ★ WRITTEN AND ILLUSTRATED BY
MEREDITH GRAN

★ ★ COLORS BY
LISA MOORE

★ ★ ★ LETTERS BY
STEVE WANDS

★ ★ COVER BY
JAB

"RESURRECTION SONG"
WRITTEN AND ILLUSTRATED BY
JEN WANG

"GRUMPY BUTT"
WRITTEN AND ILLUSTRATED BY
FAITH ERIN HICKS
COLORS BY MIRKA ANDOLFO

"FRUIT SALAD DAYS"
WRITTEN AND ILLUSTRATED BY
LIZ PRINCE

"THE BOOTLEGGER"
WRITTEN BY
YUKO OTA AND
ANANTH PANAGARIYA
ILLUSTRATED BY
YUKO OTA

"TREASURES UNTOLD"
WRITTEN AND ILLUSTRATED BY
KATE LETH

"COMMUNICATION ISSUES"
WRITTEN AND ILLUSTRATED BY
POLLY GUO

"COFFIN BREAK"
WRITTEN AND ILLUSTRATED BY
RICH TOMMASO

EDITOR
SHANNON WATTERS
DESIGNER
KASSANDRA HELLER

WITH SPECIAL THANKS TO MARISA MARIONAKIS, RICK BLANCO, CURTIS LELASH, LAURIE HALAL-ONO, KEITH MACK, KELLY CREWS AND THE WONDERFUL FOLKS AT CARTOON NETWORK.

CHAPTER ONE

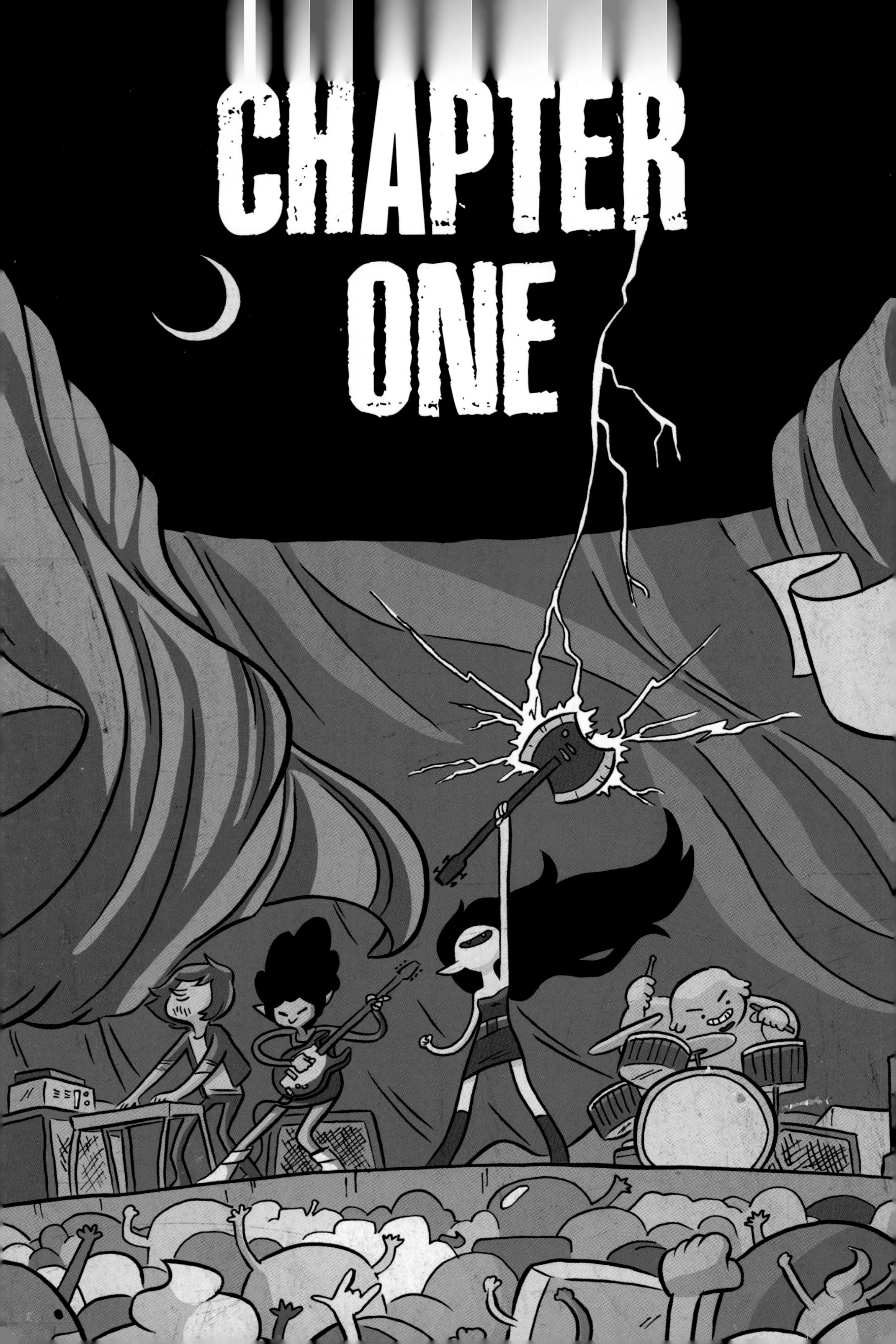

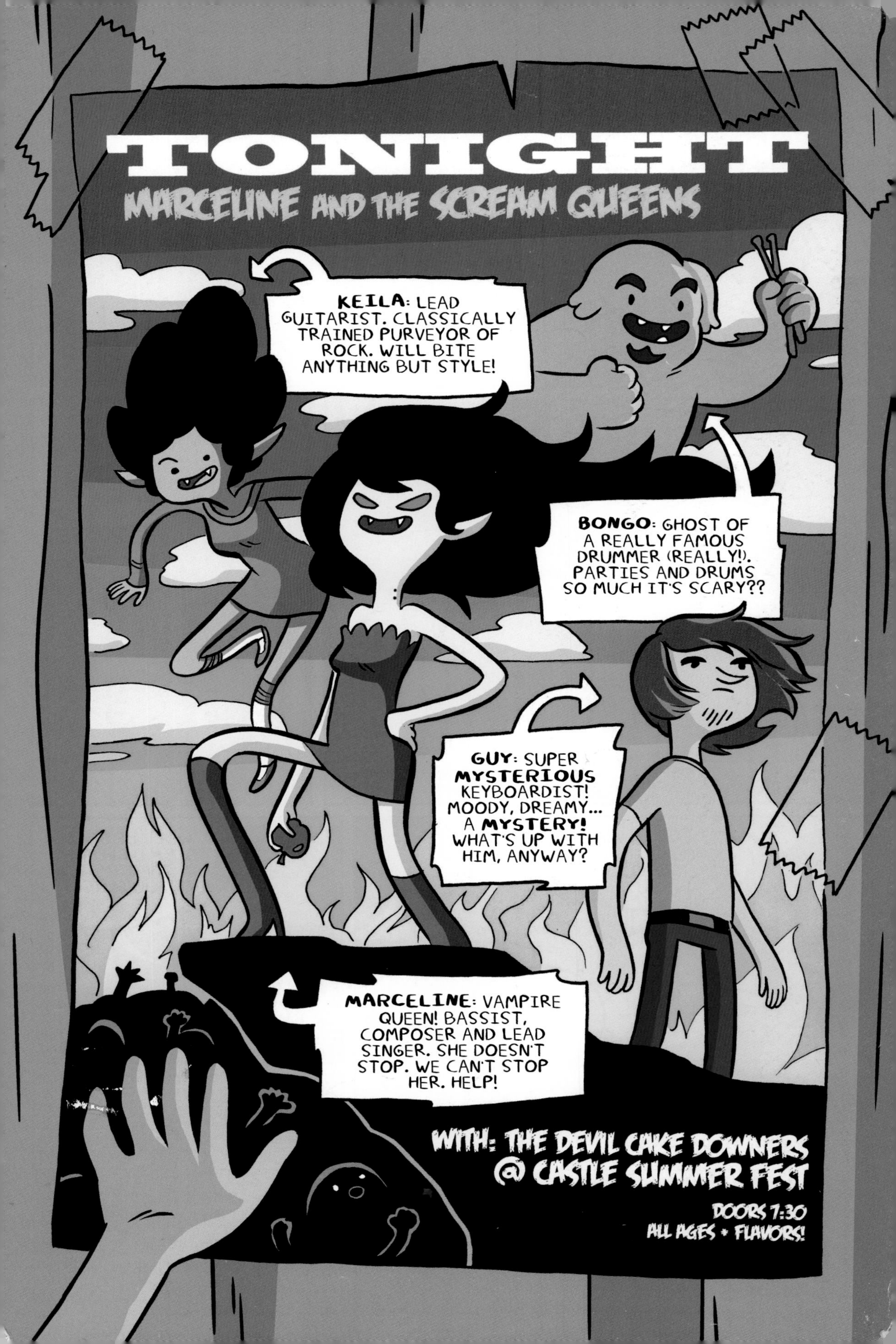
TONIGHT
MARCELINE AND THE SCREAM QUEENS
KEILA: LEAD GUITARIST. CLASSICALLY TRAINED PURVEYOR OF ROCK. WILL BITE ANYTHING BUT STYLE!
BONGO: GHOST OF A REALLY FAMOUS DRUMMER (REALLY!). PARTIES AND DRUMS SO MUCH IT'S SCARY??
GUY: SUPER MYSTERIOUS KEYBOARDIST! MOODY, DREAMY... A MYSTERY! WHAT'S UP WITH HIM, ANYWAY?
MARCELINE: VAMPIRE QUEEN! BASSIST, COMPOSER AND LEAD SINGER. SHE DOESN'T STOP. WE CAN'T STOP HER. HELP!
WITH: THE DEVIL CAKE DOWNERS
@ CASTLE SUMMER FEST
DOORS 7:30
ALL AGES + FLAVORS!

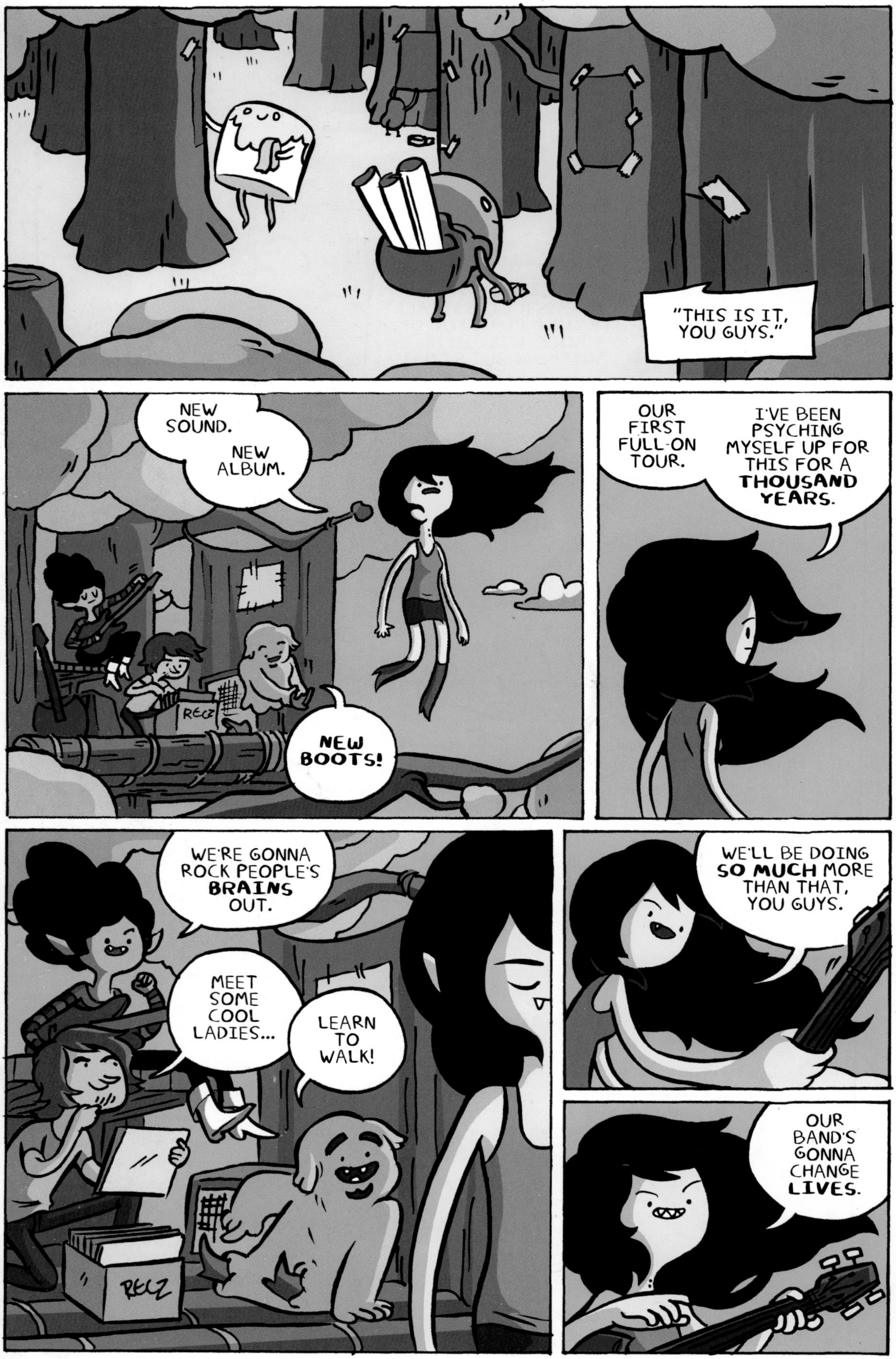
"THIS IS IT, YOU GUYS."
NEW SOUND.
NEW ALBUM.
NEW BOOTS!
OUR FIRST FULL-ON TOUR.
I'VE BEEN PSYCHING MYSELF UP FOR THIS FOR A **THOUSAND YEARS**.
WE'RE GONNA ROCK PEOPLE'S **BRAINS** OUT.
MEET SOME COOL LADIES...
LEARN TO WALK!
RECZ
WE'LL BE DOING **SO MUCH** MORE THAN THAT, YOU GUYS.
OUR BAND'S GONNA CHANGE **LIVES**.

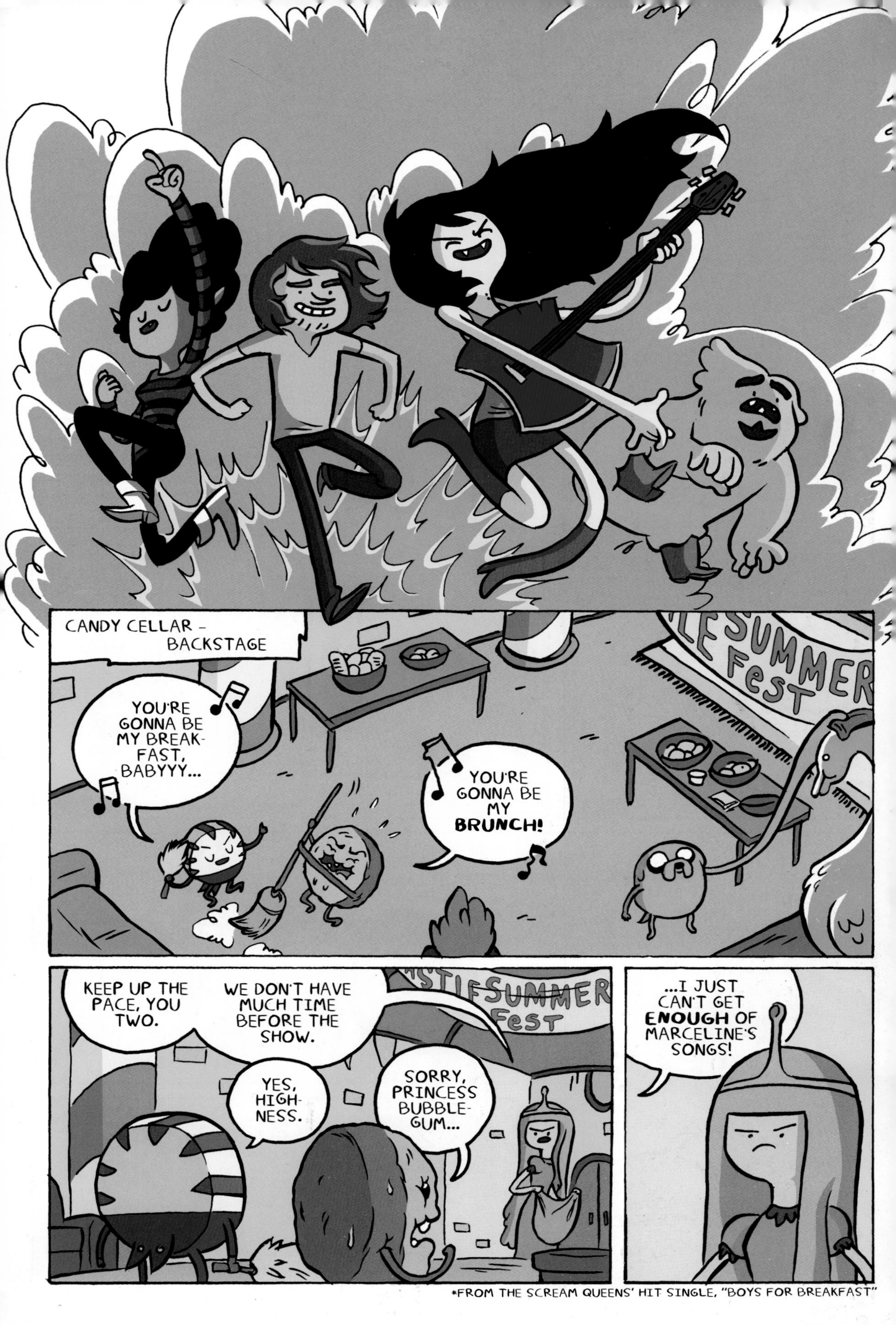
CANDY CELLAR – BACKSTAGE
YOU'RE GONNA BE MY BREAK-FAST, BABYYY...
YOU'RE GONNA BE MY **BRUNCH!**
KEEP UP THE PACE, YOU TWO.
WE DON'T HAVE MUCH TIME BEFORE THE SHOW.
YES, HIGH-NESS.
SORRY, PRINCESS BUBBLE-GUM...
...I JUST CAN'T GET **ENOUGH** OF MARCELINE'S SONGS!

*FROM THE SCREAM QUEENS' HIT SINGLE, "BOYS FOR BREAKFAST"

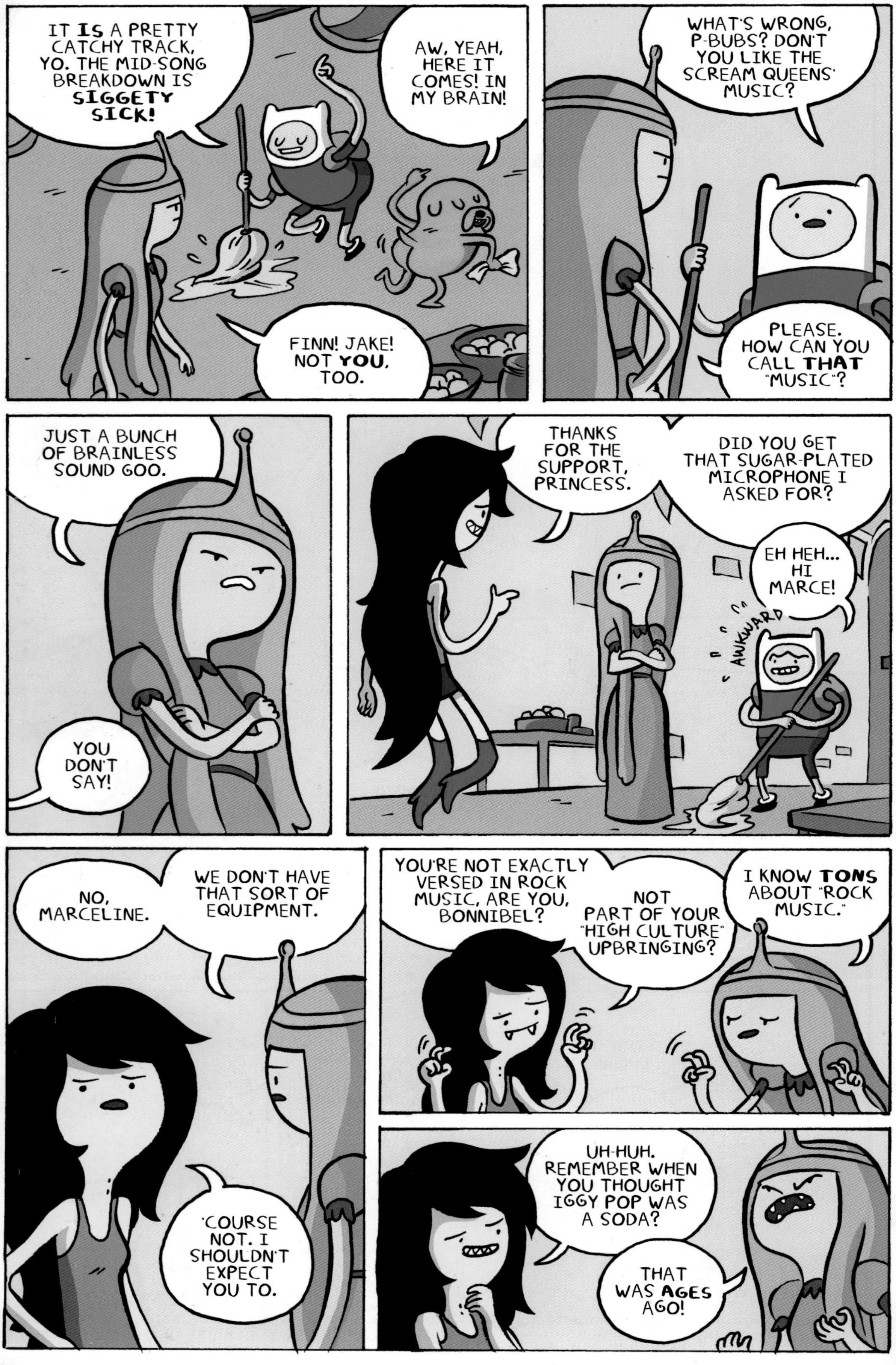
IT IS A PRETTY CATCHY TRACK, YO. THE MID-SONG BREAKDOWN IS SIGGETY SICK!
AW, YEAH, HERE IT COMES! IN MY BRAIN!
FINN! JAKE! NOT YOU, TOO.
WHAT'S WRONG, P-BUBS? DON'T YOU LIKE THE SCREAM QUEENS' MUSIC?
PLEASE. HOW CAN YOU CALL THAT "MUSIC"?
JUST A BUNCH OF BRAINLESS SOUND GOO.
YOU DON'T SAY!
THANKS FOR THE SUPPORT, PRINCESS.
DID YOU GET THAT SUGAR-PLATED MICROPHONE I ASKED FOR?
EH HEH... HI MARCE!
AWKWARD
NO, MARCELINE.
WE DON'T HAVE THAT SORT OF EQUIPMENT.
'COURSE NOT. I SHOULDN'T EXPECT YOU TO.
YOU'RE NOT EXACTLY VERSED IN ROCK MUSIC, ARE YOU, BONNIBEL?
NOT PART OF YOUR "HIGH CULTURE" UPBRINGING?
I KNOW TONS ABOUT "ROCK MUSIC."
UH-HUH. REMEMBER WHEN YOU THOUGHT IGGY POP WAS A SODA?
THAT WAS AGES AGO!

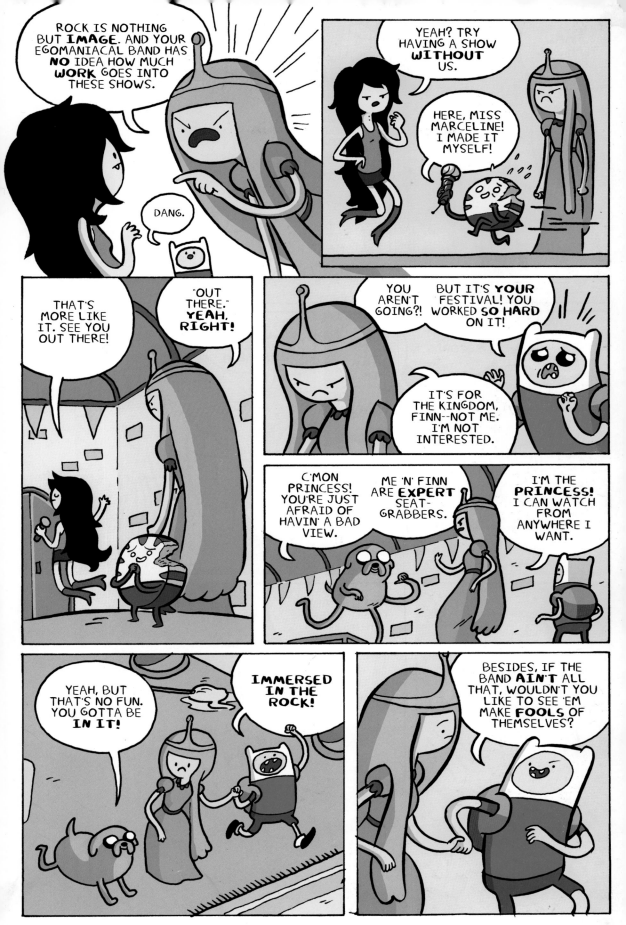

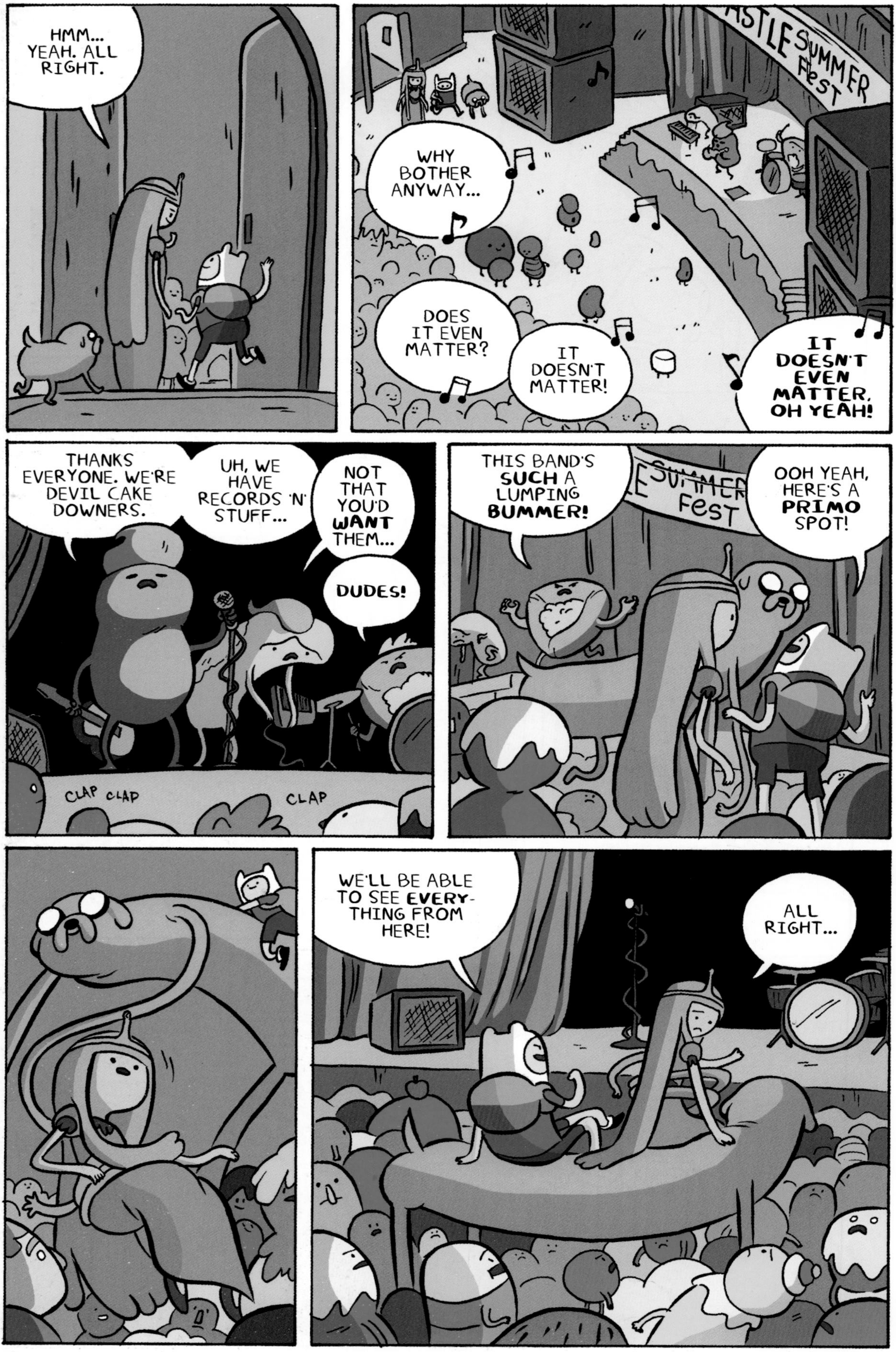
HMM... YEAH. ALL RIGHT.
ASTLE SUMMER FeST
WHY BOTHER ANYWAY...
DOES IT EVEN MATTER?
IT DOESN'T MATTER!
IT DOESN'T EVEN MATTER, OH YEAH!
THANKS EVERYONE. WE'RE DEVIL CAKE DOWNERS.
UH, WE HAVE RECORDS 'N' STUFF...
NOT THAT YOU'D **WANT** THEM...
DUDES!
CLAP CLAP
CLAP
THIS BAND'S **SUCH** A LUMPING **BUMMER!**
SUMMER FeST
OOH YEAH, HERE'S A **PRIMO** SPOT!
WE'LL BE ABLE TO SEE **EVERY-**THING FROM HERE!
ALL RIGHT...

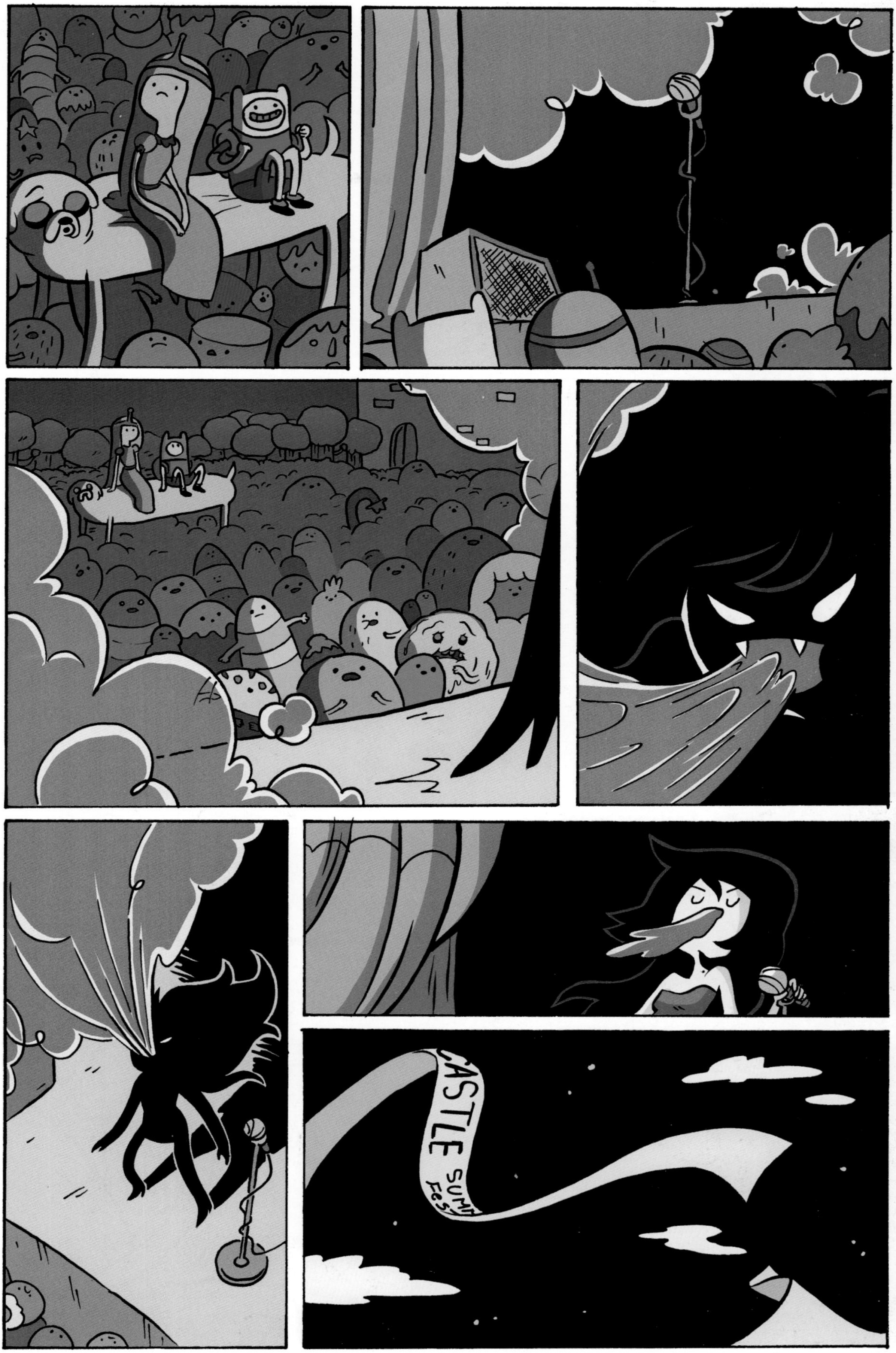
CASTLE

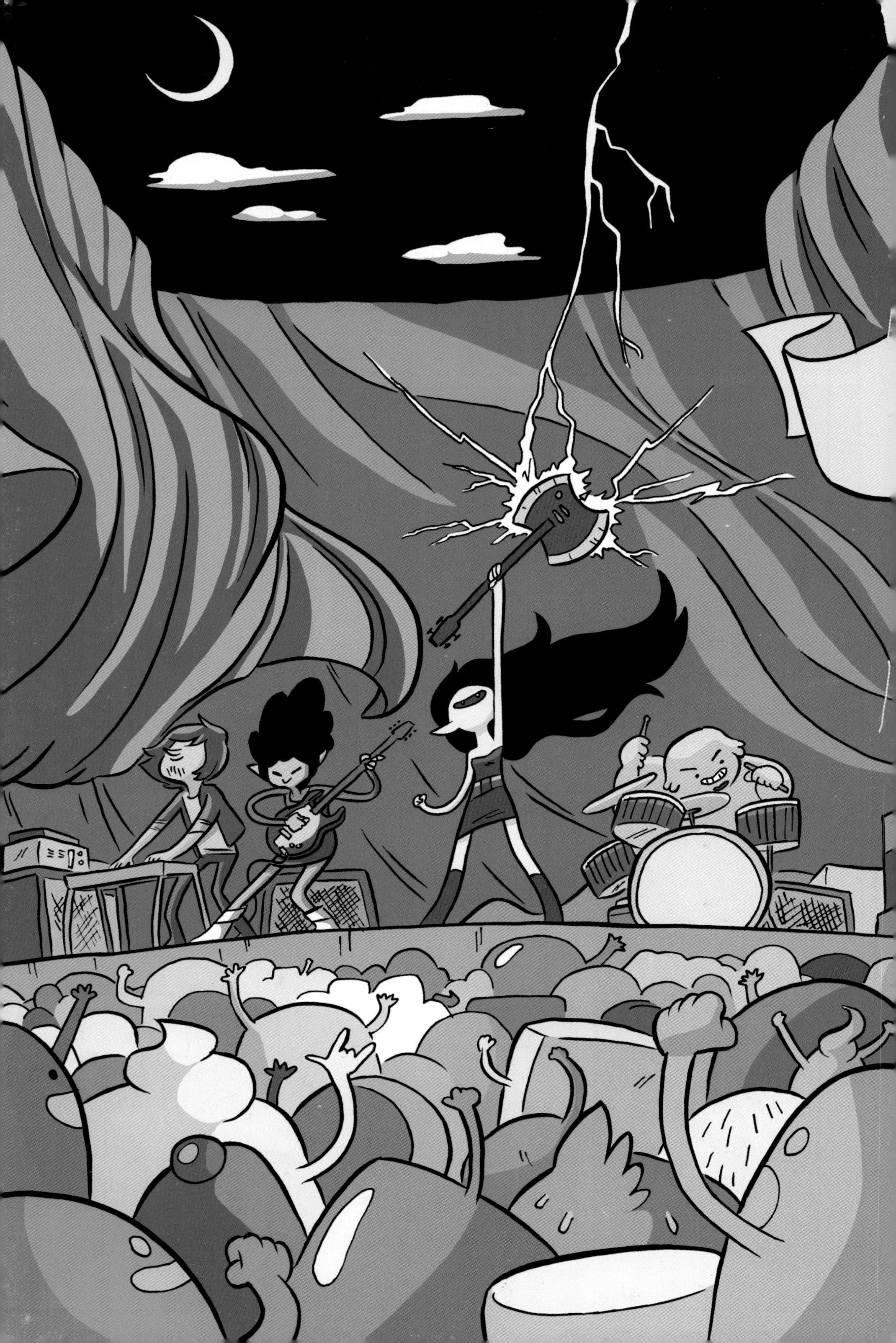

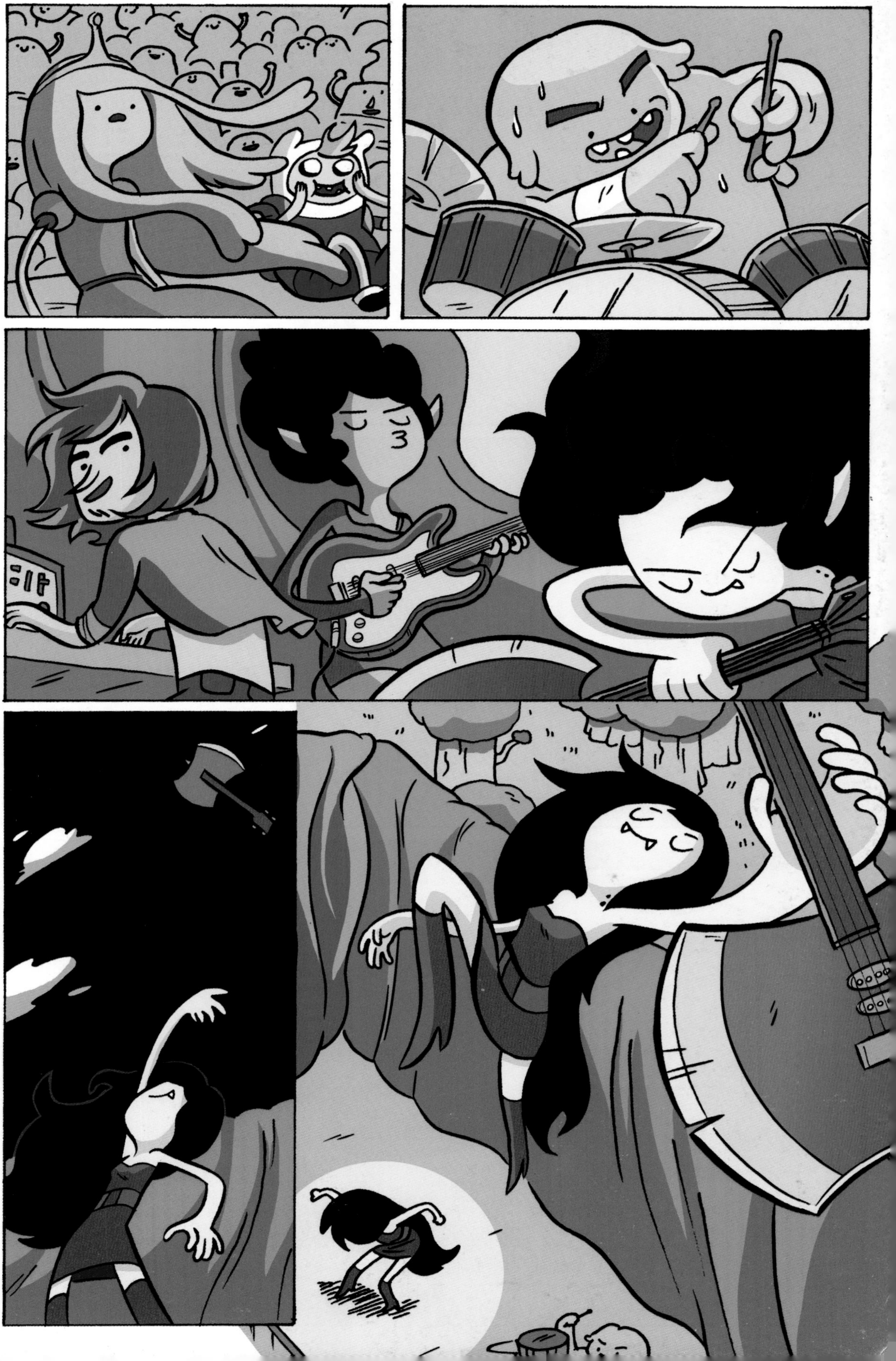

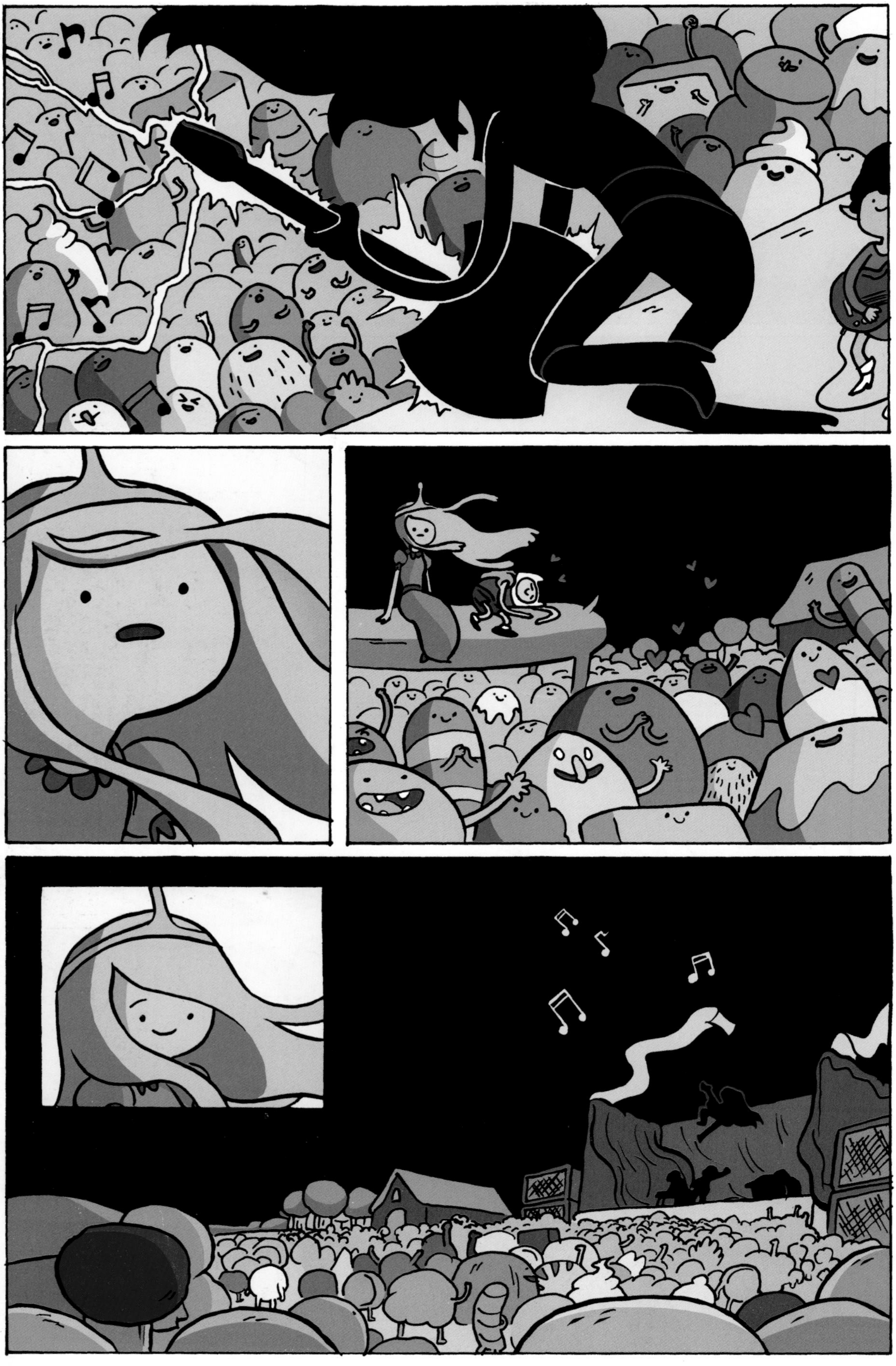

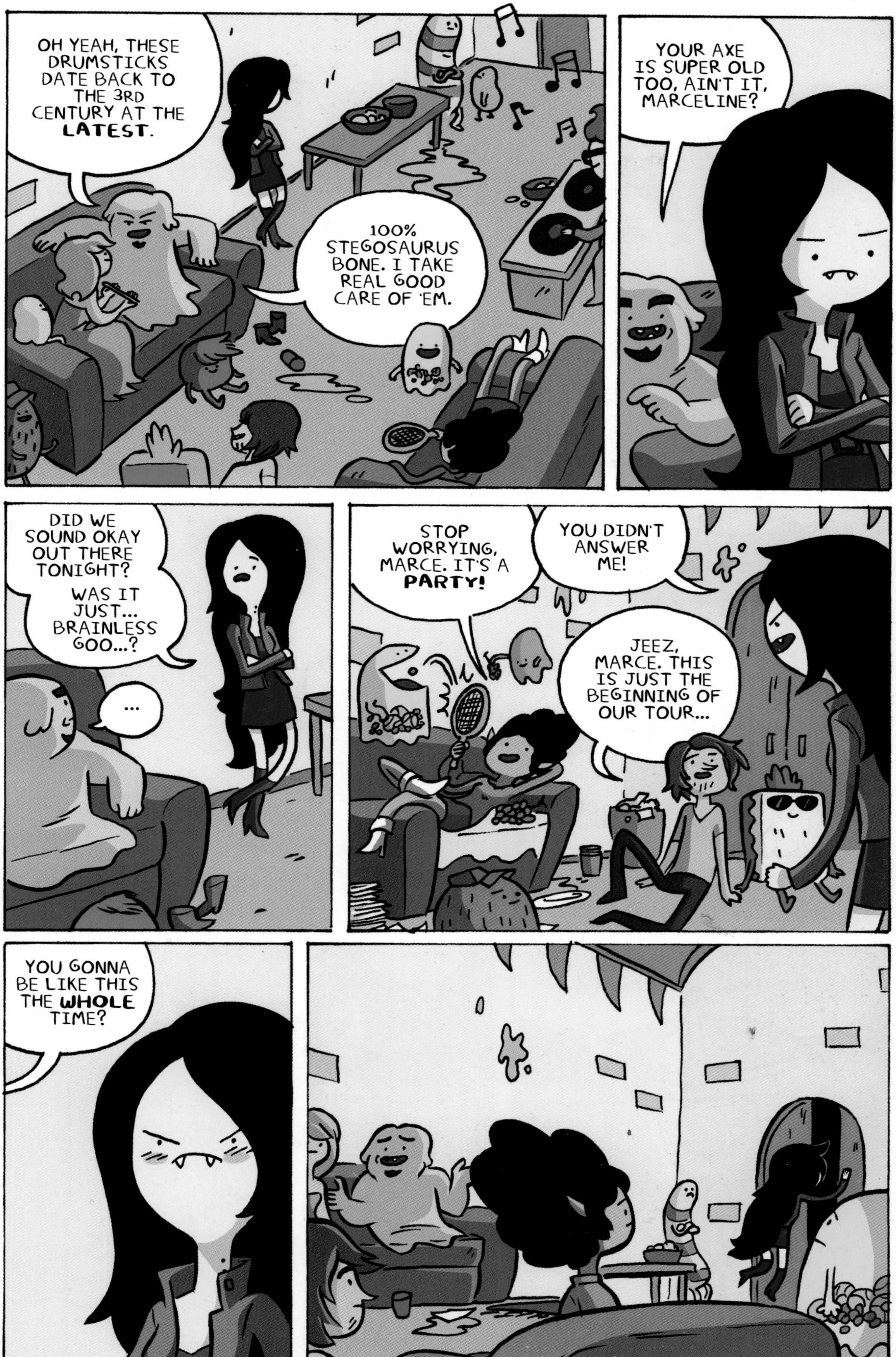

OH YEAH, THESE DRUMSTICKS DATE BACK TO THE 3RD CENTURY AT THE **LATEST**.
100% STEGOSAURUS BONE. I TAKE REAL GOOD CARE OF 'EM.
YOUR AXE IS SUPER OLD TOO, AIN'T IT, MARCELINE?
DID WE SOUND OKAY OUT THERE TONIGHT?
WAS IT JUST... BRAINLESS GOO...?
...
STOP WORRYING, MARCE. IT'S A **PARTY!**
YOU DIDN'T ANSWER ME!
JEEZ, MARCE. THIS IS JUST THE BEGINNING OF OUR TOUR...
YOU GONNA BE LIKE THIS THE **WHOLE** TIME?

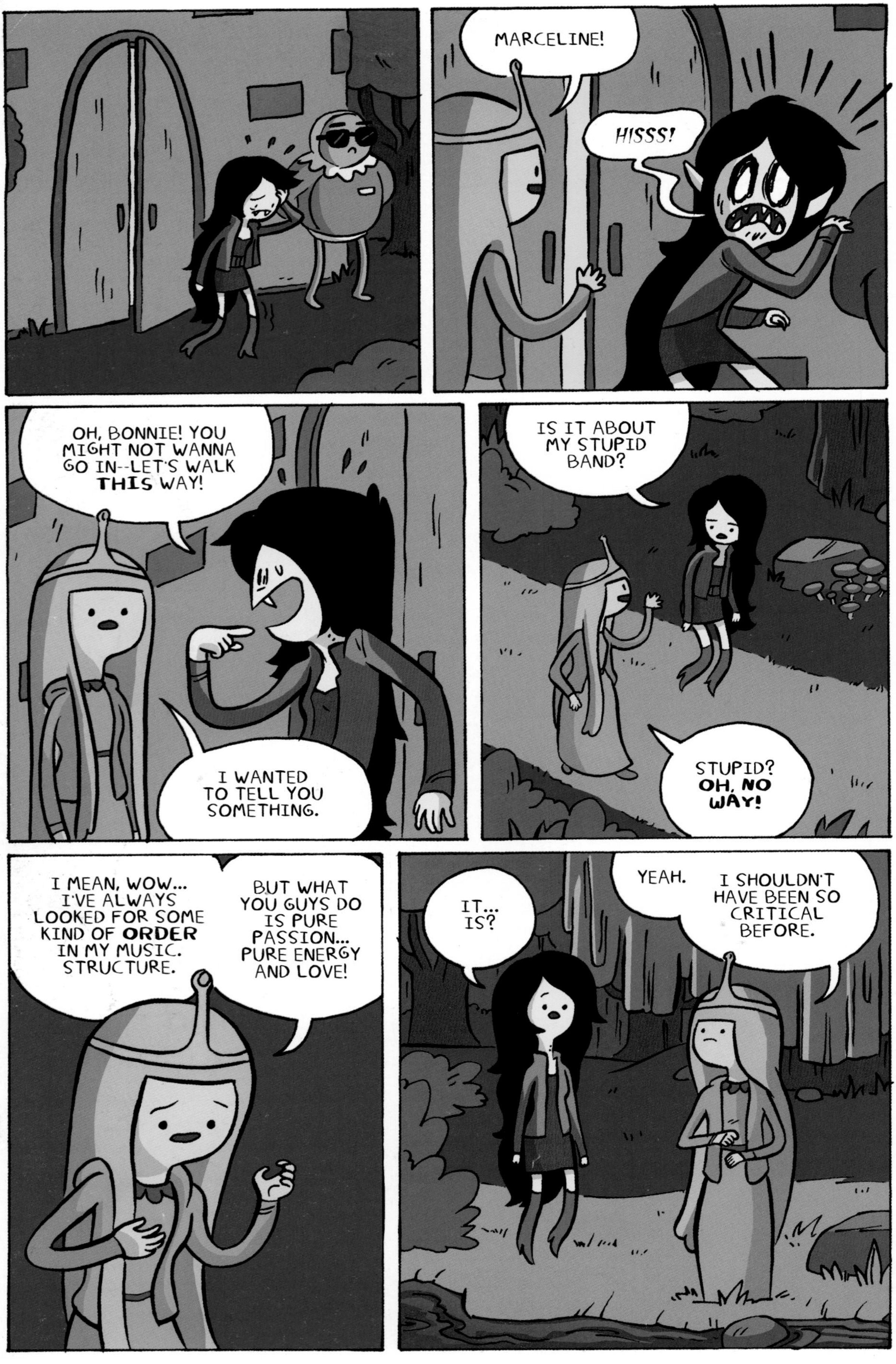
MARCELINE!
HISSS!
OH, BONNIE! YOU MIGHT NOT WANNA GO IN--LET'S WALK **THIS** WAY!
I WANTED TO TELL YOU SOMETHING.
IS IT ABOUT MY STUPID BAND?
STUPID? **OH, NO WAY!**
I MEAN, WOW... I'VE ALWAYS LOOKED FOR SOME KIND OF **ORDER** IN MY MUSIC. STRUCTURE.
BUT WHAT YOU GUYS DO IS PURE PASSION... PURE ENERGY AND LOVE!
IT... IS?
YEAH.
I SHOULDN'T HAVE BEEN SO CRITICAL BEFORE.

WELL... YOU WEREN'T **TOTALLY** WRONG.

MY BAND'S A MESS. WE CAN'T EVEN ORGANIZE OUR OWN UNDERWEAR.

I WANT THIS TOUR SO BAD...

BUT IT'S DESTINED FOR FAILURE.

MARCELINE...

WHAT IF...I CAME ON TOUR WITH YOU?

Y'KNOW, HELPED MANAGE THE BAND?

YOU'D WANNA **DO** THAT?

WELL, SURE! I CAN KEEP THINGS IN ORDER...

...AND REALLY LEARN TO APPRECIATE THE MUSIC!

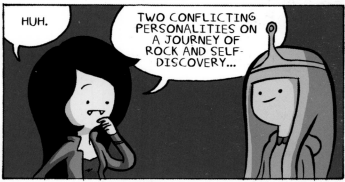
HUH.

TWO CONFLICTING PERSONALITIES ON A JOURNEY OF ROCK AND SELF-DISCOVERY...

LUMP YEAH!

GREAT IDEA, **ME!**

WITH JAKE AS THE INTERIM KING, I'LL NEED YOU ALL TO OBEY HIS WISHES.

AWW!

I'M FIRM BUT **FAIR**!

AND I'LL NEED TO KNOW **ALL** THE OFFICIAL **KING** DANCES.

ARE YOU SURE ABOUT THIS, PRINCESS? I THOUGHT THE BAND **TOTALLY** LAMED YOU **OUT**!

WHAT IF YOU COME BACK A **DIFFERENT** PERSON?

SOME GROOVIN' ROCK 'N' ROLL LADY WITH **THREE HEADS AND FIVE ARMS**?

HA HA. I WON'T!

Y'KNOW... **JAKE'S** GONNA MISS YOU A WHOLE LOT.

I WILL MISS JAKE. AND YOU **TOO**, FINN.

FRAGILE

I'LL BRING YOU A GIFT FROM MY TRIP, OKAY?

OKAY!

HAVE AN AMAZING TIME, PRINCESS.

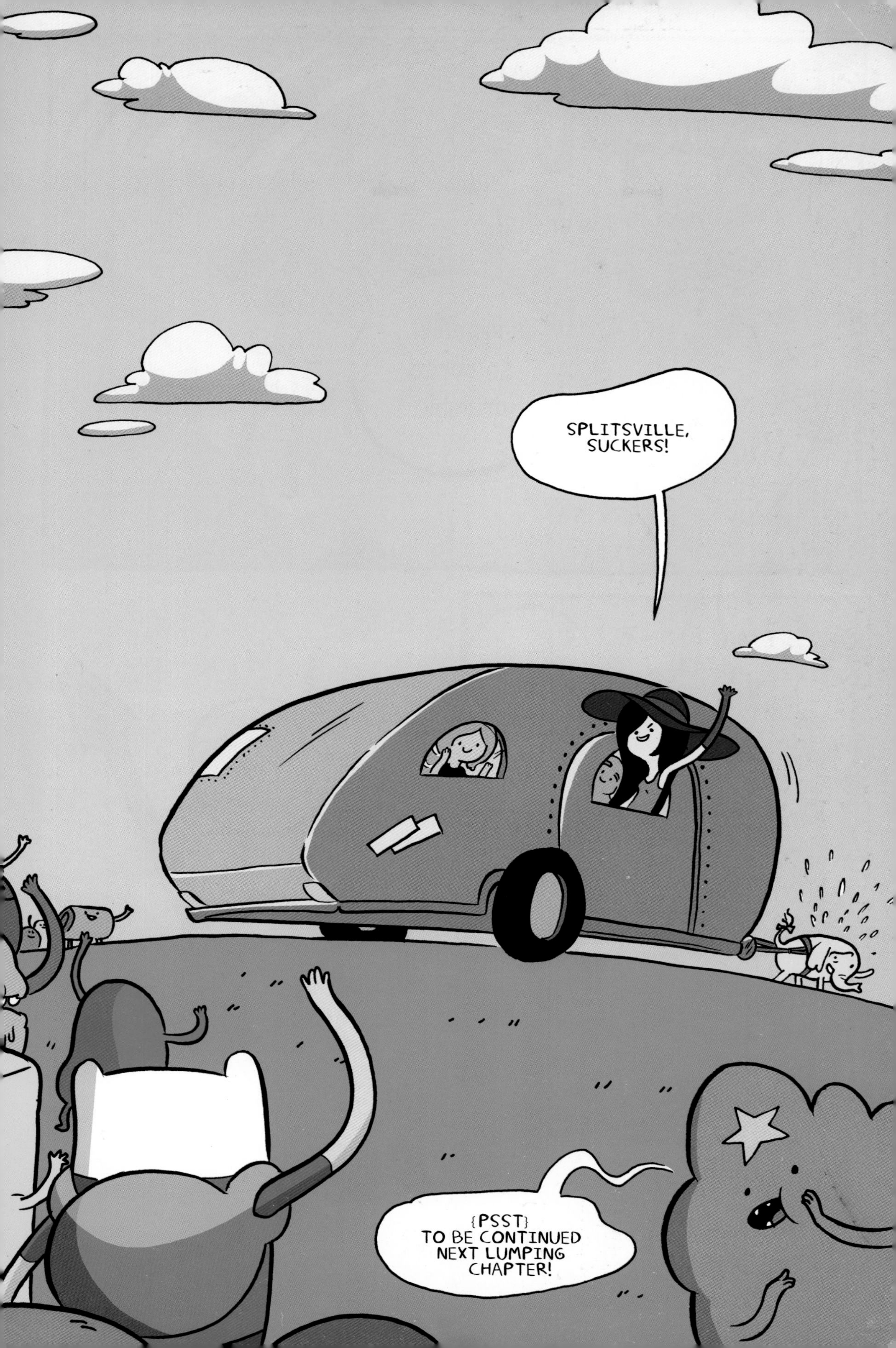
SPLITSVILLE, SUCKERS!
{PSST} TO BE CONTINUED NEXT LUMPING CHAPTER!

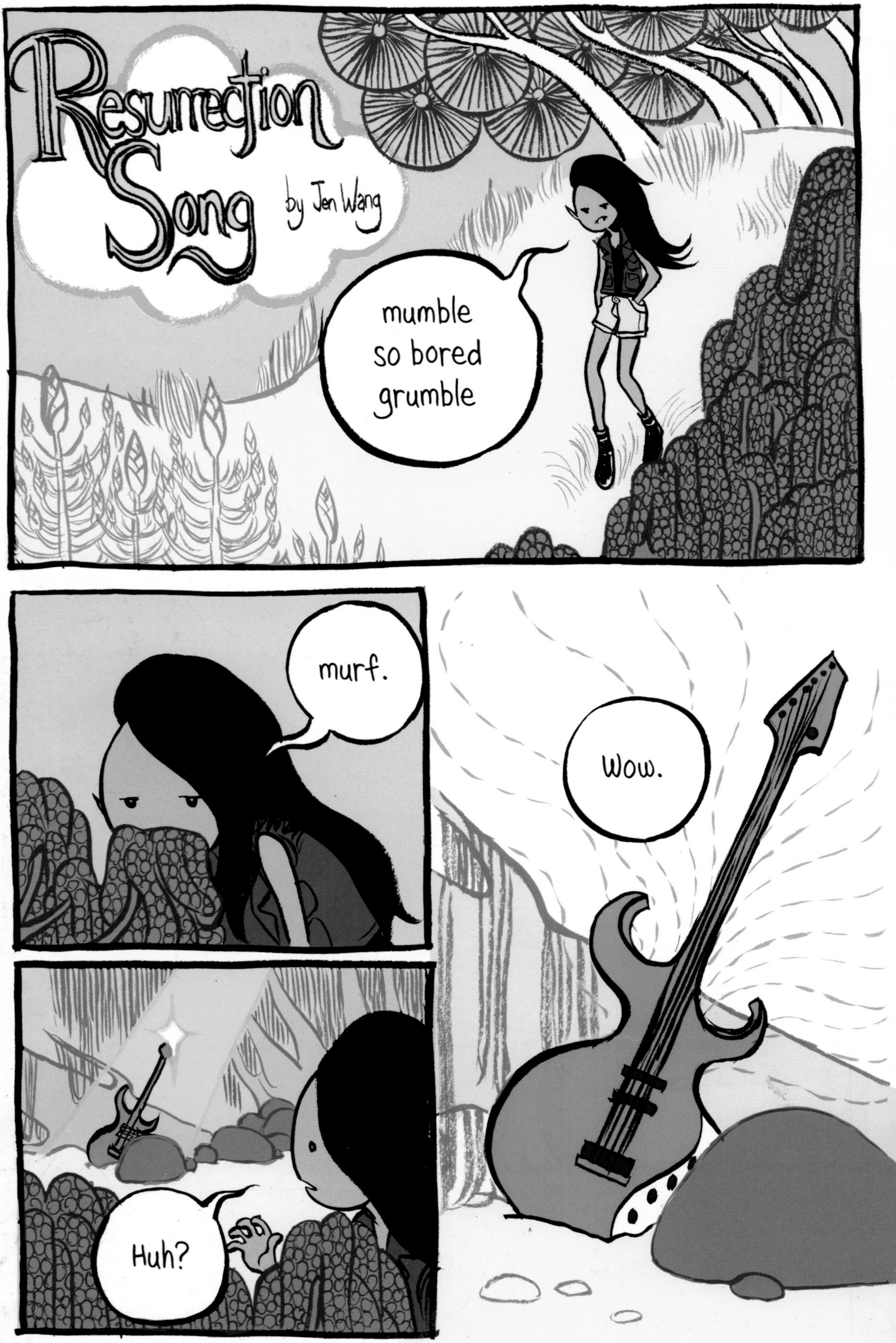

Resurrection Song
by Jen Wang
mumble so bored grumble
murf.
Huh?
Wow.

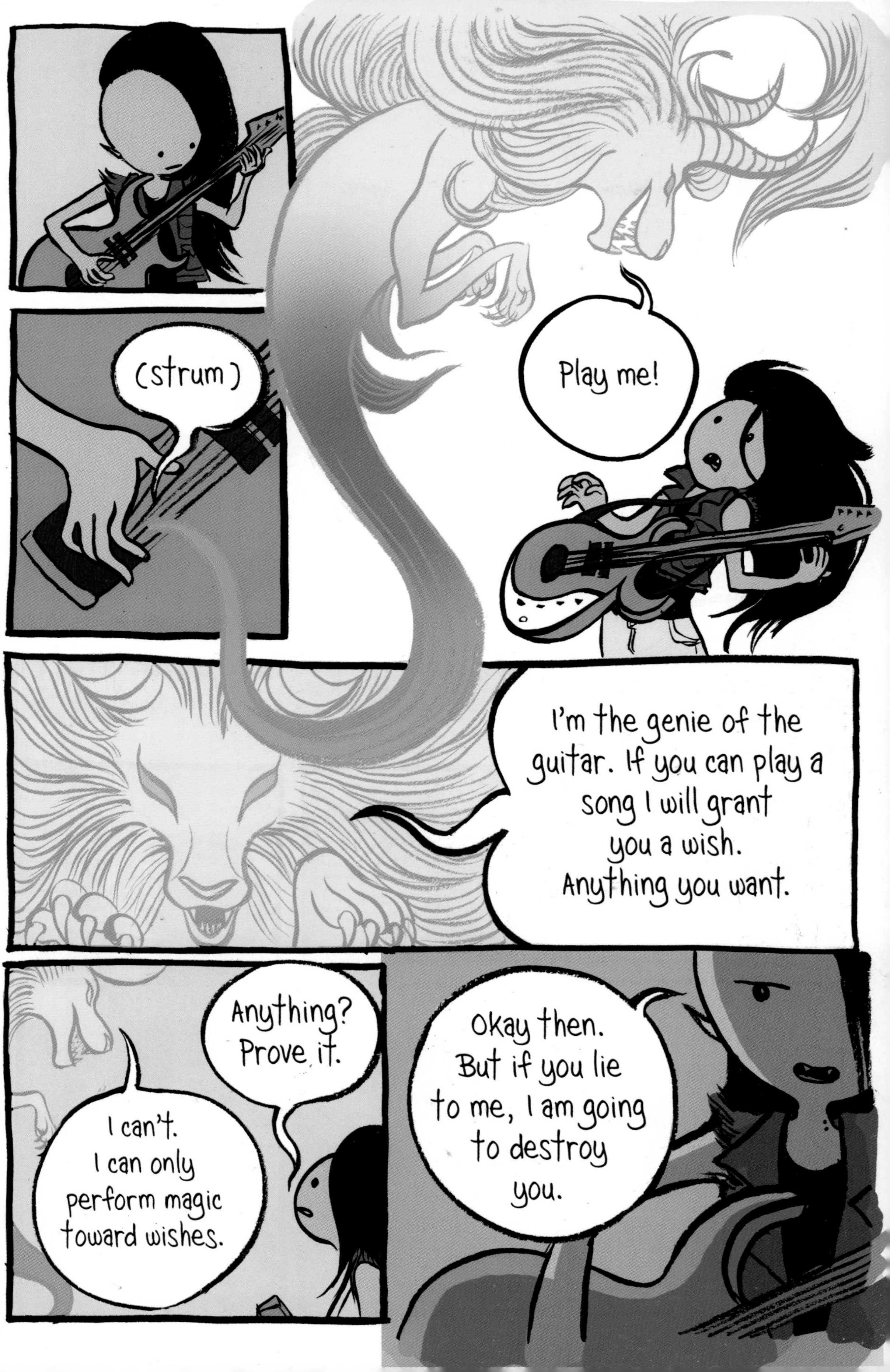
(strum)
Play me!
I'm the genie of the guitar. If you can play a song I will grant you a wish. Anything you want.
Anything? Prove it.
I can't. I can only perform magic toward wishes.
Okay then. But if you lie to me, I am going to destroy you.

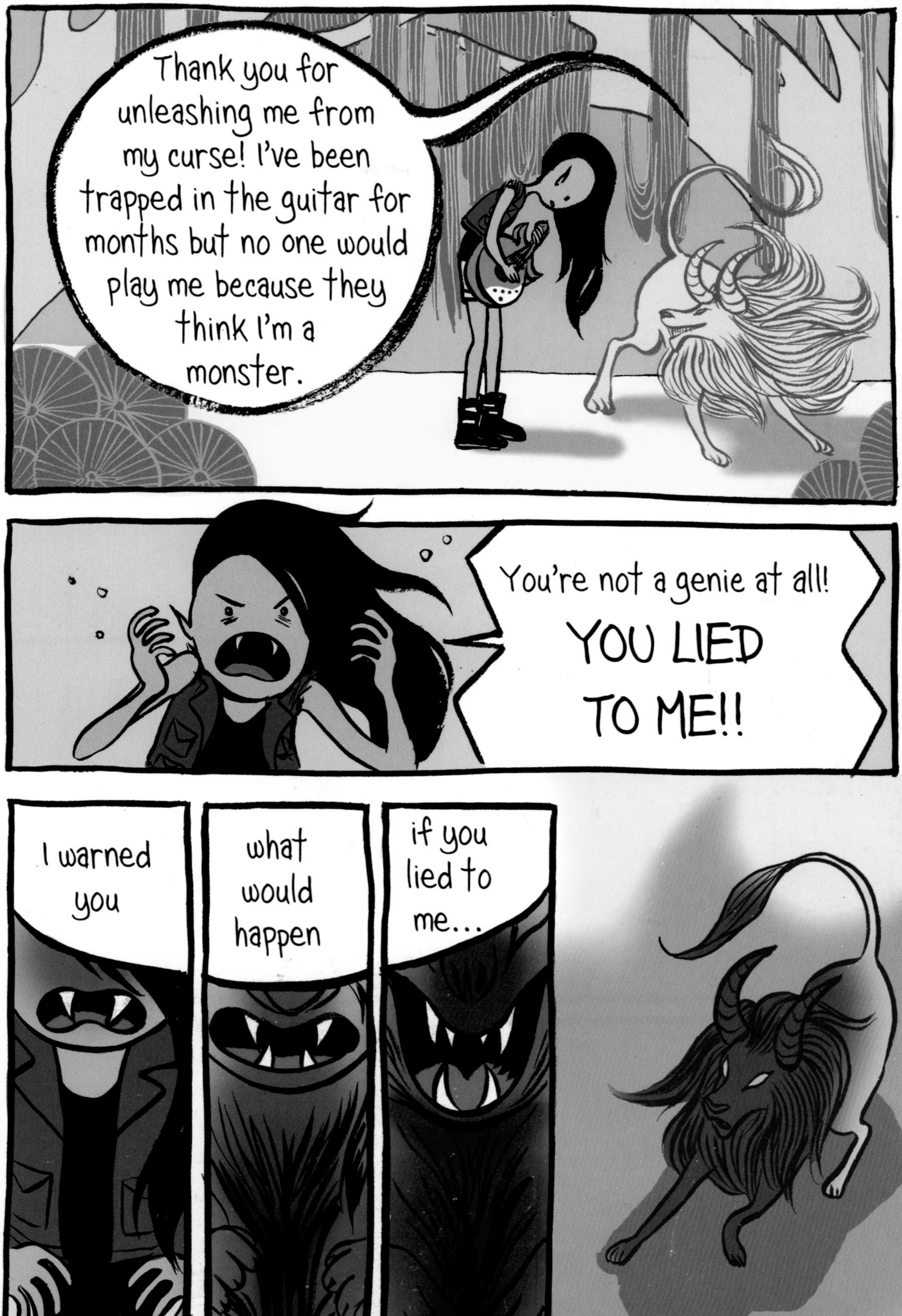
Thank you for unleashing me from my curse! I've been trapped in the guitar for months but no one would play me because they think I'm a monster.
You're not a genie at all!
YOU LIED TO ME!!
I warned you
what would happen
if you lied to me...

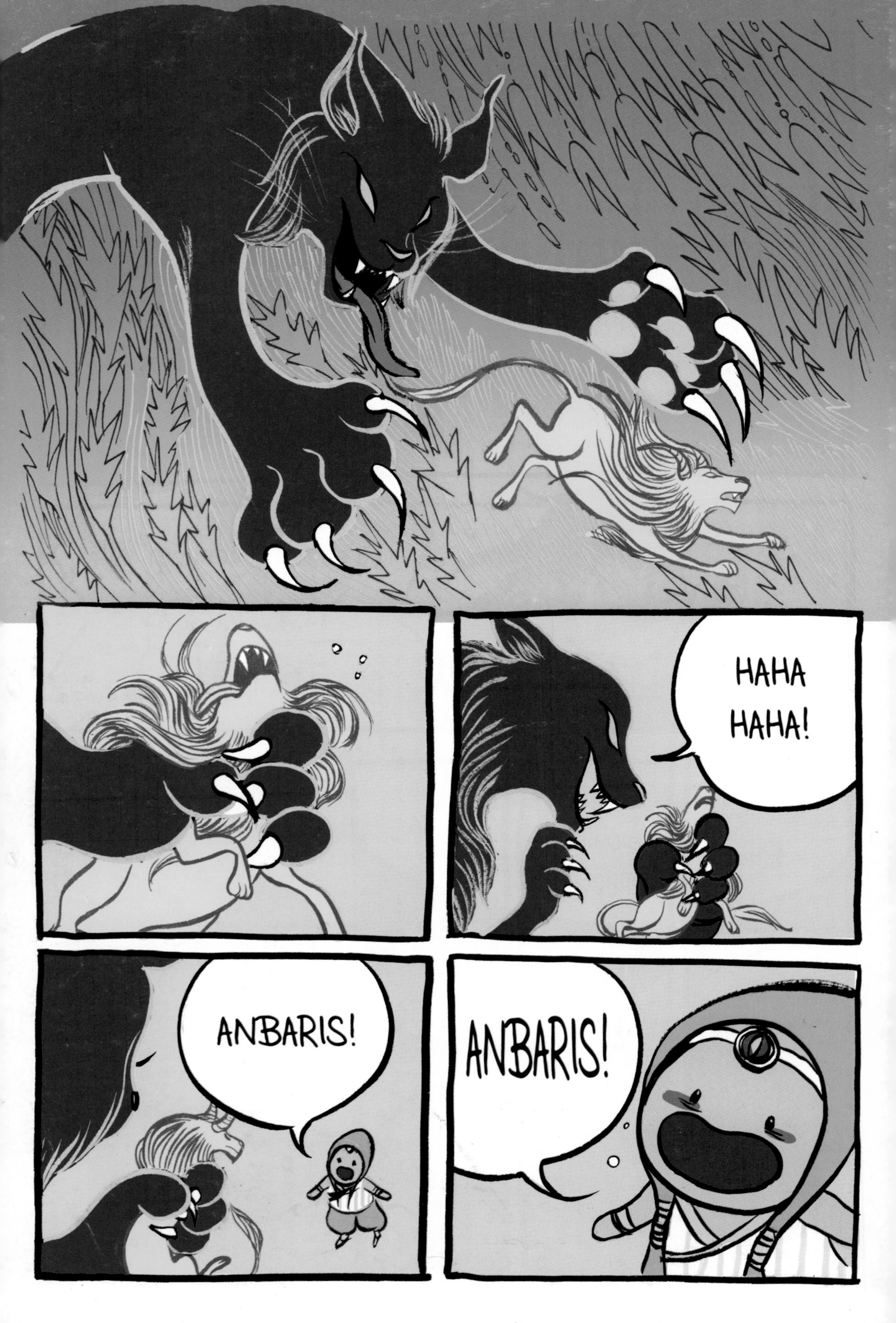
HAHA HAHA!
ANBARIS!
ANBARIS!

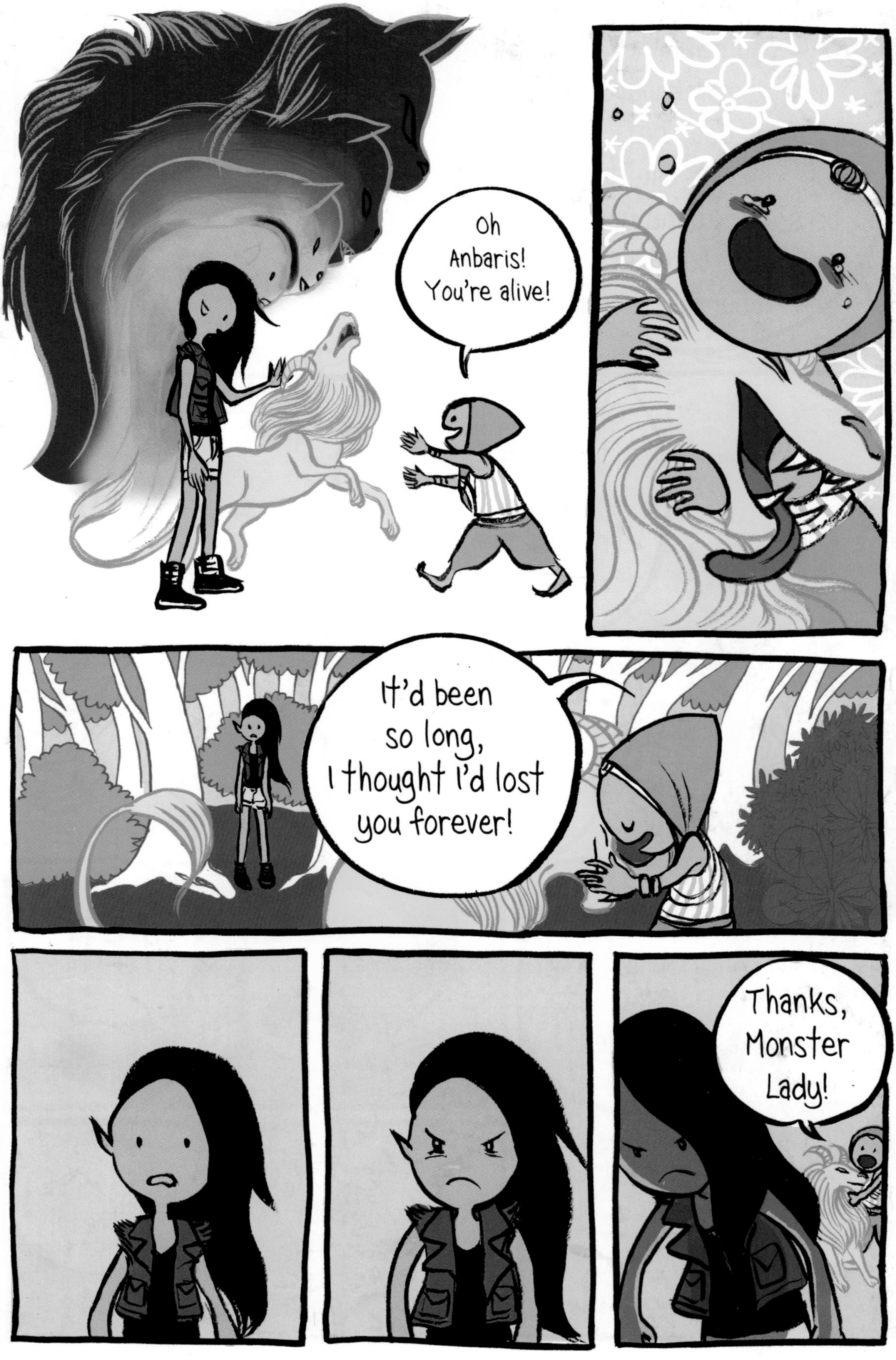
Oh
Anbaris!
You're alive!
It'd been
so long,
I thought I'd lost
you forever!
Thanks,
Monster
Lady!

CHAPTER TWO

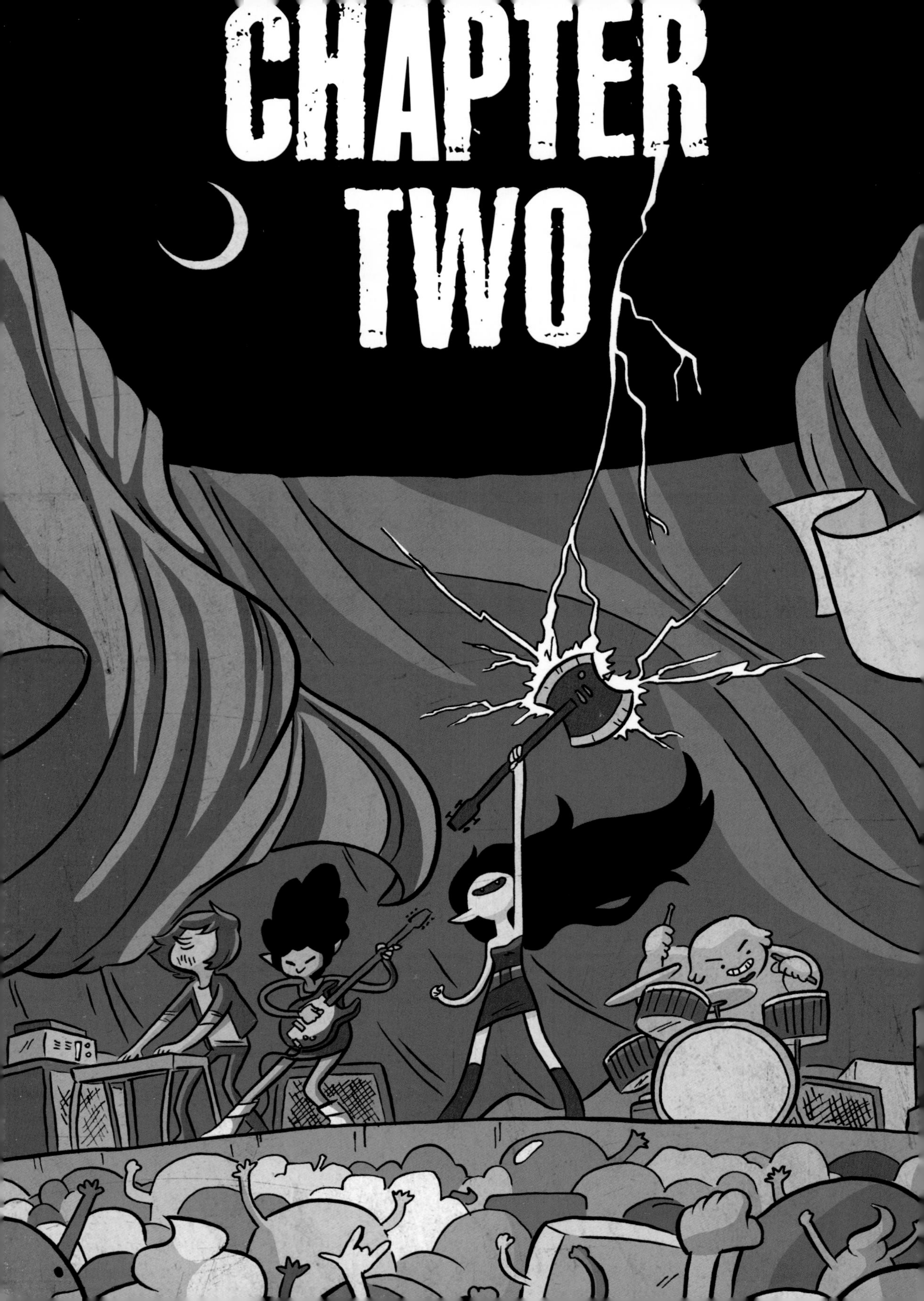

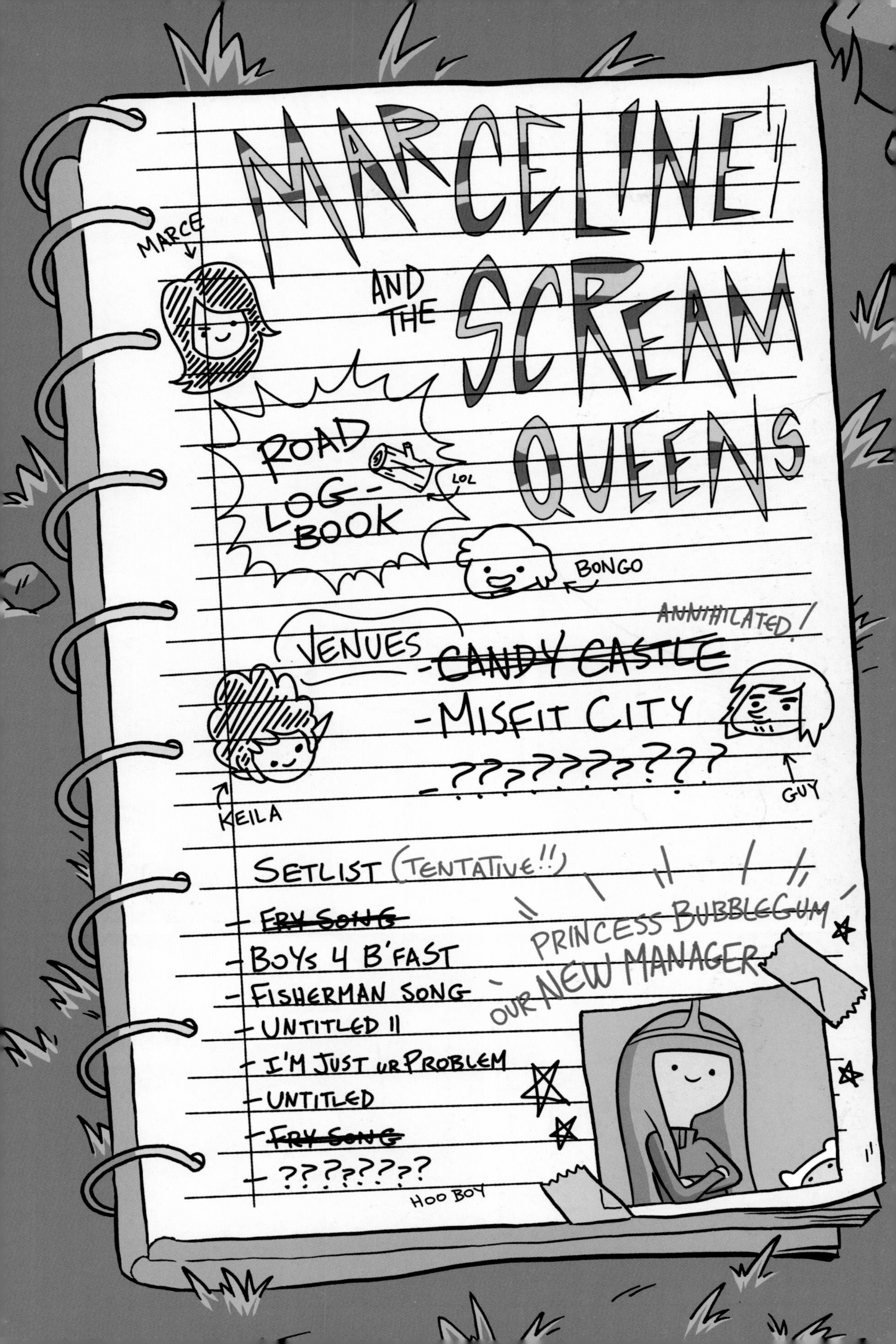
MARCELINE AND THE SCREAM QUEENS
MARCE
ROAD LOG BOOK
LOL
BONGO
ANNIHILATED!
VENUES
- CANDY CASTLE
- MISFIT CITY
- ??????????
KEILA
GUY
SETLIST (TENTATIVE!!)
- FRY SONG
- BOYS 4 B'FAST
- FISHERMAN SONG
- UNTITLED II
- I'M JUST UR PROBLEM
- UNTITLED
- FRY SONG
- ????????
HOO BOY
PRINCESS BUBBLEGUM
OUR NEW MANAGER

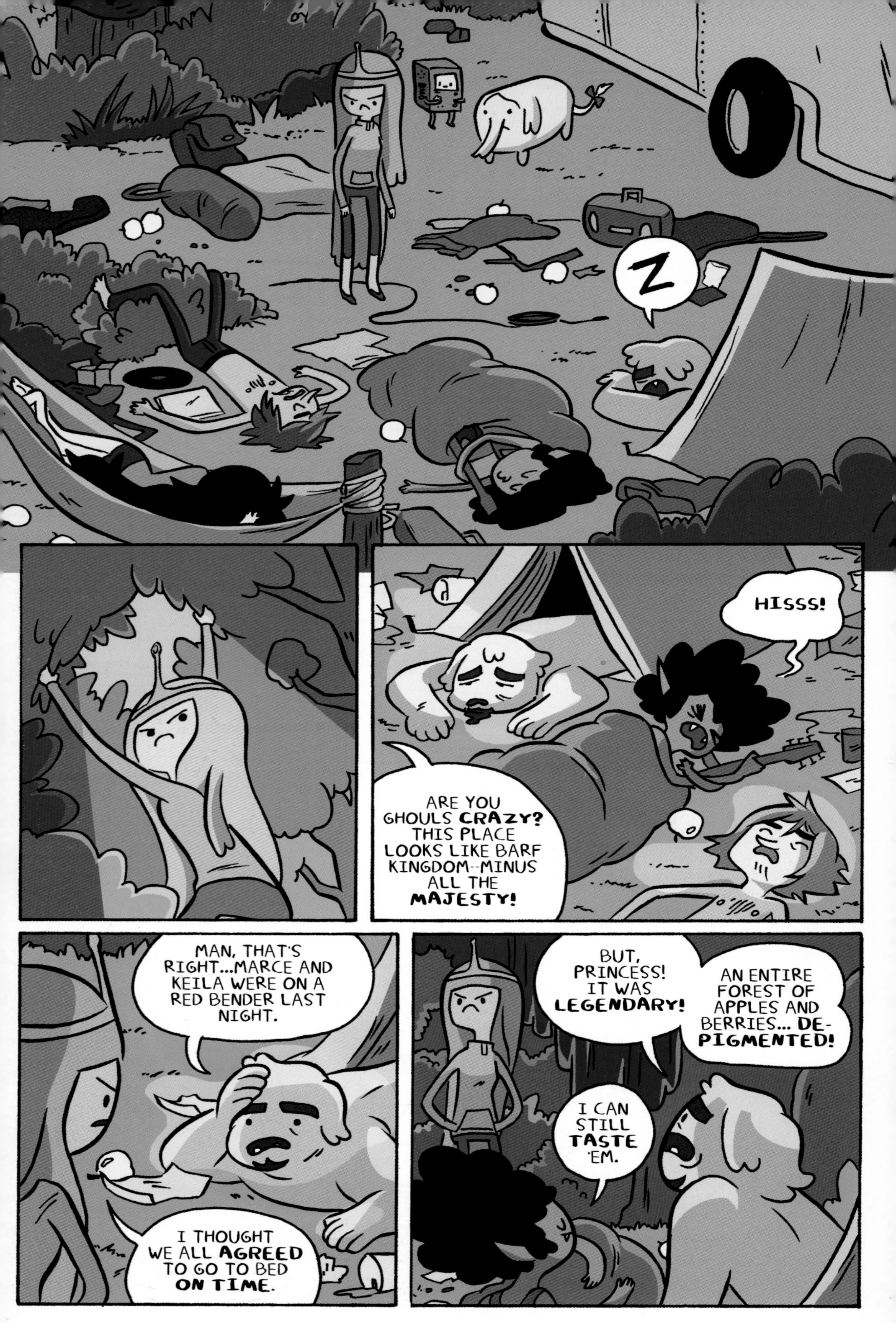
Z
HISSS!
ARE YOU GHOULS CRAZY? THIS PLACE LOOKS LIKE BARF KINGDOM--MINUS ALL THE MAJESTY!
MAN, THAT'S RIGHT...MARCE AND KEILA WERE ON A RED BENDER LAST NIGHT.
I THOUGHT WE ALL AGREED TO GO TO BED ON TIME.
BUT, PRINCESS! IT WAS LEGENDARY!
AN ENTIRE FOREST OF APPLES AND BERRIES... DE-PIGMENTED!
I CAN STILL TASTE 'EM.

S'IN MY NATURE.

IT'S IN HER **NATURE**, PRINCESS! RED FURY IS HER **THING!**

YEAH! RED FURY!

RED FURY!

RED FURY!

RED FURY!

NUTS TO THAT! I SIGNED UP TO BE YOUR MANAGER-- NOT YOUR **MOM.**

ARE A BUNCH OF SELF-MADE MUSICIANS REALLY THIS **HELPLESS?**

IT'S NOT VERY "**PUNK ROCK**" OF YOU.

WHAT?!

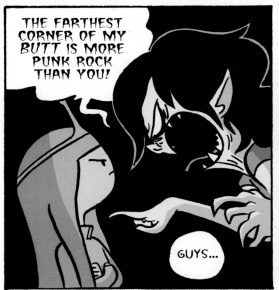

THE FARTHEST CORNER OF MY **BUTT** IS MORE PUNK ROCK THAN YOU!

GUYS...

WE'D BETTER GET READY FOR THAT INTERVIEW...IT'S IN HALF AN HOUR.

OH, **WADS!!**

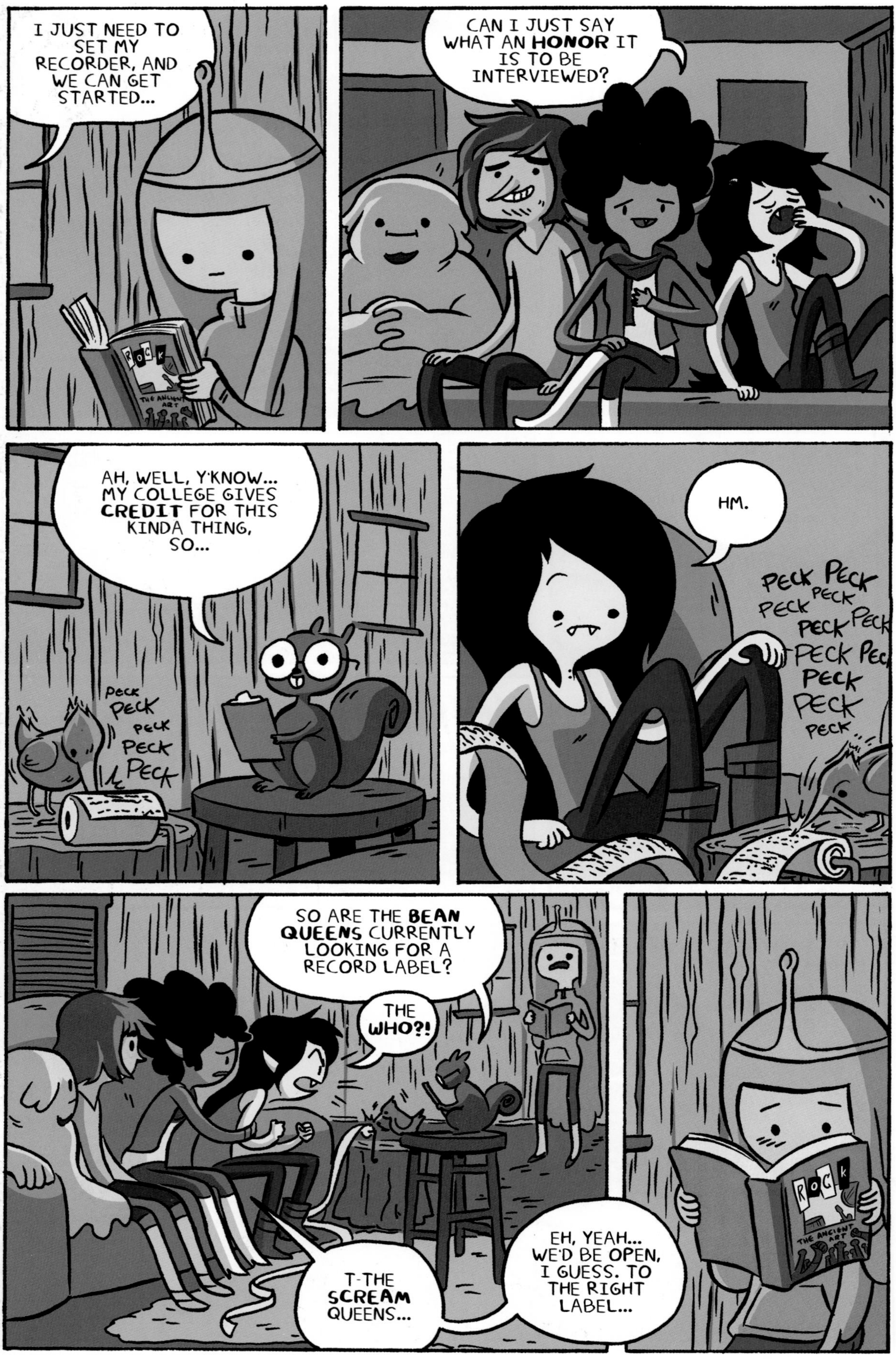
I JUST NEED TO SET MY RECORDER, AND WE CAN GET STARTED...
ROCK
THE ANCIENT ART
CAN I JUST SAY WHAT AN **HONOR** IT IS TO BE INTERVIEWED?
AH, WELL, Y'KNOW... MY COLLEGE GIVES **CREDIT** FOR THIS KINDA THING, SO...
PECK PECK PECK PECK PECK
HM.
PECK PECK PECK PECK PECK PECK PECK PECK PECK PECK PECK PECK
SO ARE THE **BEAN QUEENS** CURRENTLY LOOKING FOR A RECORD LABEL?
THE **WHO?!**
T-THE **SCREAM** QUEENS...
EH, YEAH... WE'D BE OPEN, I GUESS. TO THE RIGHT LABEL...
ROCK
THE ANCIENT ART

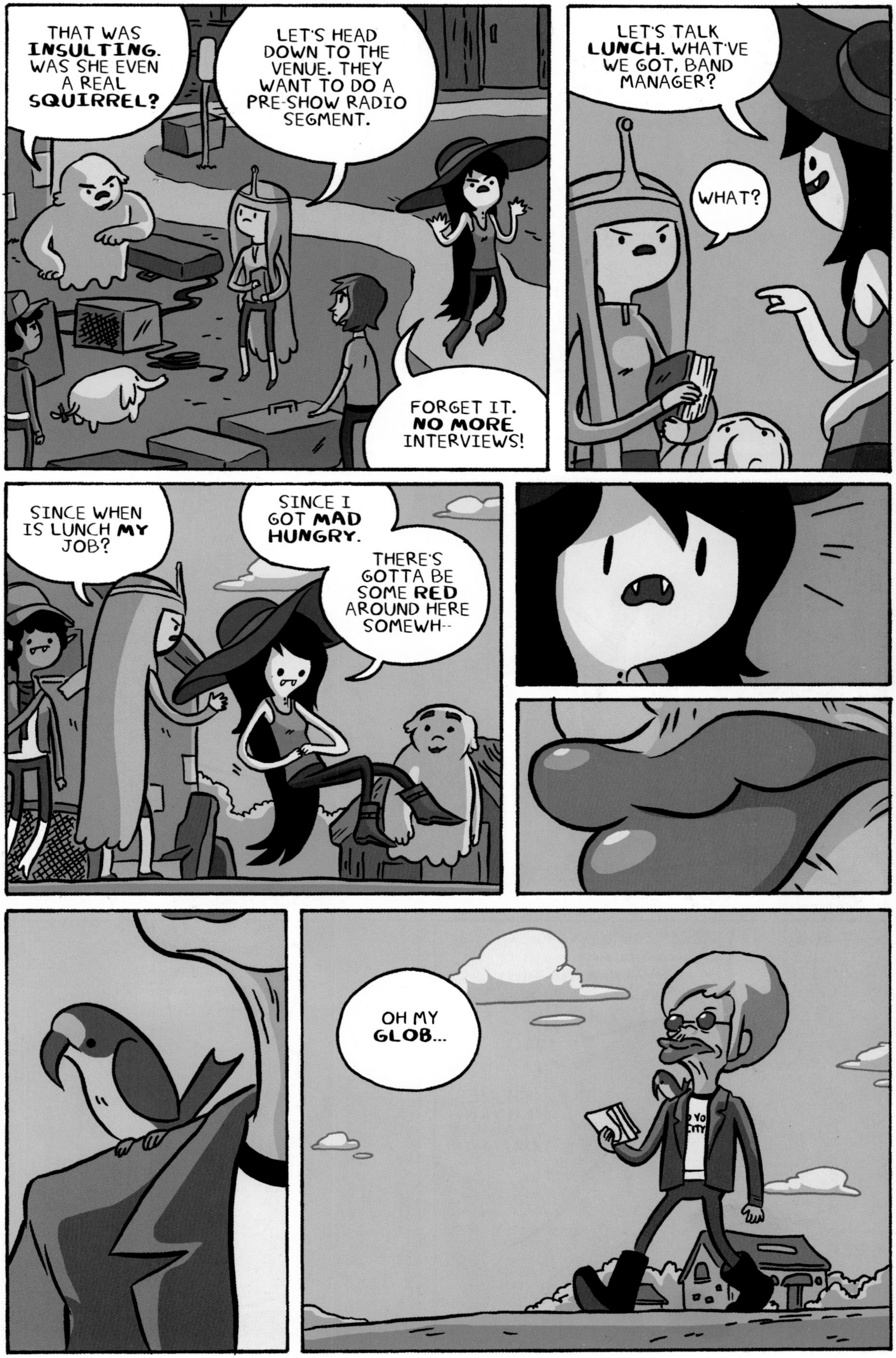
THAT WAS **INSULTING**. WAS SHE EVEN A REAL **SQUIRREL?**
LET'S HEAD DOWN TO THE VENUE. THEY WANT TO DO A PRE-SHOW RADIO SEGMENT.
FORGET IT. **NO MORE** INTERVIEWS!
LET'S TALK **LUNCH**. WHAT'VE WE GOT, BAND MANAGER?
WHAT?
SINCE WHEN IS LUNCH **MY** JOB?
SINCE I GOT **MAD HUNGRY**.
THERE'S GOTTA BE SOME **RED** AROUND HERE SOMEWH--
OH MY **GLOB**...

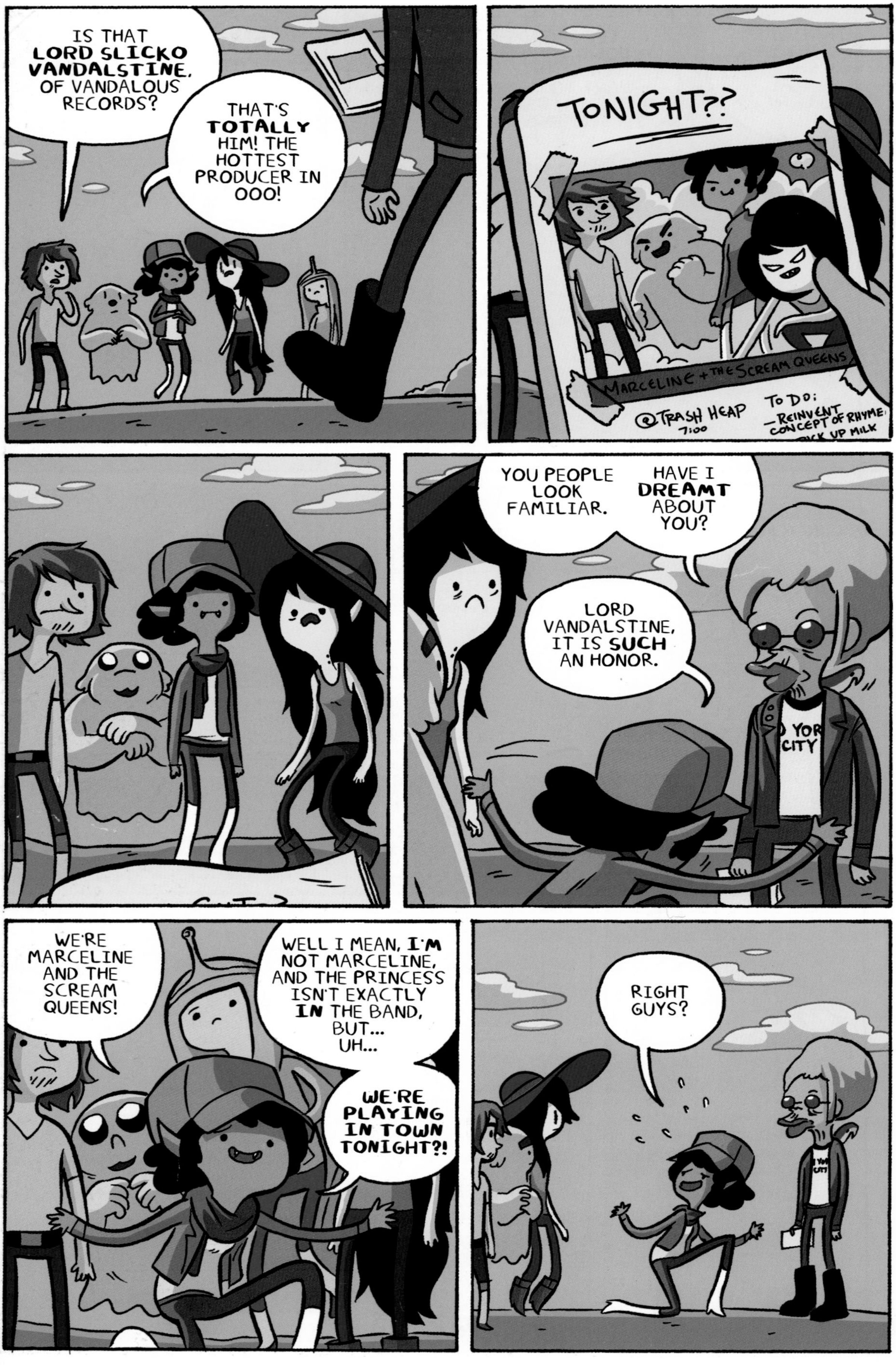
IS THAT **LORD SLICKO VANDALSTINE,** OF VANDALOUS RECORDS?
THAT'S **TOTALLY** HIM! THE HOTTEST PRODUCER IN OOO!
TONIGHT??
MARCELINE + THE SCREAM QUEENS
@ TRASH HEAP 7:00
TO DO:
—REINVENT CONCEPT OF RHYME;
YOU PEOPLE LOOK FAMILIAR.
HAVE I **DREAMT** ABOUT YOU?
LORD VANDALSTINE, IT IS **SUCH** AN HONOR.
WE'RE MARCELINE AND THE SCREAM QUEENS!
WELL I MEAN, **I'M** NOT MARCELINE, AND THE PRINCESS ISN'T EXACTLY **IN** THE BAND, BUT... UH...
WE'RE PLAYING IN TOWN TONIGHT?!
RIGHT GUYS?

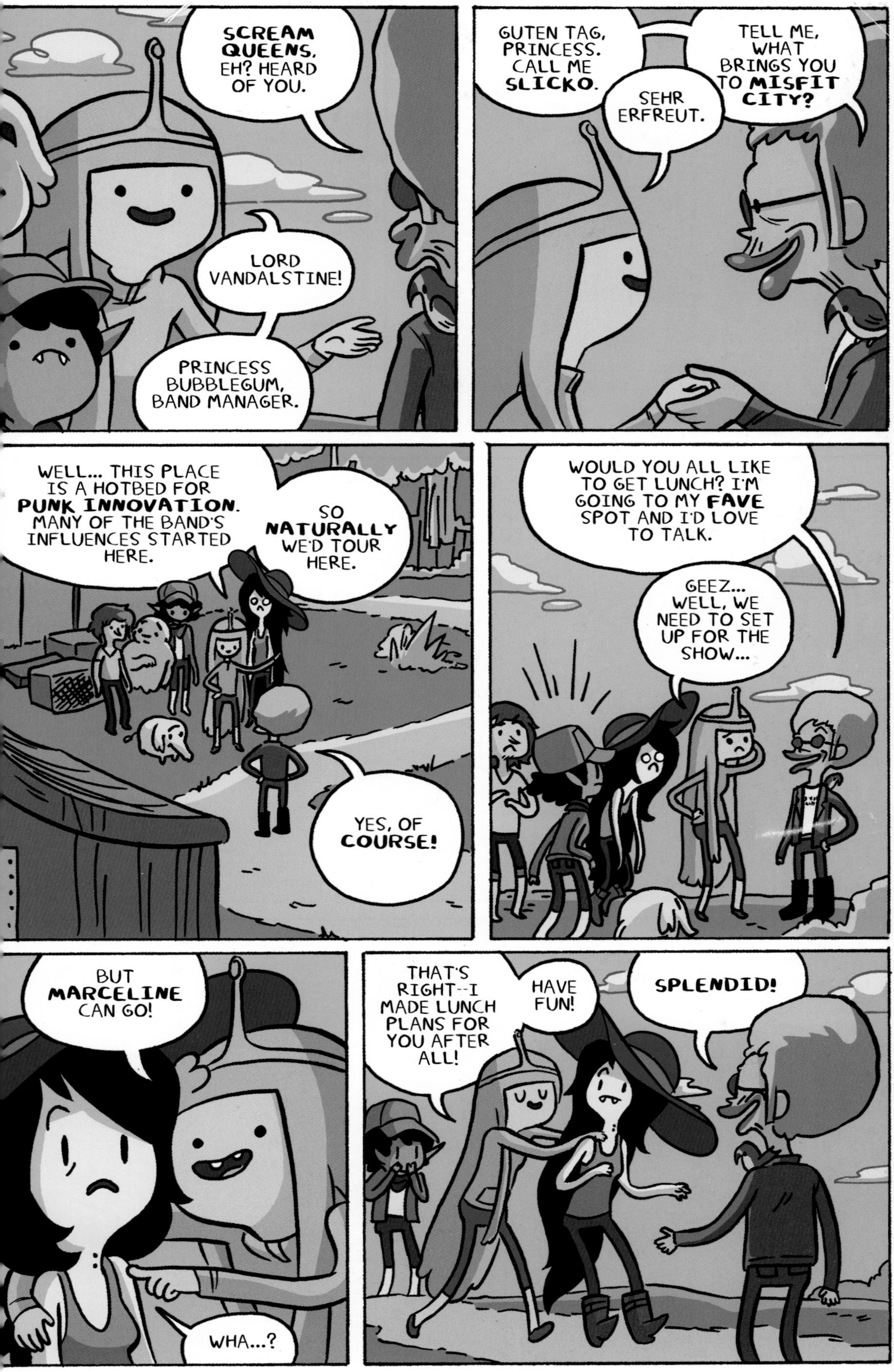
SCREAM QUEENS, EH? HEARD OF YOU.
LORD VANDALSTINE!
PRINCESS BUBBLEGUM, BAND MANAGER.
GUTEN TAG, PRINCESS. CALL ME SLICKO.
SEHR ERFREUT.
TELL ME, WHAT BRINGS YOU TO MISFIT CITY?
WELL... THIS PLACE IS A HOTBED FOR PUNK INNOVATION. MANY OF THE BAND'S INFLUENCES STARTED HERE.
SO NATURALLY WE'D TOUR HERE.
YES, OF COURSE!
WOULD YOU ALL LIKE TO GET LUNCH? I'M GOING TO MY FAVE SPOT AND I'D LOVE TO TALK.
GEEZ... WELL, WE NEED TO SET UP FOR THE SHOW...
BUT MARCELINE CAN GO!
WHA...?
THAT'S RIGHT--I MADE LUNCH PLANS FOR YOU AFTER ALL!
HAVE FUN!
SPLENDID!

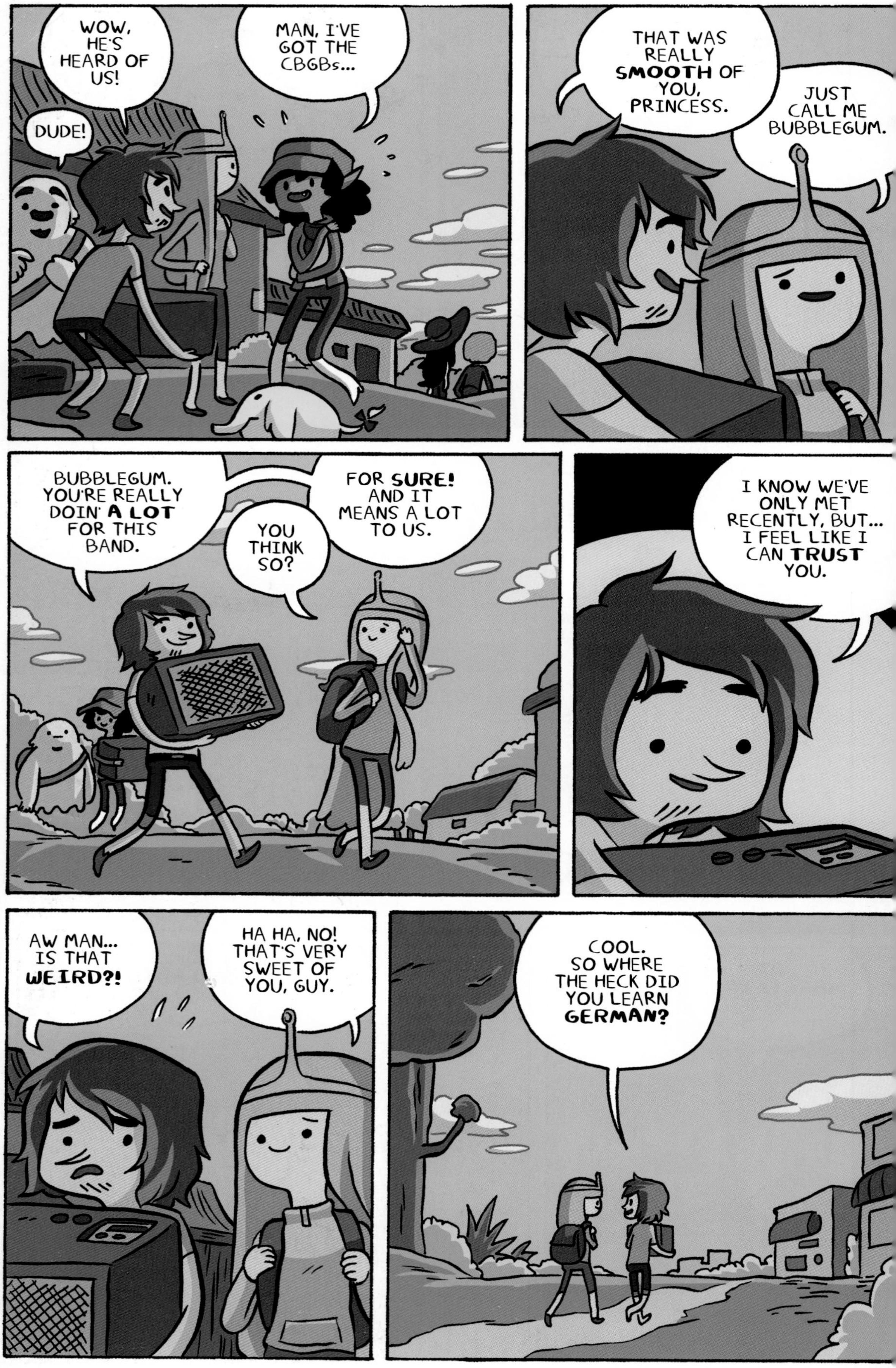

WOW, HE'S HEARD OF US!
DUDE!
MAN, I'VE GOT THE CBGBs...
THAT WAS REALLY SMOOTH OF YOU, PRINCESS.
JUST CALL ME BUBBLEGUM.
BUBBLEGUM. YOU'RE REALLY DOIN' A LOT FOR THIS BAND.
YOU THINK SO?
FOR SURE! AND IT MEANS A LOT TO US.
I KNOW WE'VE ONLY MET RECENTLY, BUT... I FEEL LIKE I CAN TRUST YOU.
AW MAN... IS THAT WEIRD?!
HA HA, NO! THAT'S VERY SWEET OF YOU, GUY.
COOL. SO WHERE THE HECK DID YOU LEARN GERMAN?

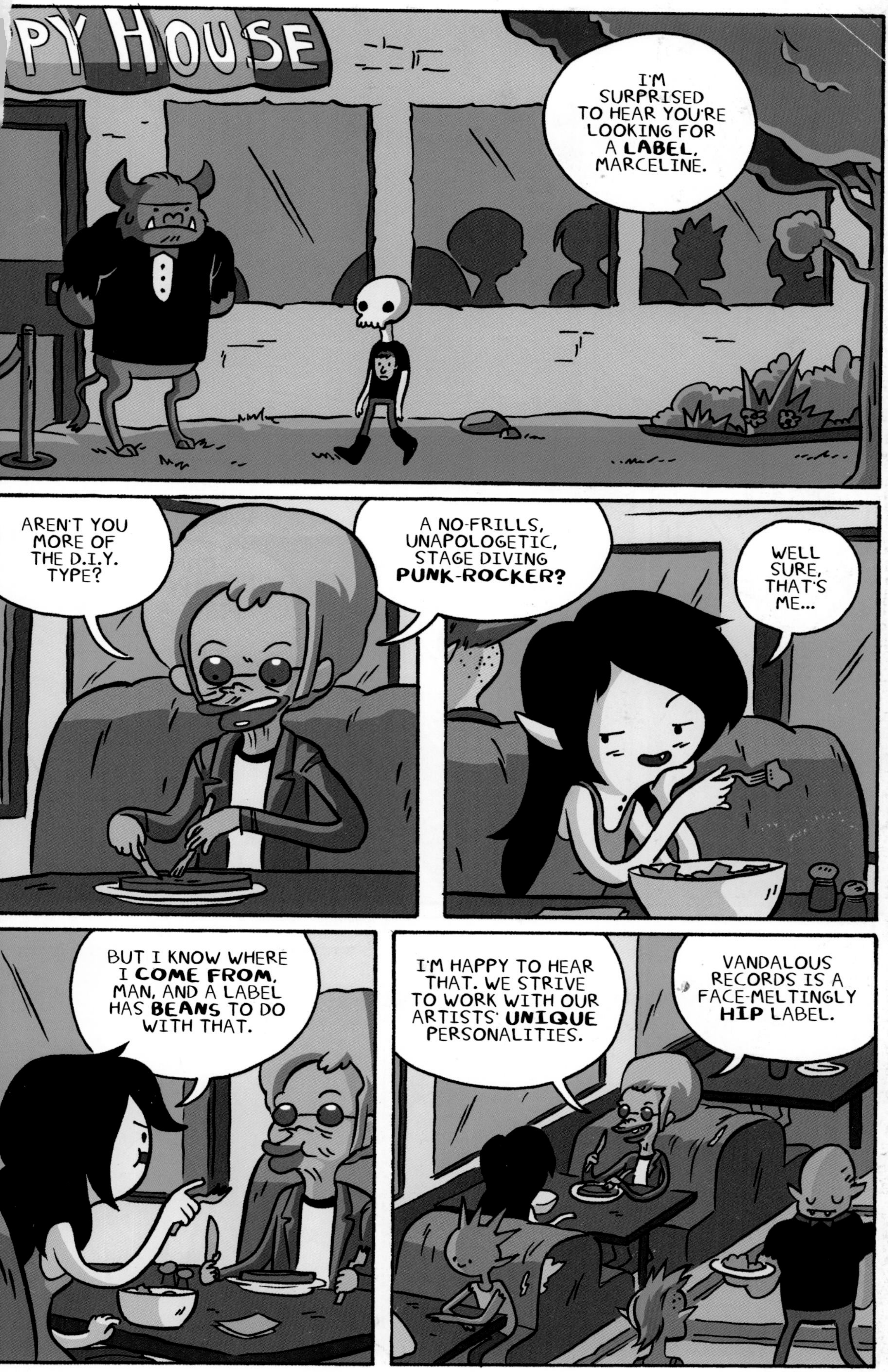
PY HOUSE
I'M SURPRISED TO HEAR YOU'RE LOOKING FOR A **LABEL**, MARCELINE.
AREN'T YOU MORE OF THE D.I.Y. TYPE?
A NO-FRILLS, UNAPOLOGETIC, STAGE DIVING **PUNK-ROCKER?**
WELL SURE, THAT'S ME...
BUT I KNOW WHERE I **COME FROM**, MAN, AND A LABEL HAS **BEANS** TO DO WITH THAT.
I'M HAPPY TO HEAR THAT. WE STRIVE TO WORK WITH OUR ARTISTS' **UNIQUE** PERSONALITIES.
VANDALOUS RECORDS IS A FACE-MELTINGLY **HIP** LABEL.

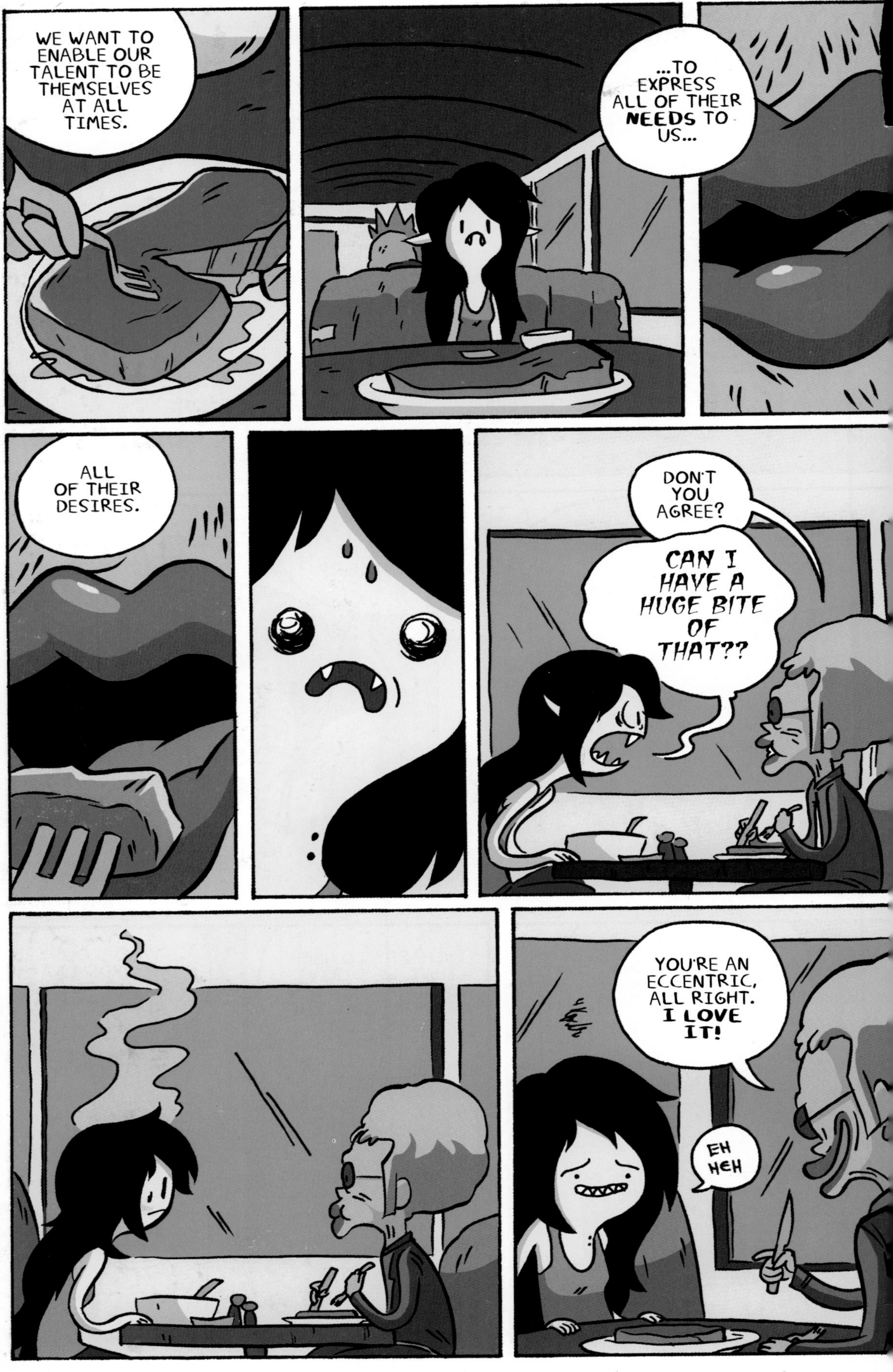
WE WANT TO ENABLE OUR TALENT TO BE THEMSELVES AT ALL TIMES.
...TO EXPRESS ALL OF THEIR **NEEDS** TO US...
ALL OF THEIR DESIRES.
DON'T YOU AGREE?
CAN I HAVE A HUGE BITE OF THAT??
YOU'RE AN ECCENTRIC, ALL RIGHT. **I LOVE IT!**
EH HEH

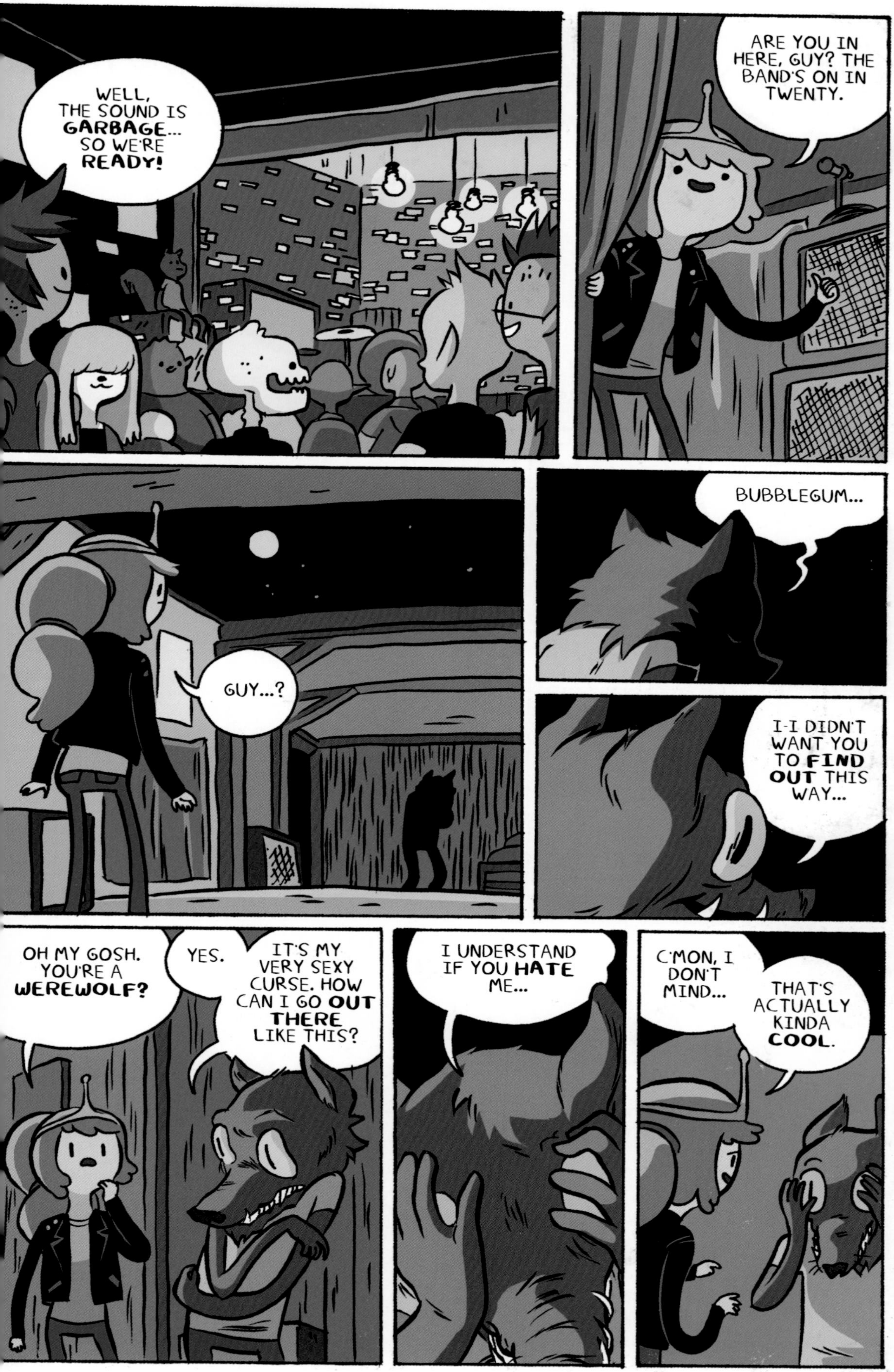
WELL, THE SOUND IS **GARBAGE**... SO WE'RE **READY!**
ARE YOU IN HERE, GUY? THE BAND'S ON IN TWENTY.
GUY...?
BUBBLEGUM...
I-I DIDN'T WANT YOU TO **FIND OUT** THIS WAY...
OH MY GOSH. YOU'RE A **WEREWOLF?**
YES.
IT'S MY VERY SEXY CURSE. HOW CAN I GO **OUT THERE** LIKE THIS?
I UNDERSTAND IF YOU **HATE** ME...
C'MON, I DON'T MIND...
THAT'S ACTUALLY KINDA **COOL**.

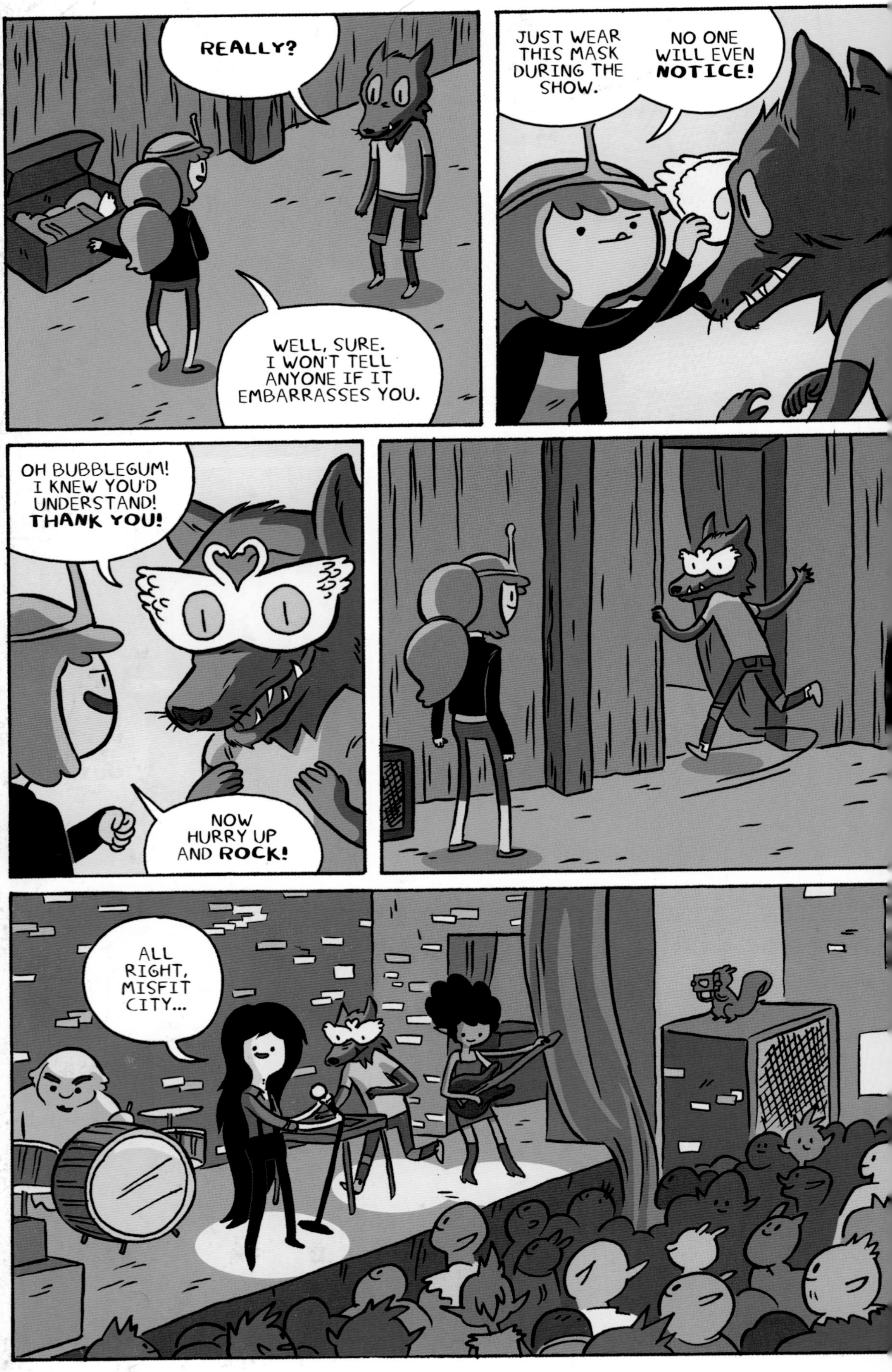
REALLY?
WELL, SURE. I WON'T TELL ANYONE IF IT EMBARRASSES YOU.
JUST WEAR THIS MASK DURING THE SHOW.
NO ONE WILL EVEN **NOTICE!**
OH BUBBLEGUM! I KNEW YOU'D UNDERSTAND! **THANK YOU!**
NOW HURRY UP AND **ROCK!**
ALL RIGHT, MISFIT CITY...

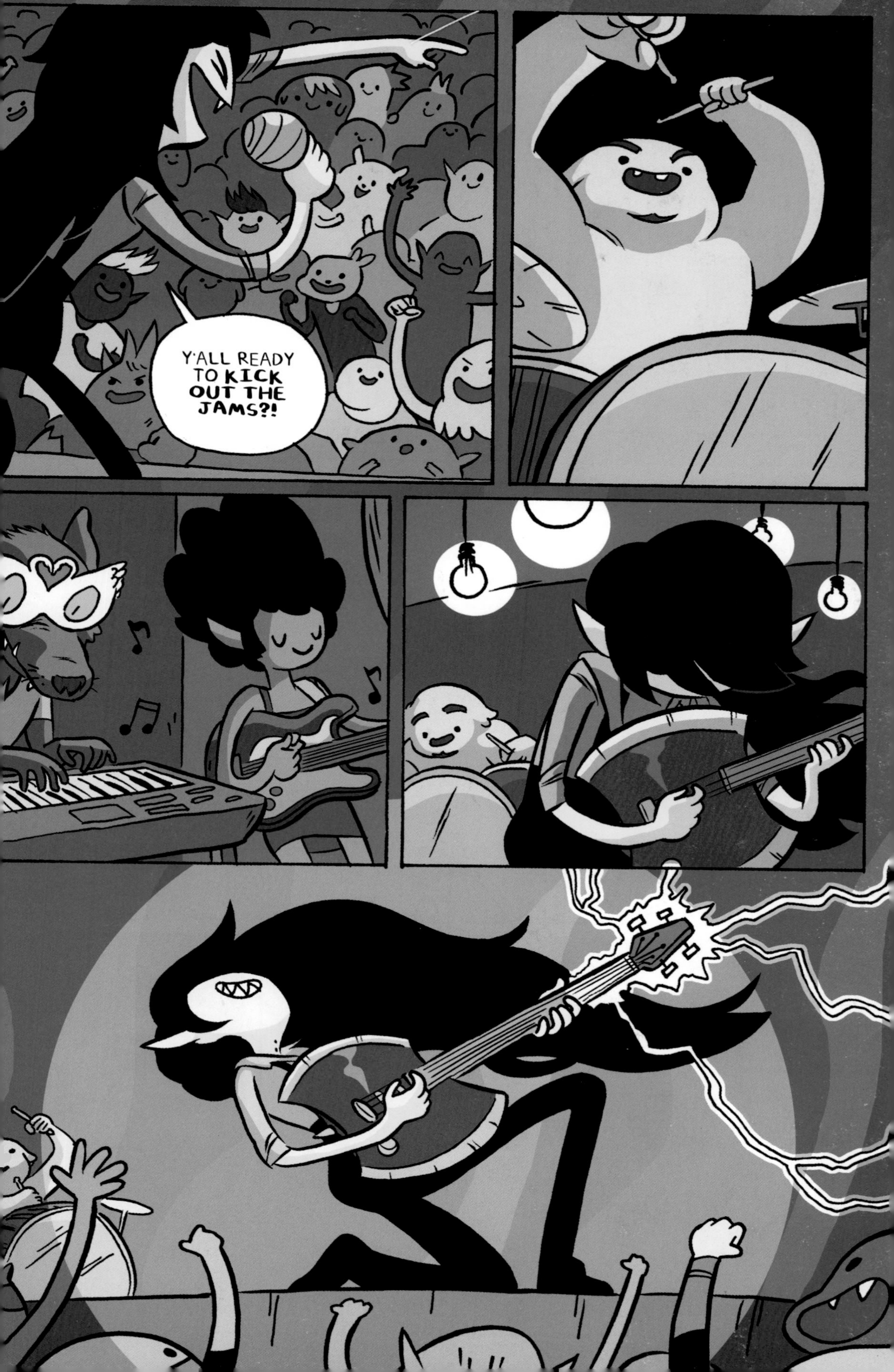
Y'ALL READY TO KICK OUT THE JAMS?!

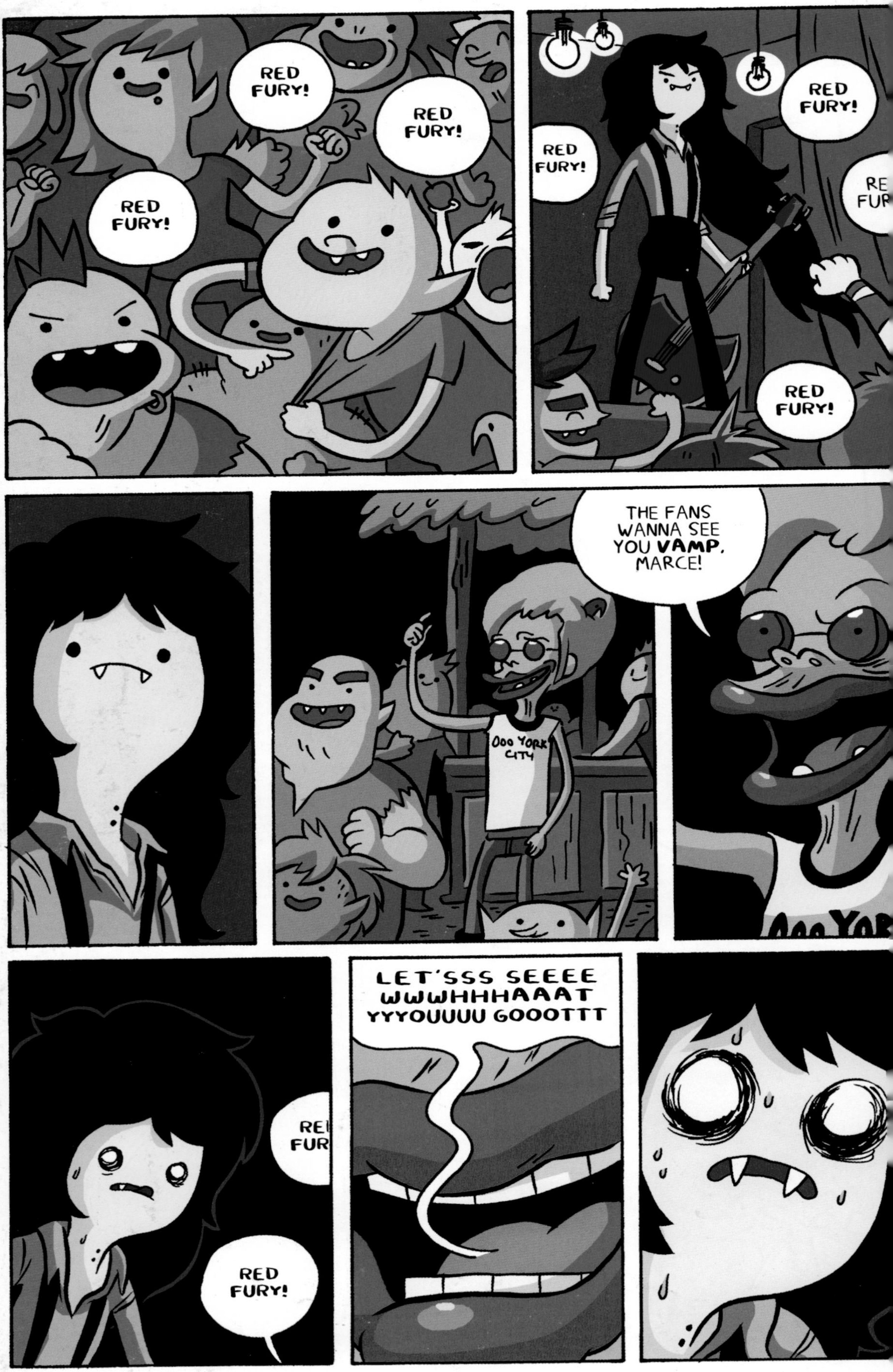
RED FURY!
RED FURY!
RED FURY!
RED FURY!
RED FURY!
RED FURY!
OOO YORK CITY
THE FANS WANNA SEE YOU **VAMP**, MARCE!
RED FURY!
LET'SSS SEEEE WWWHHHAAAT YYYOUUUU GOOOTTT

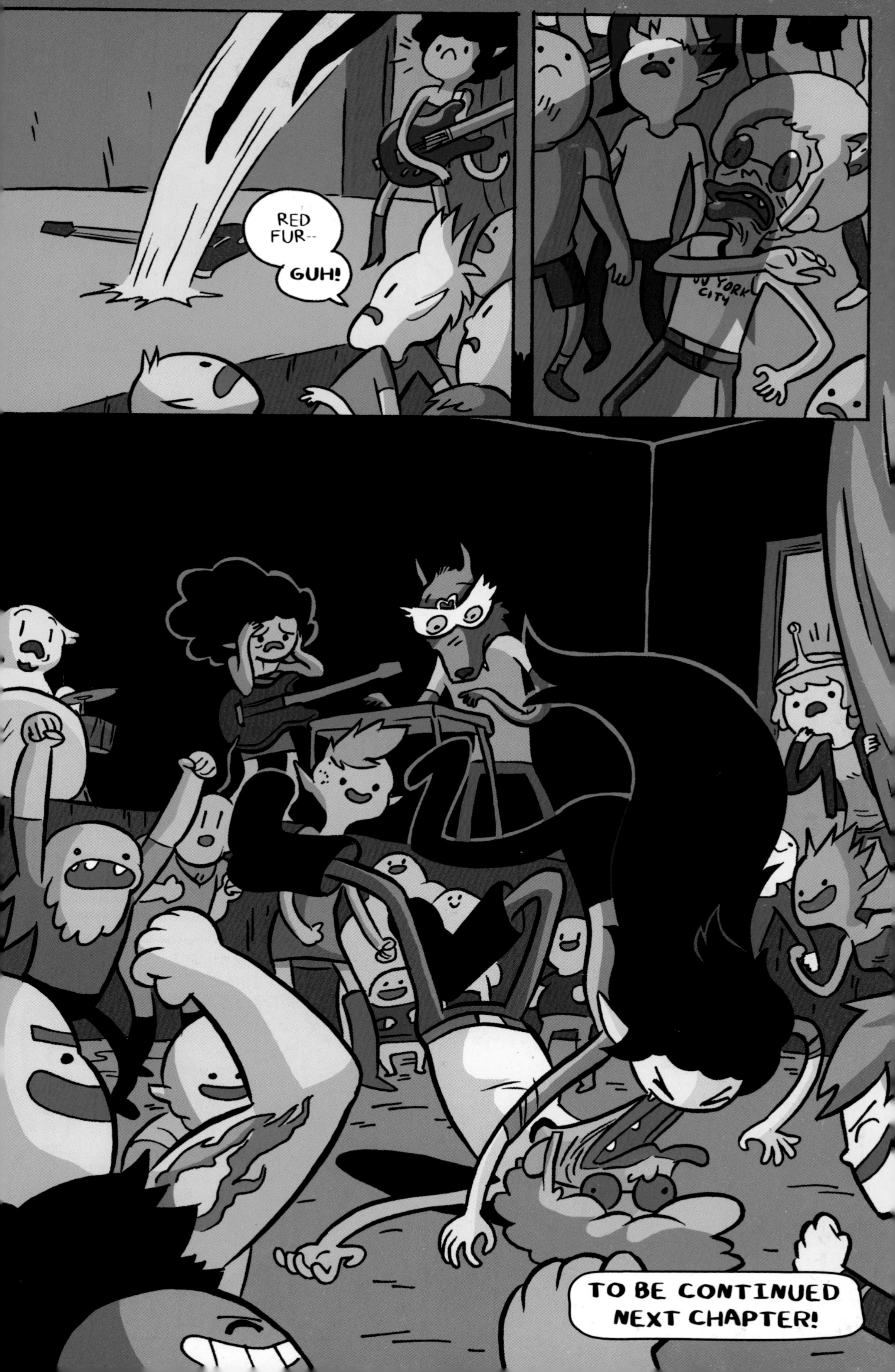
RED FUR--
GUH!
NU YORK CITY
TO BE CONTINUED NEXT CHAPTER!

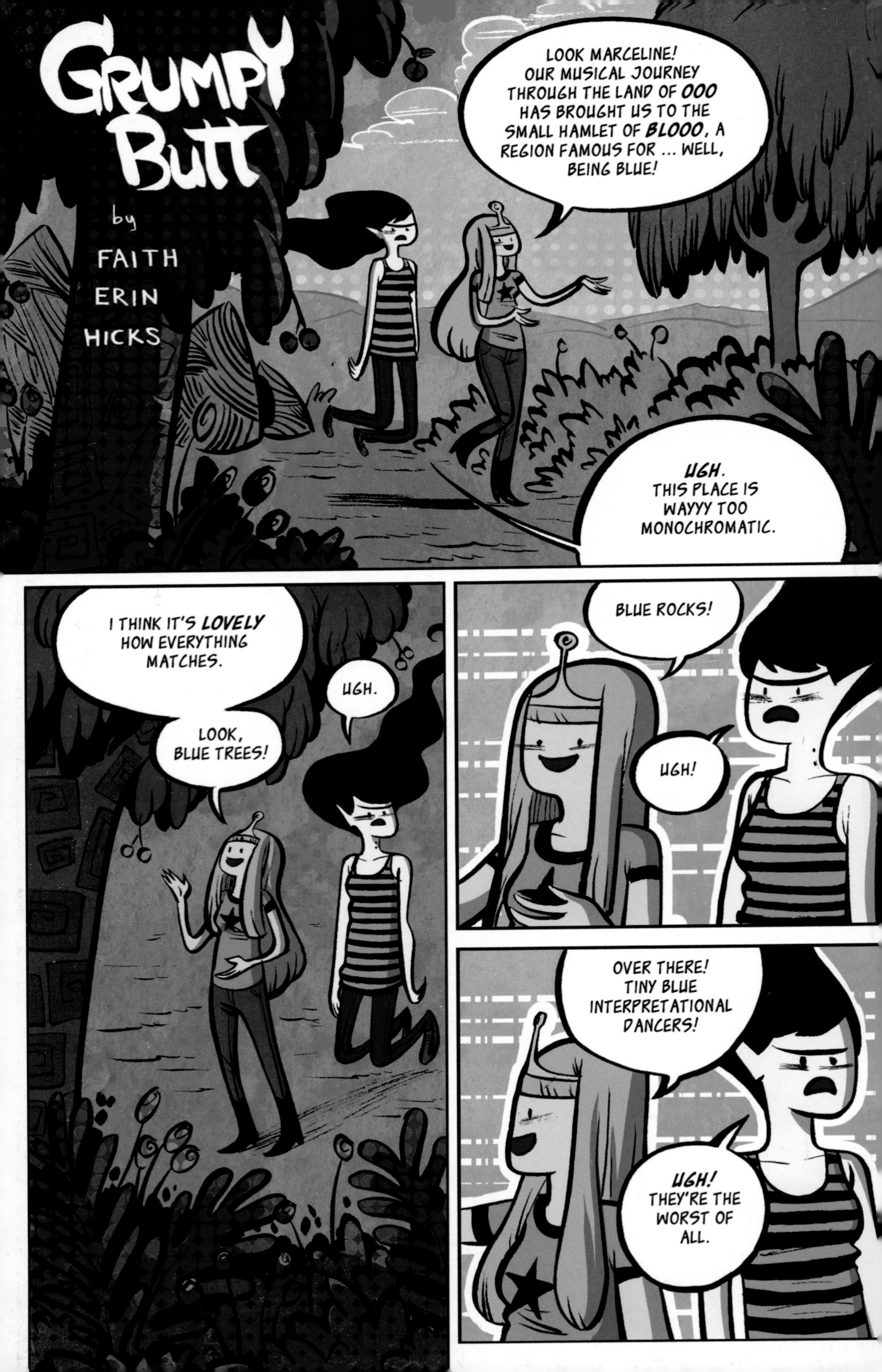
GRUMPY BUTT
by FAITH ERIN HICKS
LOOK MARCELINE! OUR MUSICAL JOURNEY THROUGH THE LAND OF OOO HAS BROUGHT US TO THE SMALL HAMLET OF BLOOO, A REGION FAMOUS FOR ... WELL, BEING BLUE!
UGH. THIS PLACE IS WAYYY TOO MONOCHROMATIC.
I THINK IT'S LOVELY HOW EVERYTHING MATCHES.
UGH.
LOOK, BLUE TREES!
BLUE ROCKS!
UGH!
OVER THERE! TINY BLUE INTERPRETATIONAL DANCERS!
UGH! THEY'RE THE WORST OF ALL.

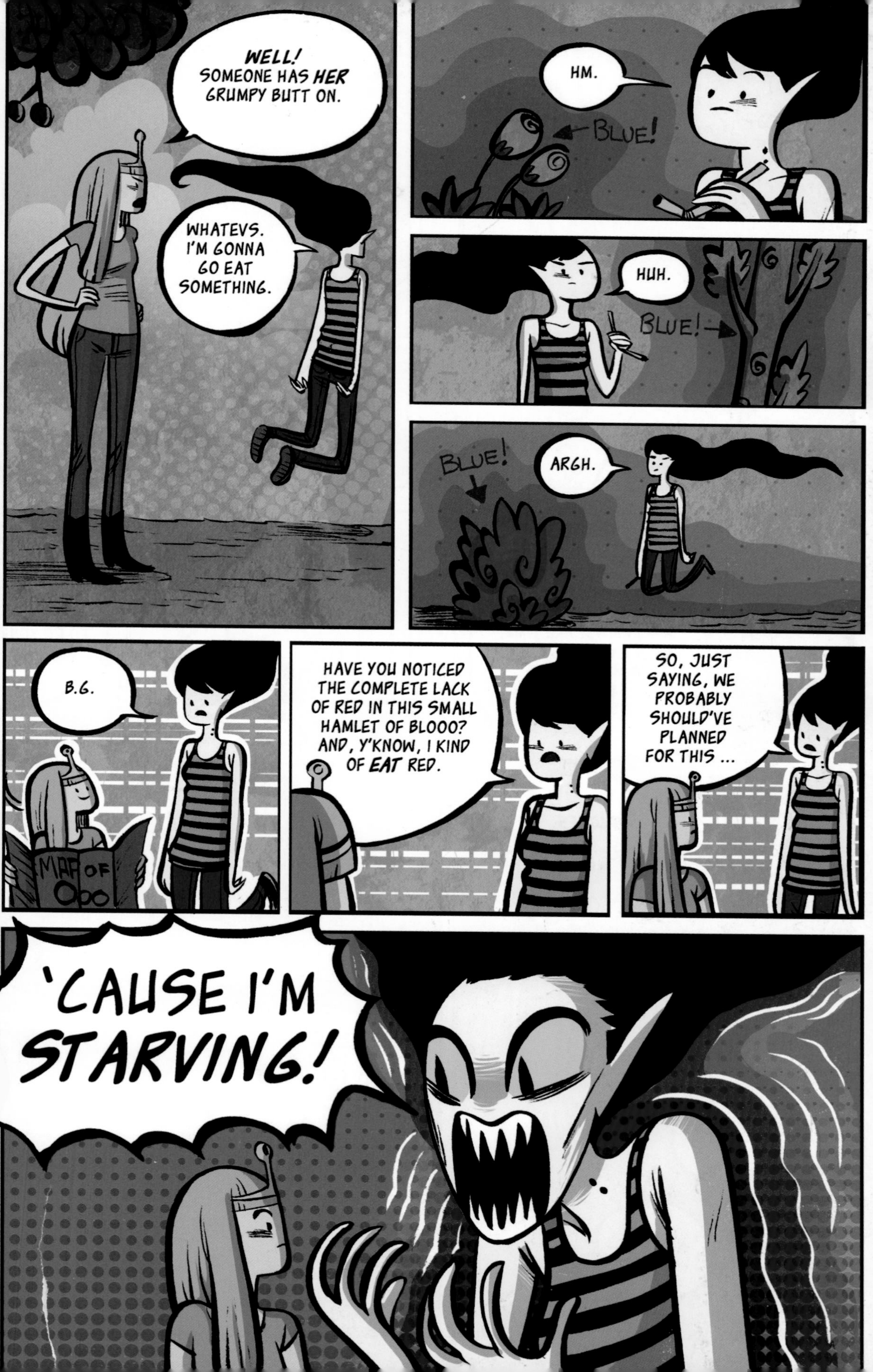
WELL! SOMEONE HAS HER GRUMPY BUTT ON.
WHATEVS. I'M GONNA GO EAT SOMETHING.
HM.
BLUE!
HUH.
BLUE!
BLUE!
ARGH.
B.G.
MAP OF Ooo
HAVE YOU NOTICED THE COMPLETE LACK OF RED IN THIS SMALL HAMLET OF BLOOO? AND, Y'KNOW, I KIND OF EAT RED.
SO, JUST SAYING, WE PROBABLY SHOULD'VE PLANNED FOR THIS ...
'CAUSE I'M STARVING!

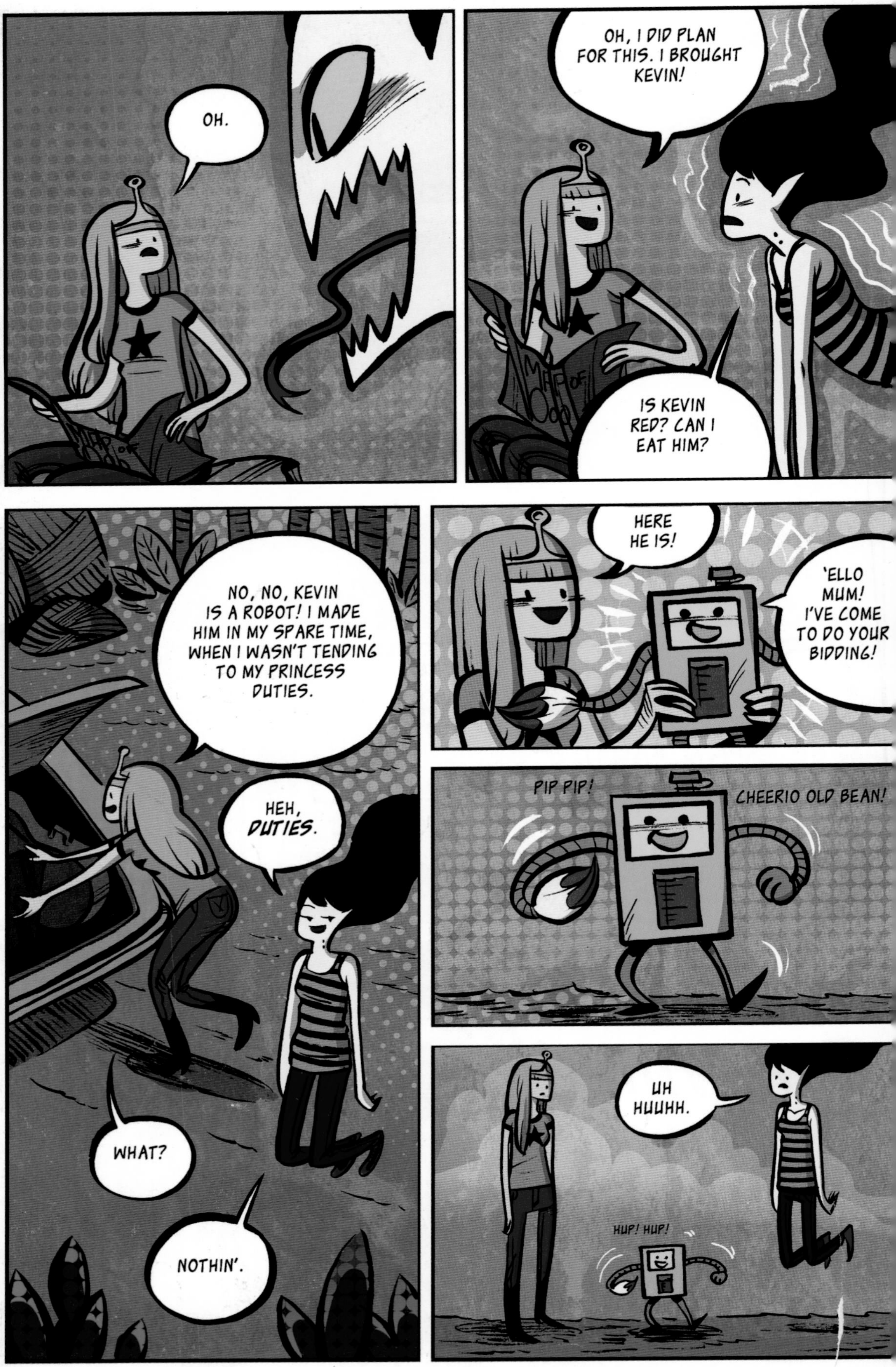
OH.
OH, I DID PLAN FOR THIS. I BROUGHT KEVIN!
IS KEVIN RED? CAN I EAT HIM?
NO, NO, KEVIN IS A ROBOT! I MADE HIM IN MY SPARE TIME, WHEN I WASN'T TENDING TO MY PRINCESS DUTIES.
HEH, *DUTIES*.
WHAT?
NOTHIN'.
HERE HE IS!
'ELLO MUM! I'VE COME TO DO YOUR BIDDING!
PIP PIP!
CHEERIO OLD BEAN!
UH HUUHH.
HUP! HUP!

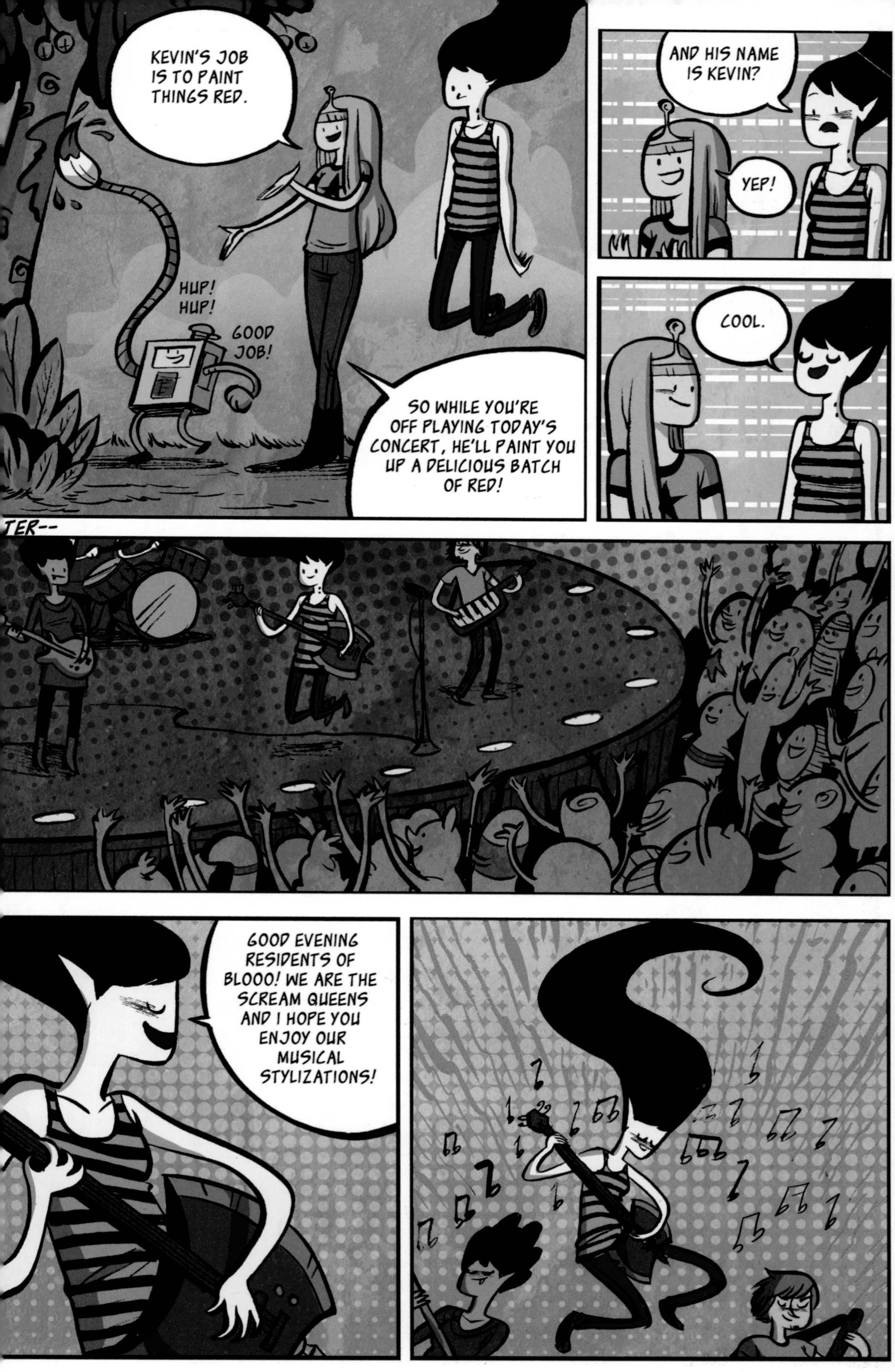
KEVIN'S JOB IS TO PAINT THINGS RED.
HUP! HUP!
GOOD JOB!
SO WHILE YOU'RE OFF PLAYING TODAY'S CONCERT, HE'LL PAINT YOU UP A DELICIOUS BATCH OF RED!
AND HIS NAME IS KEVIN?
YEP!
COOL.
TER--
GOOD EVENING RESIDENTS OF BLOOO! WE ARE THE SCREAM QUEENS AND I HOPE YOU ENJOY OUR MUSICAL STYLIZATIONS!

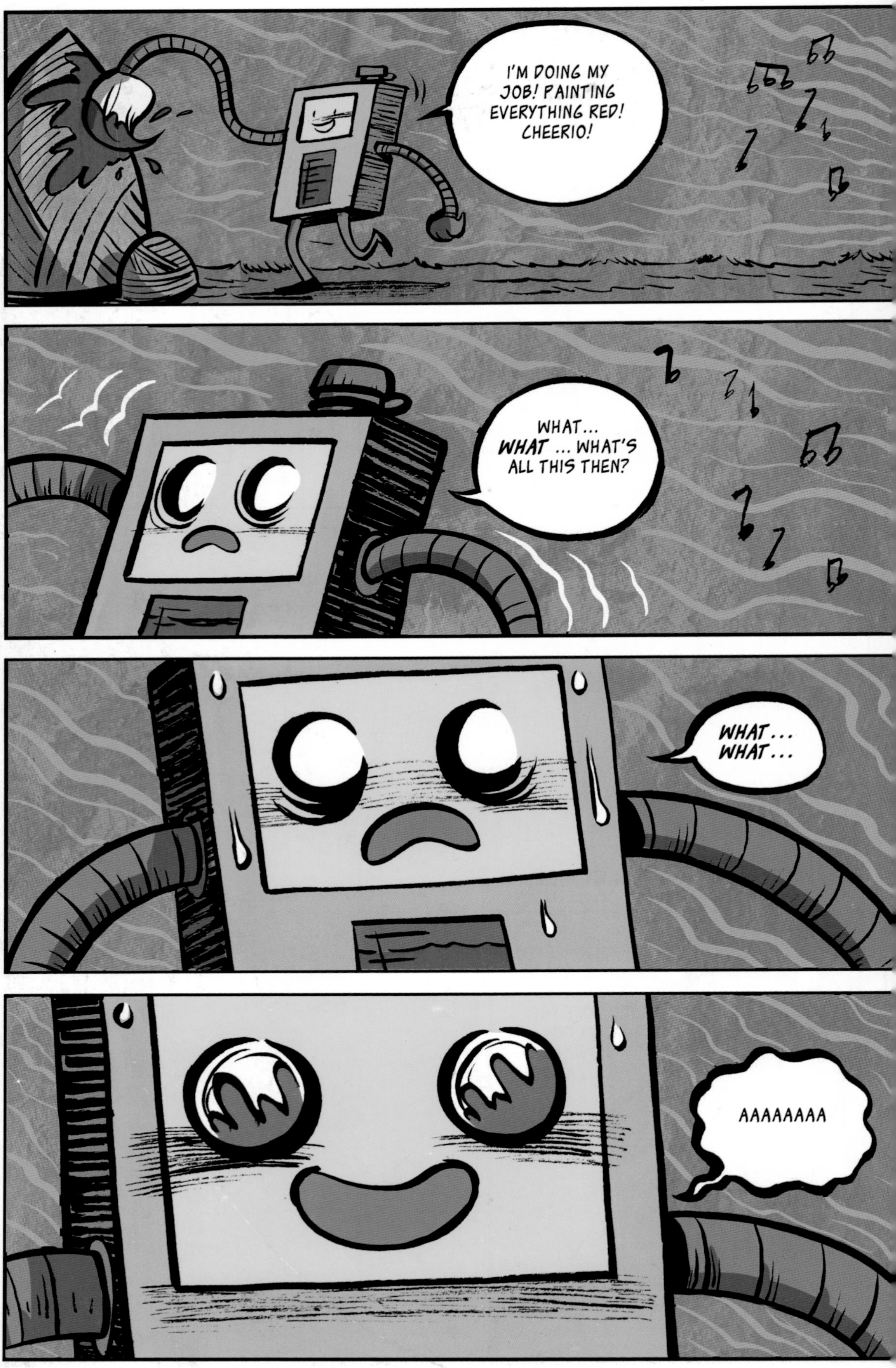
I'M DOING MY JOB! PAINTING EVERYTHING RED! CHEERIO!
WHAT... *WHAT* ... WHAT'S ALL THIS THEN?
WHAT... WHAT...
AAAAAAAA

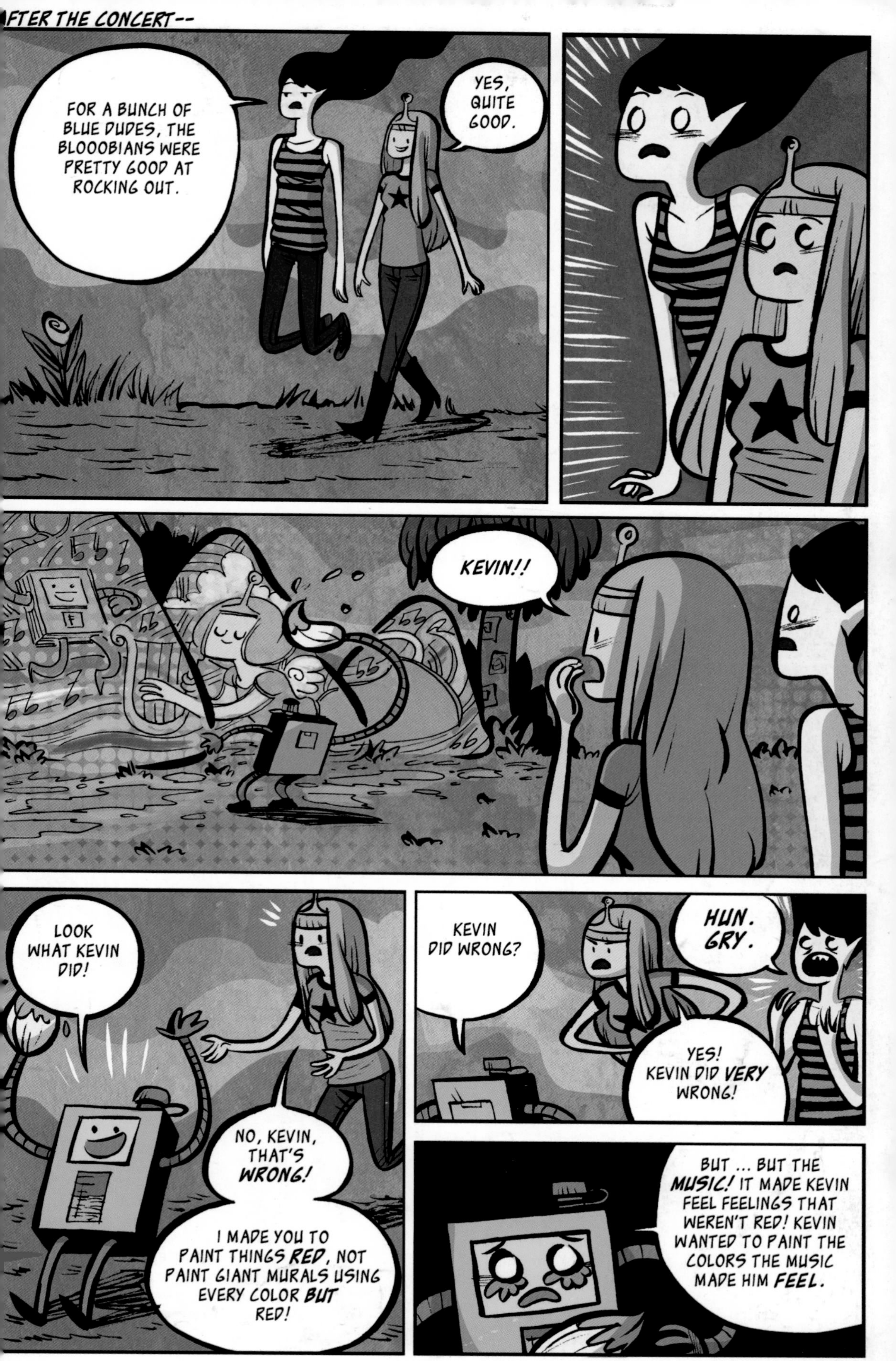
AFTER THE CONCERT--
FOR A BUNCH OF BLUE DUDES, THE BLOOOBIANS WERE PRETTY GOOD AT ROCKING OUT.
YES, QUITE GOOD.
KEVIN!!
LOOK WHAT KEVIN DID!
NO, KEVIN, THAT'S WRONG!
I MADE YOU TO PAINT THINGS RED, NOT PAINT GIANT MURALS USING EVERY COLOR BUT RED!
KEVIN DID WRONG?
HUN. GRY.
YES! KEVIN DID VERY WRONG!
BUT ... BUT THE MUSIC! IT MADE KEVIN FEEL FEELINGS THAT WEREN'T RED! KEVIN WANTED TO PAINT THE COLORS THE MUSIC MADE HIM FEEL.

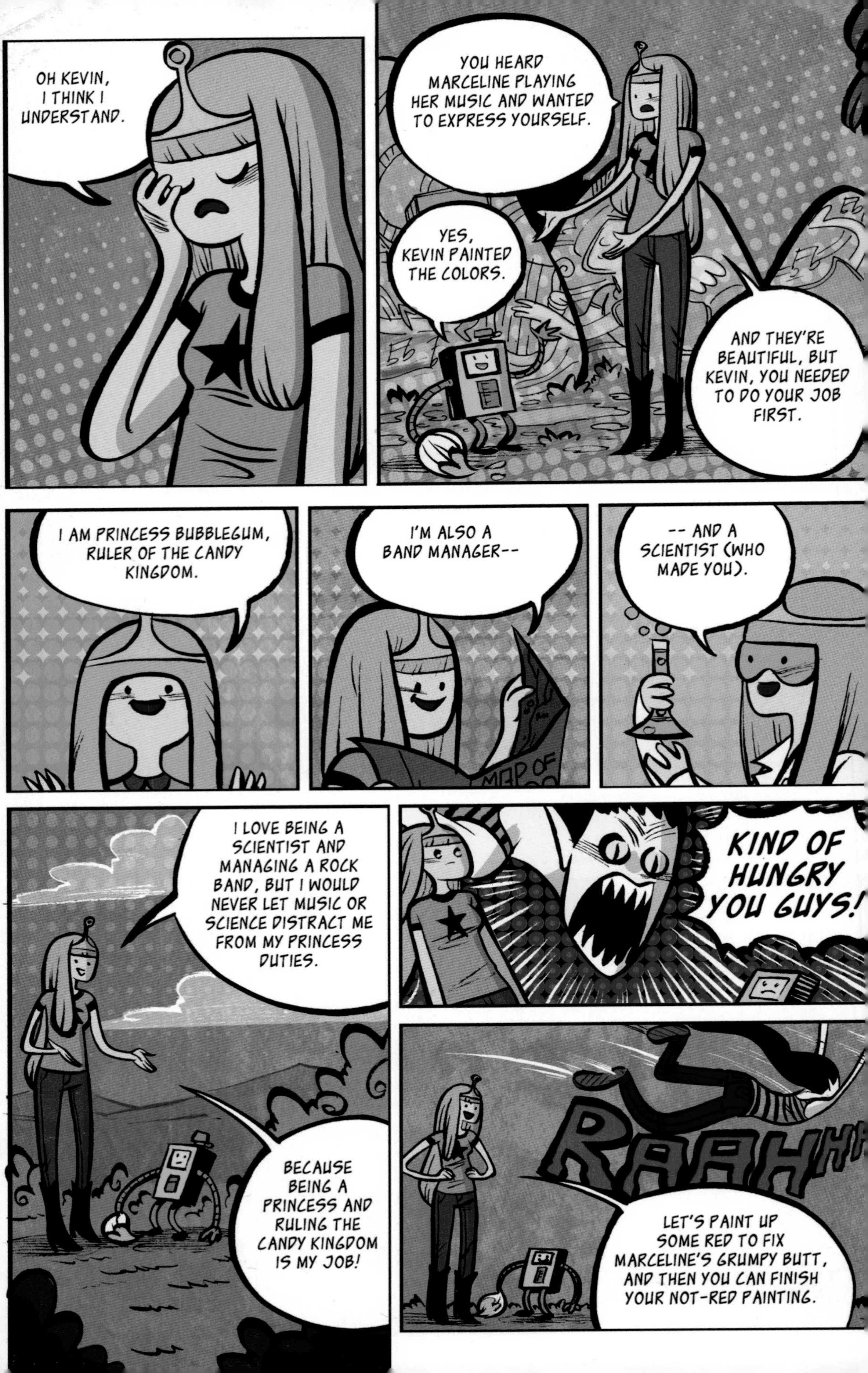
OH KEVIN, I THINK I UNDERSTAND.
YOU HEARD MARCELINE PLAYING HER MUSIC AND WANTED TO EXPRESS YOURSELF.
YES, KEVIN PAINTED THE COLORS.
AND THEY'RE BEAUTIFUL, BUT KEVIN, YOU NEEDED TO DO YOUR JOB FIRST.
I AM PRINCESS BUBBLEGUM, RULER OF THE CANDY KINGDOM.
I'M ALSO A BAND MANAGER--
-- AND A SCIENTIST (WHO MADE YOU).
I LOVE BEING A SCIENTIST AND MANAGING A ROCK BAND, BUT I WOULD NEVER LET MUSIC OR SCIENCE DISTRACT ME FROM MY PRINCESS DUTIES.
BECAUSE BEING A PRINCESS AND RULING THE CANDY KINGDOM IS MY JOB!
KIND OF HUNGRY YOU GUYS!
RAAHH
LET'S PAINT UP SOME RED TO FIX MARCELINE'S GRUMPY BUTT, AND THEN YOU CAN FINISH YOUR NOT-RED PAINTING.

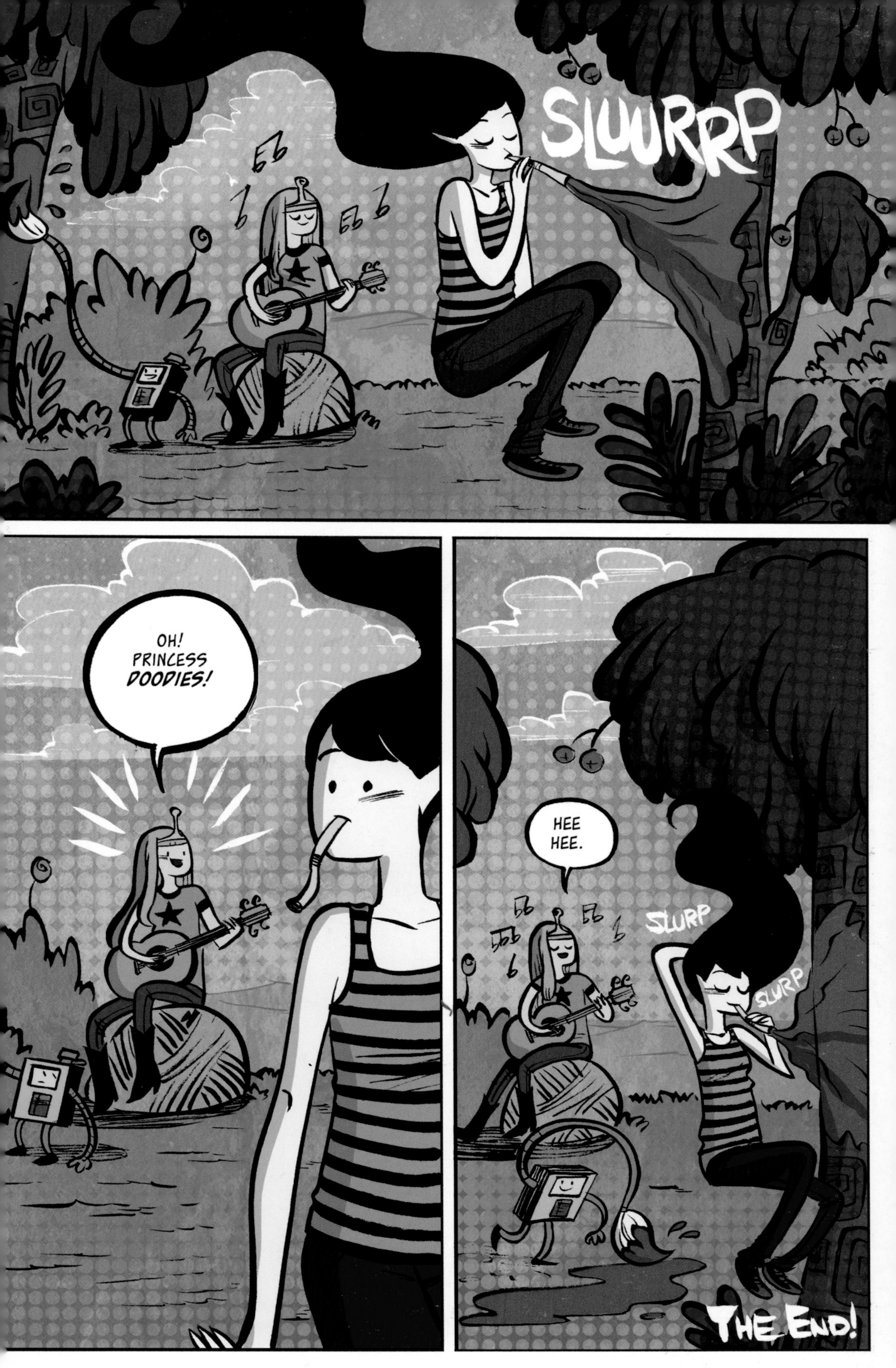
SLUURRP
OH! PRINCESS DOODIES!
HEE HEE.
SLURP
SLURP
THE END!

CHAPTER THREE

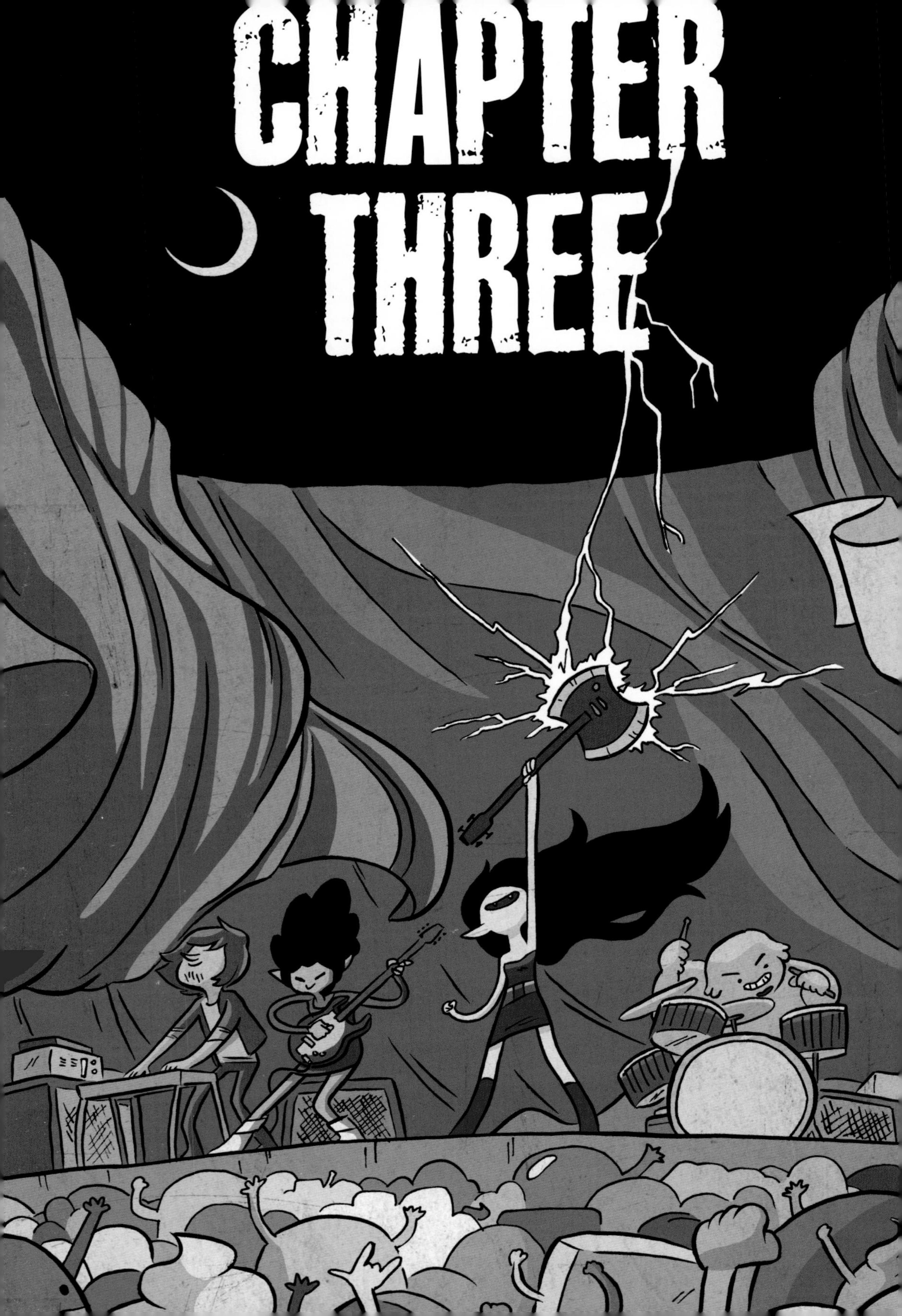

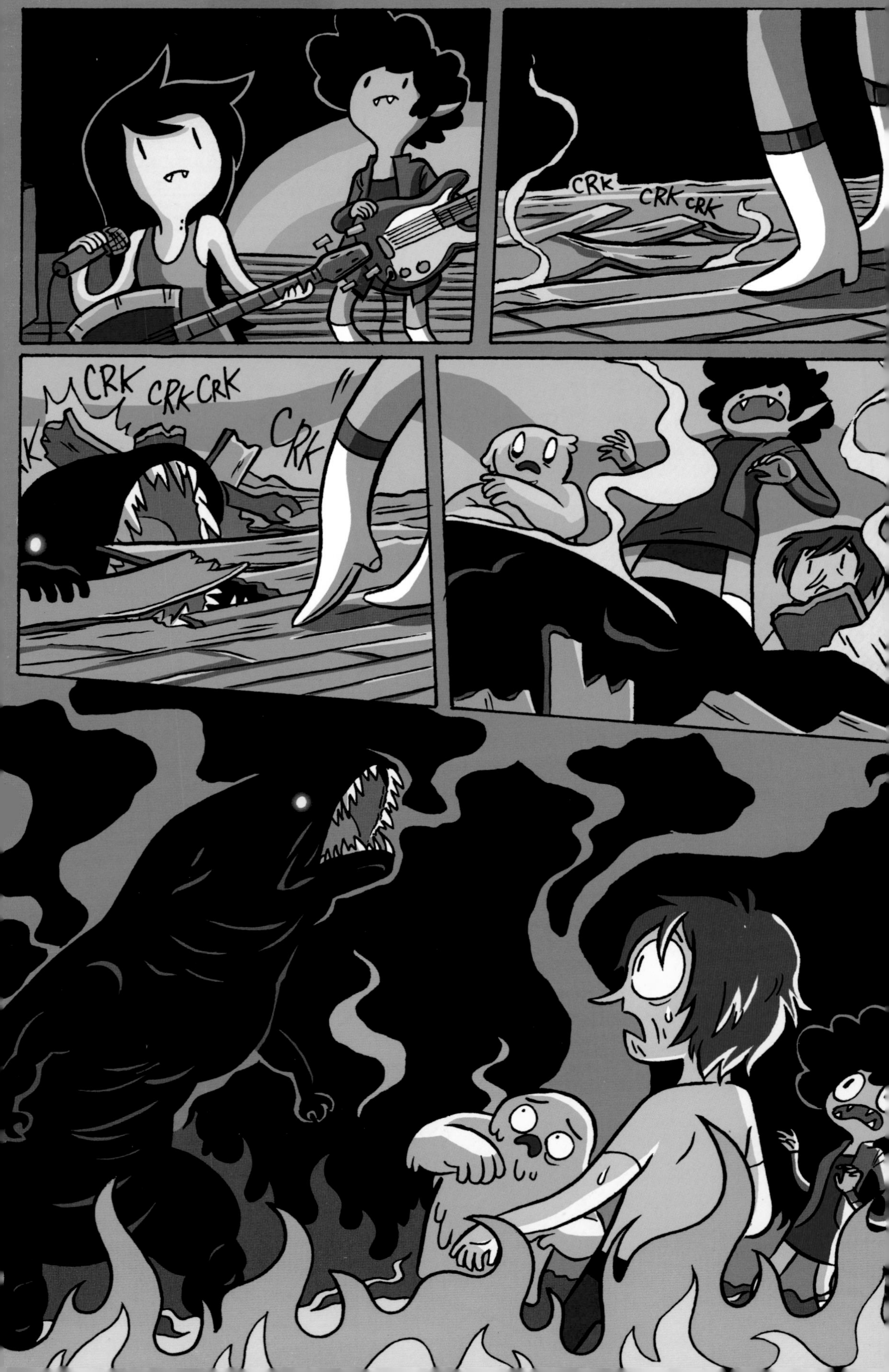

CRK
CRK CRK
CRK
CRK CRK
CRK

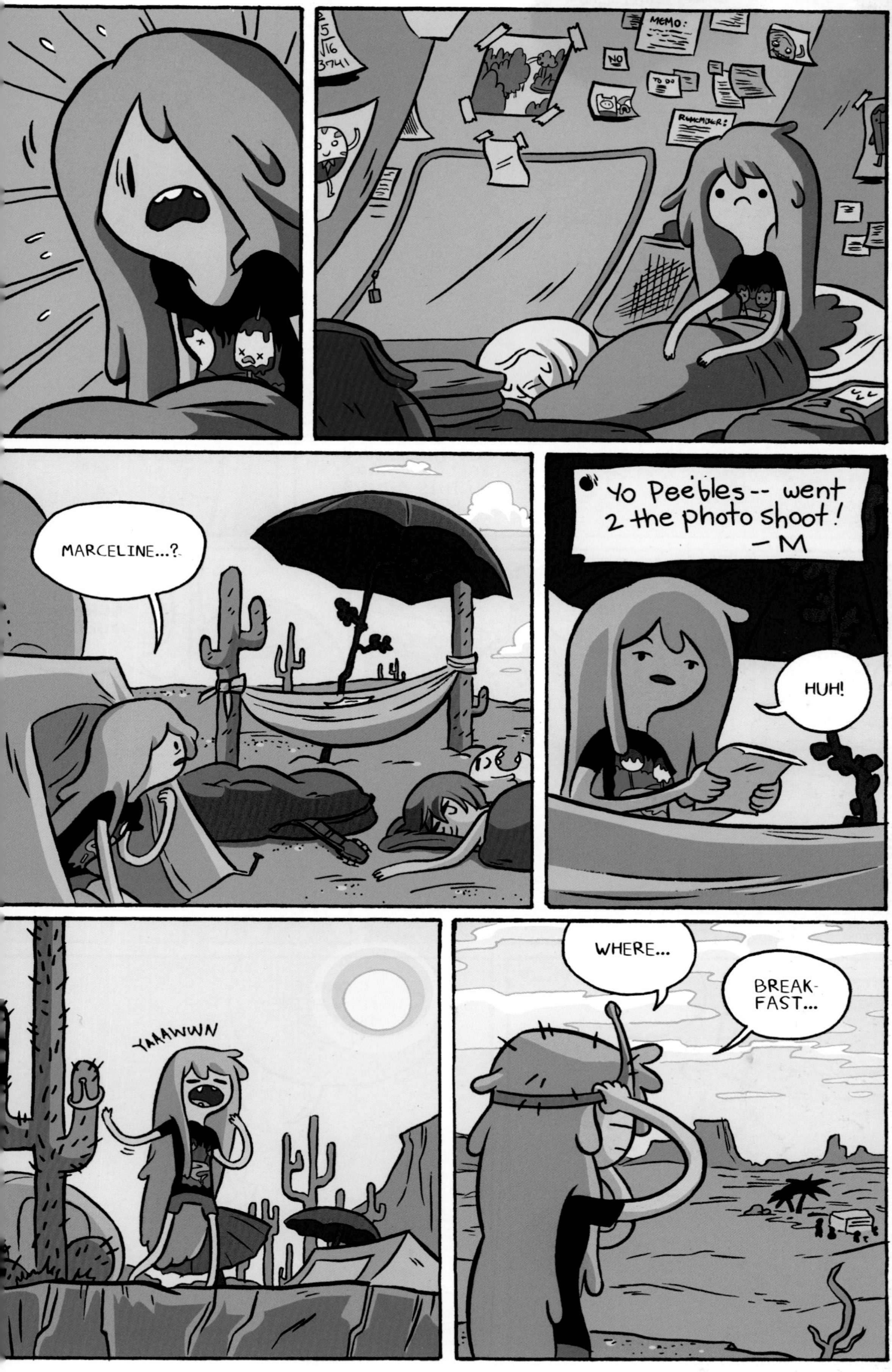
MARCELINE...?
Yo Peebles -- went 2 the photo shoot! -M
HUH!
YAAAWWN
WHERE...
BREAK-FAST...

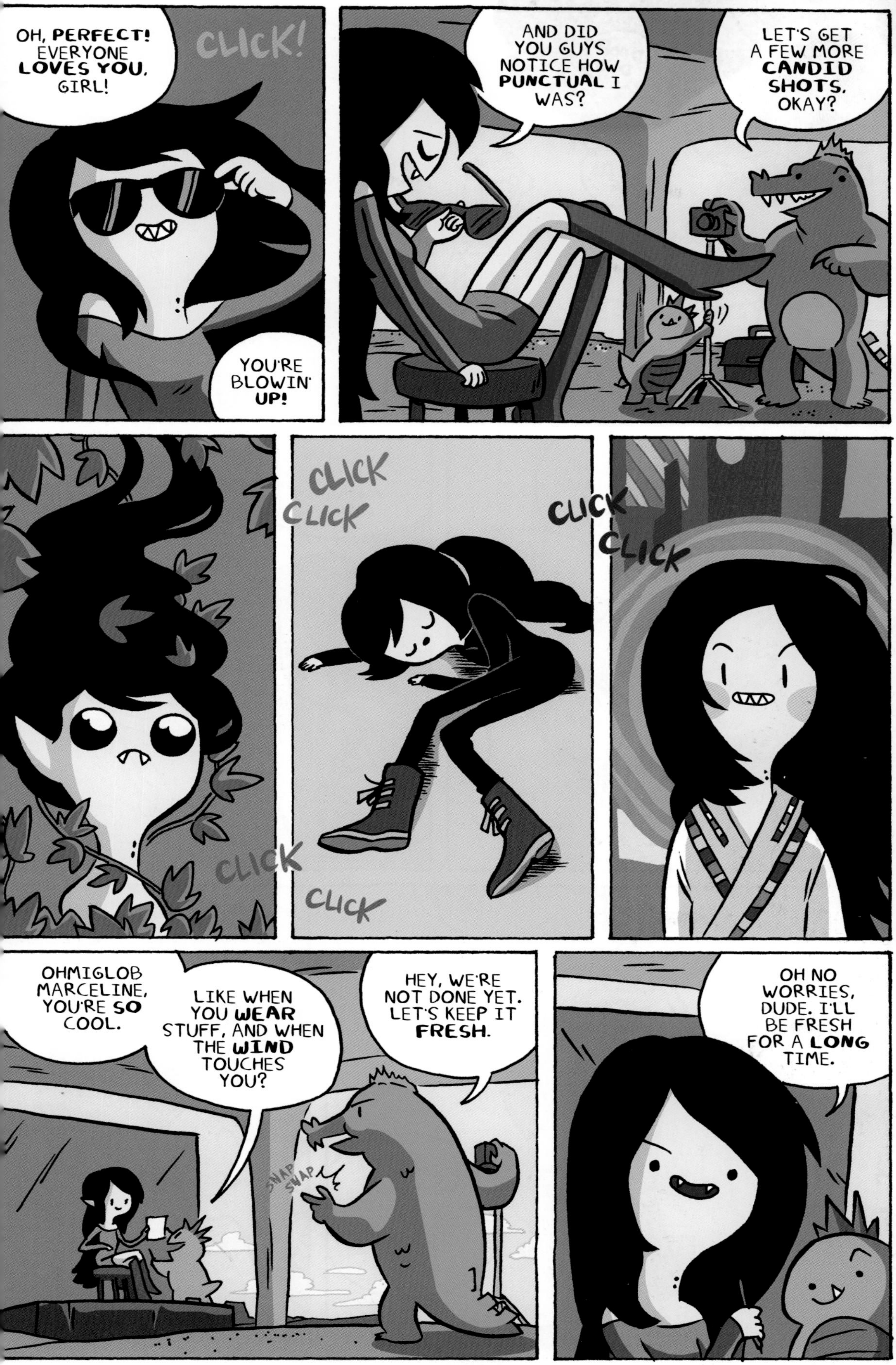
OH, PERFECT! EVERYONE LOVES YOU, GIRL!
CLICK!
YOU'RE BLOWIN' UP!
AND DID YOU GUYS NOTICE HOW PUNCTUAL I WAS?
LET'S GET A FEW MORE CANDID SHOTS, OKAY?
CLICK
CLICK
CLICK
CLICK
CLICK
CLICK
OHMIGLOB MARCELINE, YOU'RE SO COOL.
LIKE WHEN YOU WEAR STUFF, AND WHEN THE WIND TOUCHES YOU?
HEY, WE'RE NOT DONE YET. LET'S KEEP IT FRESH.
SWAP SWAP
OH NO WORRIES, DUDE. I'LL BE FRESH FOR A LONG TIME.

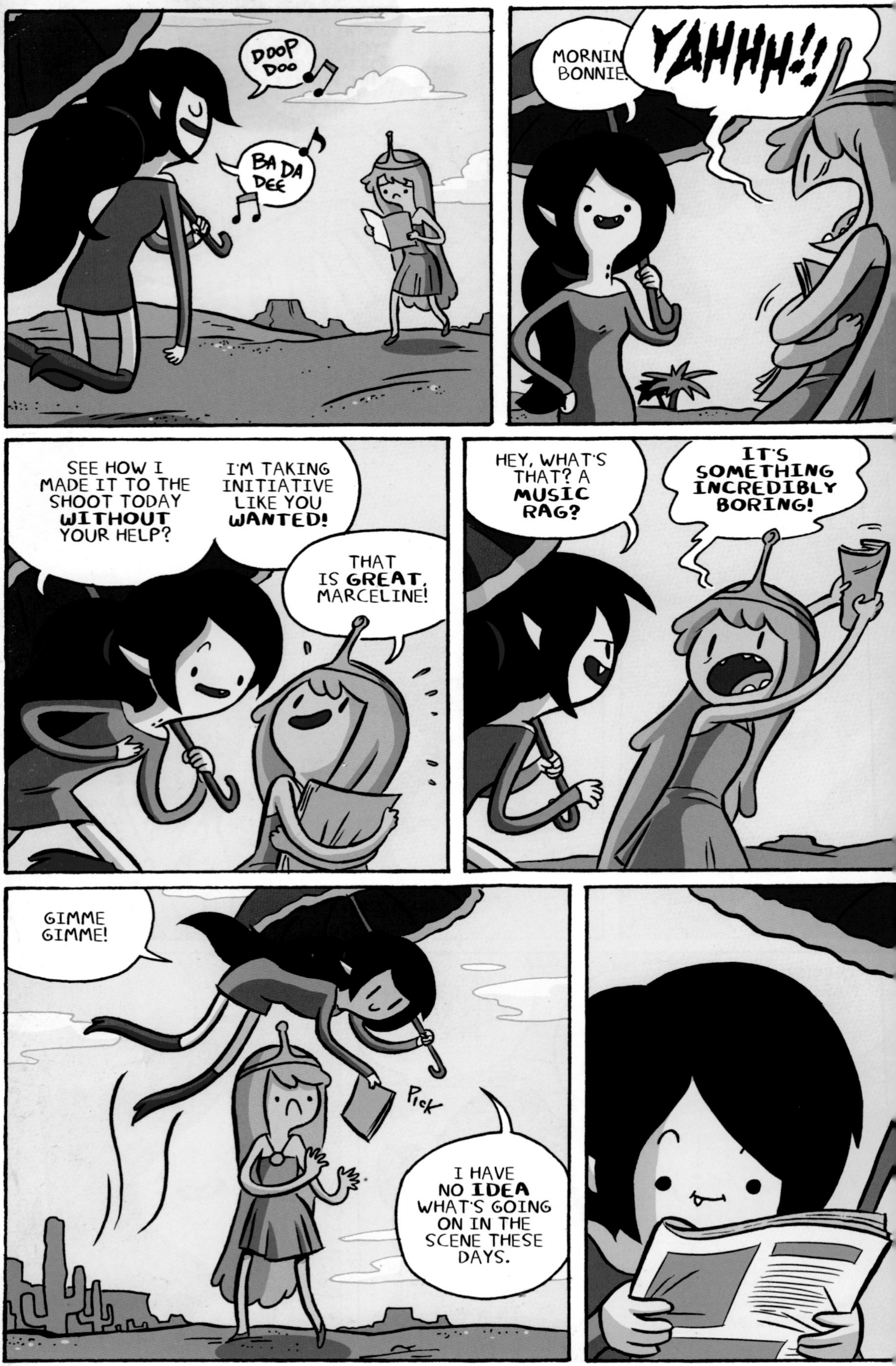

DOOP DOO
BA DA DEE
MORNIN' BONNIE!
YAHHH!!
SEE HOW I MADE IT TO THE SHOOT TODAY WITHOUT YOUR HELP?
I'M TAKING INITIATIVE LIKE YOU WANTED!
THAT IS GREAT, MARCELINE!
HEY, WHAT'S THAT? A MUSIC RAG?
IT'S SOMETHING INCREDIBLY BORING!
GIMME GIMME!
PICK
I HAVE NO IDEA WHAT'S GOING ON IN THE SCENE THESE DAYS.

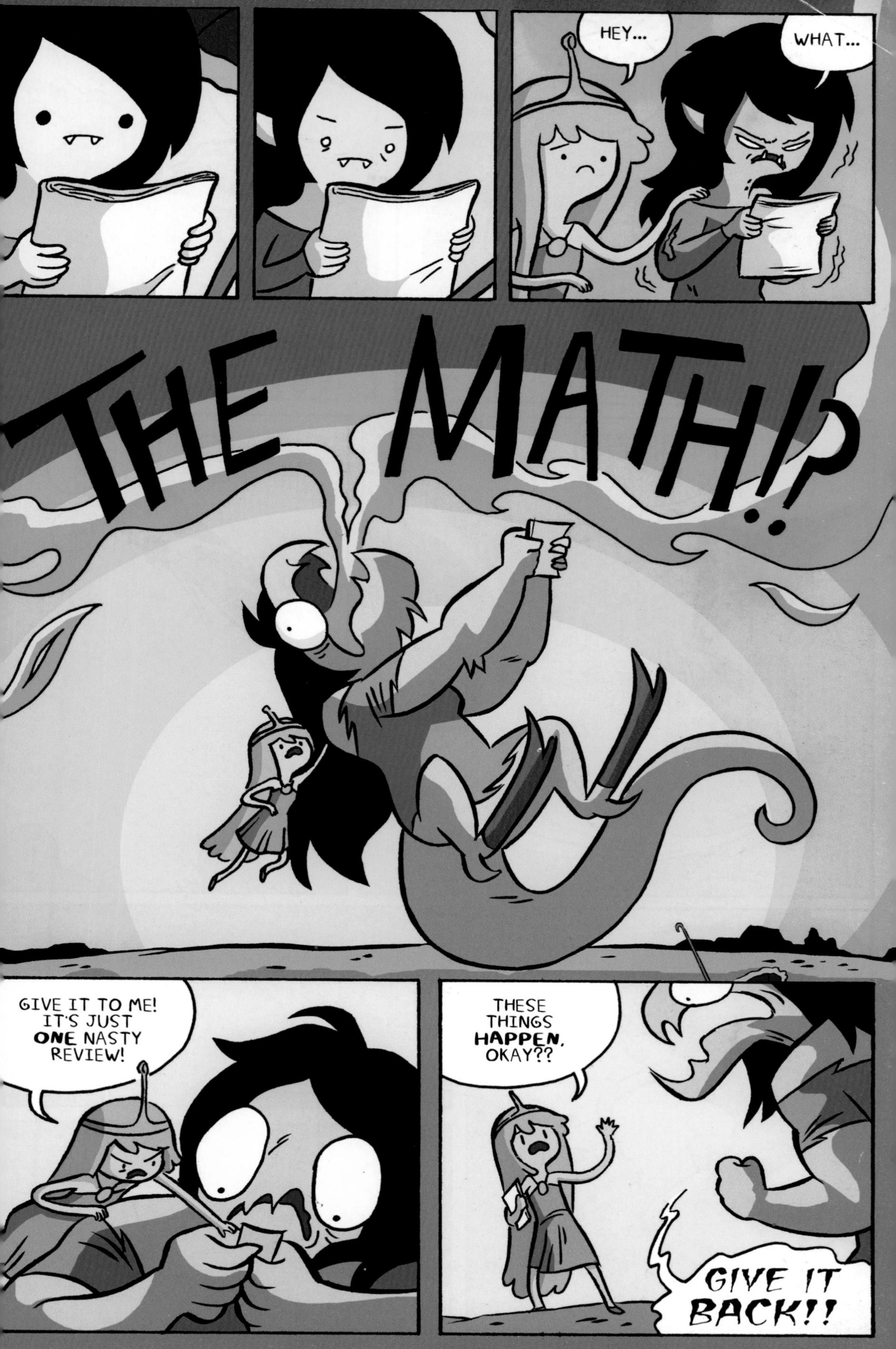
HEY...
WHAT...
THE MATH!?
GIVE IT TO ME! IT'S JUST **ONE** NASTY REVIEW!
THESE THINGS **HAPPEN**, OKAY??
GIVE IT BACK!!

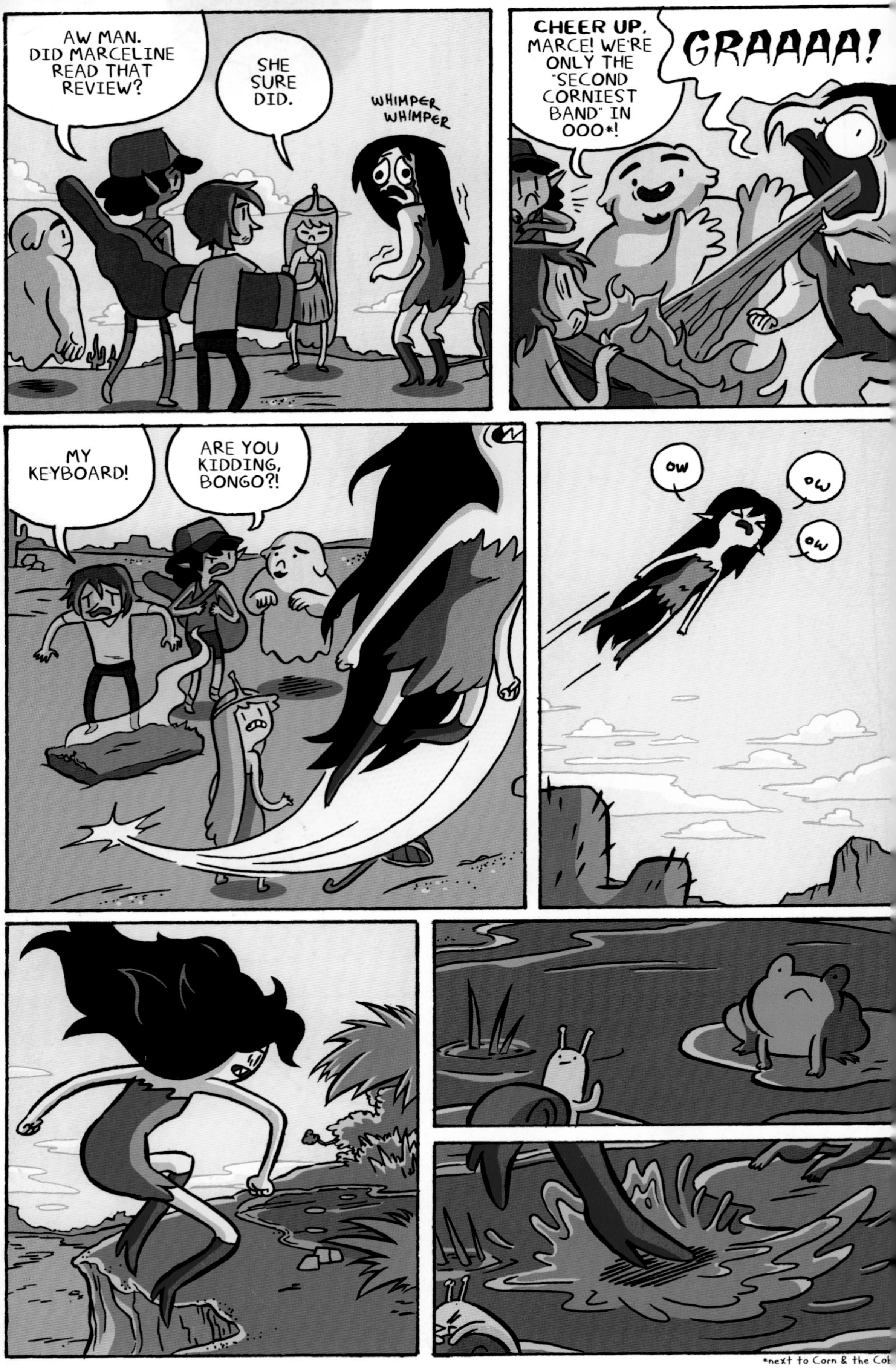
AW MAN. DID MARCELINE READ THAT REVIEW?
SHE SURE DID.
WHIMPER WHIMPER
CHEER UP, MARCE! WE'RE ONLY THE "SECOND CORNIEST BAND" IN OOO*!
GRAAAA!
MY KEYBOARD!
ARE YOU KIDDING, BONGO?!
OW
OW
OW

*next to Corn & the Co

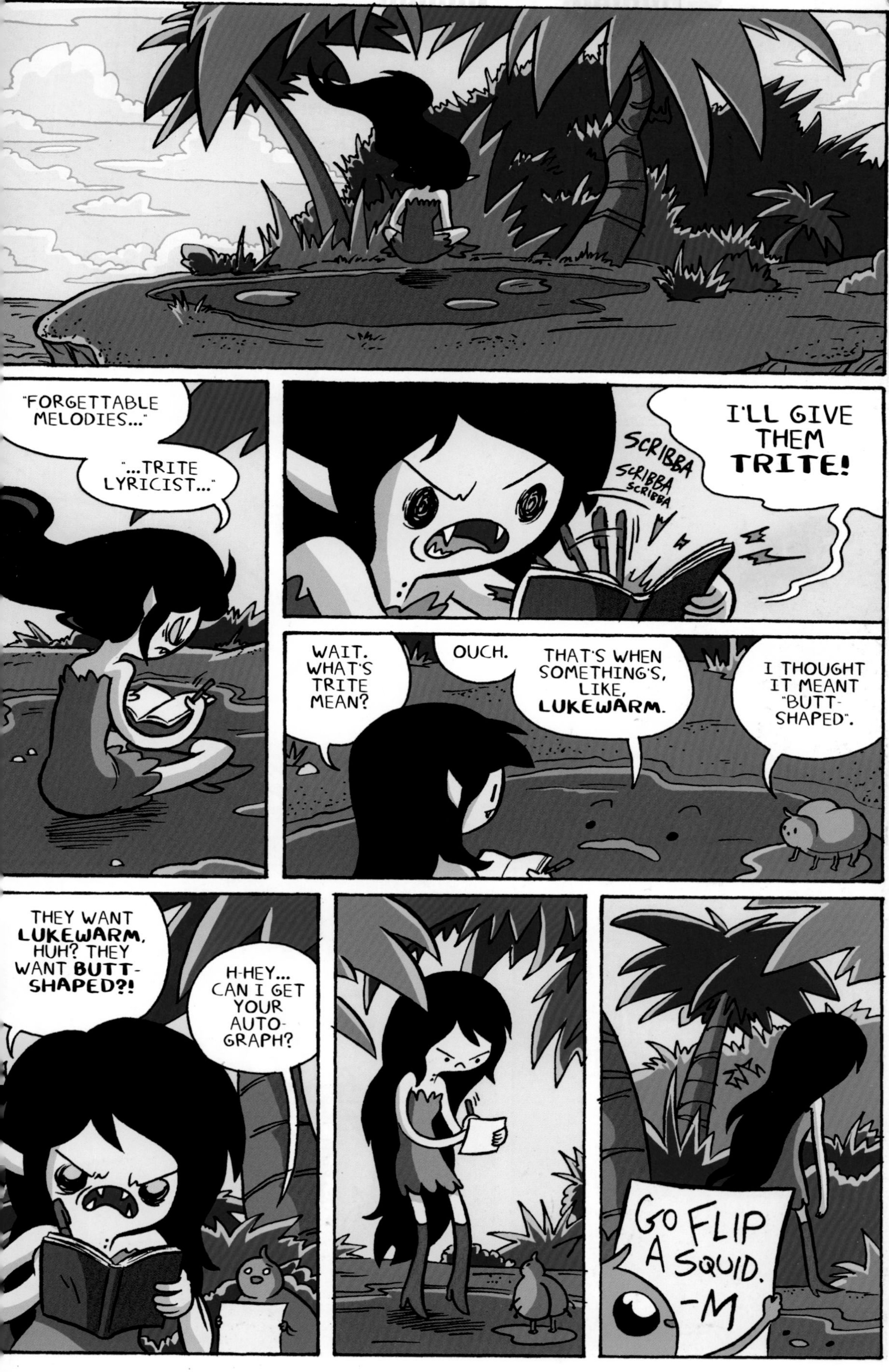
"FORGETTABLE MELODIES..."
"...TRITE LYRICIST..."
SCRIBBA SCRIBBA SCRIBBA
I'LL GIVE THEM TRITE!
WAIT. WHAT'S TRITE MEAN?
OUCH.
THAT'S WHEN SOMETHING'S, LIKE, LUKEWARM.
I THOUGHT IT MEANT "BUTT-SHAPED".
THEY WANT LUKEWARM, HUH? THEY WANT BUTT-SHAPED?!
H-HEY... CAN I GET YOUR AUTO-GRAPH?
GO FLIP A SQUID. -M

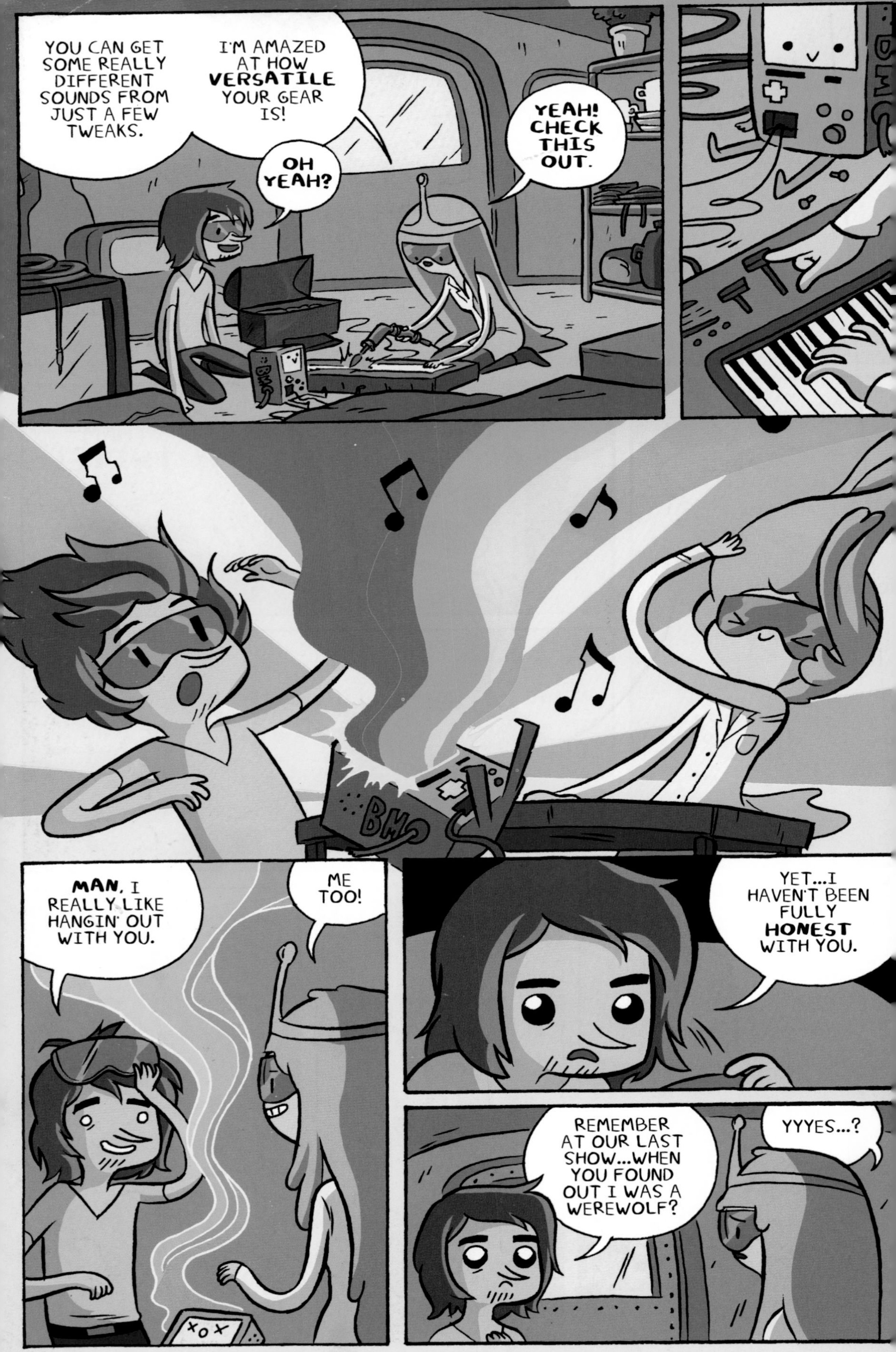
YOU CAN GET SOME REALLY DIFFERENT SOUNDS FROM JUST A FEW TWEAKS.
I'M AMAZED AT HOW VERSATILE YOUR GEAR IS!
OH YEAH?
YEAH! CHECK THIS OUT.
BMO
BMO
BMO
MAN, I REALLY LIKE HANGIN' OUT WITH YOU.
ME TOO!
YET...I HAVEN'T BEEN FULLY HONEST WITH YOU.
REMEMBER AT OUR LAST SHOW...WHEN YOU FOUND OUT I WAS A WEREWOLF?
YYYES...?

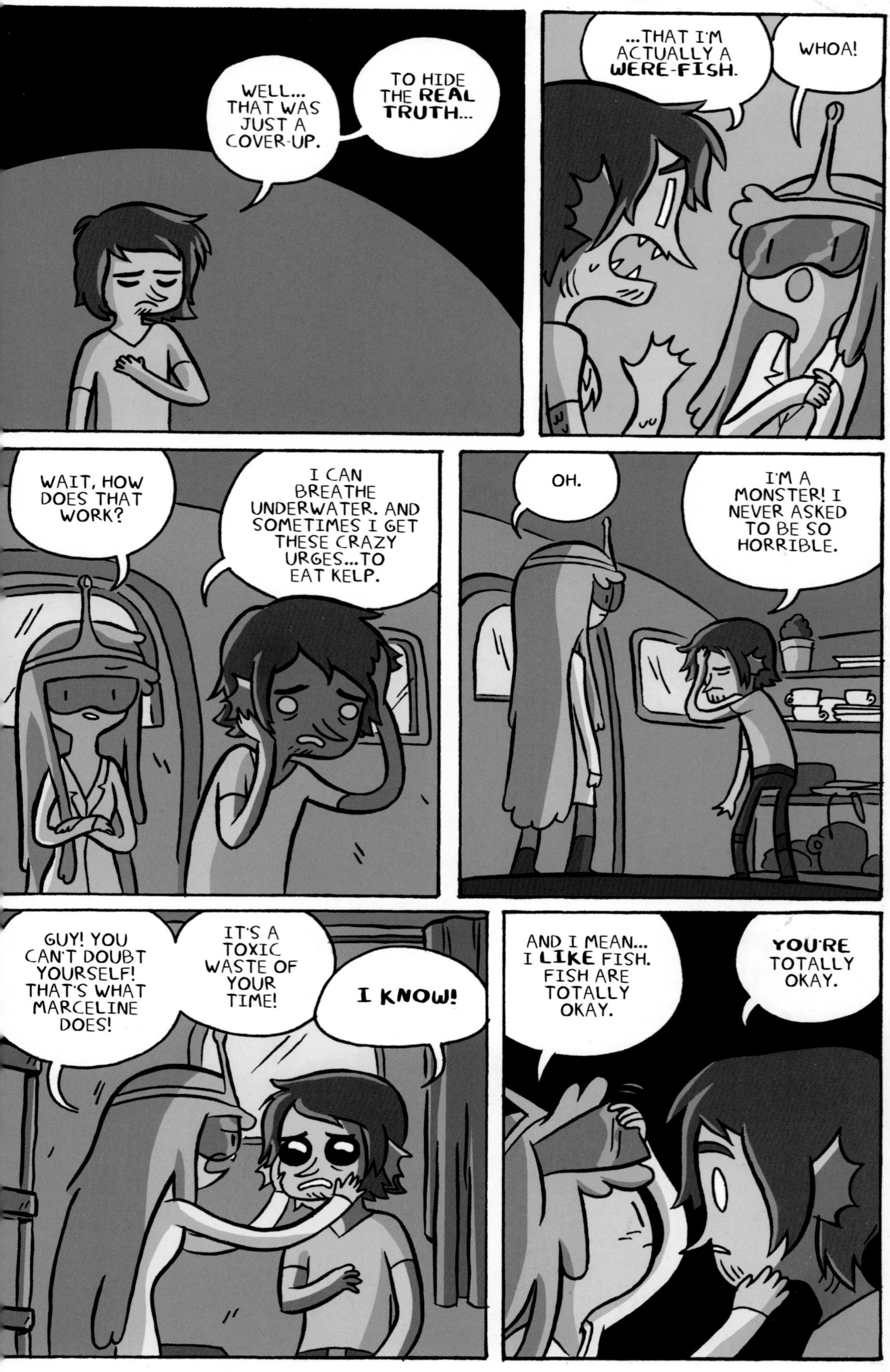
WELL... THAT WAS JUST A COVER-UP.
TO HIDE THE **REAL TRUTH**...
...THAT I'M ACTUALLY A **WERE-FISH**.
WHOA!
WAIT, HOW DOES THAT WORK?
I CAN BREATHE UNDERWATER. AND SOMETIMES I GET THESE CRAZY URGES...TO EAT KELP.
OH.
I'M A MONSTER! I NEVER ASKED TO BE SO HORRIBLE.
GUY! YOU CAN'T DOUBT YOURSELF! THAT'S WHAT MARCELINE DOES!
IT'S A TOXIC WASTE OF YOUR TIME!
I KNOW!
AND I MEAN... I **LIKE** FISH. FISH ARE TOTALLY OKAY.
YOU'RE TOTALLY OKAY.

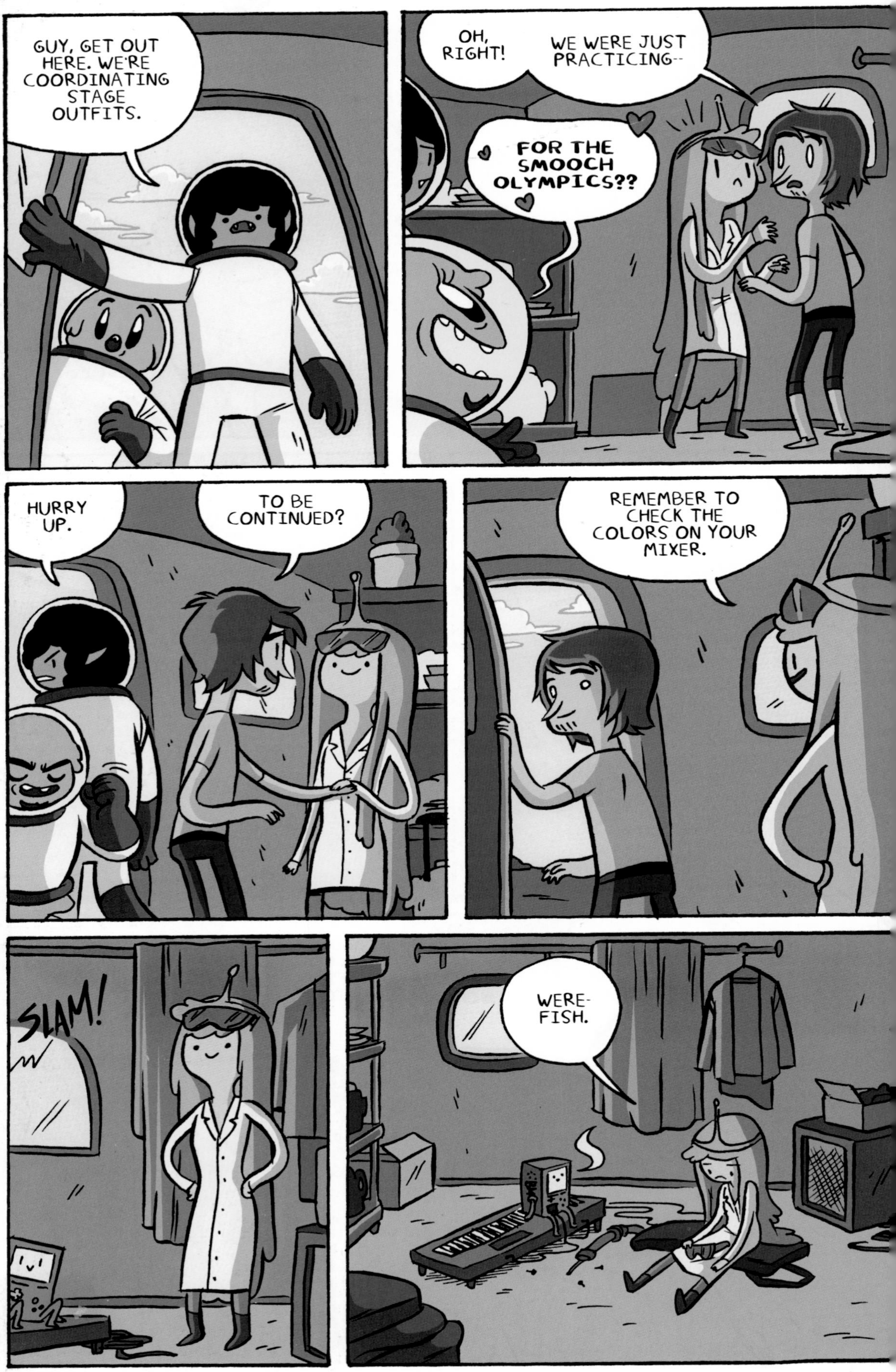
GUY, GET OUT HERE. WE'RE COORDINATING STAGE OUTFITS.
OH, RIGHT!
WE WERE JUST PRACTICING--
FOR THE SMOOCH OLYMPICS??
HURRY UP.
TO BE CONTINUED?
REMEMBER TO CHECK THE COLORS ON YOUR MIXER.
SLAM!
WERE-FISH.

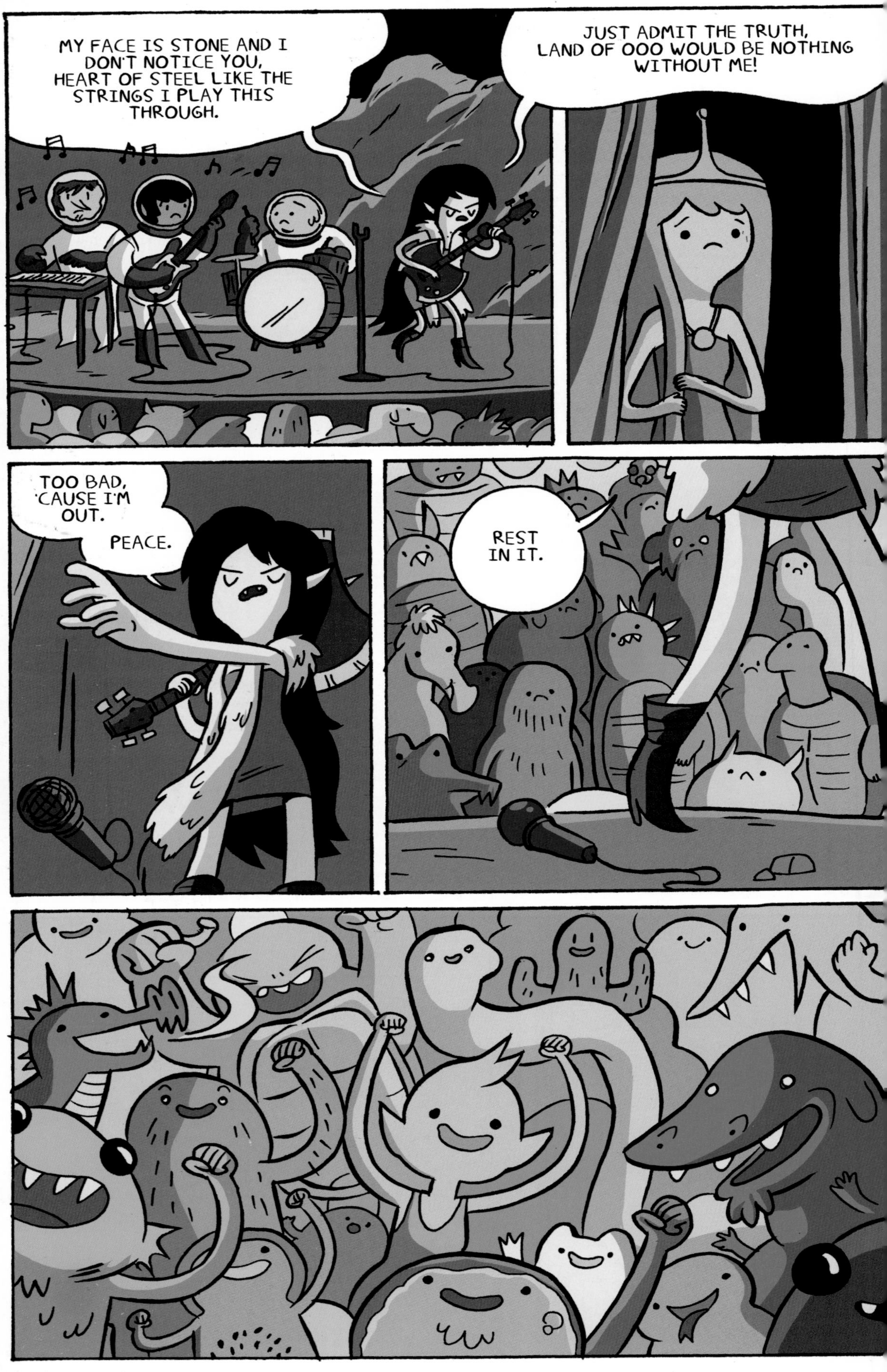
MY FACE IS STONE AND I DON'T NOTICE YOU, HEART OF STEEL LIKE THE STRINGS I PLAY THIS THROUGH.
JUST ADMIT THE TRUTH, LAND OF OOO WOULD BE NOTHING WITHOUT ME!
TOO BAD, 'CAUSE I'M OUT.
PEACE.
REST IN IT.

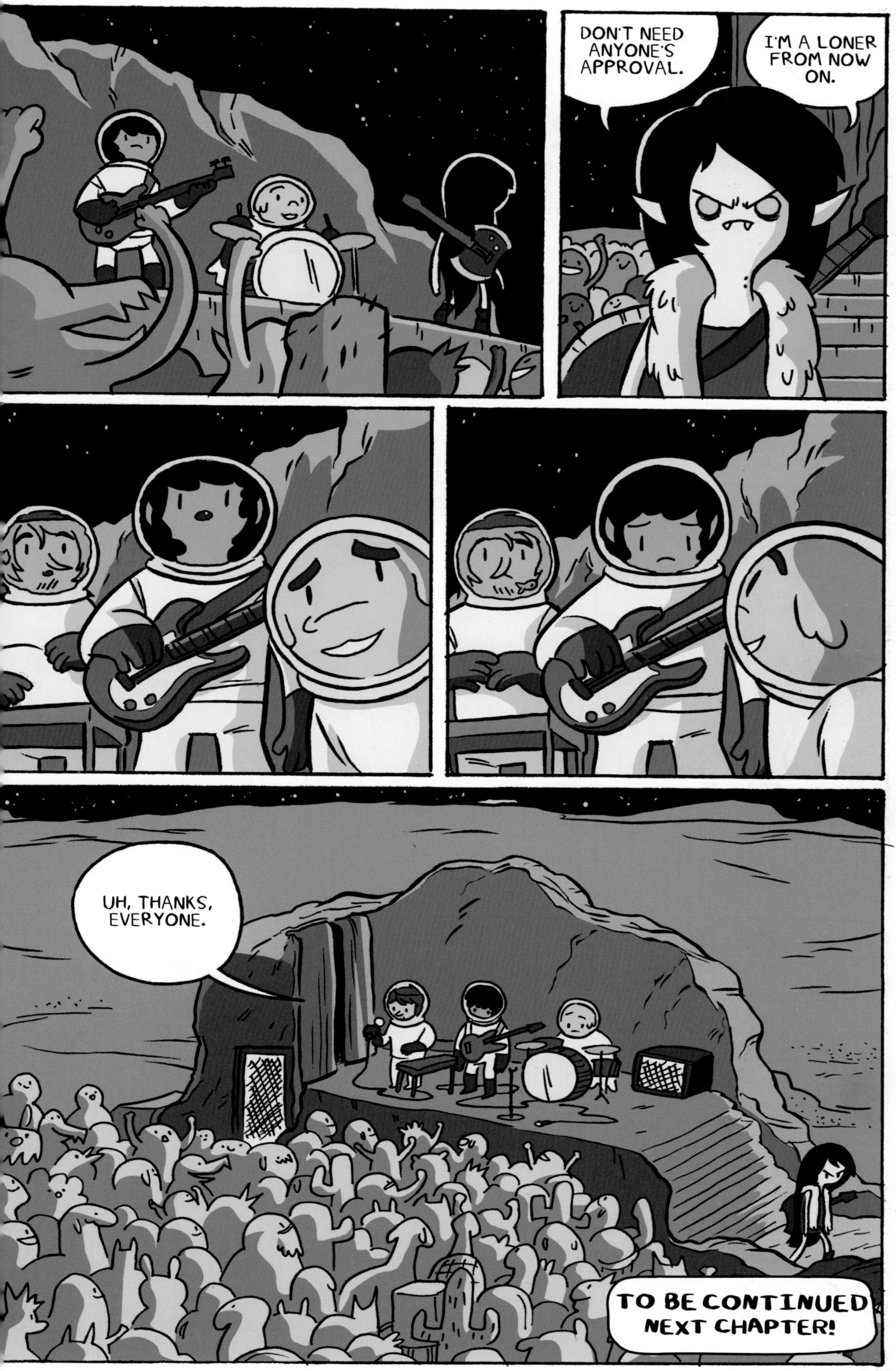
DON'T NEED ANYONE'S APPROVAL.
I'M A LONER FROM NOW ON.
UH, THANKS, EVERYONE.
TO BE CONTINUED NEXT CHAPTER!

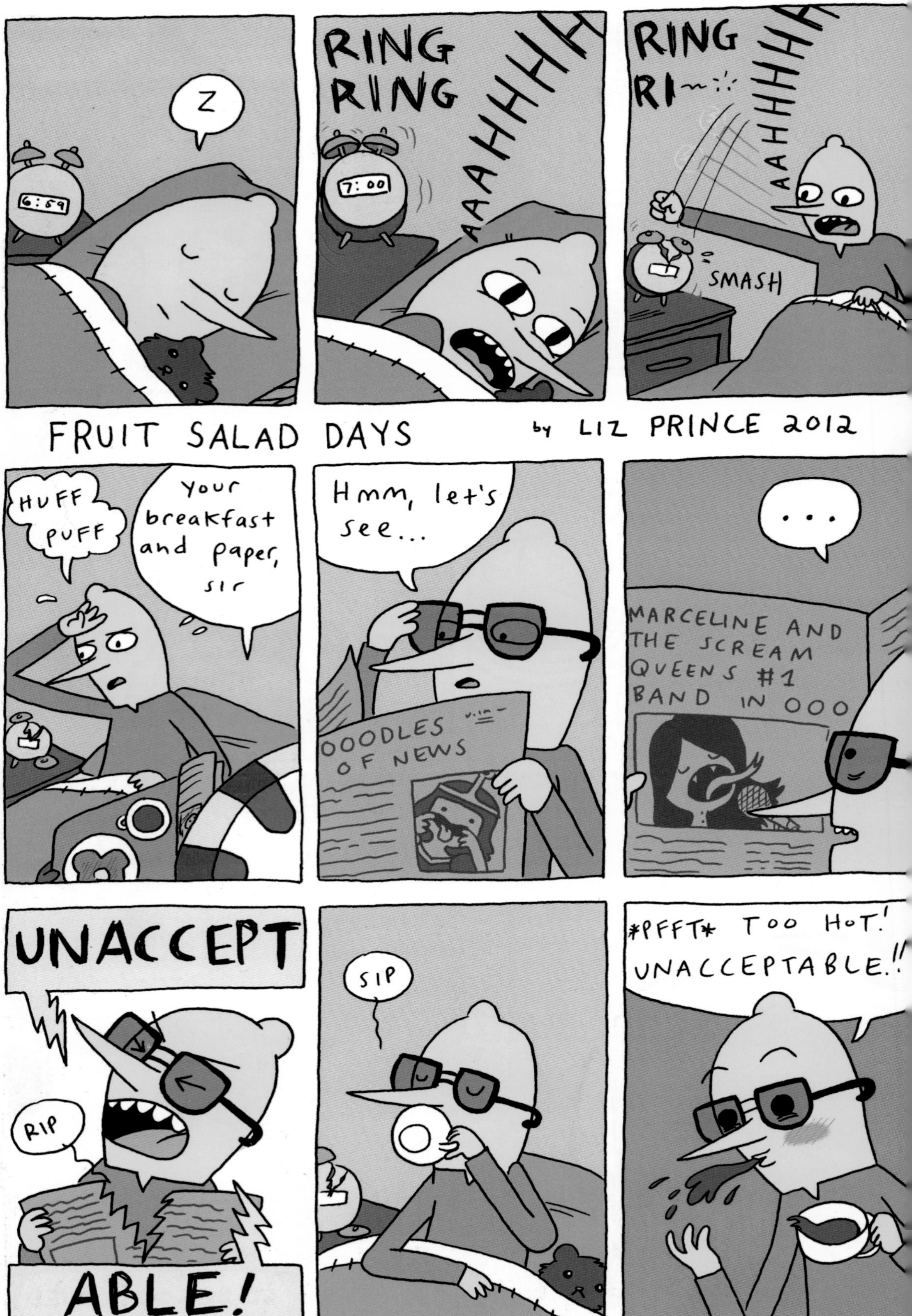
Z
6:59
RING
RING
AAAHHHHH
7:00
RING
RI~
AAHHHHHH
SMASH
FRUIT SALAD DAYS
by LIZ PRINCE 2012
HUFF PUFF
your breakfast and paper, sir
Hmm, let's see...
OOODLES OF NEWS
...
MARCELINE AND THE SCREAM QUEENS #1 BAND IN OOO
UNACCEPT
RIP
ABLE!
SIP
PFFT TOO HOT! UNACCEPTABLE!!

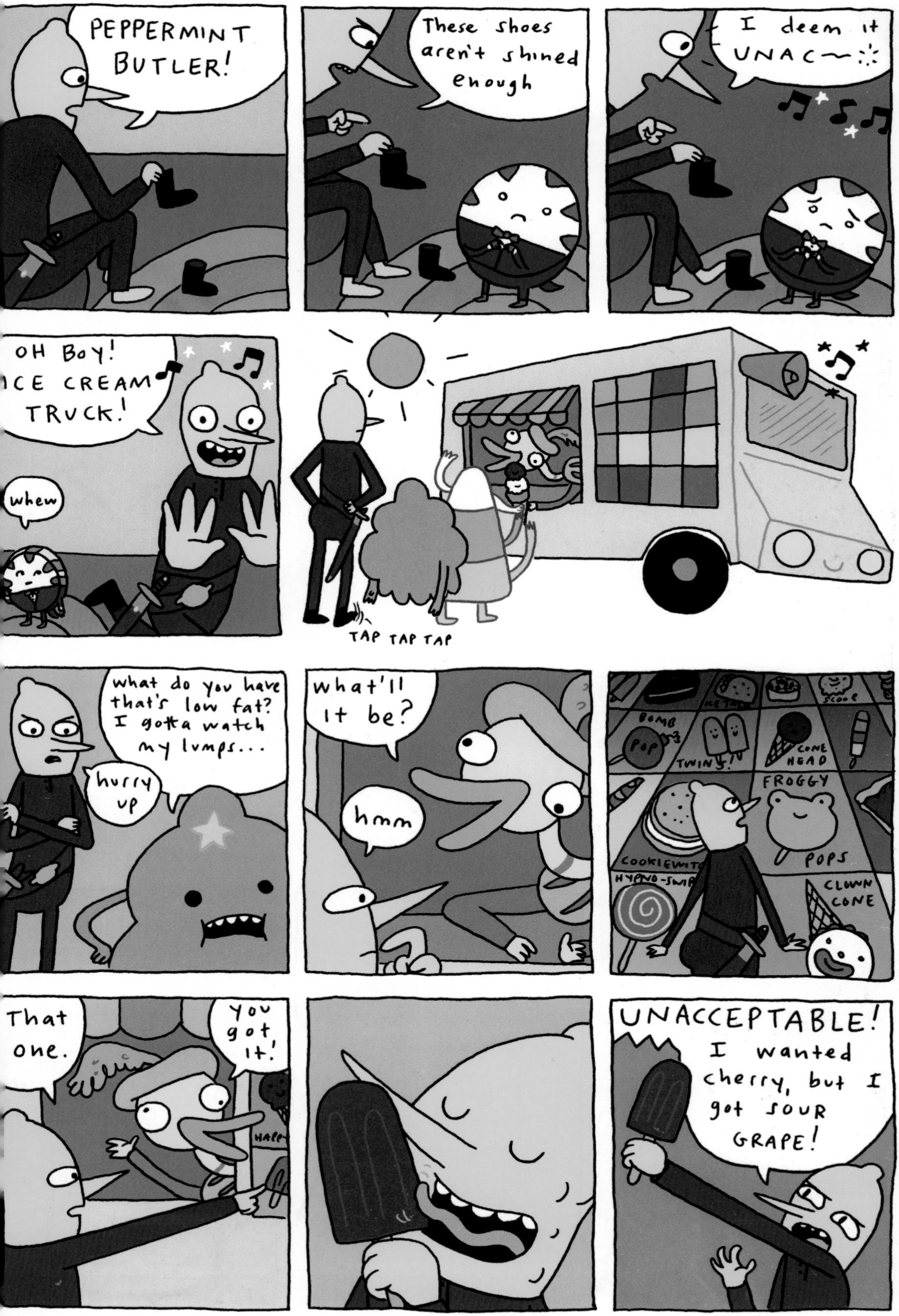
PEPPERMINT BUTLER!
These shoes aren't shined enough
I deem it UNAC~
OH BOY! ICE CREAM TRUCK!
whew
TAP TAP TAP
what do you have that's low fat? I gotta watch my lumps...
hurry up
what'll it be?
hmm
BOMB POP
TWINS!
CONE HEAD
FROGGY POPS
COOKIEWIT
HYPNO-SWIR
CLOWN CONE
That one.
You got it!
UNACCEPTABLE! I wanted cherry, but I got SOUR GRAPE!

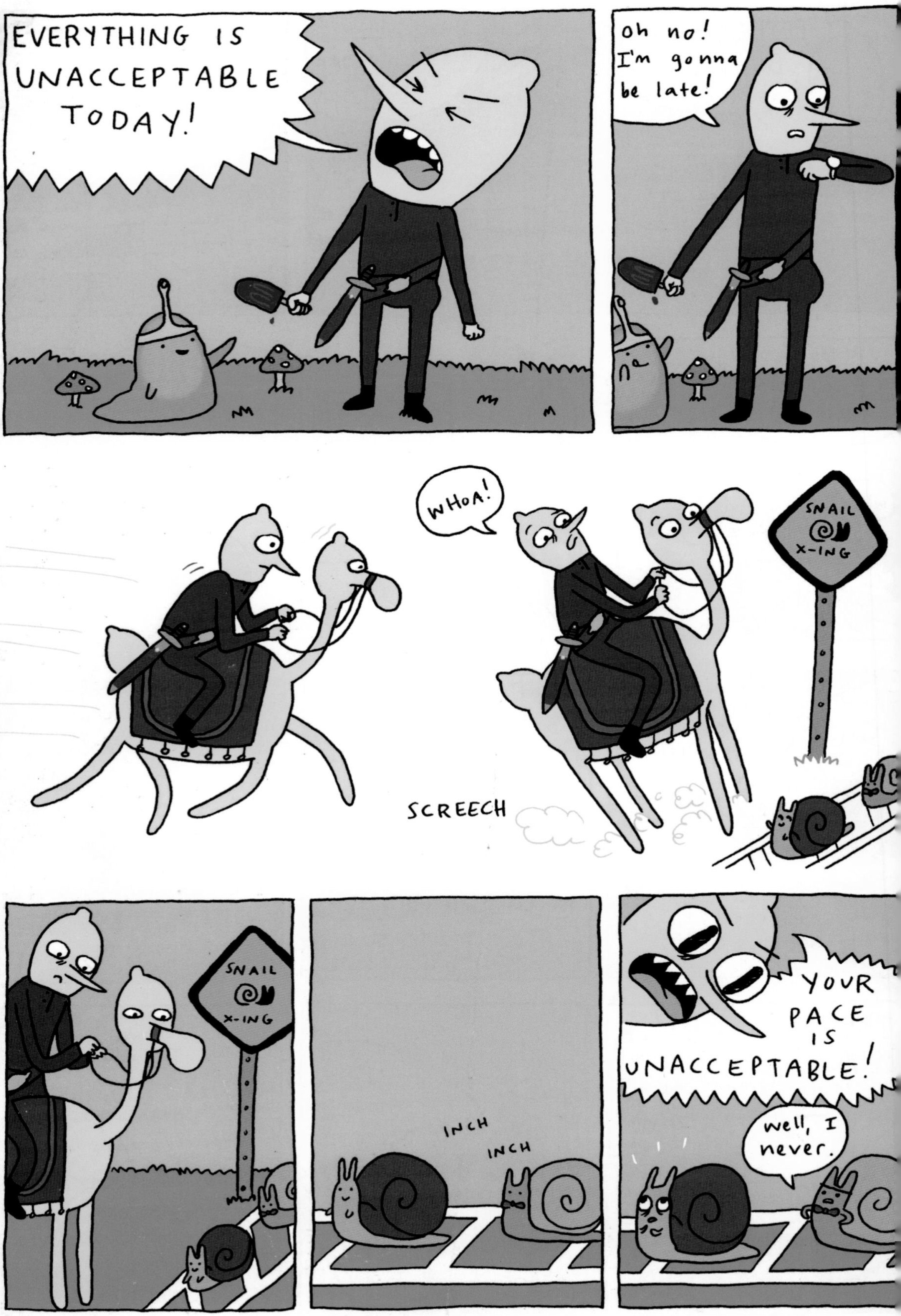
EVERYTHING IS UNACCEPTABLE TODAY!
oh no! I'm gonna be late!
WHOA!
SCREECH
SNAIL X-ING
SNAIL X-ING
INCH
INCH
YOUR PACE IS UNACCEPTABLE!
well, I never.

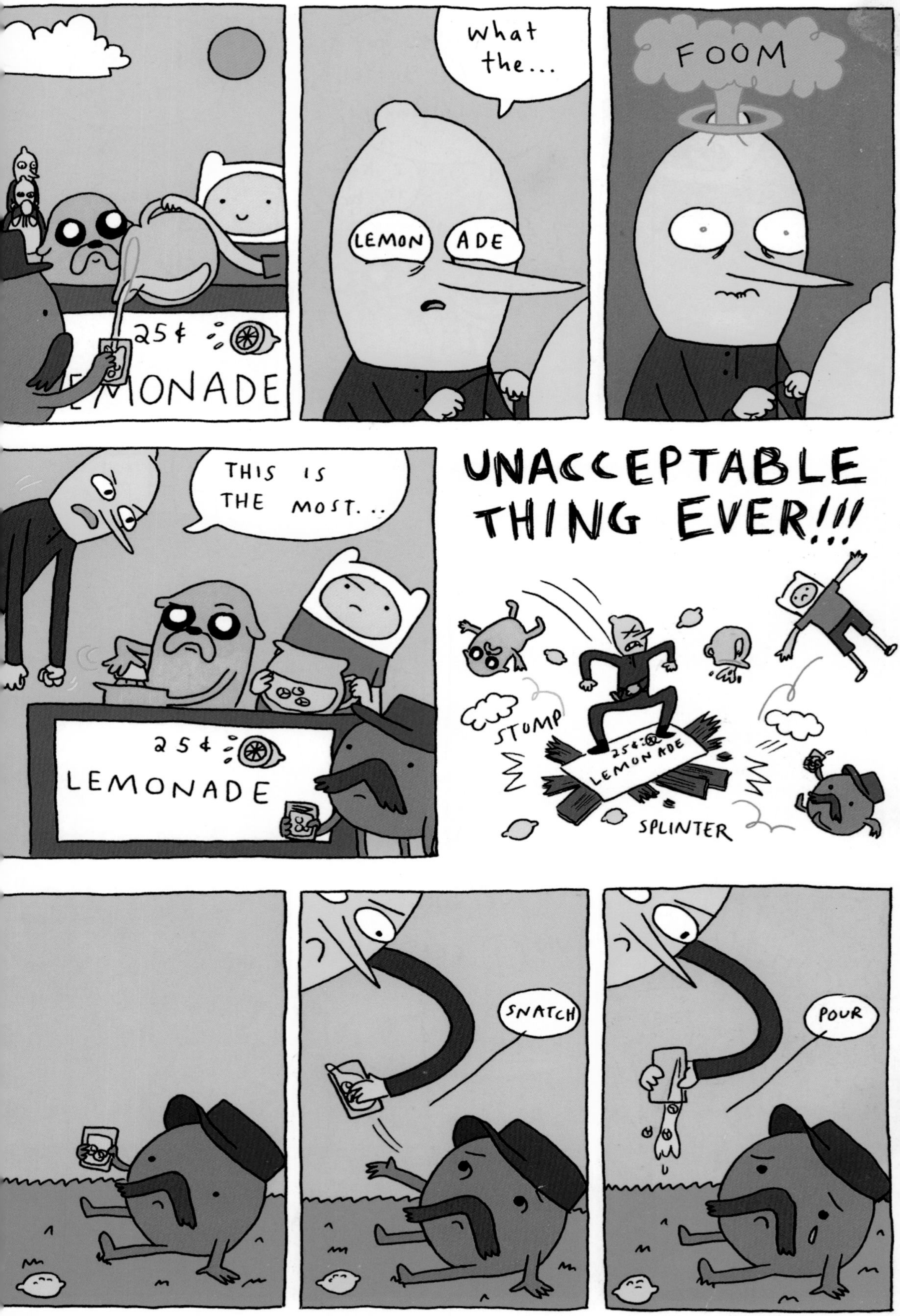
25¢
LEMONADE
what the...
LEMON
ADE
FOOM
THIS IS THE MOST...
25¢
LEMONADE
UNACCEPTABLE THING EVER!!!
STOMP
25¢ LEMONADE
SPLINTER
SNATCH
POUR

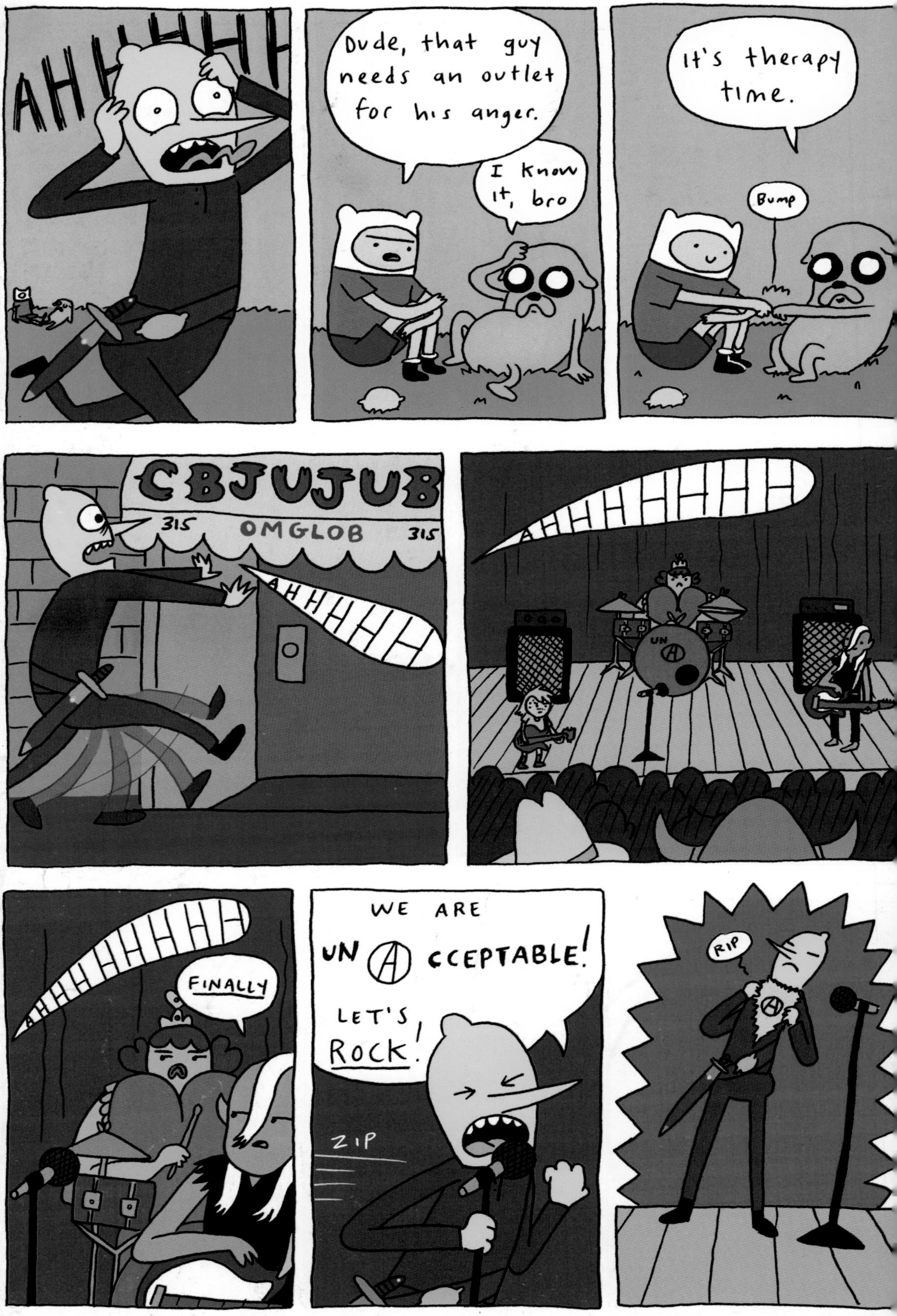
AHHHHHH
Dude, that guy needs an outlet for his anger.
I know it, bro
It's therapy time.
Bump
CBJUJUB
315
OMGLOB
315
AHHHHHH
AHHHHHHHHHHH
UN
AHHHHHHHHHHHH
FINALLY
WE ARE UN A CCEPTABLE!
LET'S ROCK!
ZIP
RIP

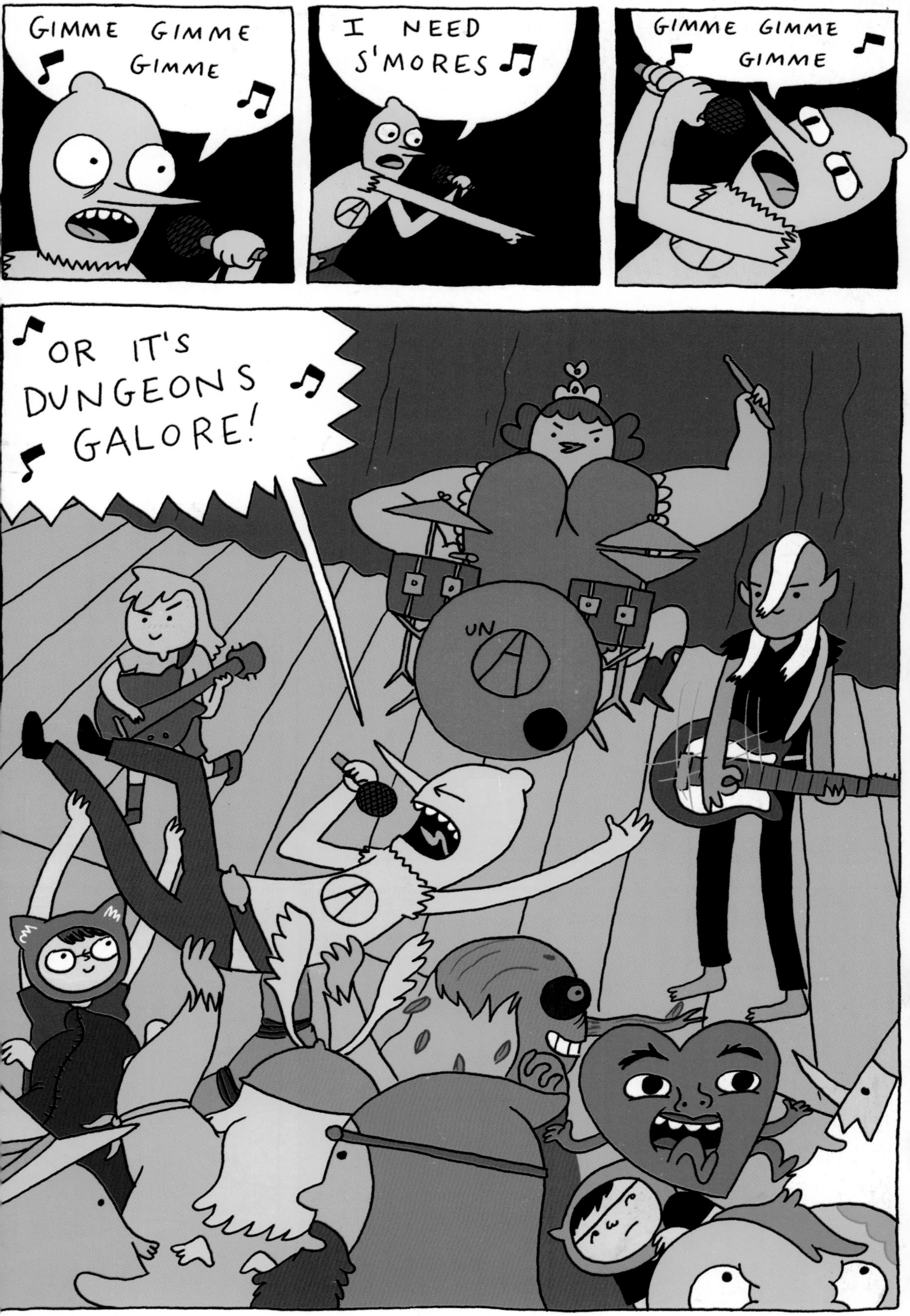
GIMME GIMME GIMME
I NEED S'MORES
GIMME GIMME GIMME
OR IT'S DUNGEONS GALORE!
UN

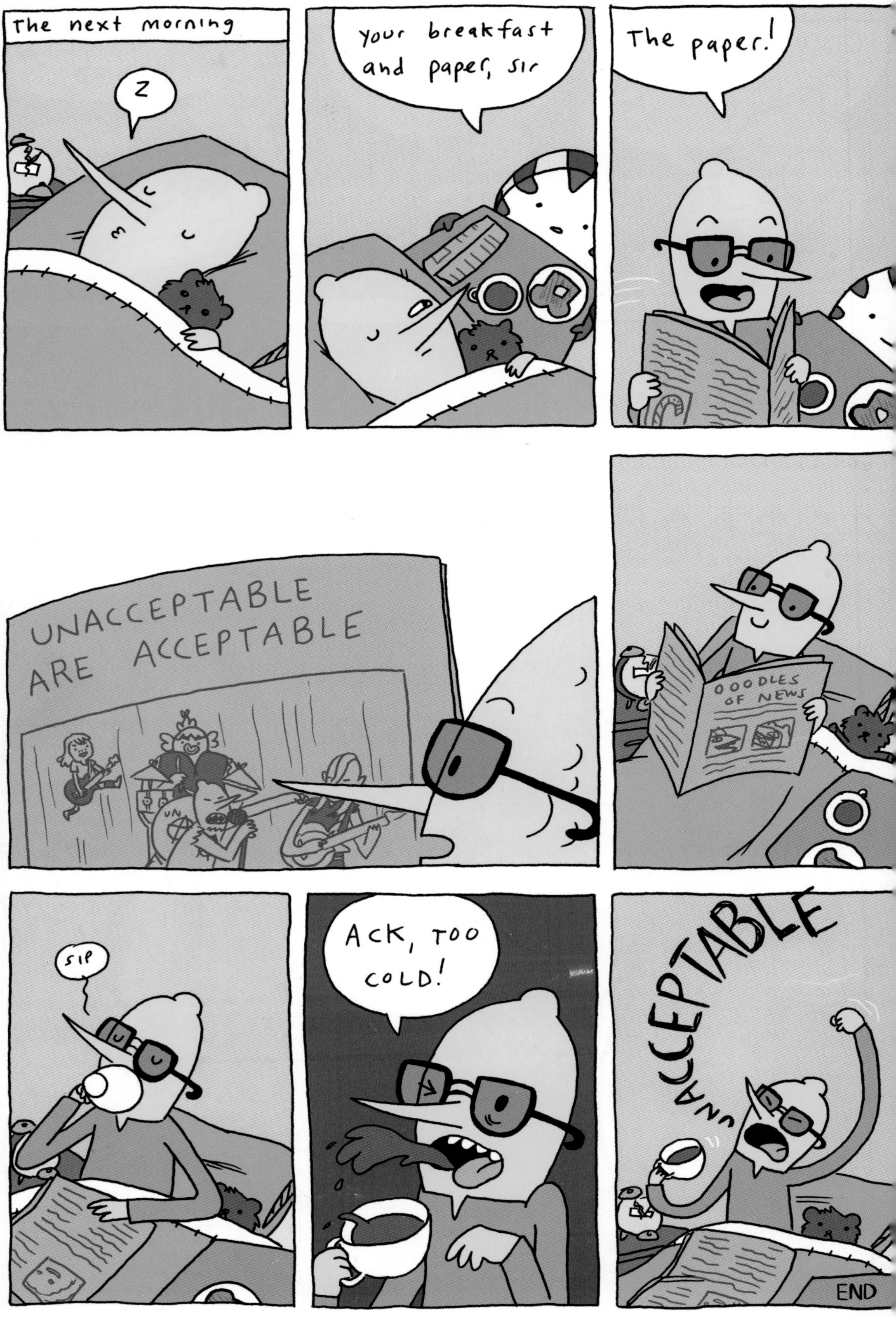
The next morning
Z
your breakfast and paper, sir
The paper!
UNACCEPTABLE ARE ACCEPTABLE
UN
OOODLES OF NEWS
SIP
ACK, TOO COLD!
UNACCEPTABLE
END

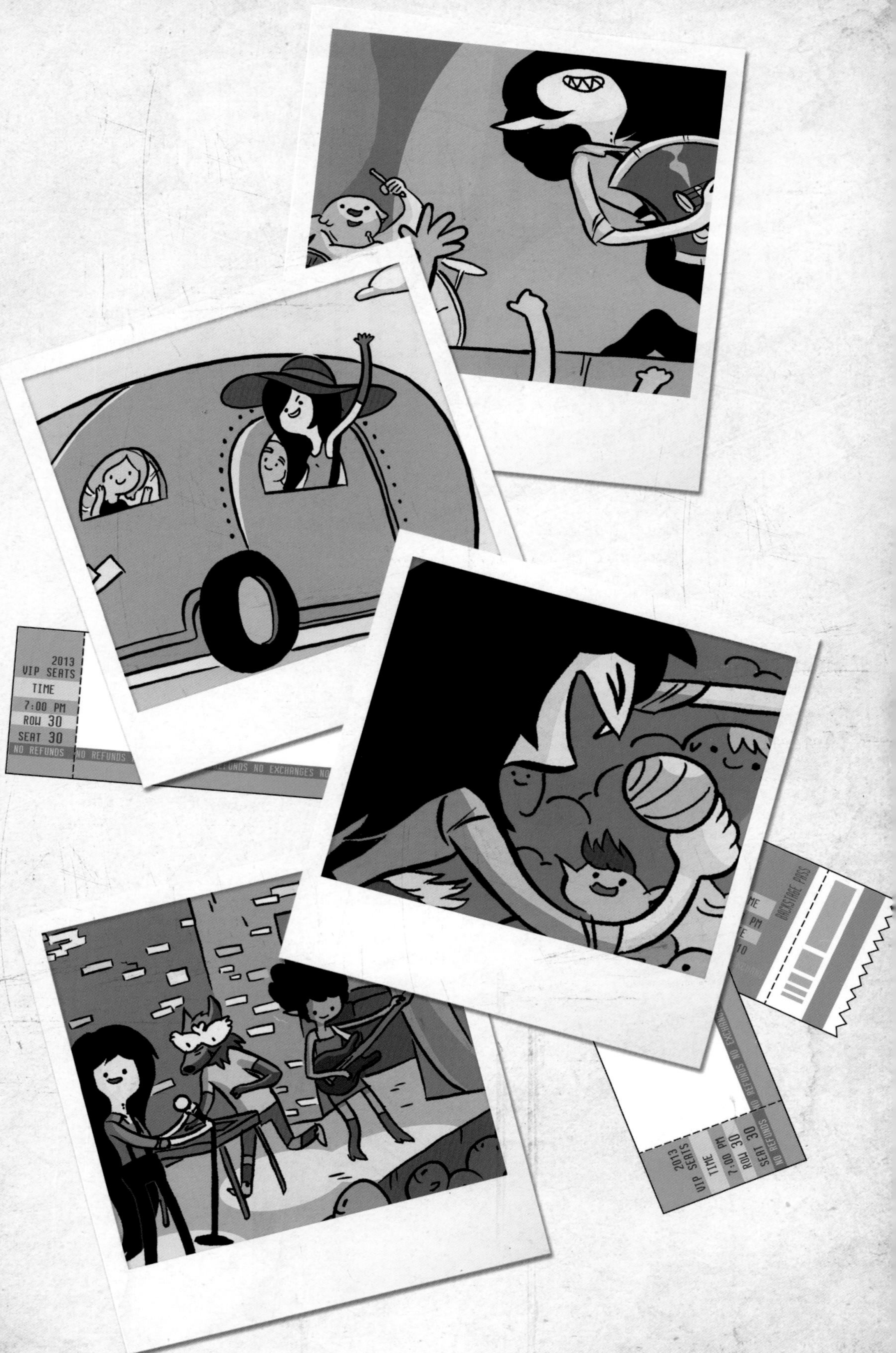
2013
VIP SEATS
TIME
7:00 PM
ROW 30
SEAT 30
NO REFUNDS
NO REFUNDS
NO EXCHANGES
BACKSTAGE PASS
2013
VIP SEATS
TIME
7:00 PM
ROW 30
SEAT 30
NO REFUNDS
NO REFUNDS NO EXCHANGES

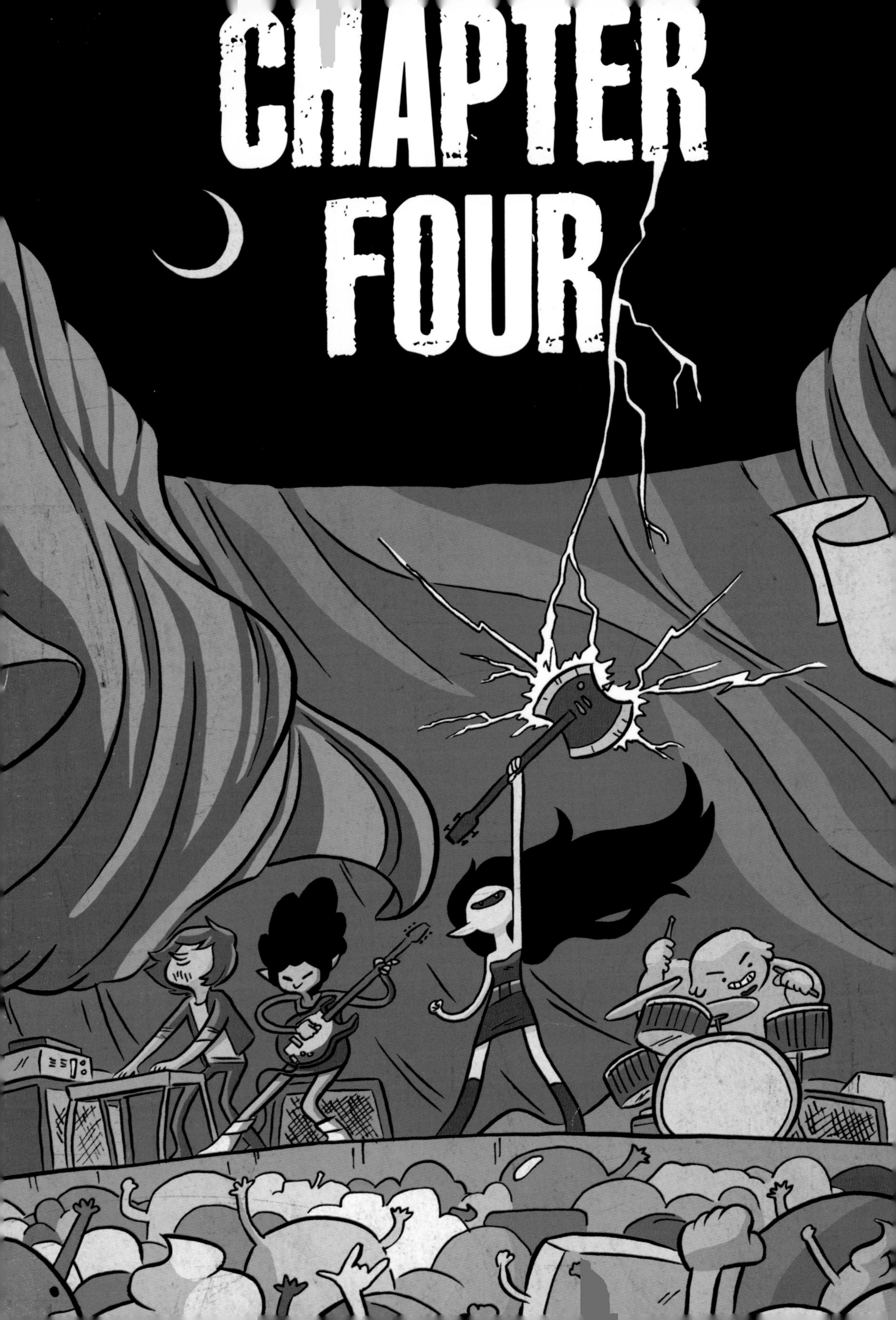
CHAPTER
FOUR

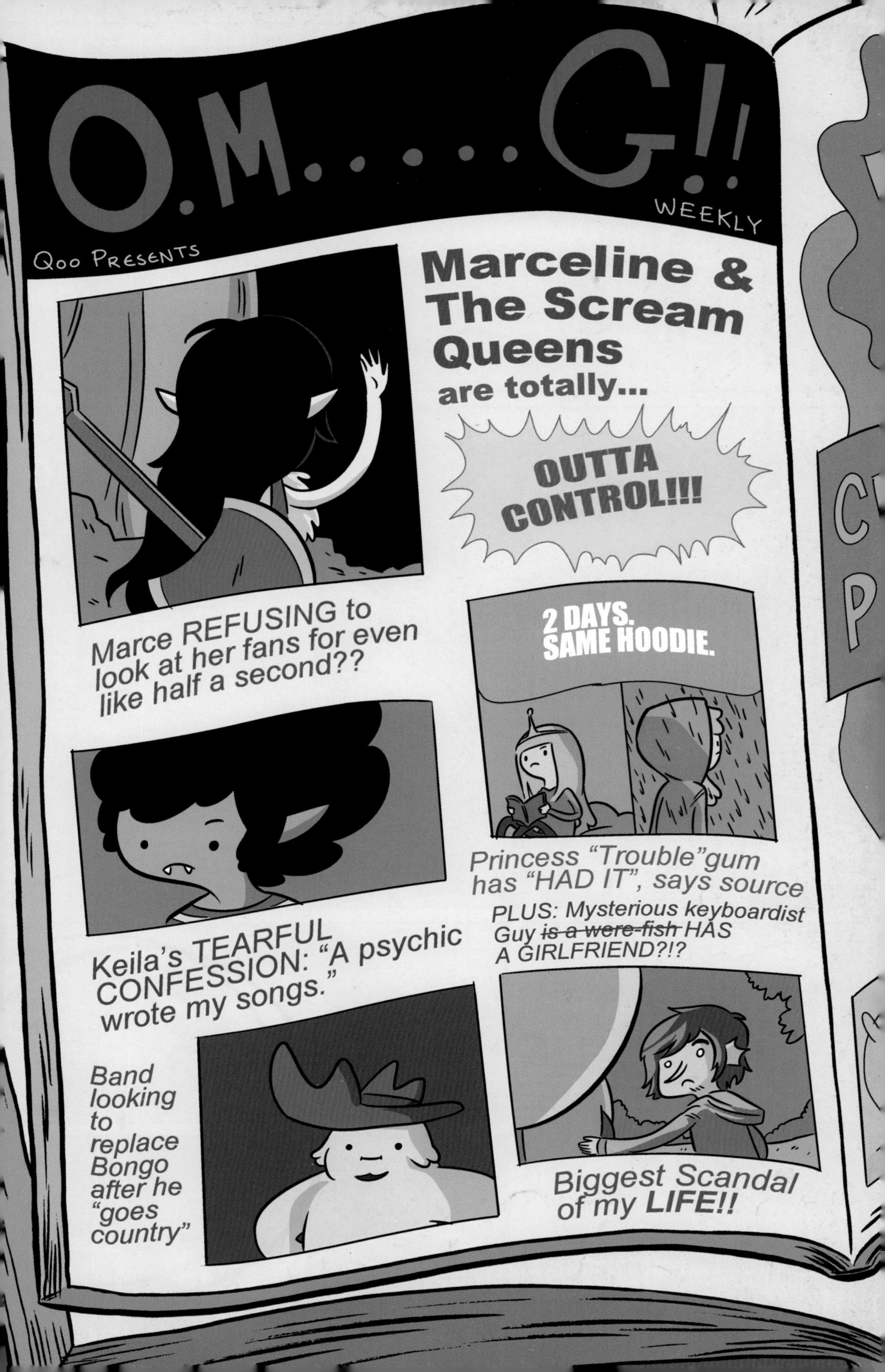
O.M...G!!
WEEKLY
Qoo Presents
Marceline & The Scream Queens are totally...
OUTTA CONTROL!!!
Marce REFUSING to look at her fans for even like half a second??
2 DAYS. SAME HOODIE.
Princess "Trouble"gum has "HAD IT", says source
PLUS: Mysterious keyboardist Guy ~~is a were-fish~~ HAS A GIRLFRIEND?!?
Keila's TEARFUL CONFESSION: "A psychic wrote my songs."
Band looking to replace Bongo after he "goes country"
Biggest Scandal of my LIFE!!

UH.

W-WHAT WAS I JUST SINGING?

FISHER-MAN SONG!

THE MIGHTY TIDE!

WHAT THE HECK SONG IS **THAT?**

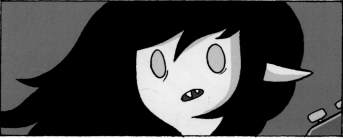

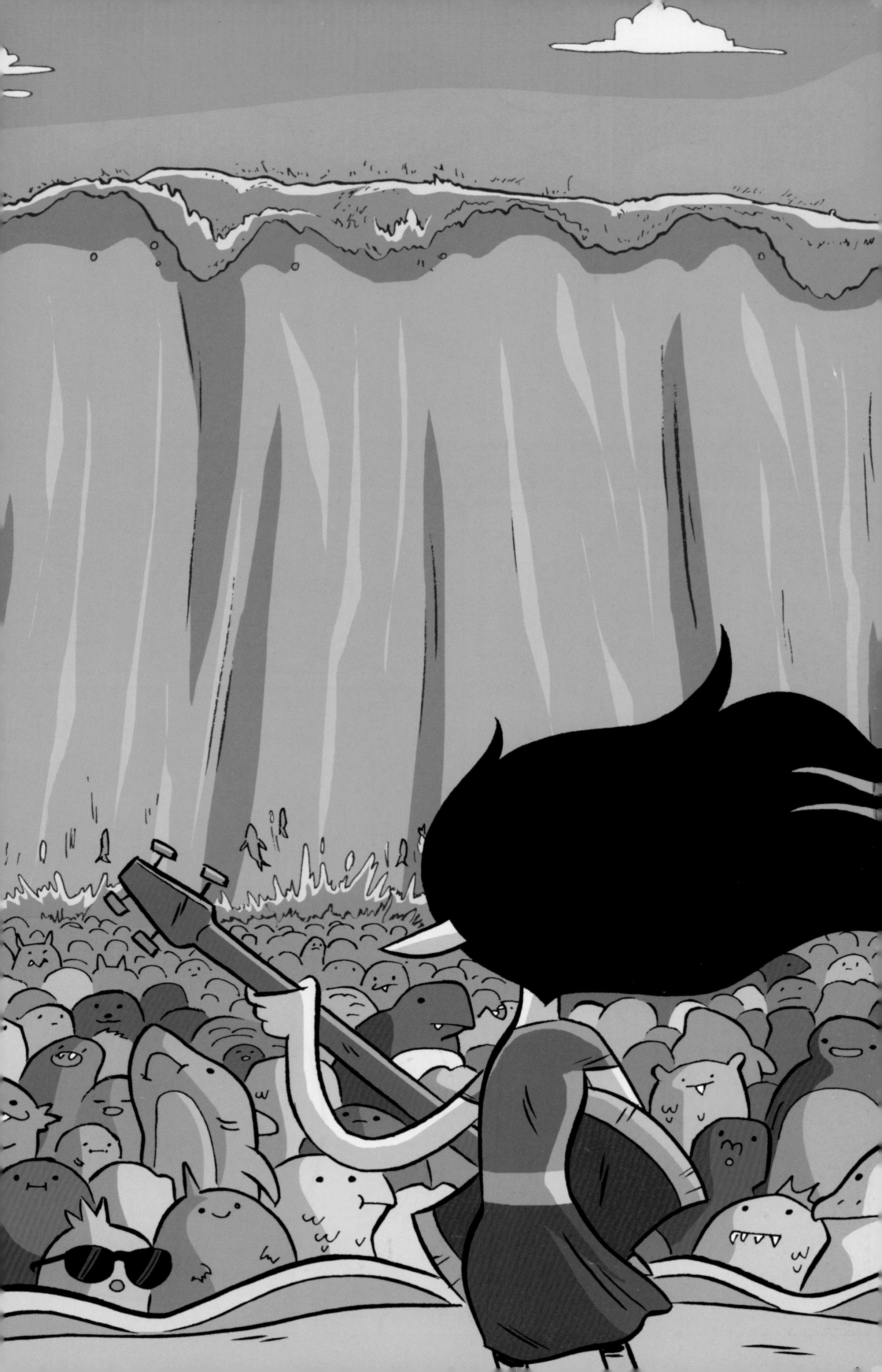

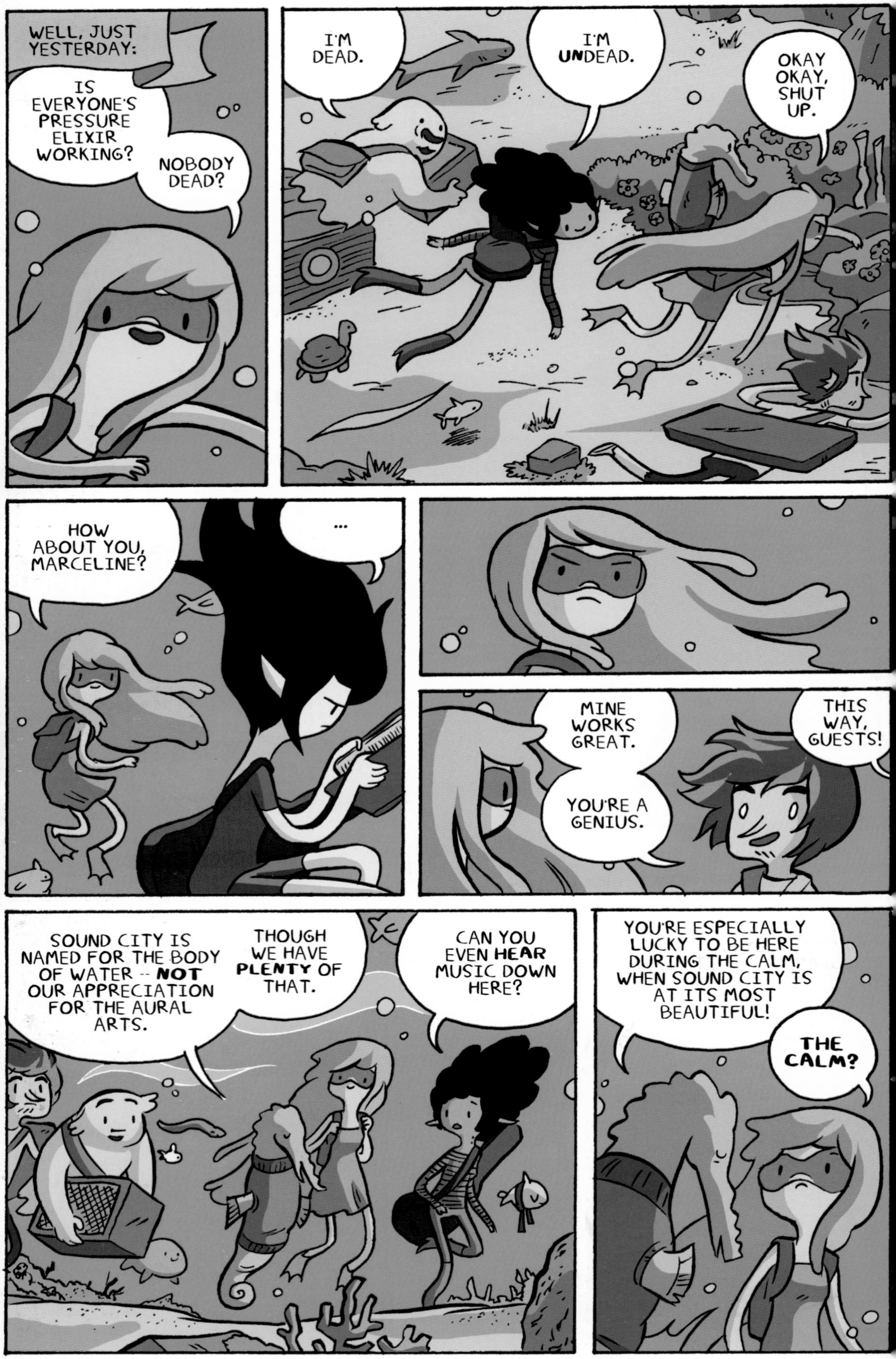
WELL, JUST YESTERDAY:
IS EVERYONE'S PRESSURE ELIXIR WORKING?
NOBODY DEAD?
I'M DEAD.
I'M UNDEAD.
OKAY OKAY, SHUT UP.
HOW ABOUT YOU, MARCELINE?
...
MINE WORKS GREAT.
YOU'RE A GENIUS.
THIS WAY, GUESTS!
SOUND CITY IS NAMED FOR THE BODY OF WATER -- NOT OUR APPRECIATION FOR THE AURAL ARTS.
THOUGH WE HAVE PLENTY OF THAT.
CAN YOU EVEN HEAR MUSIC DOWN HERE?
YOU'RE ESPECIALLY LUCKY TO BE HERE DURING THE CALM, WHEN SOUND CITY IS AT ITS MOST BEAUTIFUL!
THE CALM?

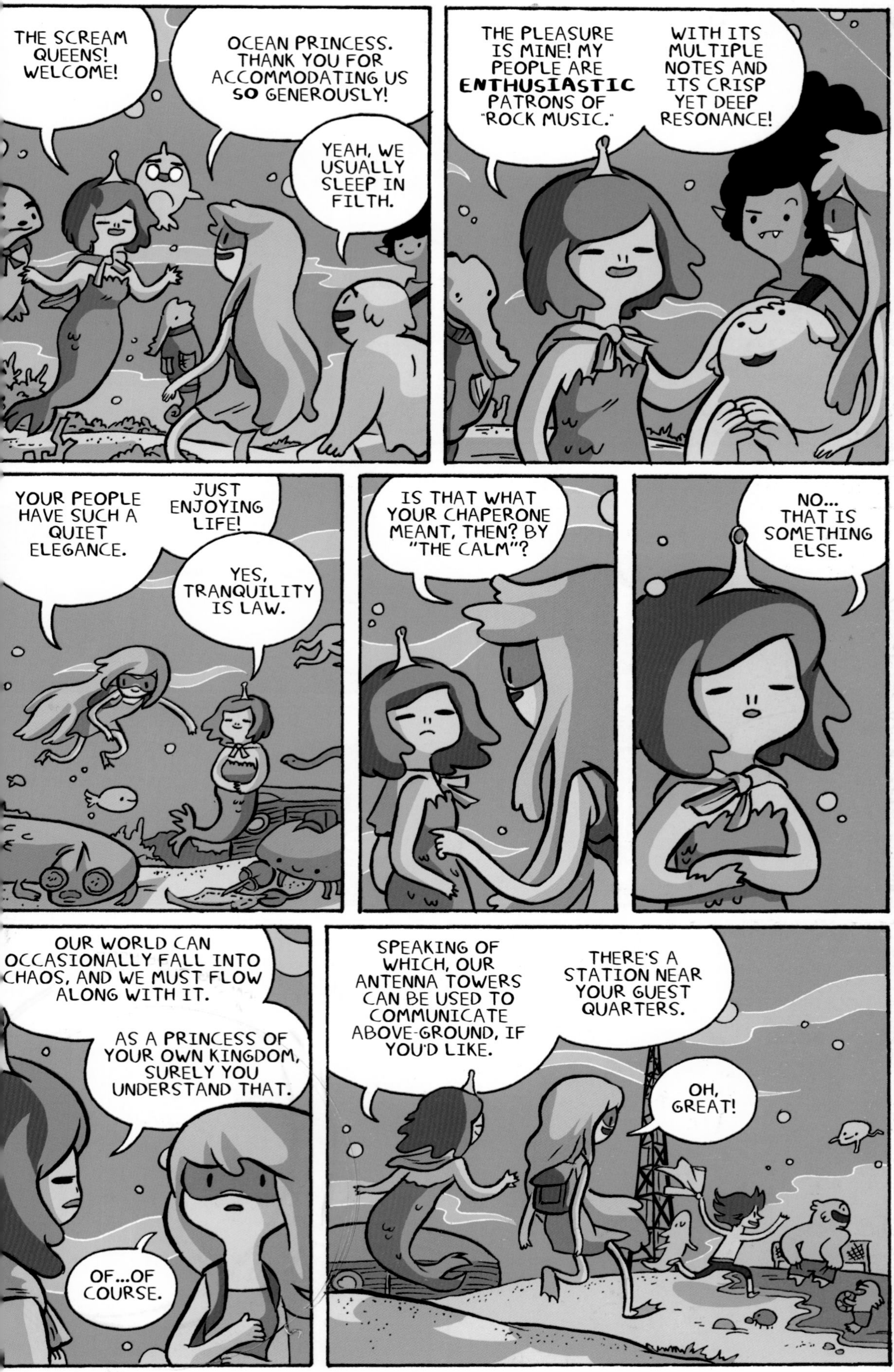
THE SCREAM QUEENS! WELCOME!
OCEAN PRINCESS. THANK YOU FOR ACCOMMODATING US SO GENEROUSLY!
YEAH, WE USUALLY SLEEP IN FILTH.
THE PLEASURE IS MINE! MY PEOPLE ARE ENTHUSIASTIC PATRONS OF "ROCK MUSIC."
WITH ITS MULTIPLE NOTES AND ITS CRISP YET DEEP RESONANCE!
YOUR PEOPLE HAVE SUCH A QUIET ELEGANCE.
JUST ENJOYING LIFE!
YES, TRANQUILITY IS LAW.
IS THAT WHAT YOUR CHAPERONE MEANT, THEN? BY "THE CALM"?
NO... THAT IS SOMETHING ELSE.
OUR WORLD CAN OCCASIONALLY FALL INTO CHAOS, AND WE MUST FLOW ALONG WITH IT.
AS A PRINCESS OF YOUR OWN KINGDOM, SURELY YOU UNDERSTAND THAT.
OF...OF COURSE.
SPEAKING OF WHICH, OUR ANTENNA TOWERS CAN BE USED TO COMMUNICATE ABOVE-GROUND, IF YOU'D LIKE.
THERE'S A STATION NEAR YOUR GUEST QUARTERS.
OH, GREAT!

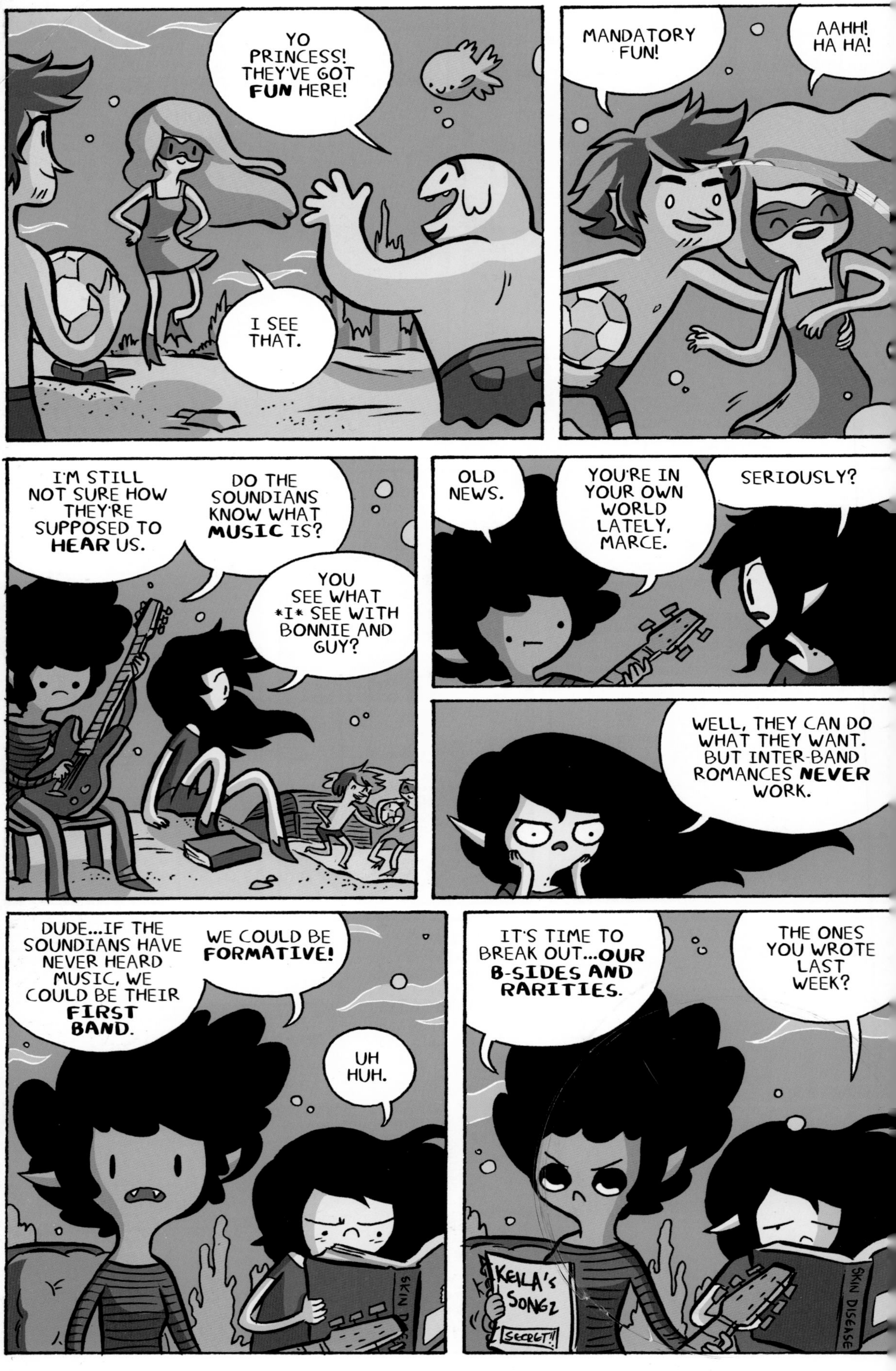
YO PRINCESS! THEY'VE GOT **FUN** HERE!
I SEE THAT.
MANDATORY FUN!
AAHH! HA HA!
I'M STILL NOT SURE HOW THEY'RE SUPPOSED TO **HEAR** US.
DO THE SOUNDIANS KNOW WHAT **MUSIC** IS?
YOU SEE WHAT *I* SEE WITH BONNIE AND GUY?
OLD NEWS.
YOU'RE IN YOUR OWN WORLD LATELY, MARCE.
SERIOUSLY?
WELL, THEY CAN DO WHAT THEY WANT. BUT INTER-BAND ROMANCES **NEVER** WORK.
DUDE...IF THE SOUNDIANS HAVE NEVER HEARD MUSIC, WE COULD BE THEIR **FIRST BAND**.
WE COULD BE **FORMATIVE!**
UH HUH.
IT'S TIME TO BREAK OUT...**OUR B-SIDES AND RARITIES**.
THE ONES YOU WROTE LAST WEEK?
KEILA's SONGZ
SECRET!!
SKIN DISEASE

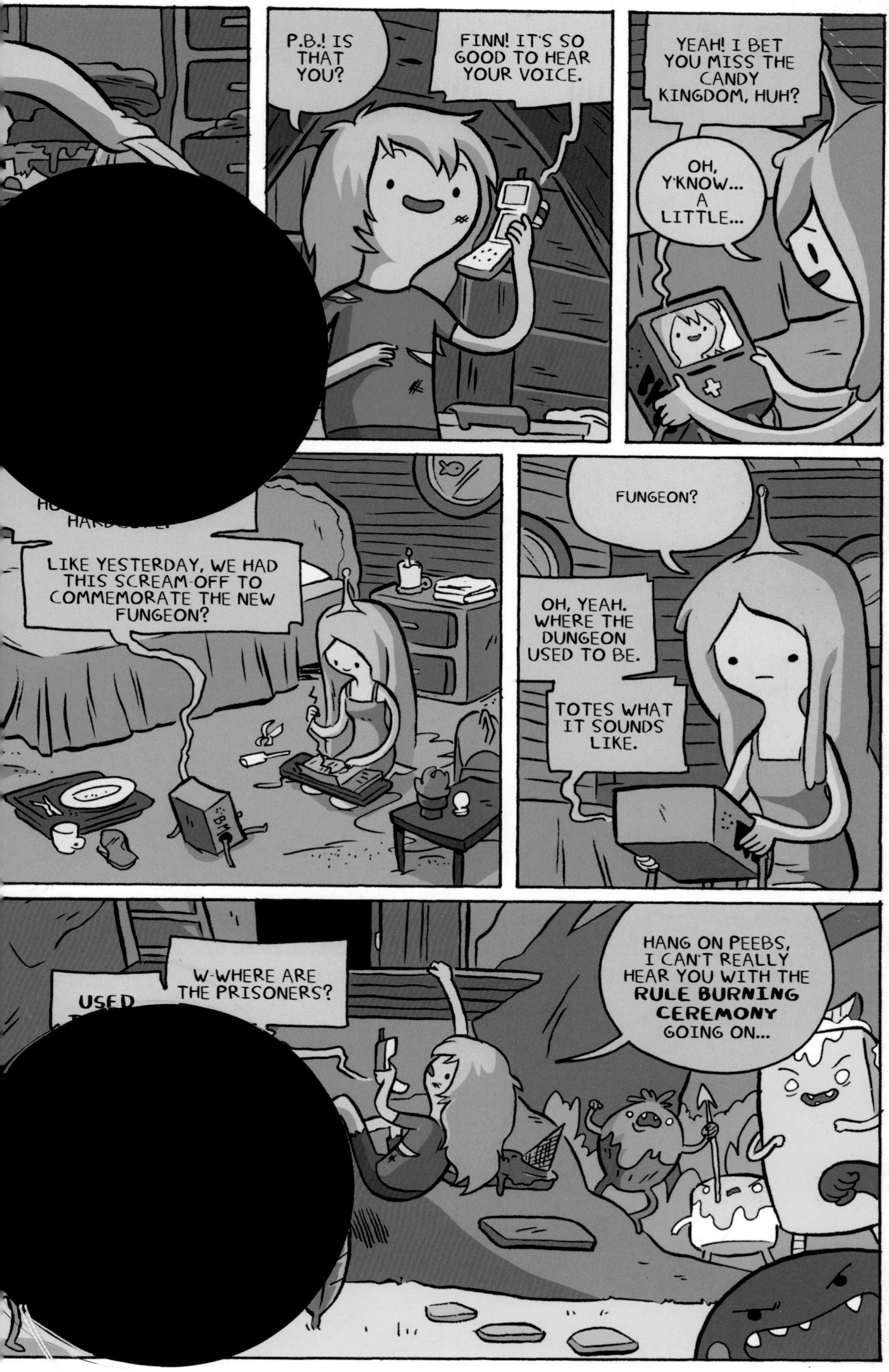

[redacted]
P.B.! IS THAT YOU?
FINN! IT'S SO GOOD TO HEAR YOUR VOICE.
YEAH! I BET YOU MISS THE CANDY KINGDOM, HUH?
OH, Y'KNOW... A LITTLE...
[redacted]
LIKE YESTERDAY, WE HAD THIS SCREAM-OFF TO COMMEMORATE THE NEW FUNGEON?
FUNGEON?
OH, YEAH. WHERE THE DUNGEON USED TO BE.
TOTES WHAT IT SOUNDS LIKE.
W-WHERE ARE THE PRISONERS?
USED [redacted]
HANG ON PEEBS, I CAN'T REALLY HEAR YOU WITH THE **RULE BURNING CEREMONY** GOING ON...

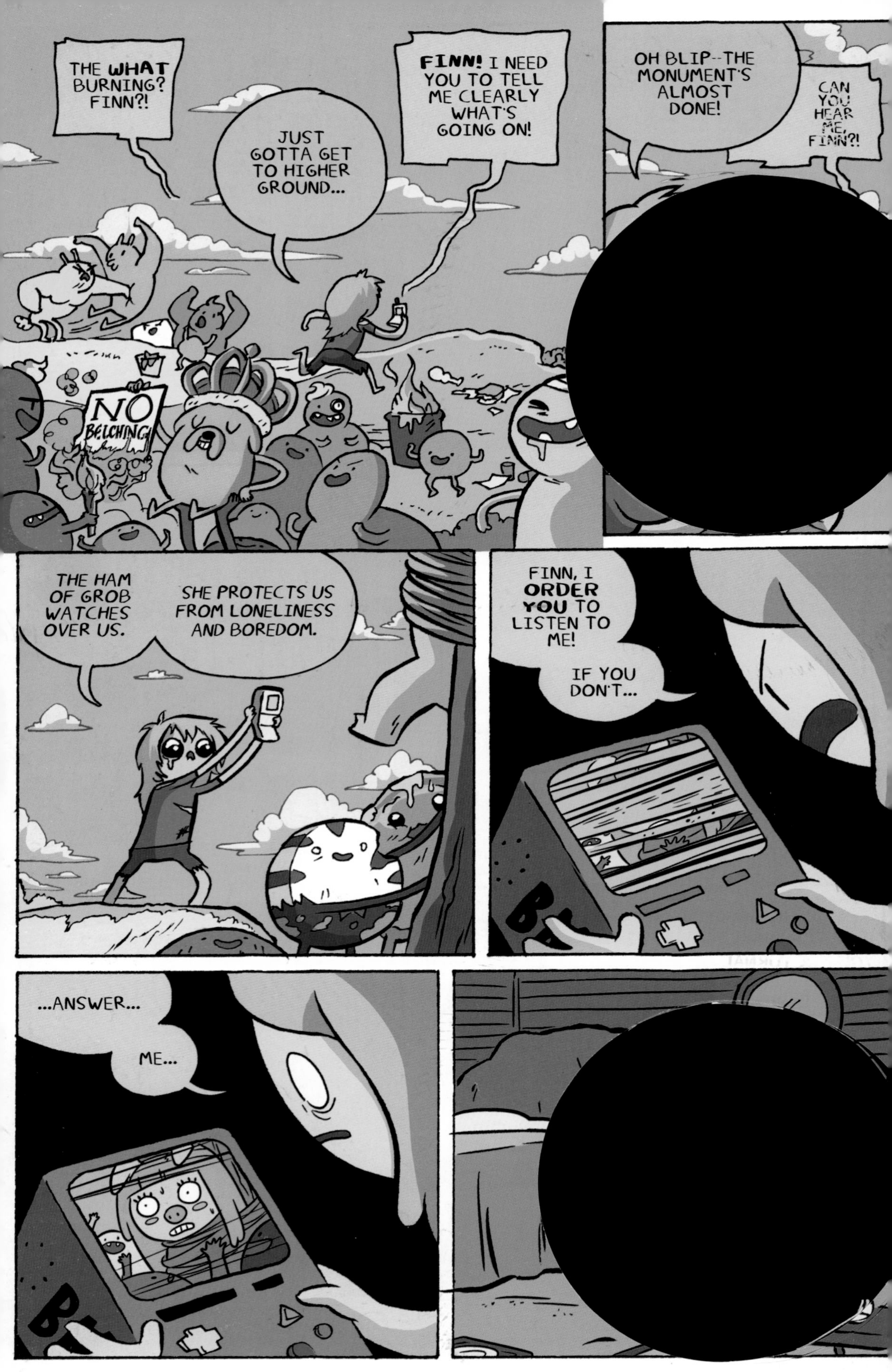

THE WHAT BURNING? FINN?!
JUST GOTTA GET TO HIGHER GROUND...
FINN! I NEED YOU TO TELL ME CLEARLY WHAT'S GOING ON!
NO BELCHING!
OH BLIP--THE MONUMENT'S ALMOST DONE!
CAN YOU HEAR ME, FINN?!
THE HAM OF GROB WATCHES OVER US.
SHE PROTECTS US FROM LONELINESS AND BOREDOM.
FINN, I ORDER YOU TO LISTEN TO ME!
IF YOU DON'T...
...ANSWER...
ME...

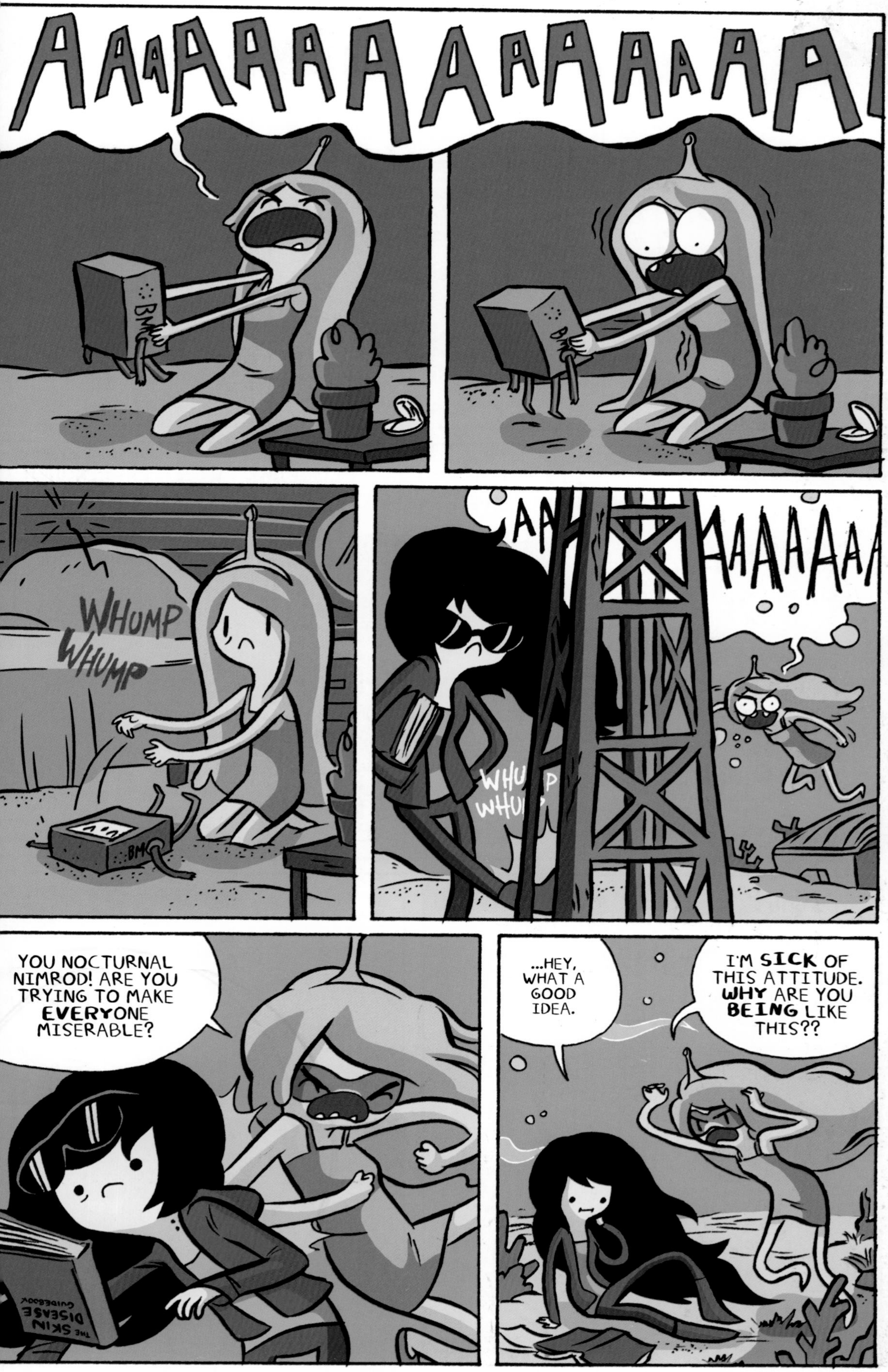
AAAAAAAAAAAAA
WHUMP
WHUMP
AAAAAAAAA
WHUMP
WHUMP
YOU NOCTURNAL NIMROD! ARE YOU TRYING TO MAKE EVERYONE MISERABLE?
THE SKIN DISEASE GUIDEBOOK
...HEY, WHAT A GOOD IDEA.
I'M SICK OF THIS ATTITUDE. WHY ARE YOU BEING LIKE THIS??

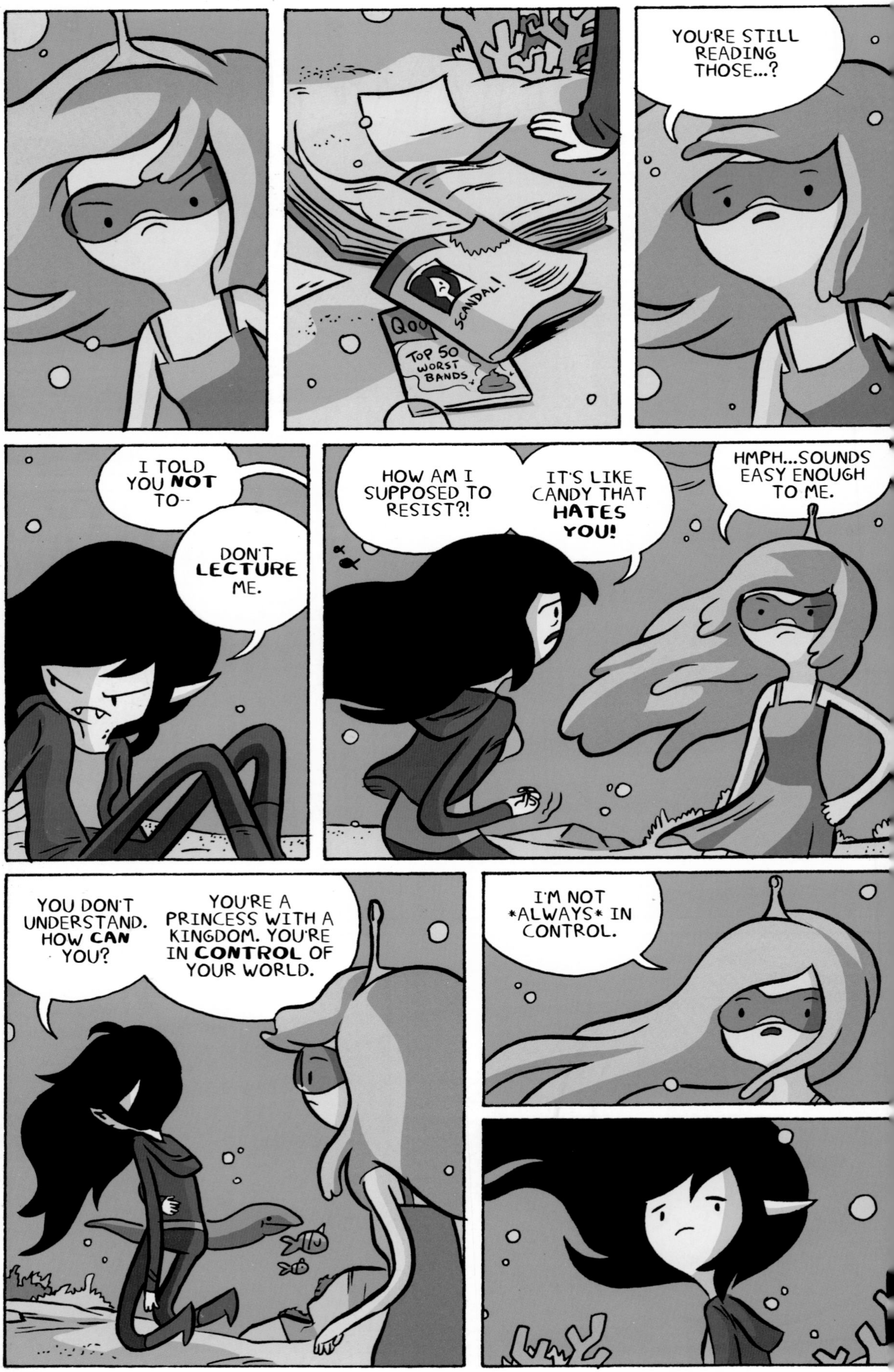
SCANDAL!
QOO
TOP 50 WORST BANDS
YOU'RE STILL READING THOSE...?
I TOLD YOU **NOT** TO--
DON'T **LECTURE** ME.
HOW AM I SUPPOSED TO RESIST?!
IT'S LIKE CANDY THAT **HATES YOU!**
HMPH...SOUNDS EASY ENOUGH TO ME.
YOU DON'T UNDERSTAND. HOW **CAN** YOU?
YOU'RE A PRINCESS WITH A KINGDOM. YOU'RE IN **CONTROL** OF YOUR WORLD.
I'M NOT *ALWAYS* IN CONTROL.

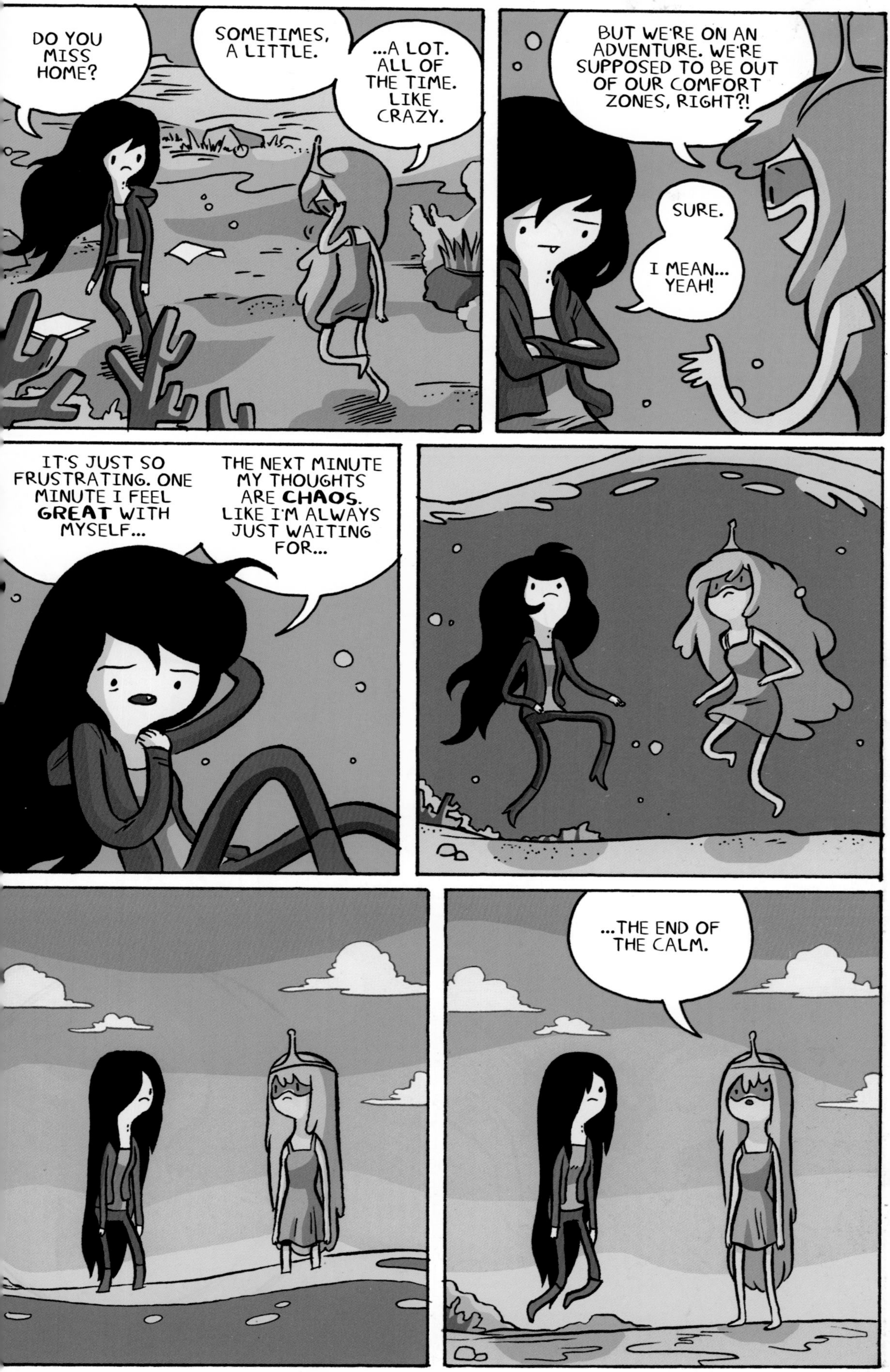
DO YOU MISS HOME?
SOMETIMES, A LITTLE.
...A LOT. ALL OF THE TIME. LIKE CRAZY.
BUT WE'RE ON AN ADVENTURE. WE'RE SUPPOSED TO BE OUT OF OUR COMFORT ZONES, RIGHT?!
SURE.
I MEAN... YEAH!
IT'S JUST SO FRUSTRATING. ONE MINUTE I FEEL **GREAT** WITH MYSELF...
THE NEXT MINUTE MY THOUGHTS ARE **CHAOS**. LIKE I'M ALWAYS JUST WAITING FOR...
...THE END OF THE CALM.

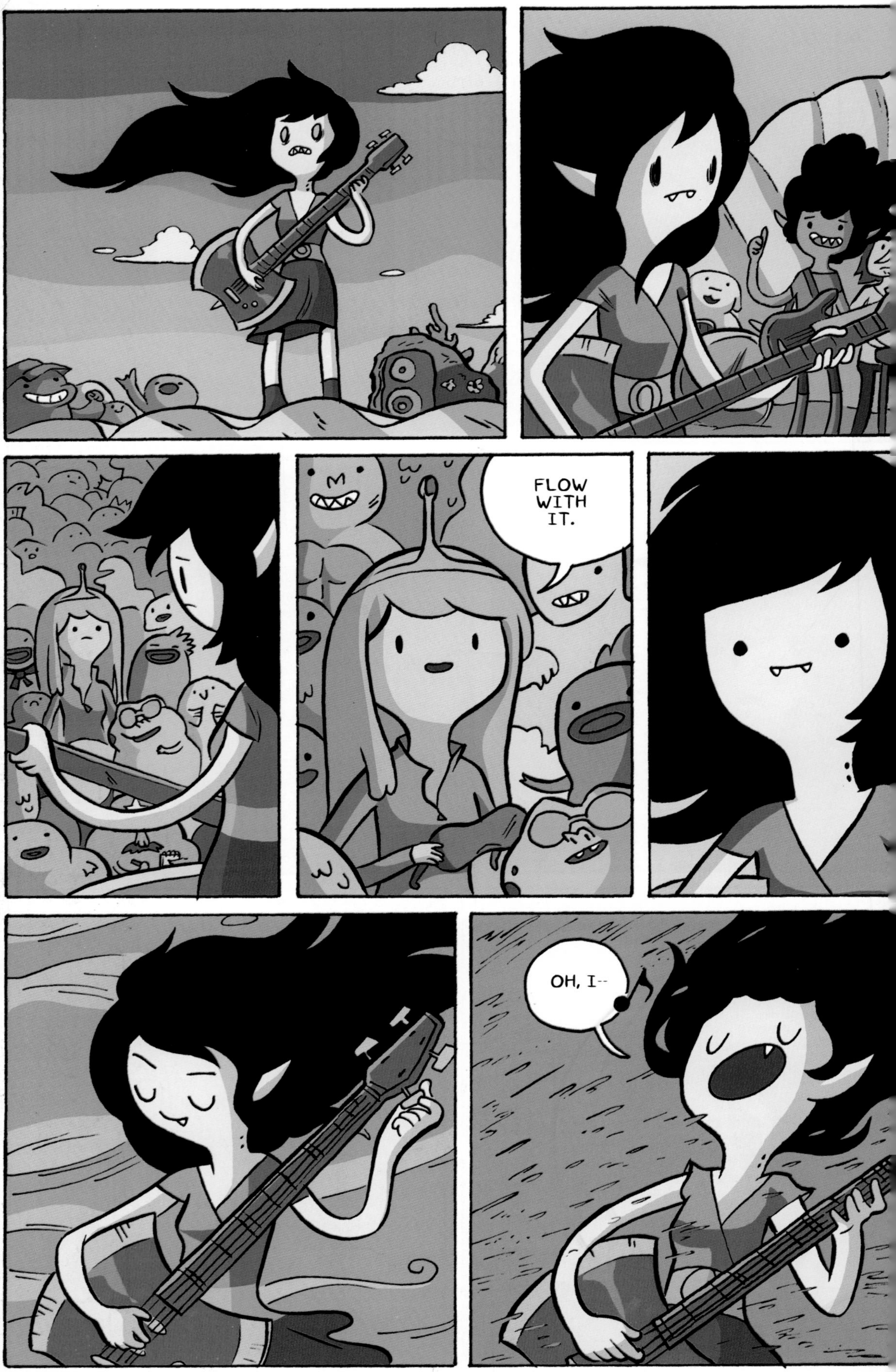
FLOW WITH IT.
OH, I--

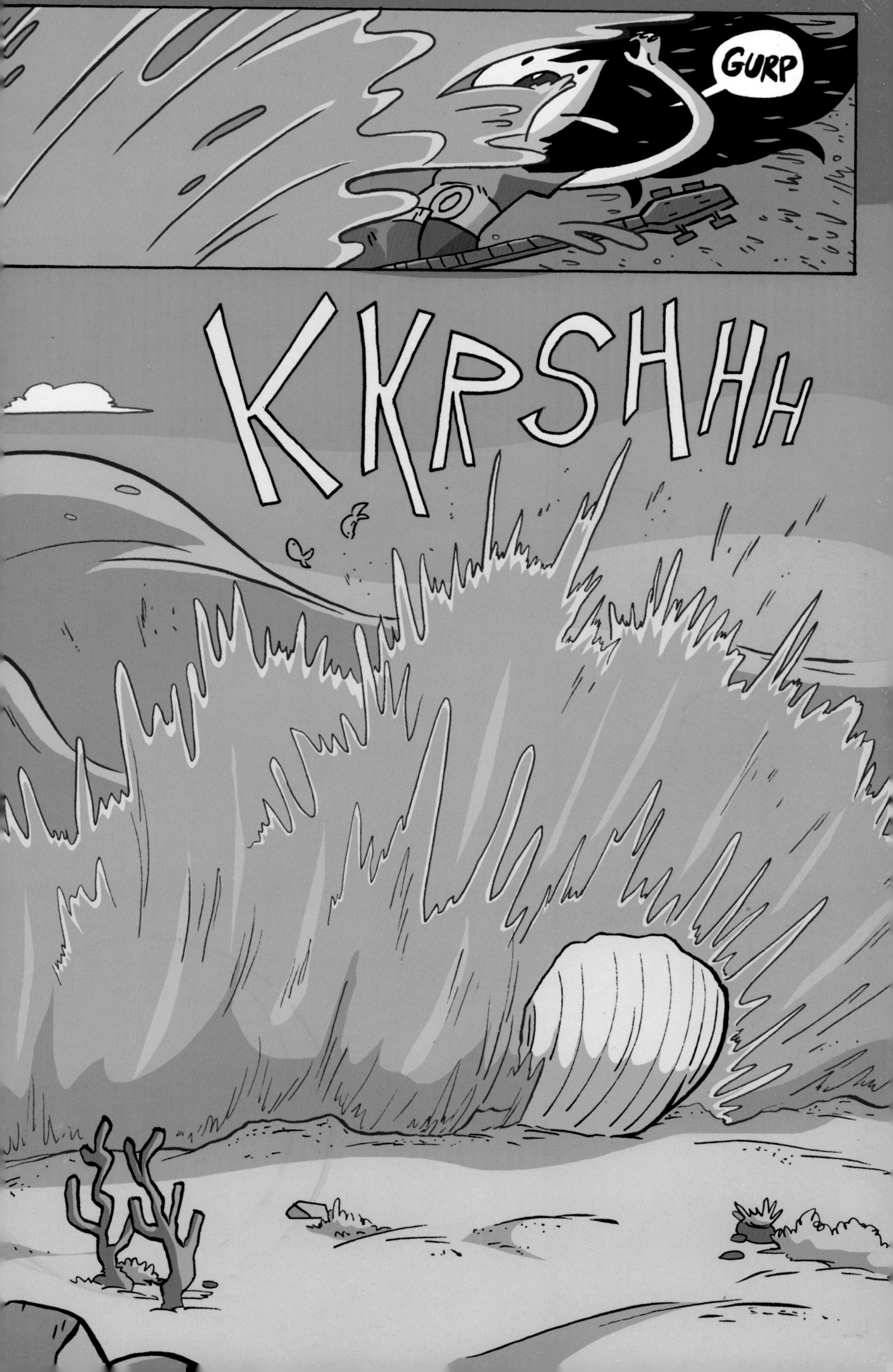
GURP
KKRSHHH

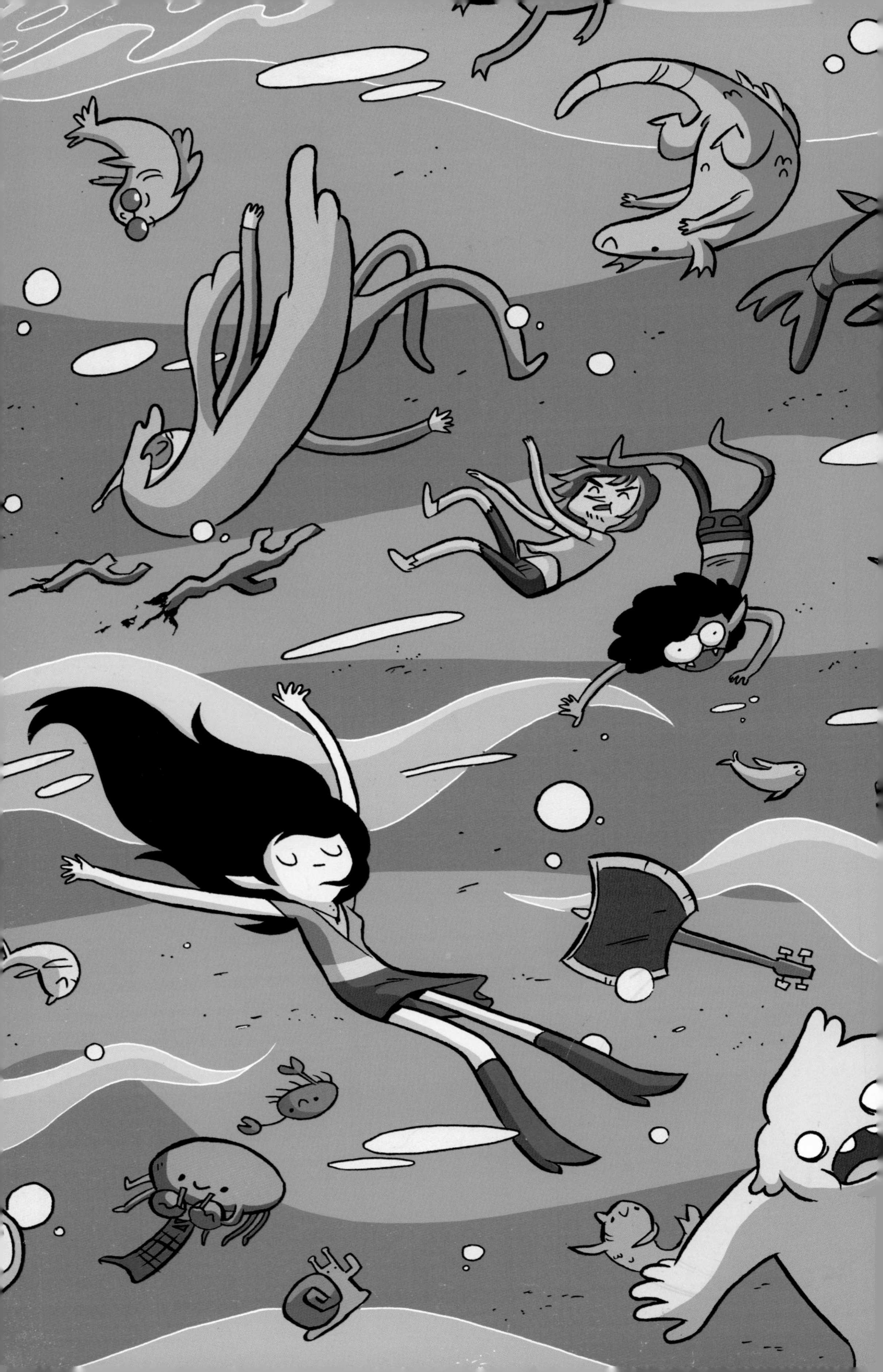

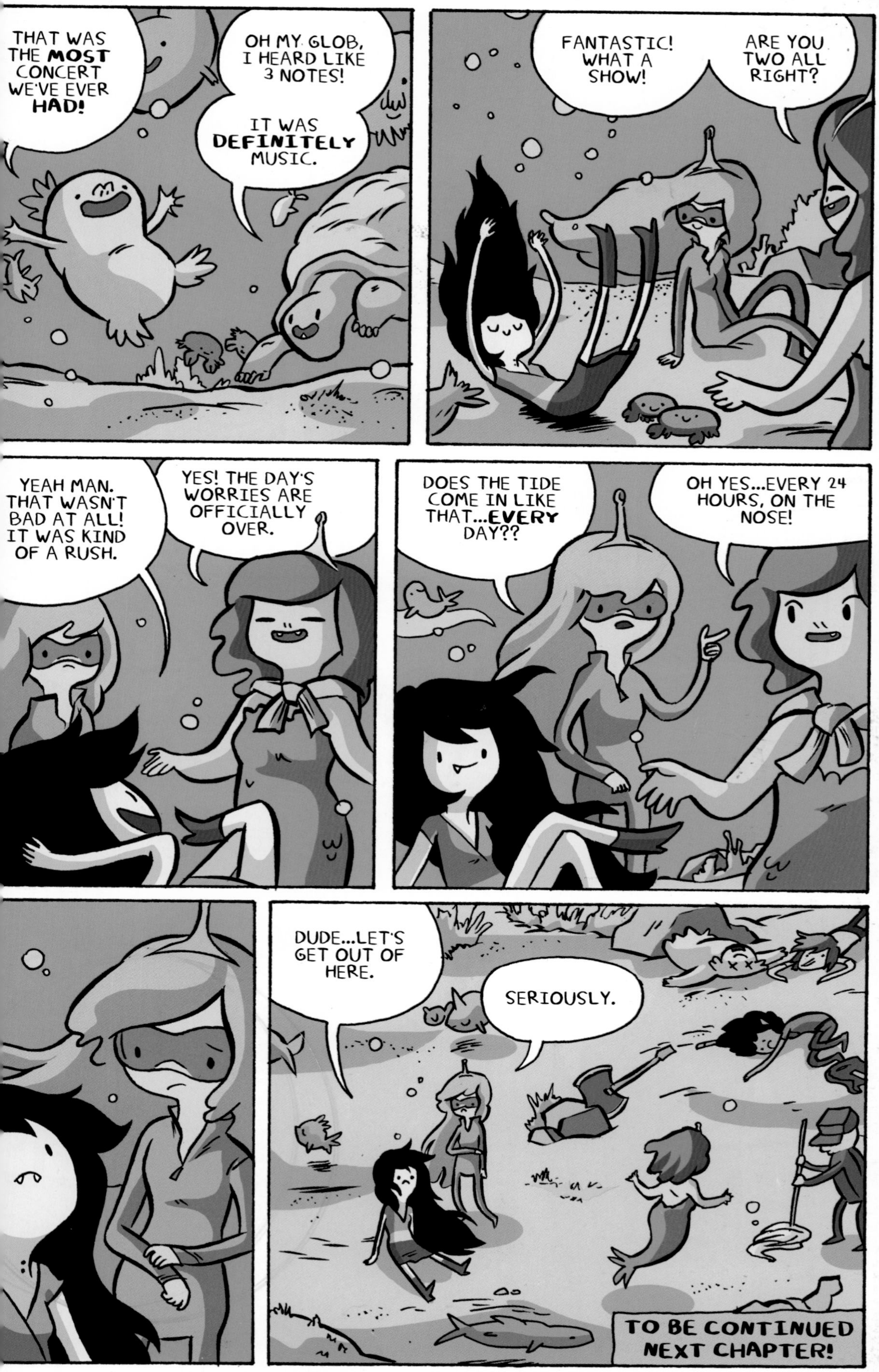

THAT WAS THE **MOST** CONCERT WE'VE EVER **HAD!**
OH MY GLOB, I HEARD LIKE 3 NOTES!
IT WAS **DEFINITELY** MUSIC.
FANTASTIC! WHAT A SHOW!
ARE YOU TWO ALL RIGHT?
YEAH MAN. THAT WASN'T BAD AT ALL! IT WAS KIND OF A RUSH.
YES! THE DAY'S WORRIES ARE OFFICIALLY OVER.
DOES THE TIDE COME IN LIKE THAT...**EVERY** DAY??
OH YES...EVERY 24 HOURS, ON THE NOSE!
DUDE...LET'S GET OUT OF HERE.
SERIOUSLY.
TO BE CONTINUED NEXT CHAPTER!

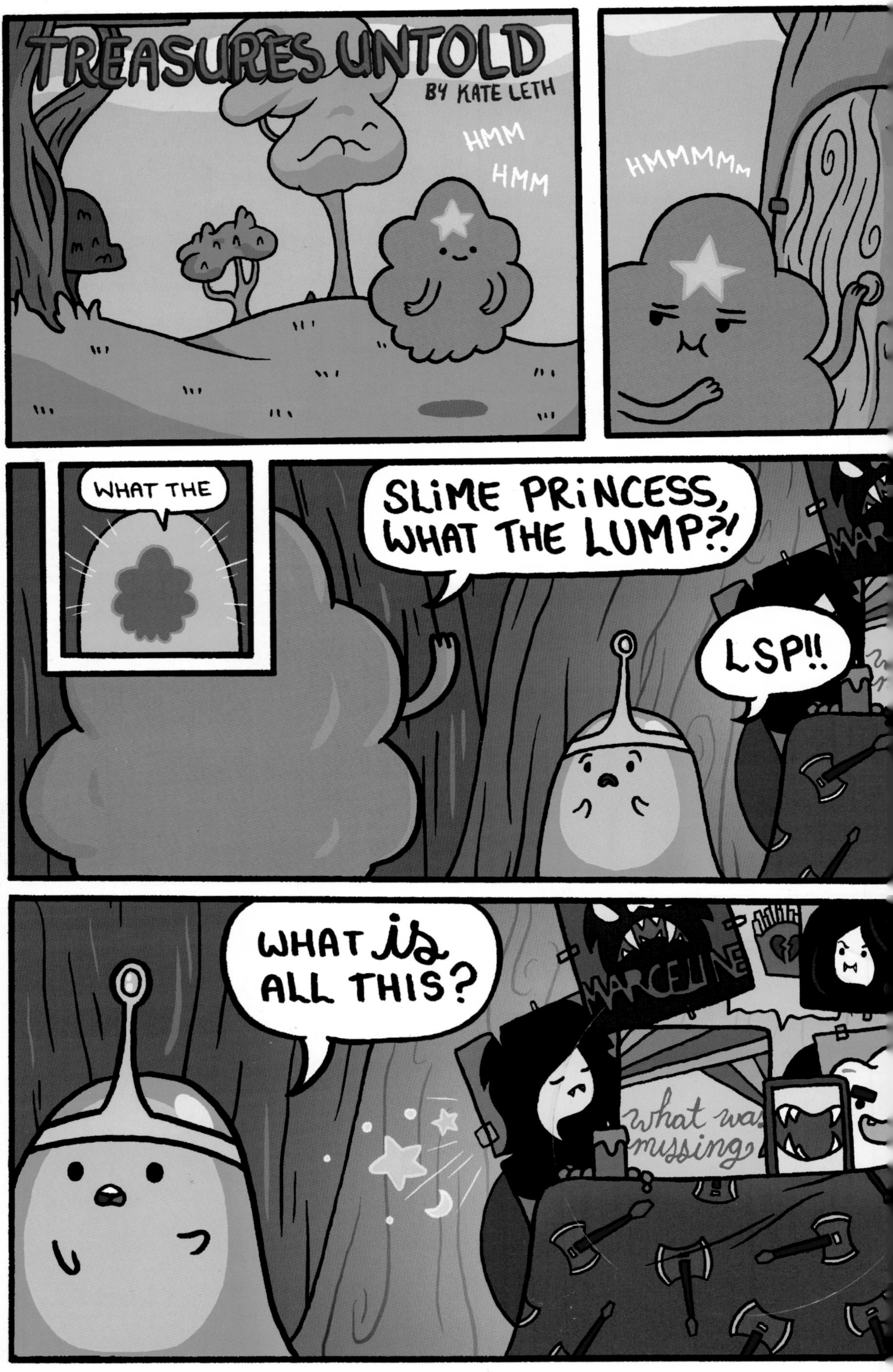

TREASURES UNTOLD
BY KATE LETH
HMM
HMM
HMMMMM
WHAT THE
SLIME PRINCESS, WHAT THE LUMP?!
LSP!!
WHAT is ALL THIS?
MARCELINE
what was missing

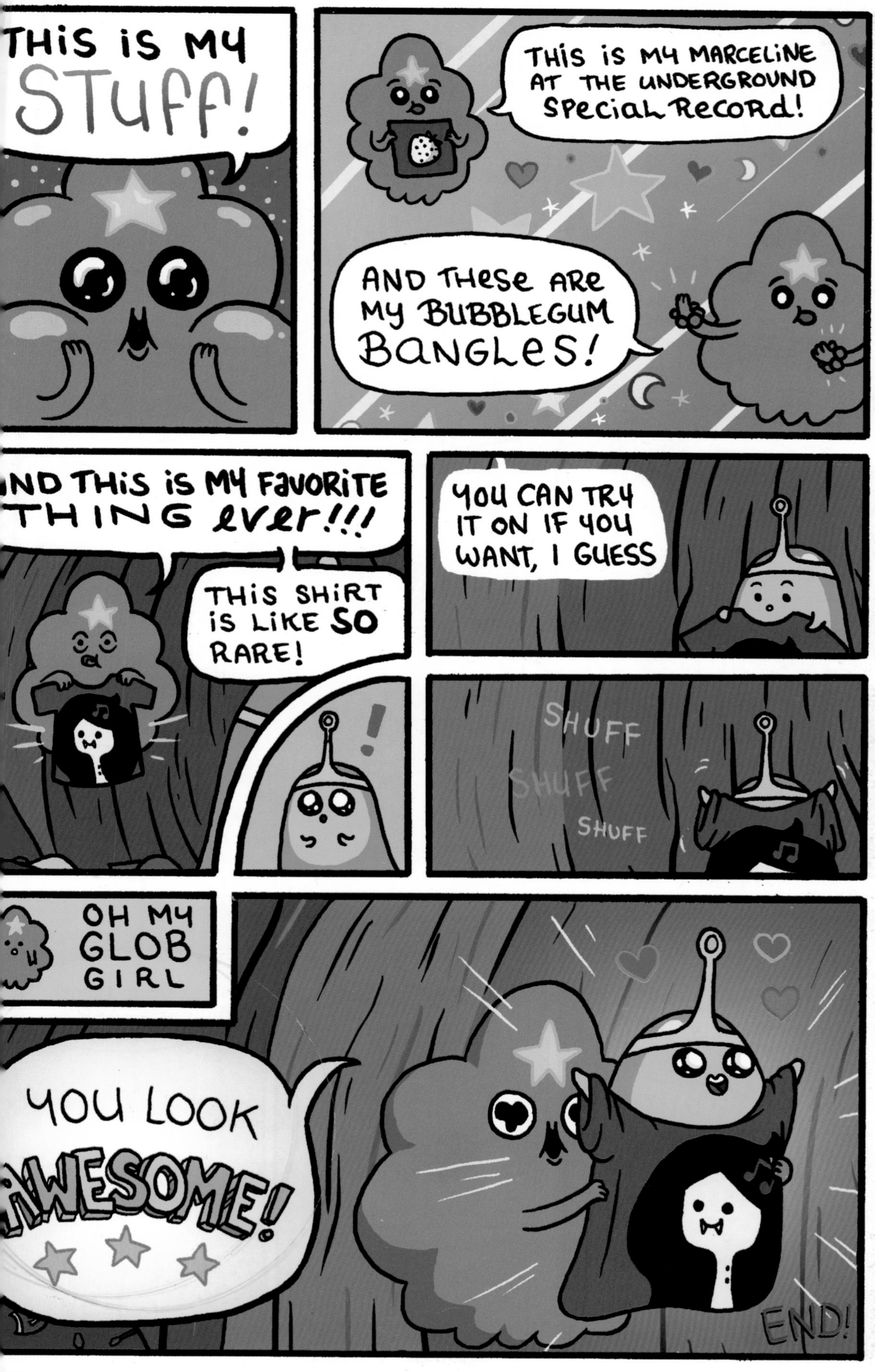
THIS IS MY STUFF!
THIS IS MY MARCELINE AT THE UNDERGROUND SPECIAL RECORD!
AND THESE ARE MY BUBBLEGUM BANGLES!
ND THIS IS MY FAVORITE THING ever!!!
THIS SHIRT IS LIKE SO RARE!
YOU CAN TRY IT ON IF YOU WANT, I GUESS
SHUFF
SHUFF
SHUFF
OH MY GLOB GIRL
YOU LOOK AWESOME!
END!

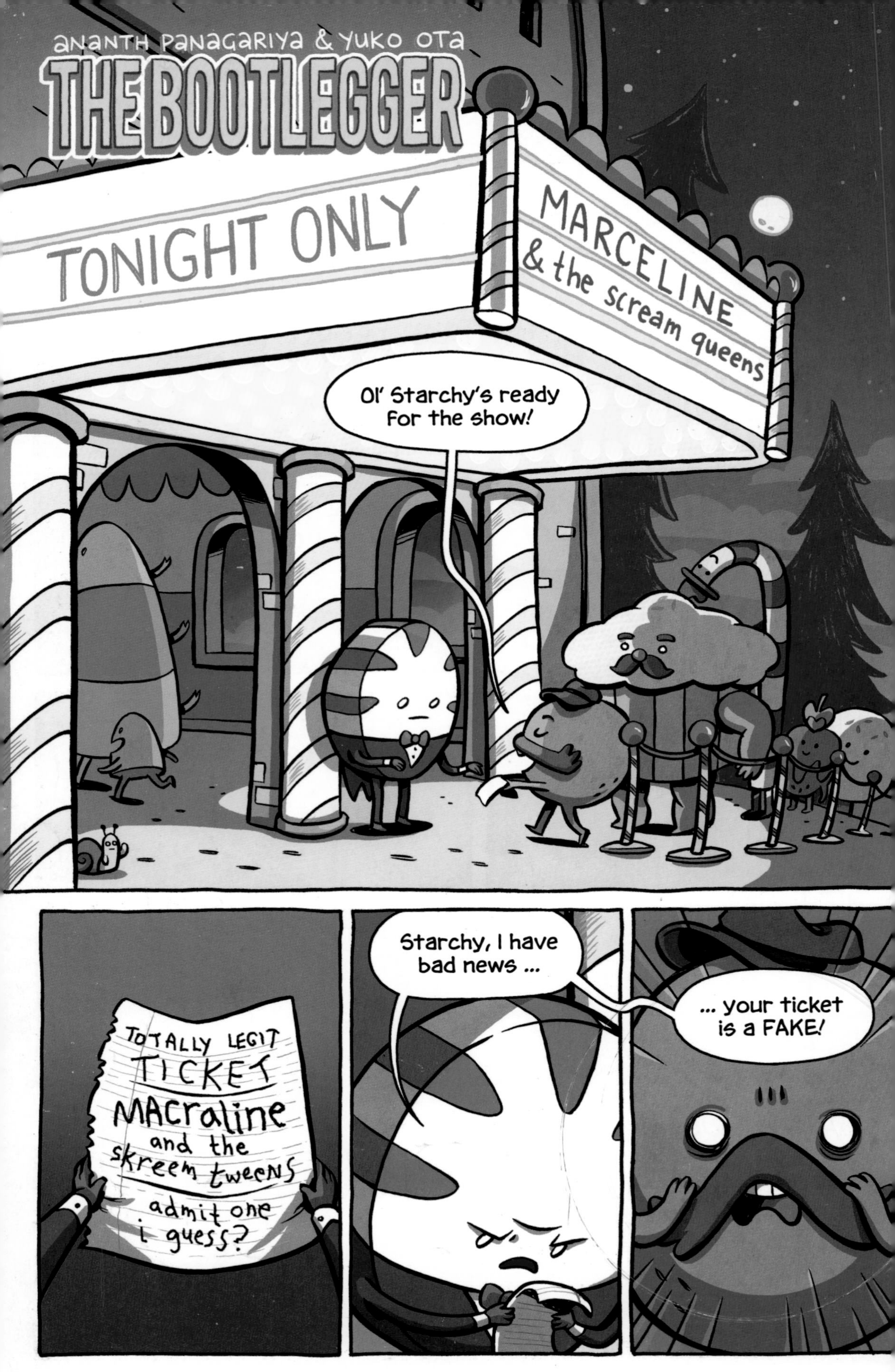
ananth panagariya & yuko ota
THE BOOTLEGGER
TONIGHT ONLY
MARCELINE & the scream queens
Ol' Starchy's ready for the show!
TOTALLY LEGIT TICKET MACraline and the skreem tweens admit one i guess?
Starchy, I have bad news ...
... your ticket is a FAKE!

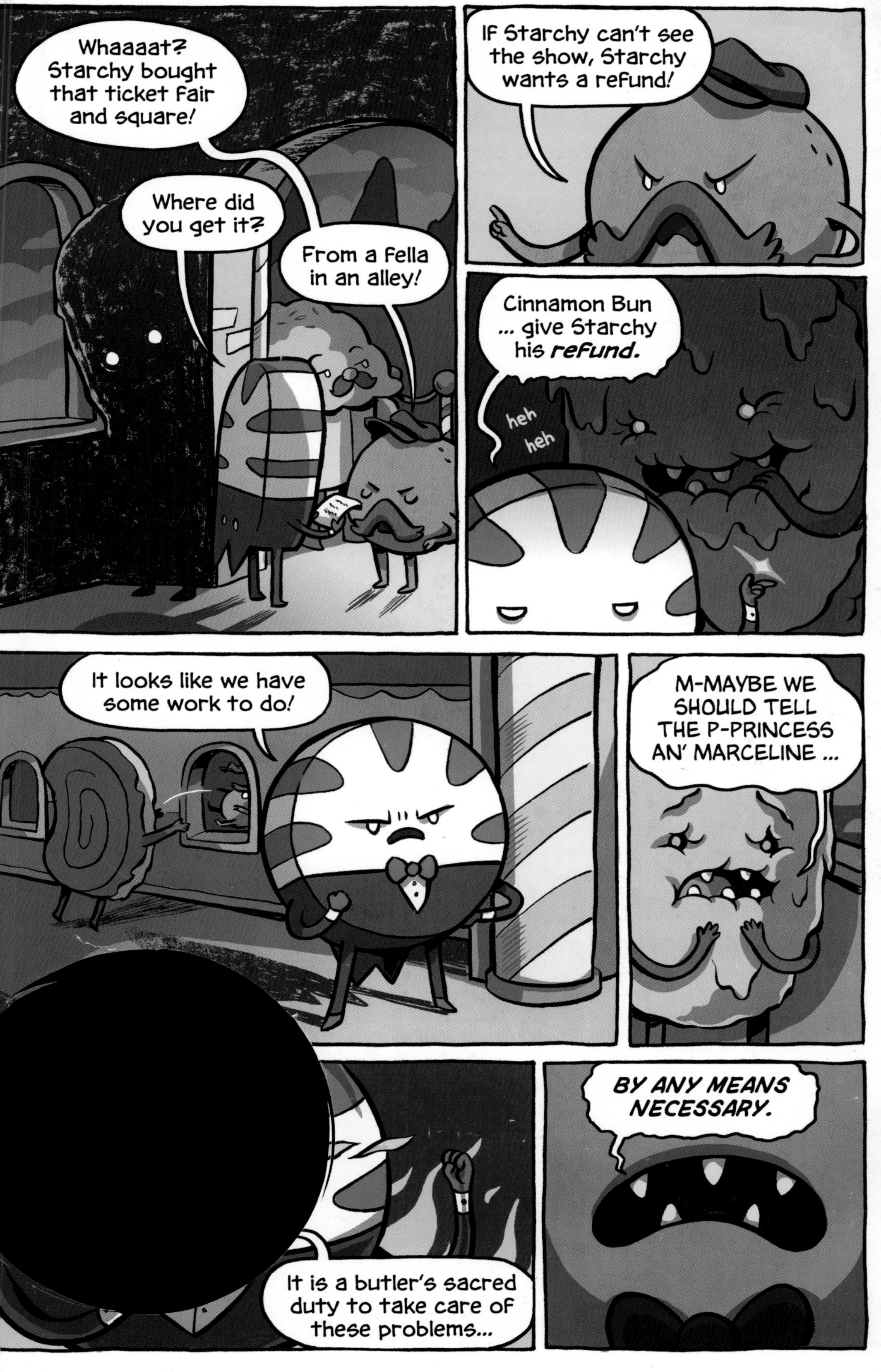

Whaaaat? Starchy bought that ticket fair and square!
Where did you get it?
From a fella in an alley!
If Starchy can't see the show, Starchy wants a refund!
Cinnamon Bun ... give Starchy his *refund.*
heh heh
It looks like we have some work to do!
M-MAYBE WE SHOULD TELL THE P-PRINCESS AN' MARCELINE ...
It is a butler's sacred duty to take care of these problems...
BY ANY MEANS NECESSARY.

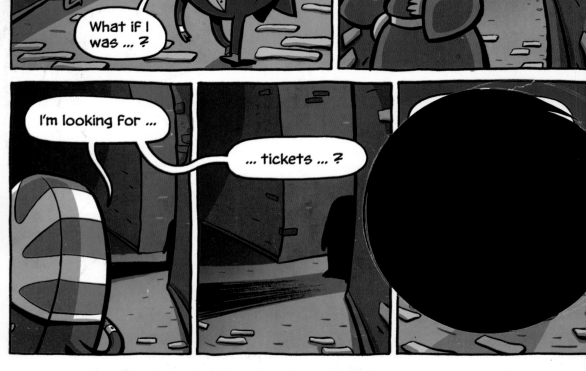

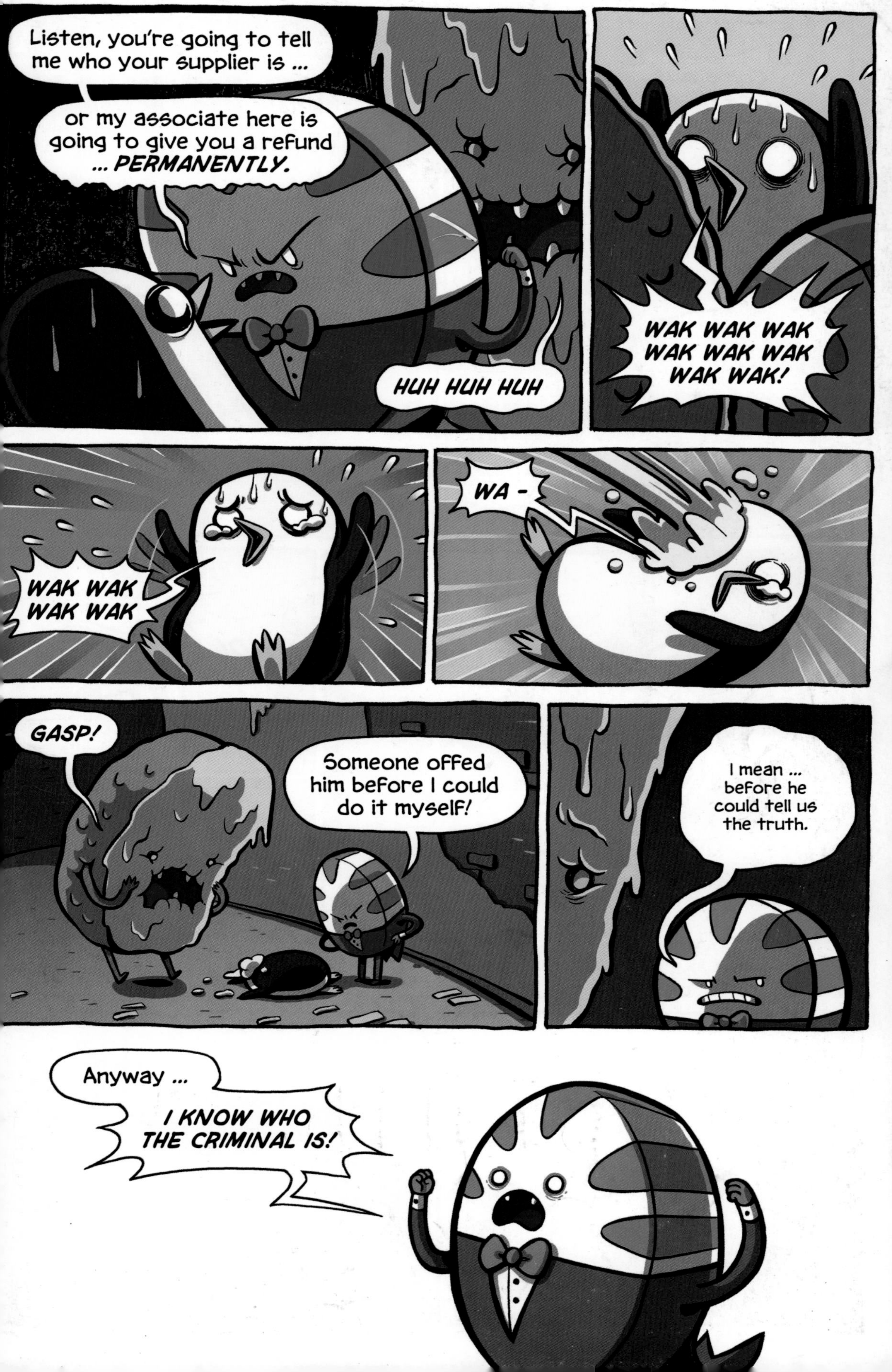
Listen, you're going to tell me who your supplier is ...
or my associate here is going to give you a refund ... PERMANENTLY.
HUH HUH HUH
WAK WAK WAK WAK WAK WAK WAK WAK!
WAK WAK WAK WAK
WA -
GASP!
Someone offed him before I could do it myself!
I mean ... before he could tell us the truth.
Anyway ...
I KNOW WHO THE CRIMINAL IS!

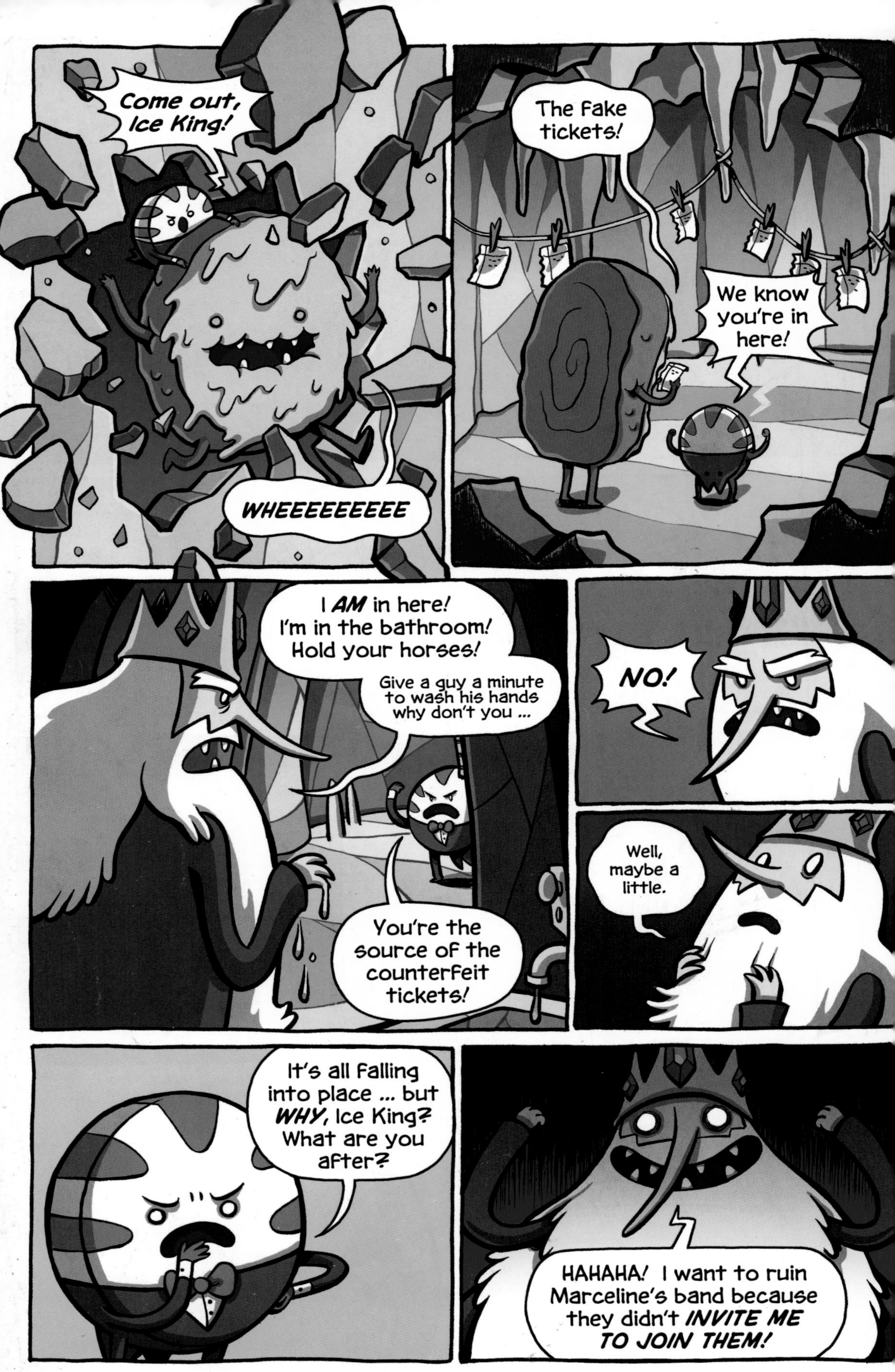
Come out, Ice King!
WHEEEEEEEEEE
The fake tickets!
We know you're in here!
I AM in here! I'm in the bathroom! Hold your horses!
Give a guy a minute to wash his hands why don't you ...
You're the source of the counterfeit tickets!
NO!
Well, maybe a little.
It's all falling into place ... but WHY, Ice King? What are you after?
HAHAHA! I want to ruin Marceline's band because they didn't INVITE ME TO JOIN THEM!

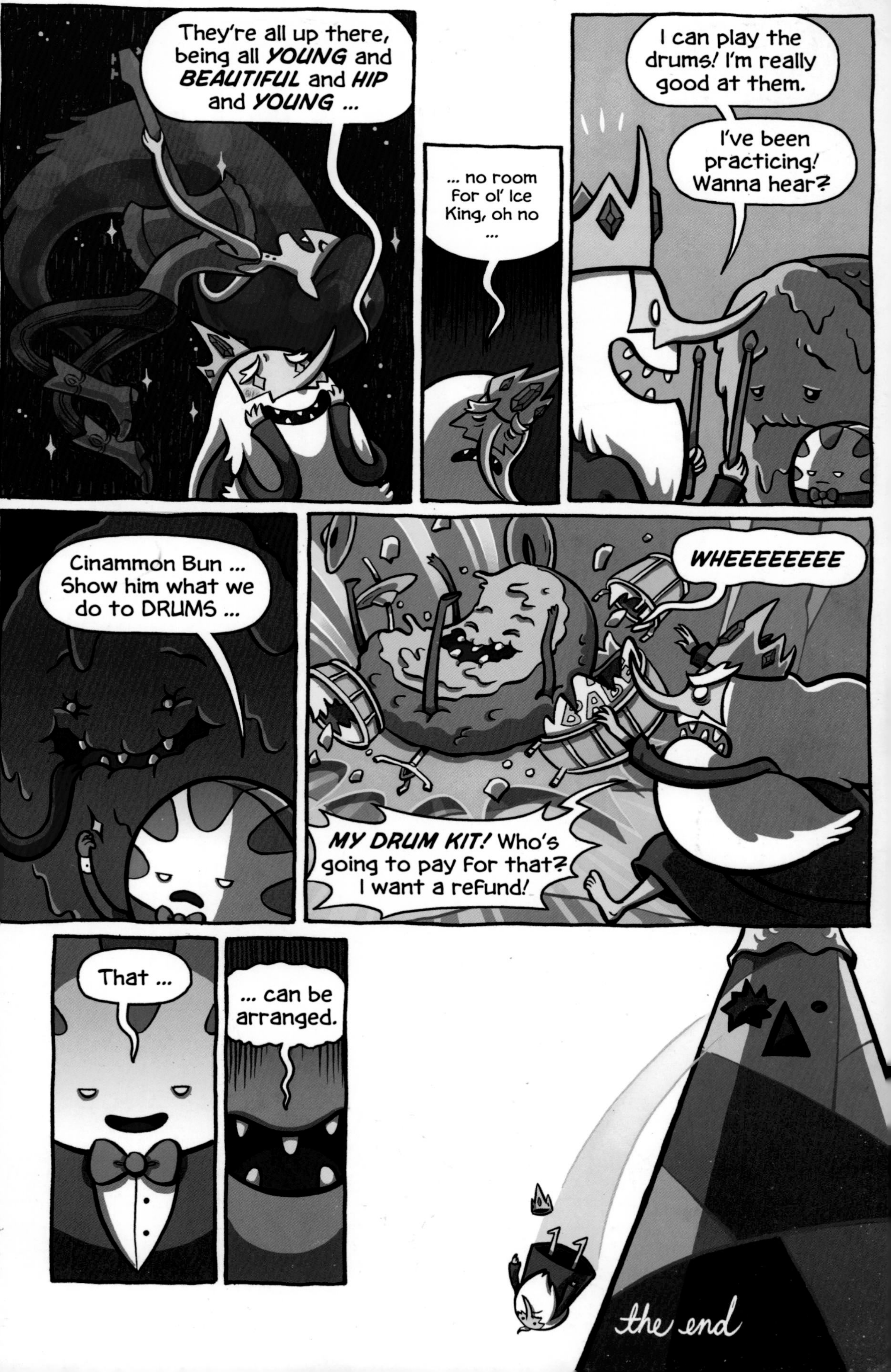
They're all up there, being all YOUNG and BEAUTIFUL and HIP and YOUNG ...
... no room for ol' Ice King, oh no ...
I can play the drums! I'm really good at them.
I've been practicing! Wanna hear?
Cinammon Bun ... Show him what we do to DRUMS ...
WHEEEEEEEE
MY DRUM KIT! Who's going to pay for that? I want a refund!
That ...
... can be arranged.
the end

CHAPTER FIVE

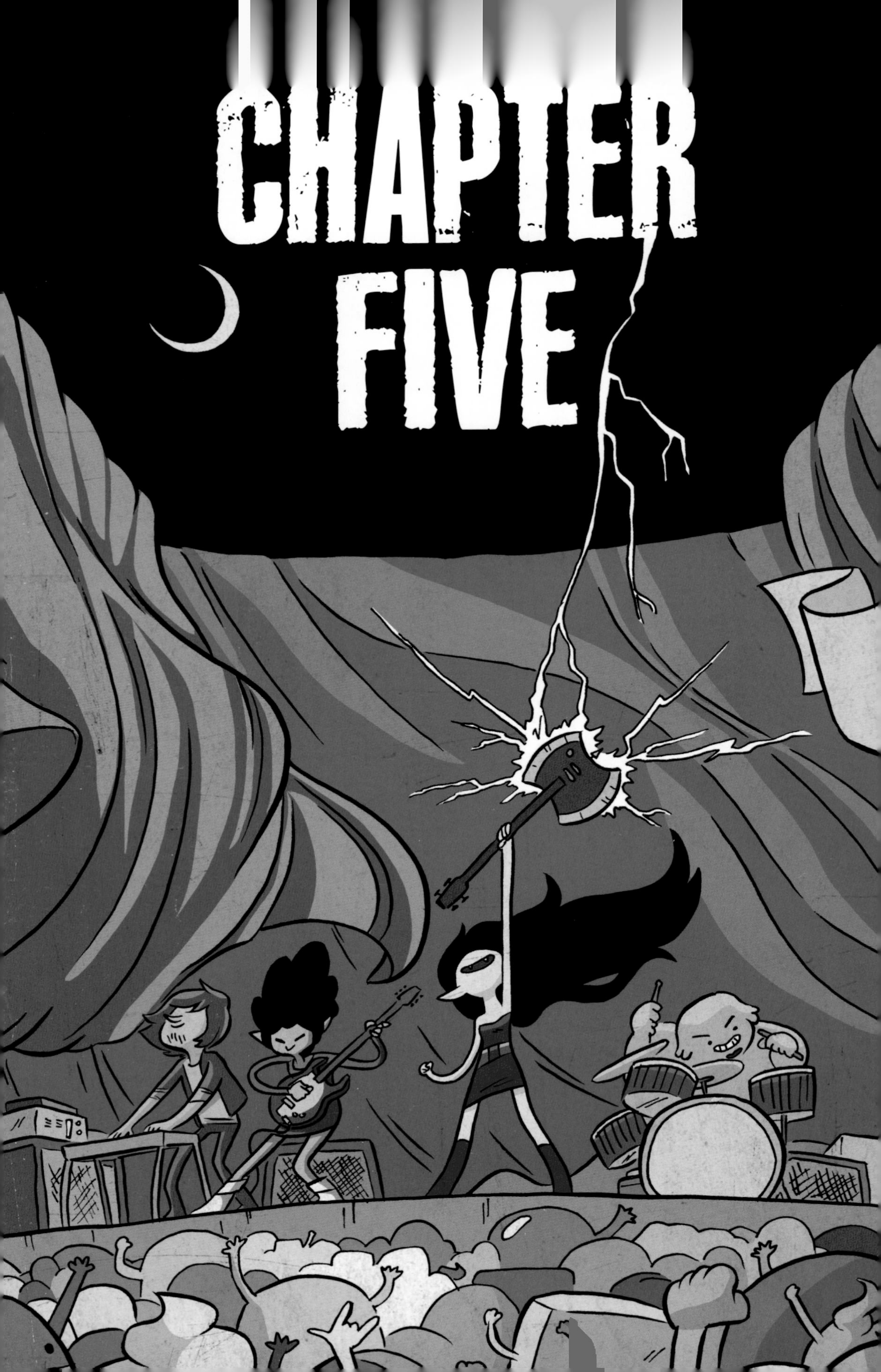

MEMORANDUM

This contract hereby grants
MARCELINE + THE SCREAM QUEENS (The **"Talent"**)
and _PRINCESS BUBBLEGUM_ (The **"Manager"**)
one (1) two-way passage to the Nightosphere to
play their next live show. The Talent agrees to provide
one (1) *Apple Pie* (The **"Work"**) in exchange for
these services, to be delivered immediately
and deliciously.

MALOSO VOBISCUM ET CUM SPIRITUM!

COME **ON**, BONGO...!

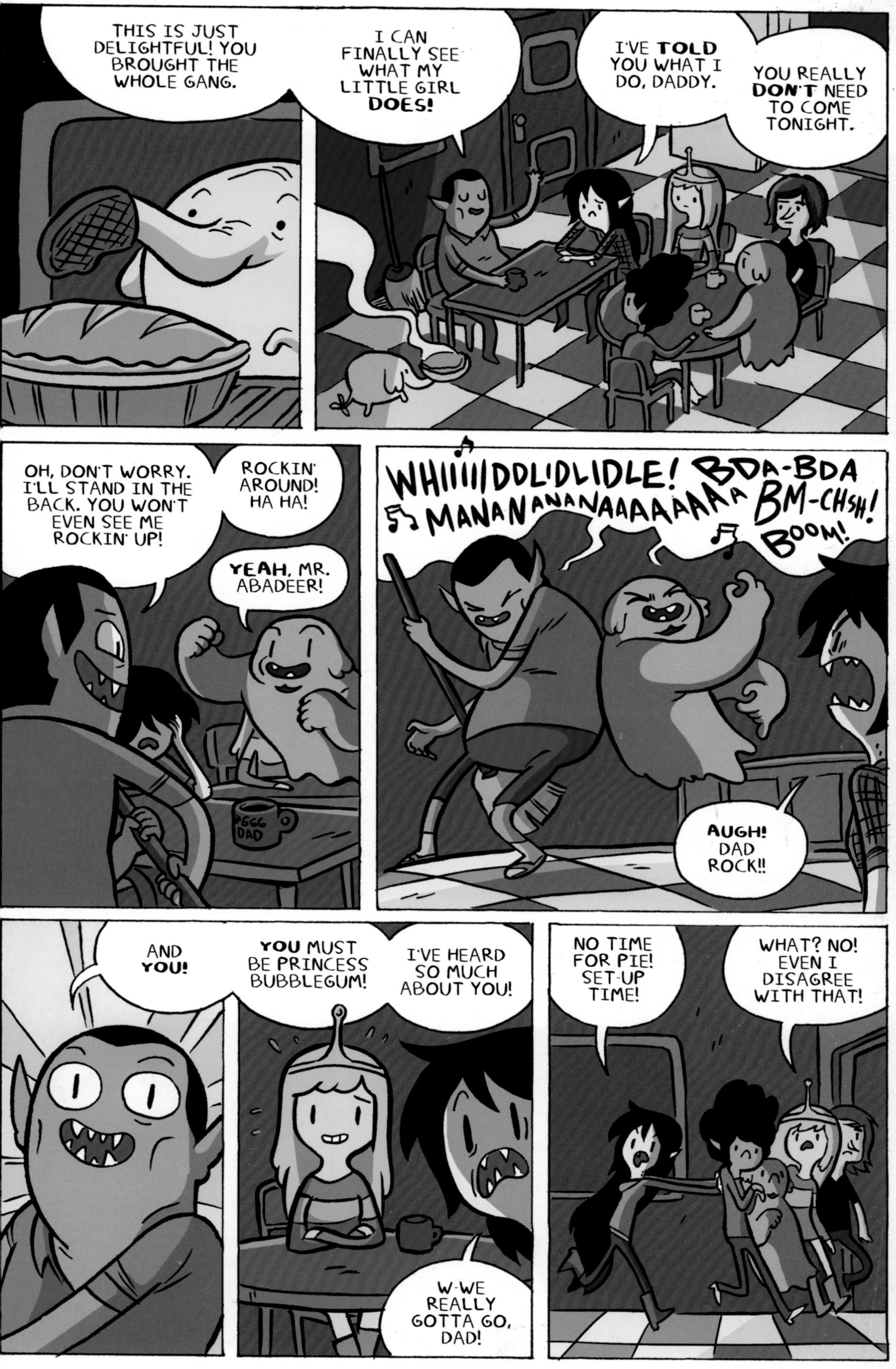

THIS IS JUST DELIGHTFUL! YOU BROUGHT THE WHOLE GANG.
I CAN FINALLY SEE WHAT MY LITTLE GIRL **DOES!**
I'VE **TOLD** YOU WHAT I DO, DADDY.
YOU REALLY **DON'T** NEED TO COME TONIGHT.
OH, DON'T WORRY. I'LL STAND IN THE BACK. YOU WON'T EVEN SEE ME ROCKIN' UP!
ROCKIN' AROUND! HA HA!
YEAH, MR. ABADEER!
#666 DAD
WHIIIIIDDLIDLIDLE! BDA-BDA
MANANANANAAAAAAAAA
BM-CHSH!
BOOM!
AUGH! DAD ROCK!!
AND **YOU!**
YOU MUST BE PRINCESS BUBBLEGUM!
I'VE HEARD SO MUCH ABOUT YOU!
W-WE REALLY GOTTA GO, DAD!
NO TIME FOR PIE! SET-UP TIME!
WHAT? NO! EVEN I DISAGREE WITH THAT!

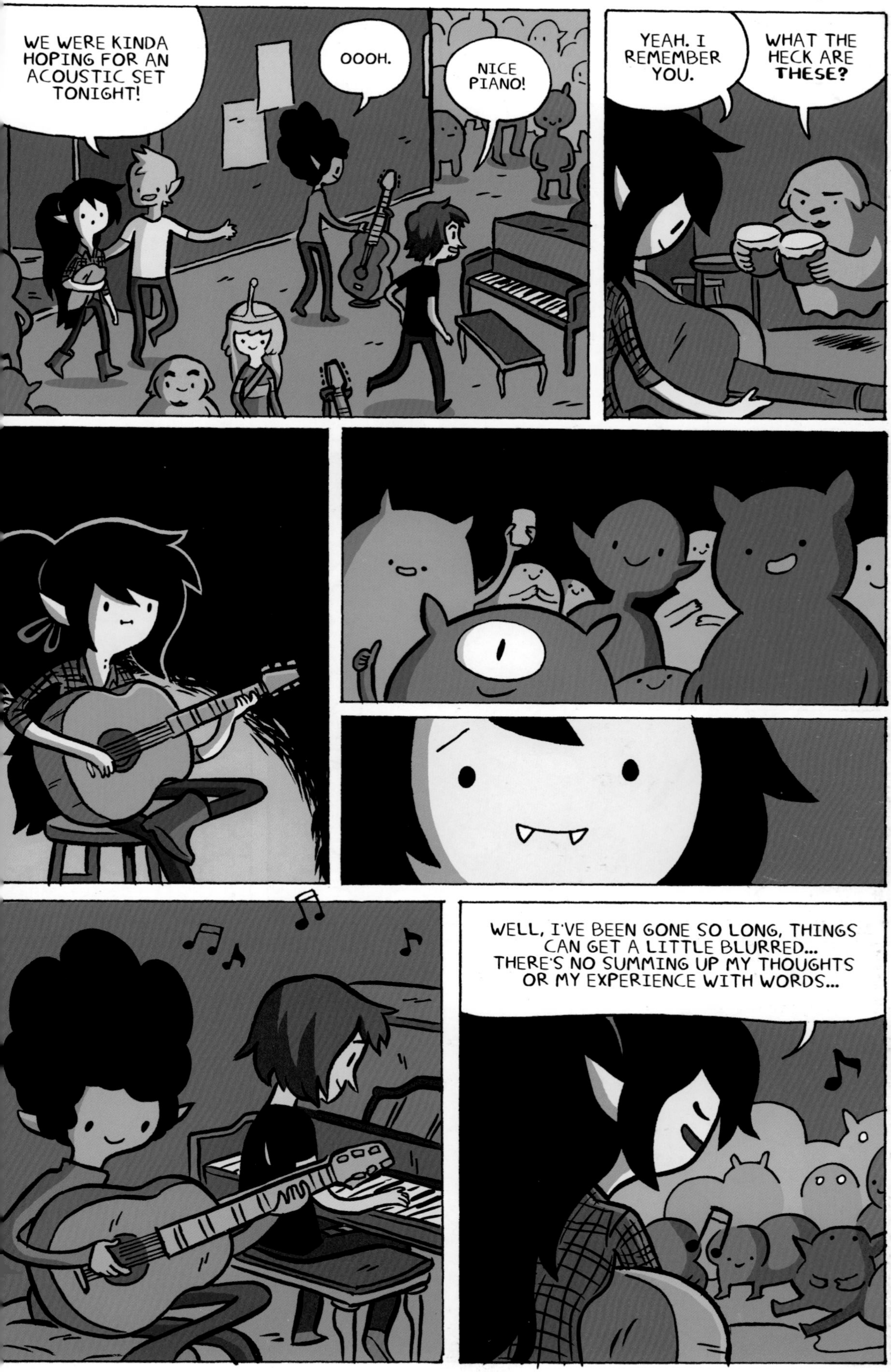
WE WERE KINDA HOPING FOR AN ACOUSTIC SET TONIGHT!
OOOH.
NICE PIANO!
YEAH. I REMEMBER YOU.
WHAT THE HECK ARE **THESE?**
WELL, I'VE BEEN GONE SO LONG, THINGS CAN GET A LITTLE BLURRED... THERE'S NO SUMMING UP MY THOUGHTS OR MY EXPERIENCE WITH WORDS...

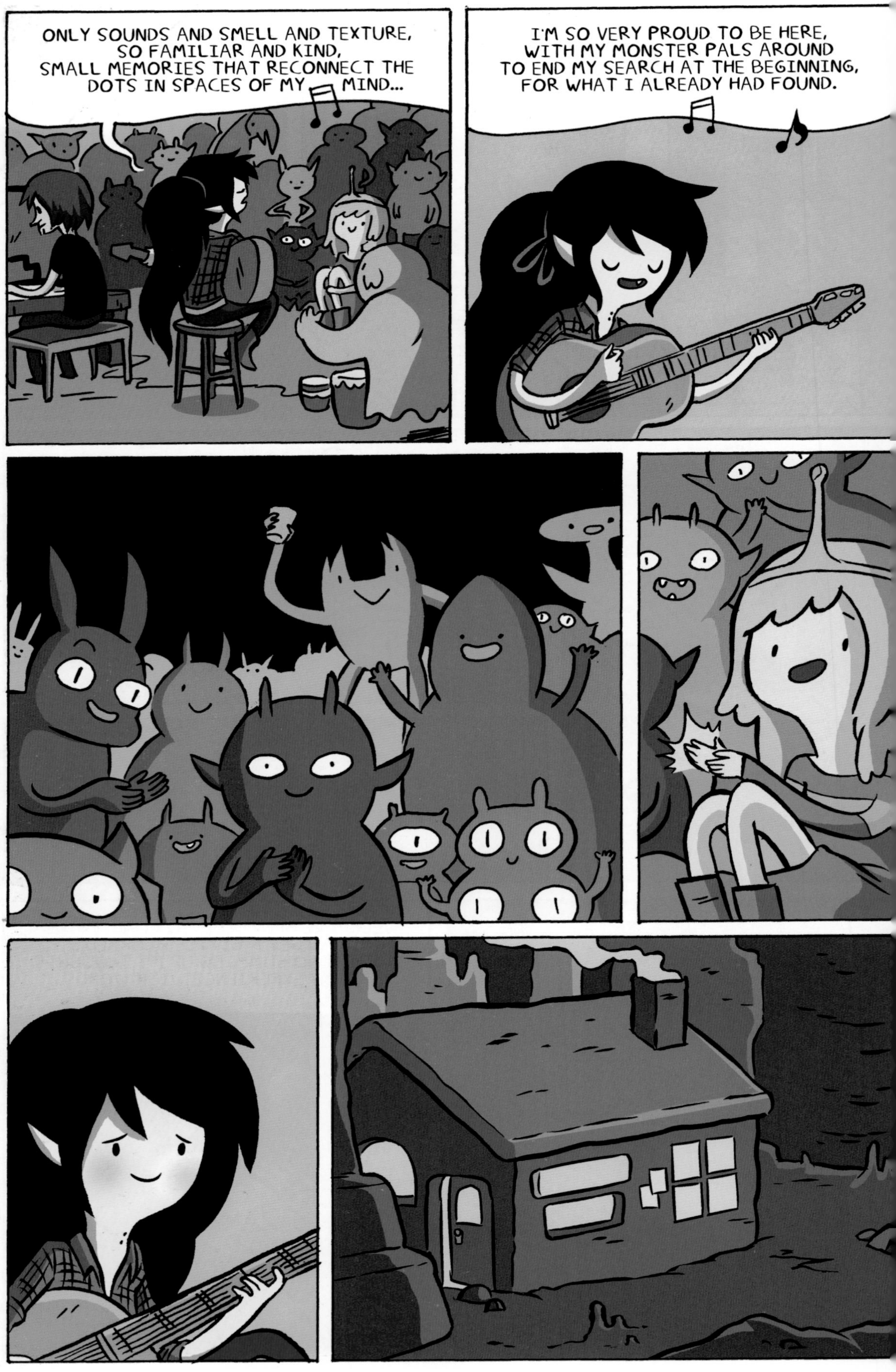
ONLY SOUNDS AND SMELL AND TEXTURE, SO FAMILIAR AND KIND, SMALL MEMORIES THAT RECONNECT THE DOTS IN SPACES OF MY MIND...
I'M SO VERY PROUD TO BE HERE, WITH MY MONSTER PALS AROUND TO END MY SEARCH AT THE BEGINNING, FOR WHAT I ALREADY HAD FOUND.

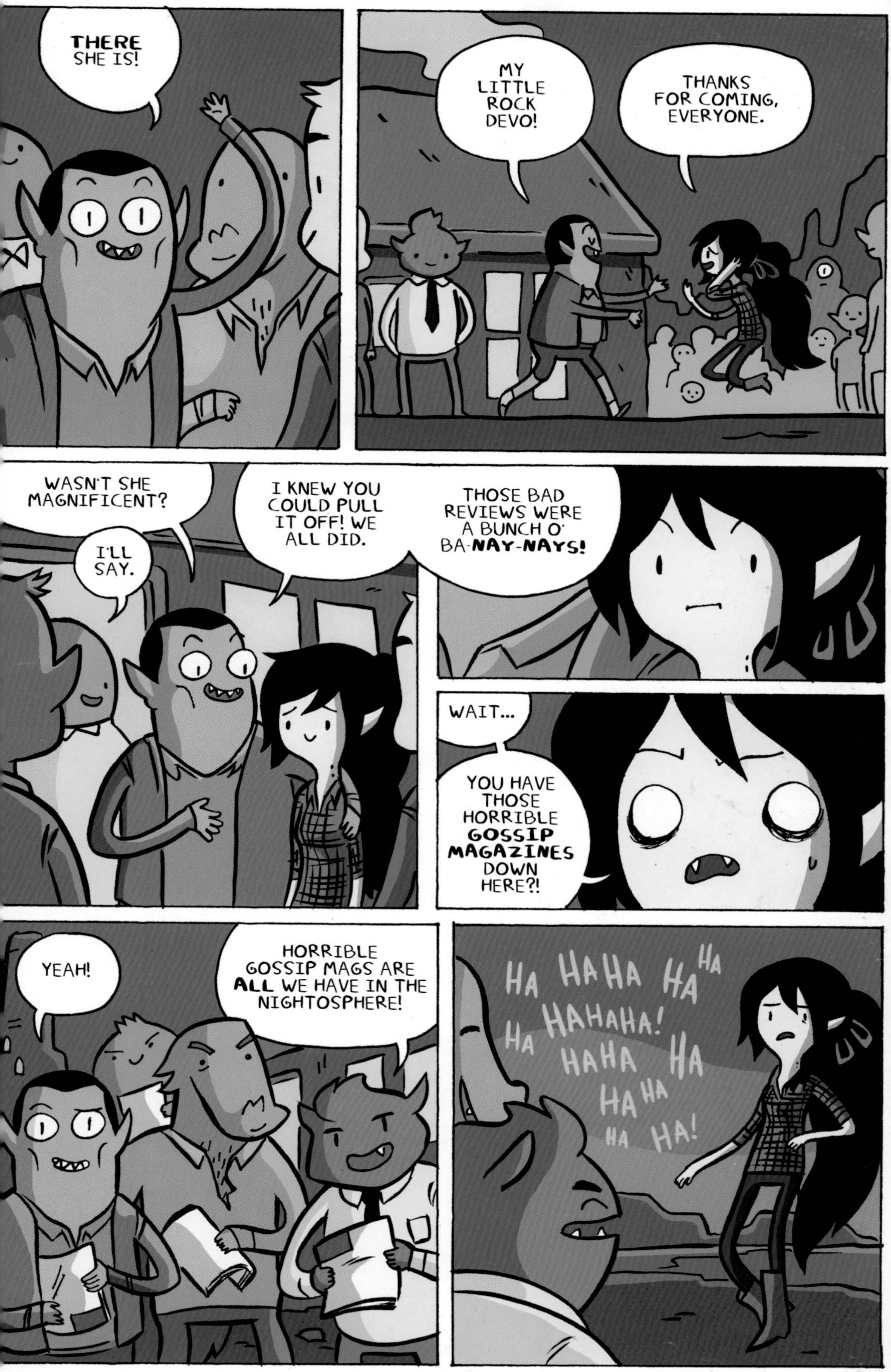

THERE SHE IS!
MY LITTLE ROCK DEVO!
THANKS FOR COMING, EVERYONE.
WASN'T SHE MAGNIFICENT?
I'LL SAY.
I KNEW YOU COULD PULL IT OFF! WE ALL DID.
THOSE BAD REVIEWS WERE A BUNCH O' BA-NAY-NAYS!
WAIT...
YOU HAVE THOSE HORRIBLE GOSSIP MAGAZINES DOWN HERE?!
YEAH!
HORRIBLE GOSSIP MAGS ARE ALL WE HAVE IN THE NIGHTOSPHERE!
HA HA HA HA HA HAHAHA! HA HAHA HA HA HA HA HA!

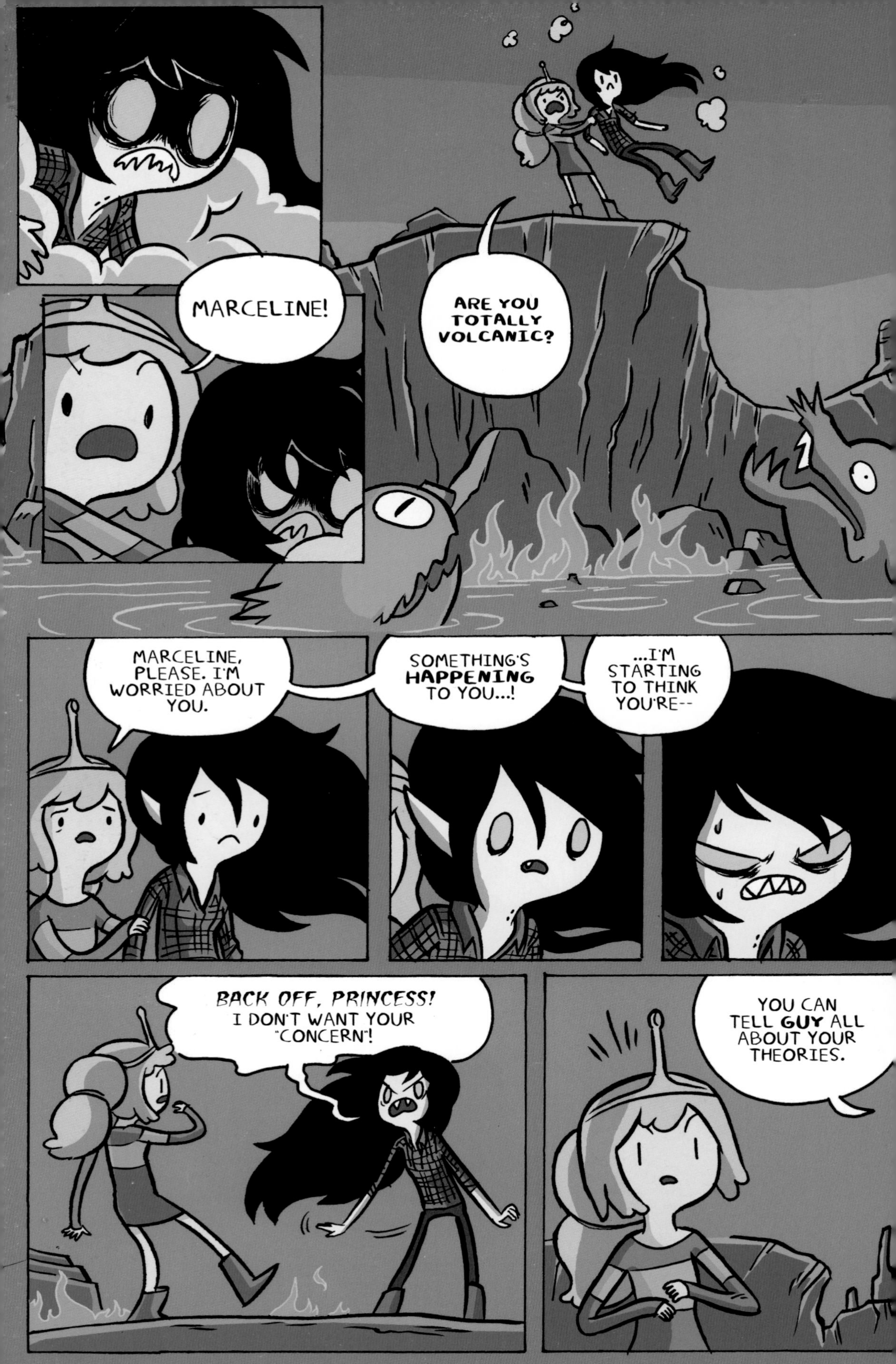
MARCELINE!
ARE YOU TOTALLY VOLCANIC?
MARCELINE, PLEASE. I'M WORRIED ABOUT YOU.
SOMETHING'S **HAPPENING** TO YOU...!
...I'M STARTING TO THINK YOU'RE--
BACK OFF, PRINCESS! I DON'T WANT YOUR "CONCERN"!
YOU CAN TELL **GUY** ALL ABOUT YOUR THEORIES.

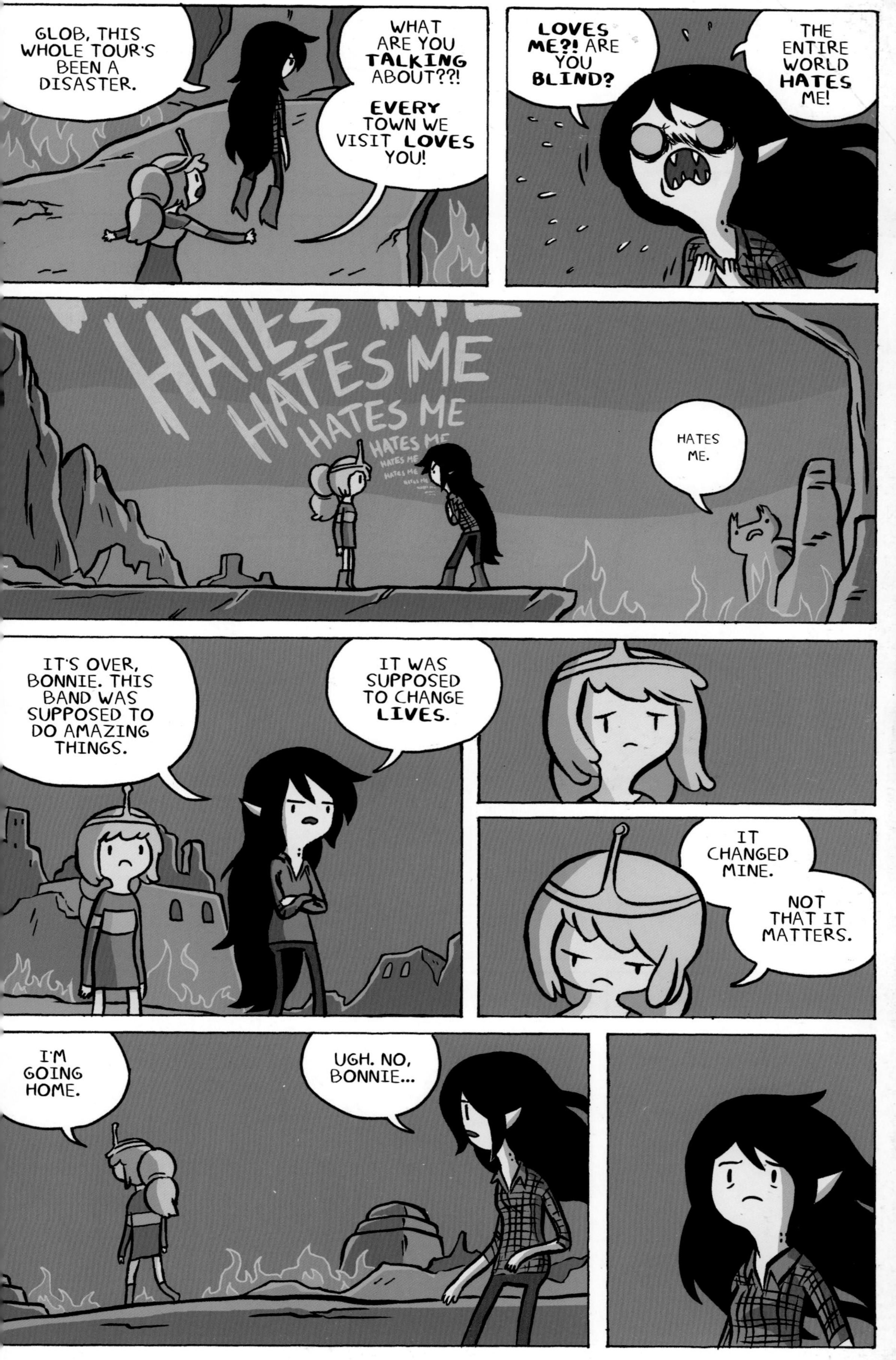

GLOB, THIS WHOLE TOUR'S BEEN A DISASTER.
WHAT ARE YOU **TALKING** ABOUT??!
EVERY TOWN WE VISIT **LOVES** YOU!
LOVES ME?! ARE YOU **BLIND?**
THE ENTIRE WORLD **HATES** ME!
HATES ME
HATES ME
HATES ME
HATES ME
HATES ME
HATES ME
HATES ME.
IT'S OVER, BONNIE. THIS BAND WAS SUPPOSED TO DO AMAZING THINGS.
IT WAS SUPPOSED TO CHANGE **LIVES**.
IT CHANGED MINE.
NOT THAT IT MATTERS.
I'M GOING HOME.
UGH. NO, BONNIE...

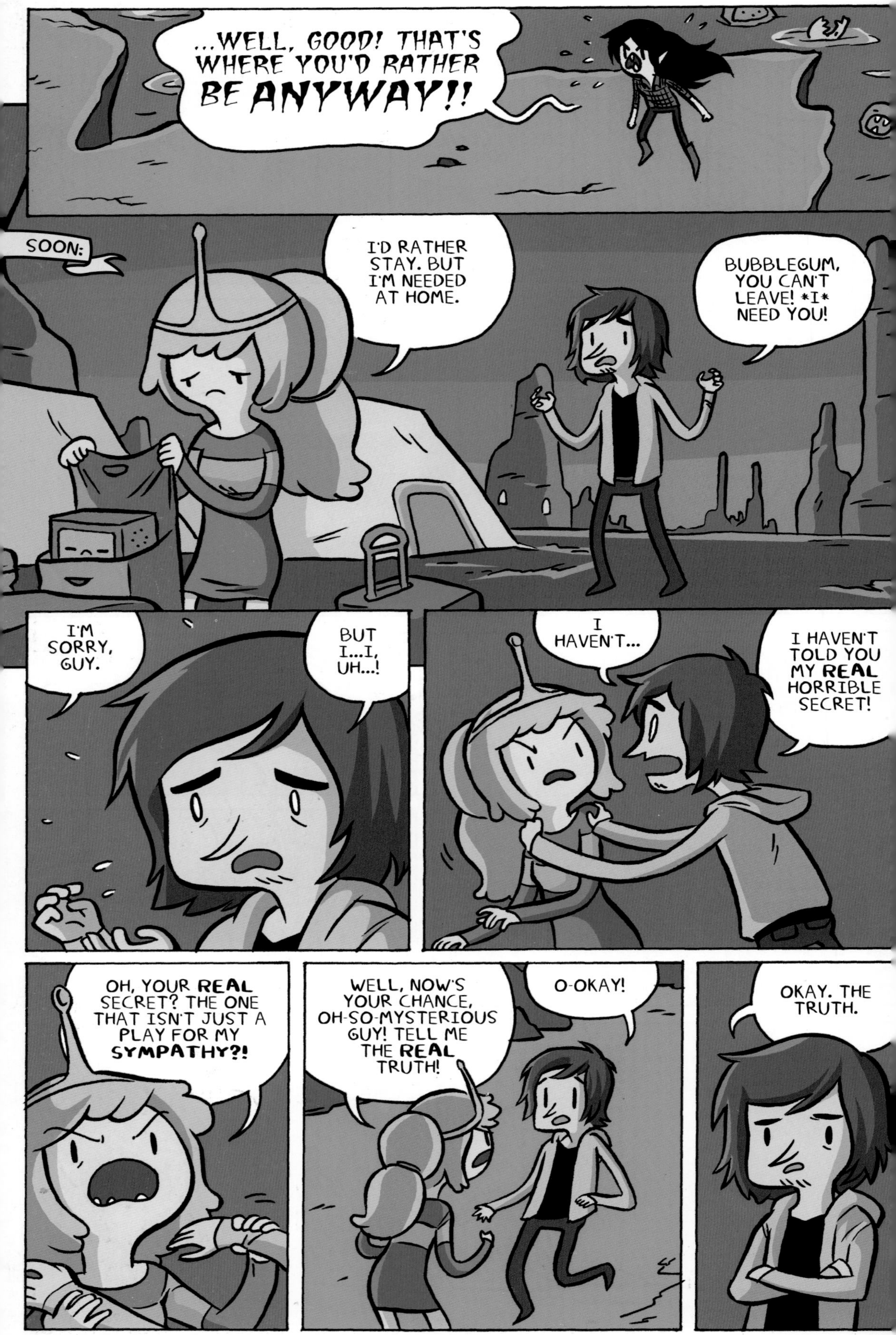
...WELL, GOOD! THAT'S WHERE YOU'D RATHER BE ANYWAY!!
SOON:
I'D RATHER STAY. BUT I'M NEEDED AT HOME.
BUBBLEGUM, YOU CAN'T LEAVE! *I* NEED YOU!
I'M SORRY, GUY.
BUT I...I, UH...!
I HAVEN'T...
I HAVEN'T TOLD YOU MY REAL HORRIBLE SECRET!
OH, YOUR REAL SECRET? THE ONE THAT ISN'T JUST A PLAY FOR MY SYMPATHY?!
WELL, NOW'S YOUR CHANCE, OH-SO-MYSTERIOUS GUY! TELL ME THE REAL TRUTH!
O-OKAY!
OKAY. THE TRUTH.

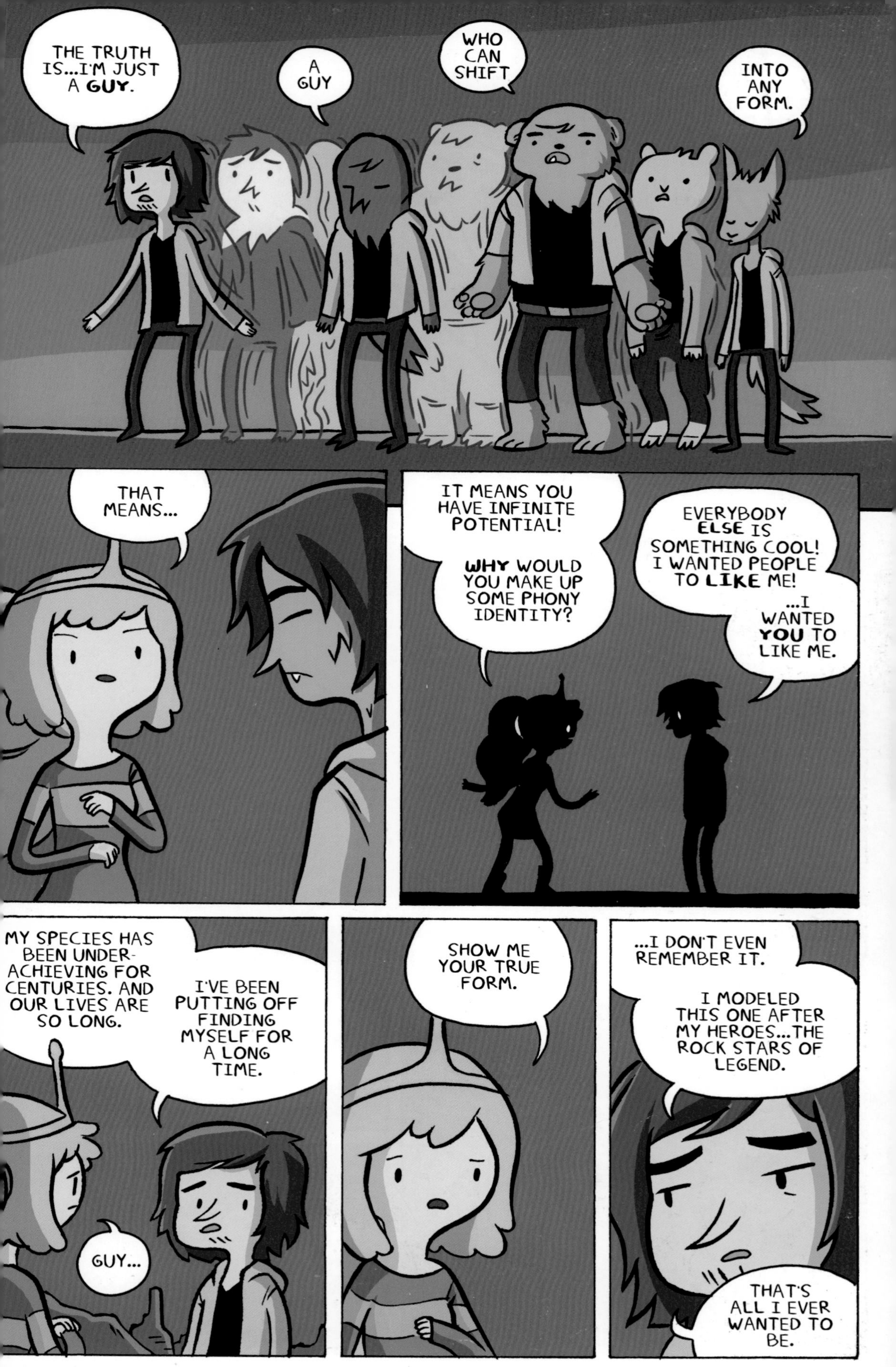
THE TRUTH IS...I'M JUST A **GUY**.
A GUY
WHO CAN SHIFT
INTO ANY FORM.
THAT MEANS...
IT MEANS YOU HAVE INFINITE POTENTIAL!
WHY WOULD YOU MAKE UP SOME PHONY IDENTITY?
EVERYBODY **ELSE** IS SOMETHING COOL! I WANTED PEOPLE TO **LIKE** ME!
...I WANTED **YOU** TO LIKE ME.
MY SPECIES HAS BEEN UNDER-ACHIEVING FOR CENTURIES. AND OUR LIVES ARE SO LONG.
I'VE BEEN PUTTING OFF FINDING MYSELF FOR A LONG TIME.
GUY...
SHOW ME YOUR TRUE FORM.
...I DON'T EVEN REMEMBER IT.
I MODELED THIS ONE AFTER MY HEROES...THE ROCK STARS OF LEGEND.
THAT'S ALL I EVER WANTED TO BE.

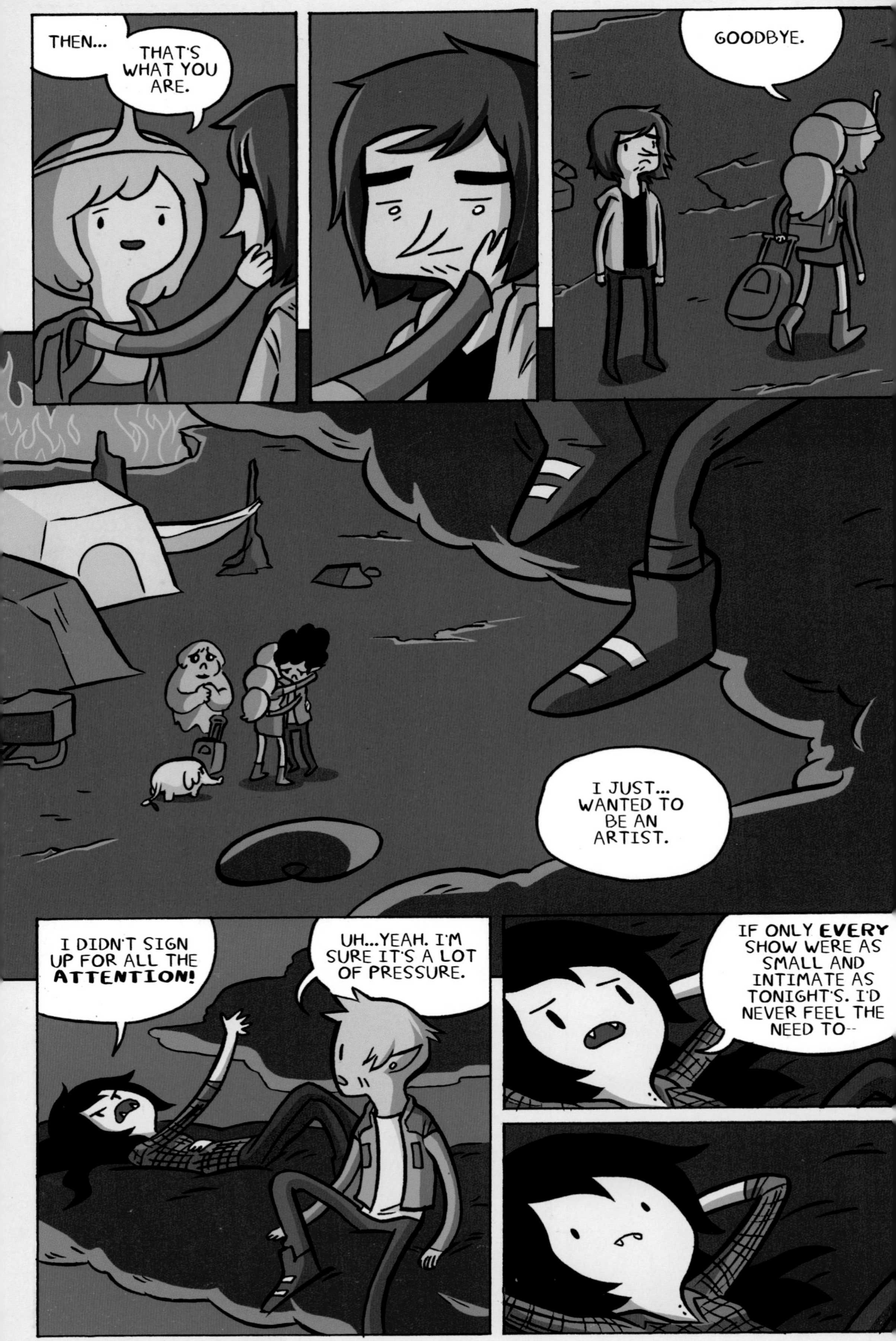
THEN...
THAT'S WHAT YOU ARE.
GOODBYE.
I JUST... WANTED TO BE AN ARTIST.
I DIDN'T SIGN UP FOR ALL THE **ATTENTION!**
UH...YEAH. I'M SURE IT'S A LOT OF PRESSURE.
IF ONLY **EVERY** SHOW WERE AS SMALL AND INTIMATE AS TONIGHT'S. I'D NEVER FEEL THE NEED TO--

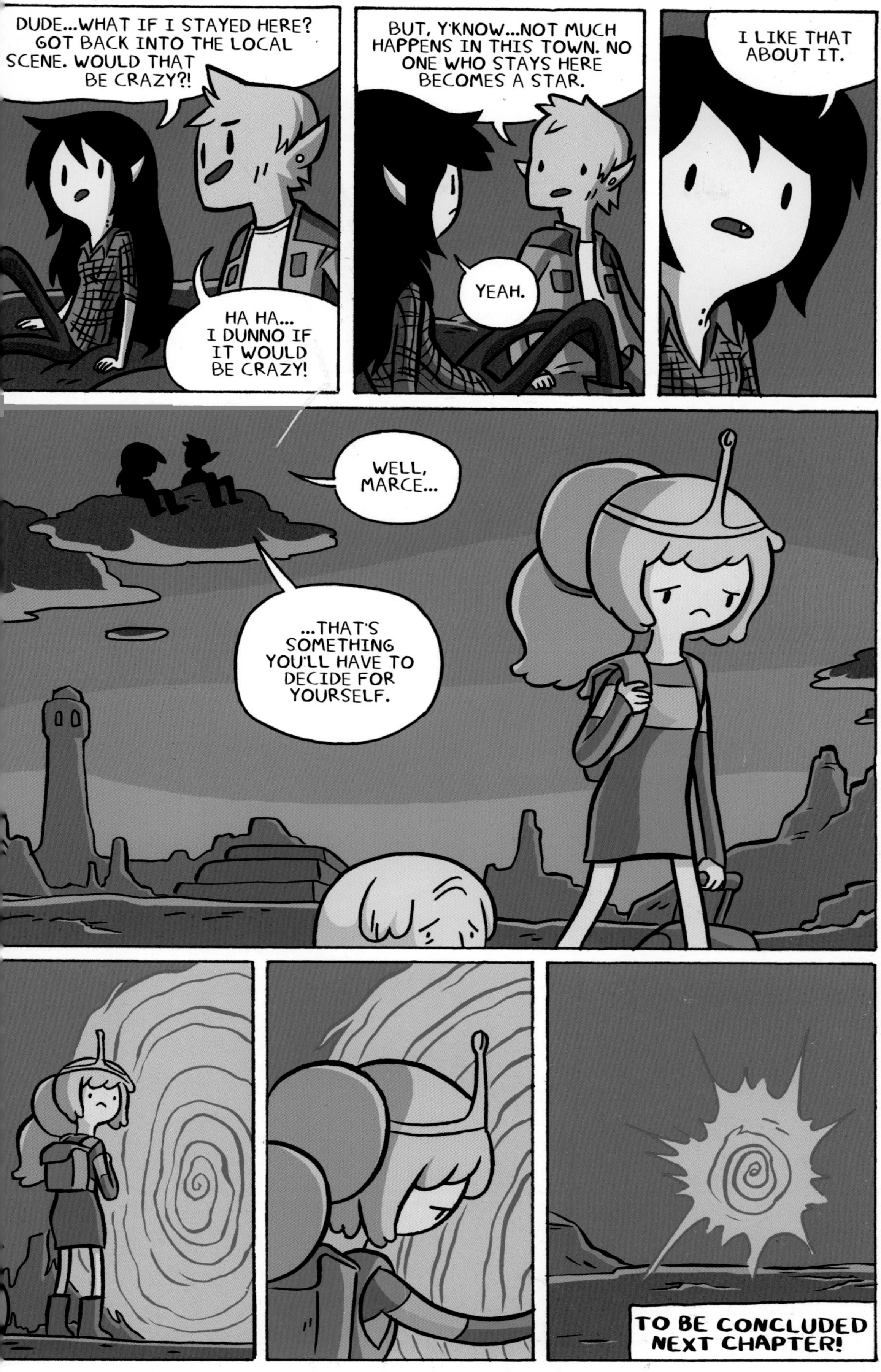
DUDE...WHAT IF I STAYED HERE? GOT BACK INTO THE LOCAL SCENE. WOULD THAT BE CRAZY?!
HA HA... I DUNNO IF IT WOULD BE CRAZY!
BUT, Y'KNOW...NOT MUCH HAPPENS IN THIS TOWN. NO ONE WHO STAYS HERE BECOMES A STAR.
YEAH.
I LIKE THAT ABOUT IT.
WELL, MARCE...
...THAT'S SOMETHING YOU'LL HAVE TO DECIDE FOR YOURSELF.
TO BE CONCLUDED NEXT CHAPTER!

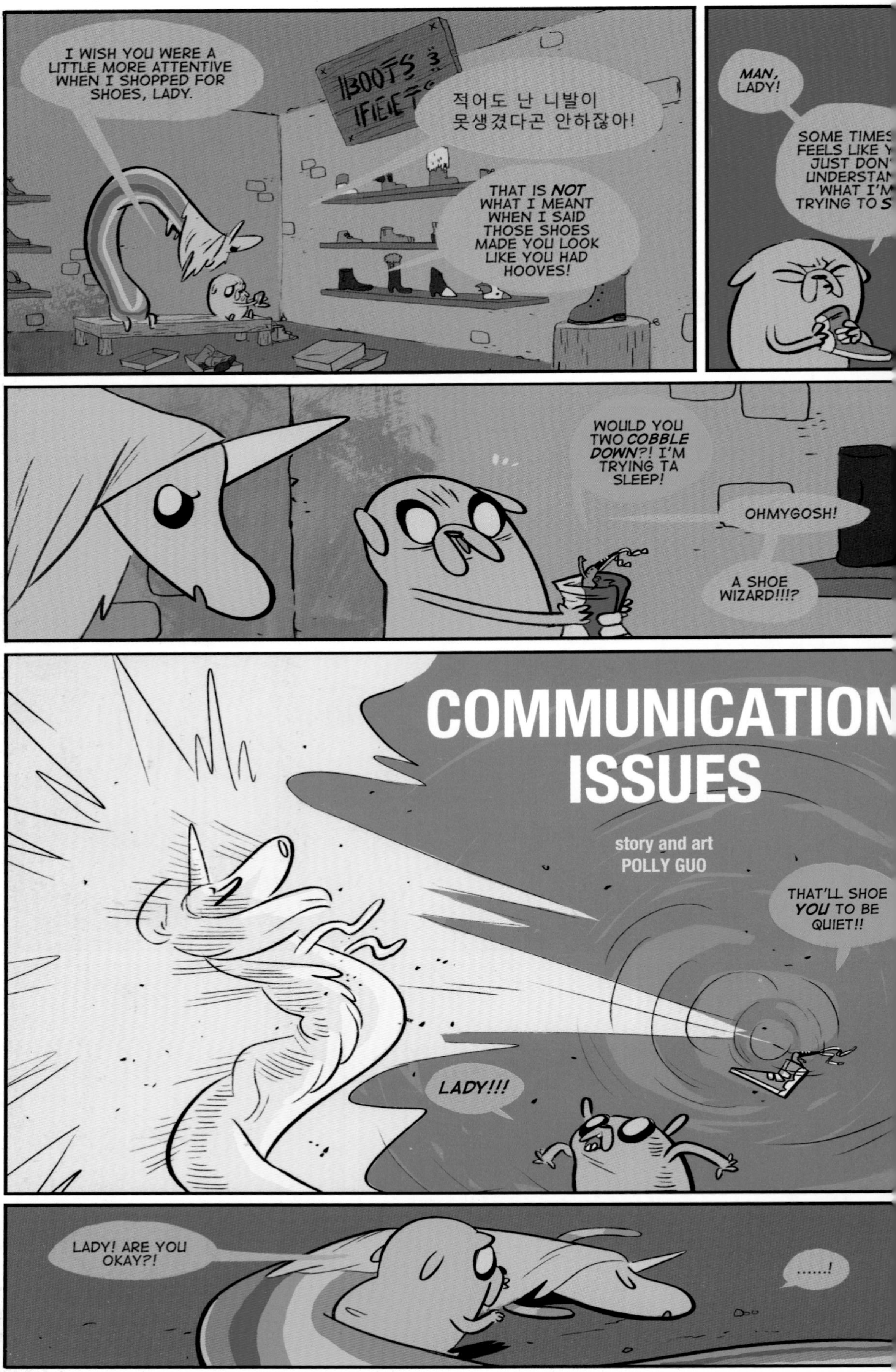
I WISH YOU WERE A LITTLE MORE ATTENTIVE WHEN I SHOPPED FOR SHOES, LADY.
적어도 난 니발이 못생겼다곤 안하잖아!
THAT IS *NOT* WHAT I MEANT WHEN I SAID THOSE SHOES MADE YOU LOOK LIKE YOU HAD HOOVES!
MAN, LADY!
SOME TIMES FEELS LIKE Y JUST DON' UNDERSTAN WHAT I'M TRYING TO *S*
WOULD YOU TWO *COBBLE DOWN*?! I'M TRYING TA SLEEP!
OHMYGOSH!
A SHOE WIZARD!!!?
COMMUNICATION ISSUES
story and art
POLLY GUO
THAT'LL SHOE *YOU* TO BE QUIET!!
LADY!!!
LADY! ARE YOU OKAY?!
......!

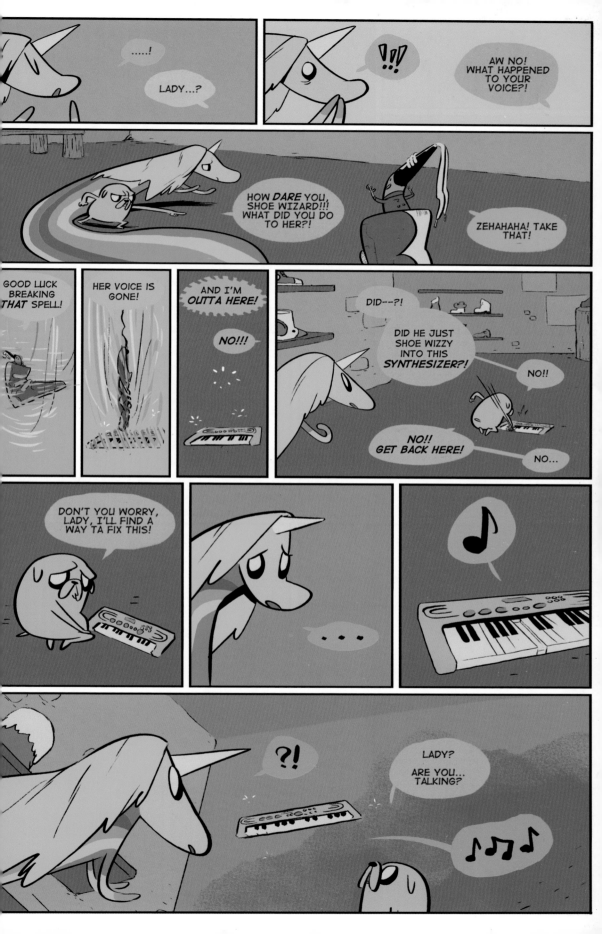

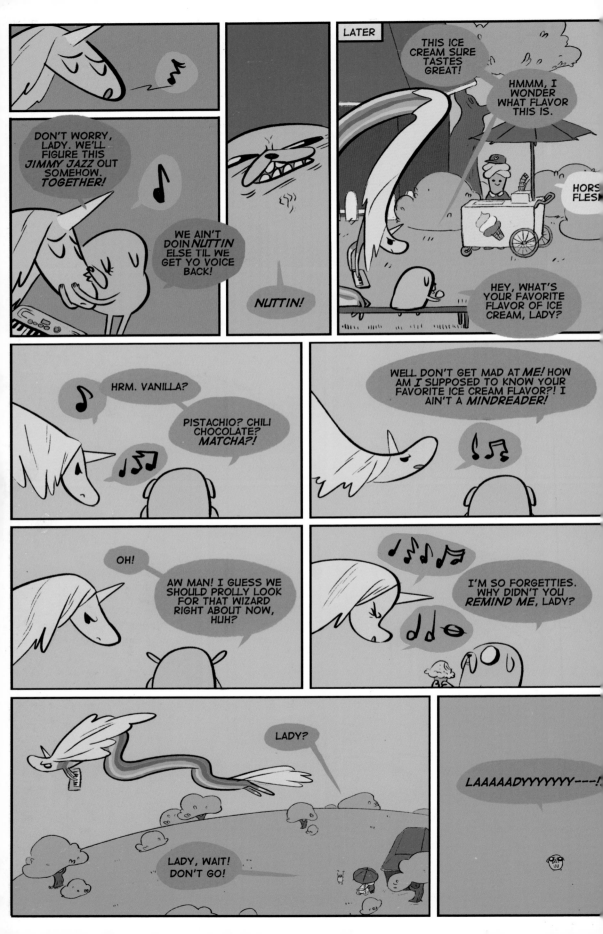

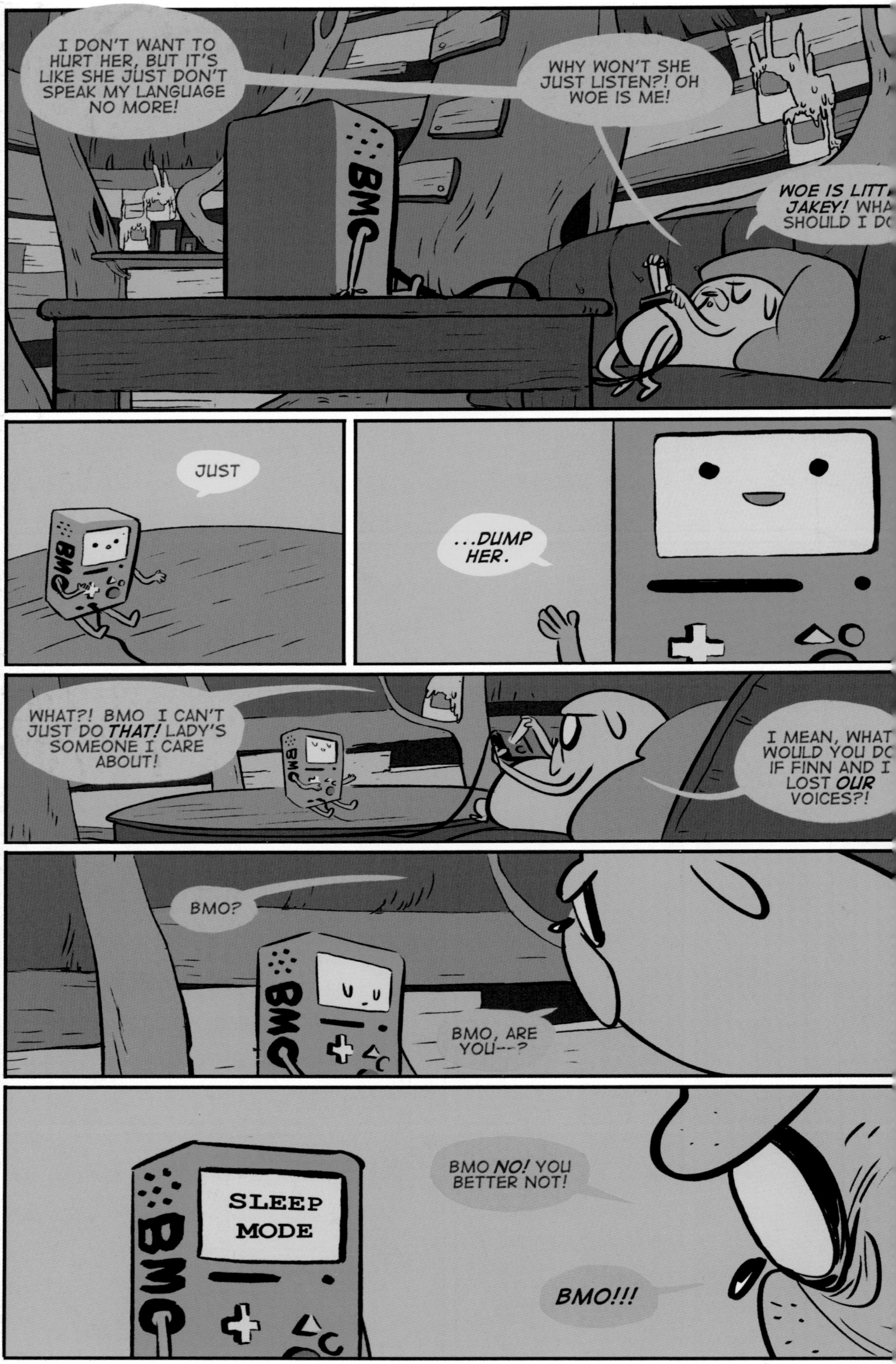
I DON'T WANT TO HURT HER, BUT IT'S LIKE SHE JUST DON'T SPEAK MY LANGUAGE NO MORE!
WHY WON'T SHE JUST LISTEN?! OH WOE IS ME!
WOE IS LITT JAKEY! WHA SHOULD I DO
BMO
JUST
...DUMP HER.
WHAT?! BMO I CAN'T JUST DO THAT! LADY'S SOMEONE I CARE ABOUT!
I MEAN, WHAT WOULD YOU DO IF FINN AND I LOST OUR VOICES?!
BMO?
BMO, ARE YOU--?
SLEEP MODE
BMO NO! YOU BETTER NOT!
BMO!!!

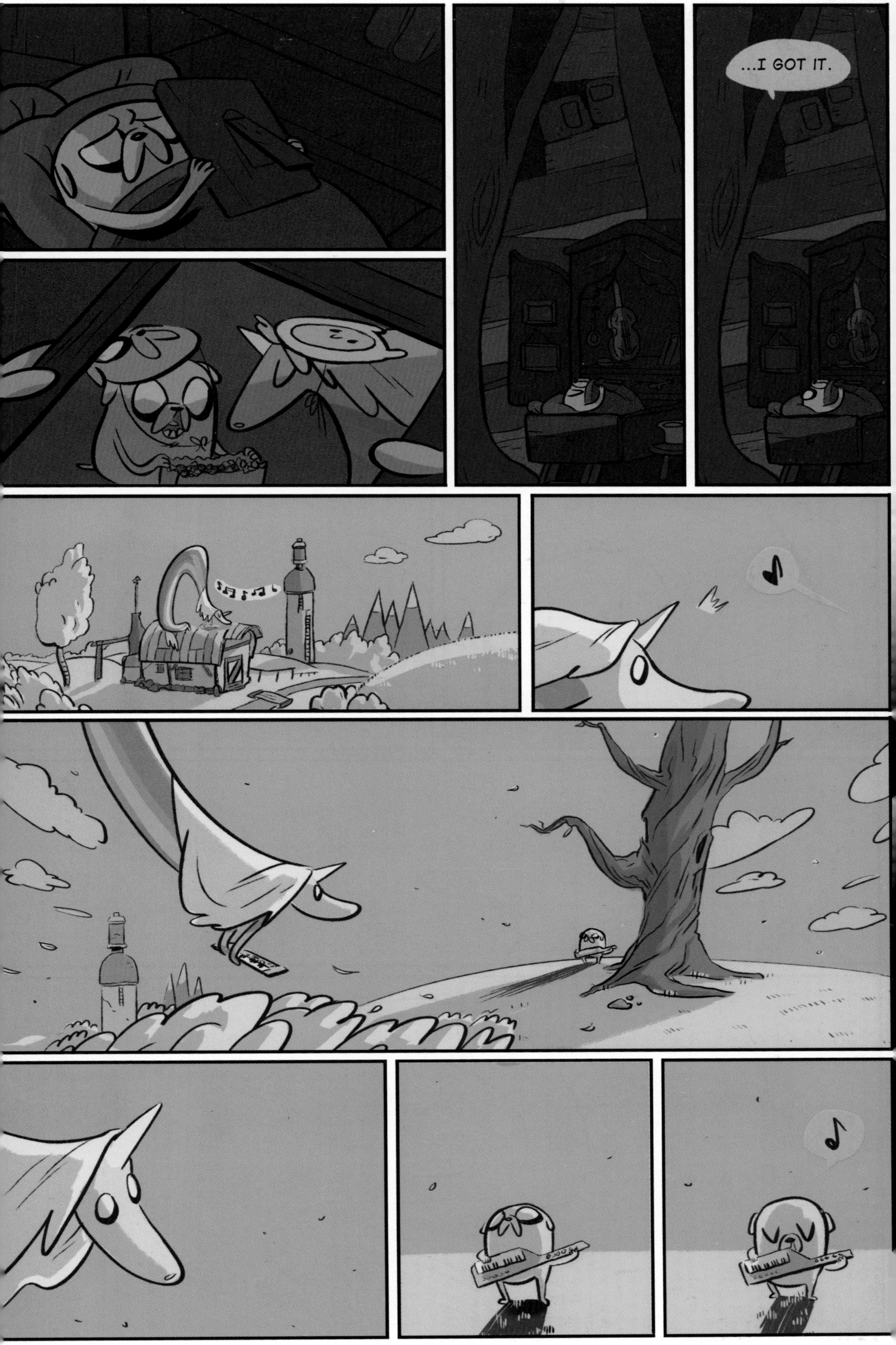
...I GOT IT.

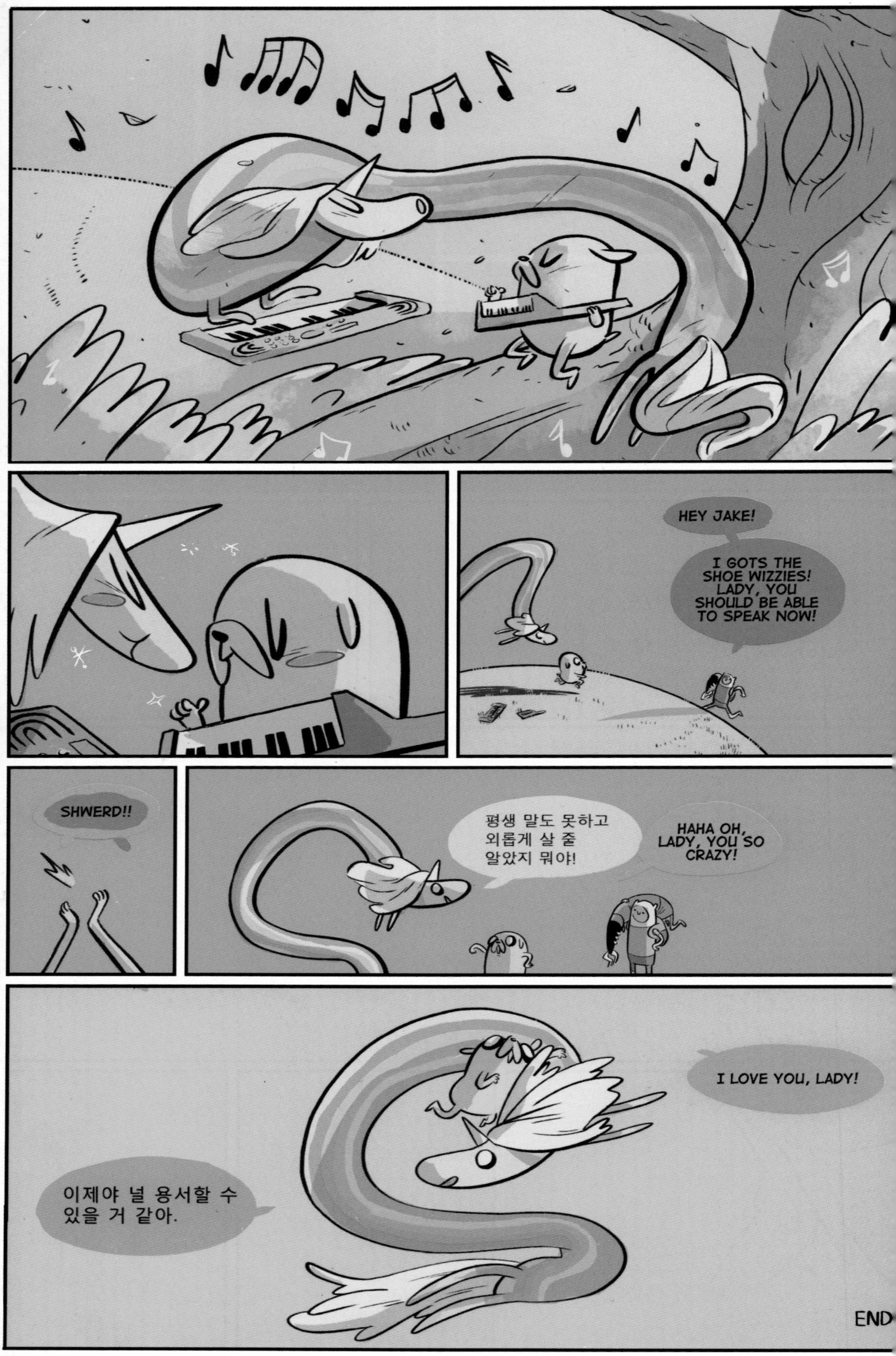
HEY JAKE!
I GOTS THE SHOE WIZZIES! LADY, YOU SHOULD BE ABLE TO SPEAK NOW!
SHWERD!!
평생 말도 못하고 외롭게 살 줄 알았지 뭐야!
HAHA OH, LADY, YOU SO CRAZY!
I LOVE YOU, LADY!
이제야 널 용서할 수 있을 거 같아.
END

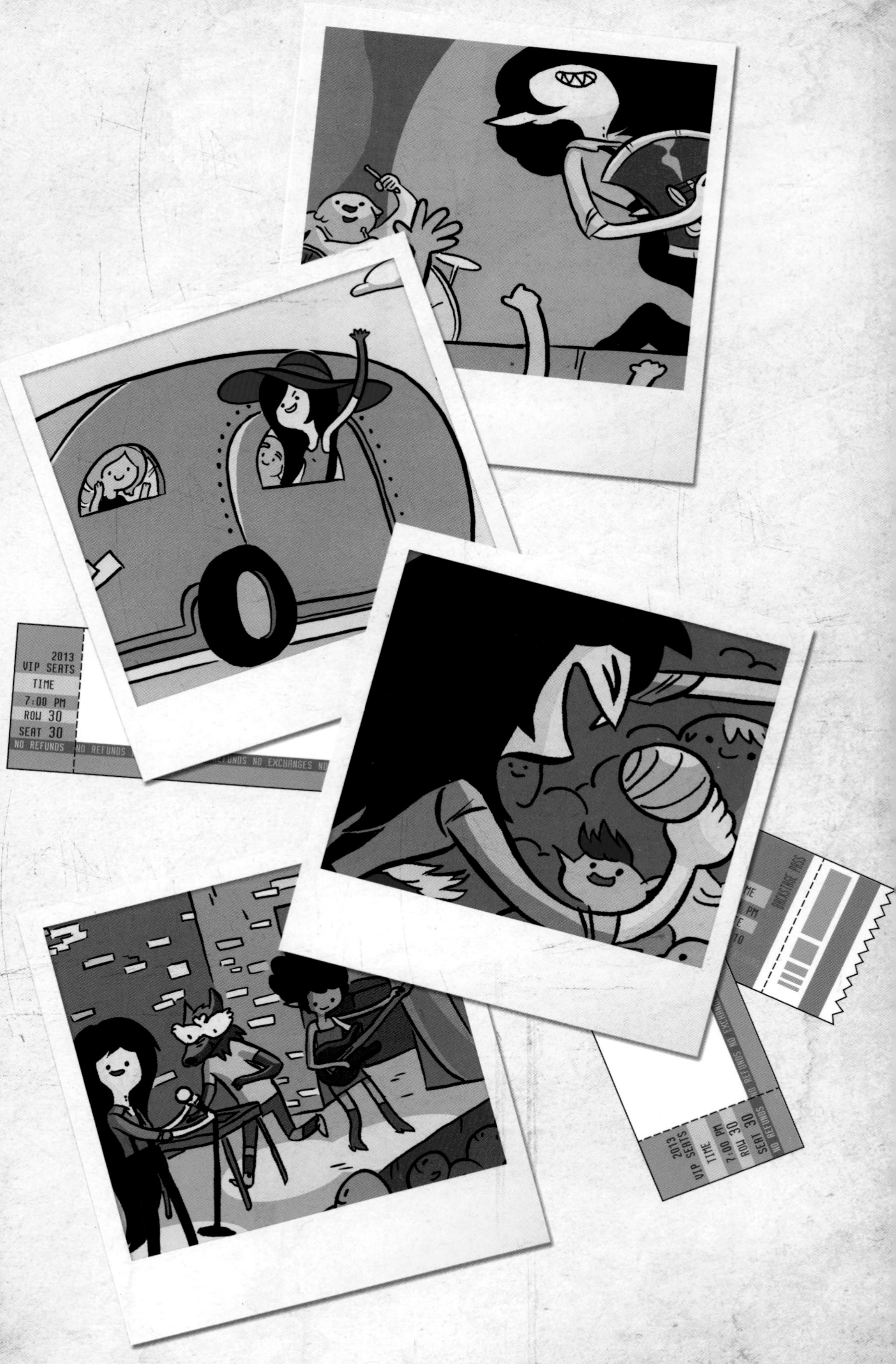
2013
VIP SEATS
TIME
7:00 PM
ROW 30
SEAT 30
NO REFUNDS
NO REFUNDS
REFUNDS NO EXCHANGES NO
BACKSTAGE PASS
2013
VIP SEATS
TIME
7:00 PM
ROW 30
SEAT 30
NO REFUNDS
NO REFUNDS NO EXCHANGES

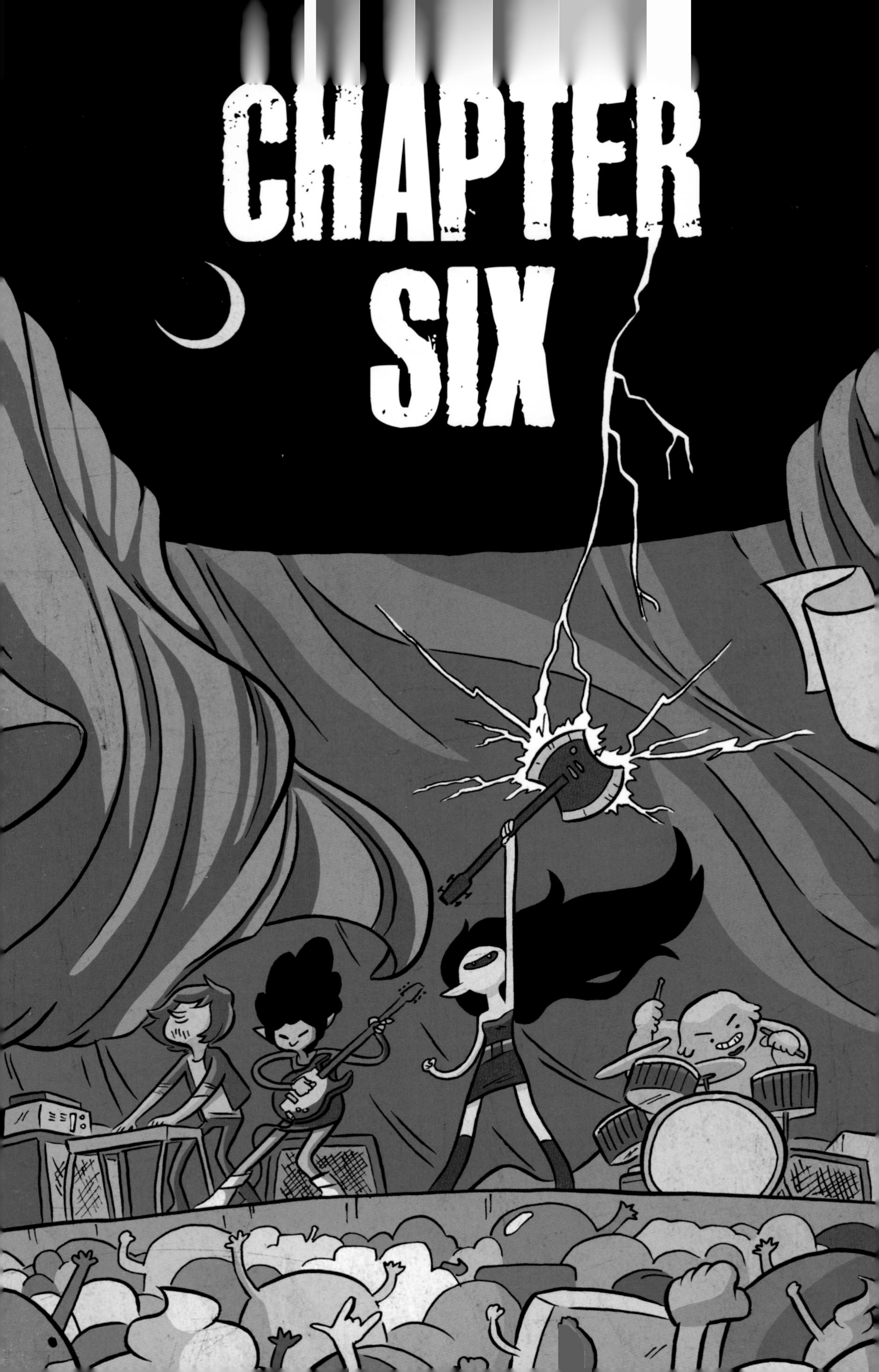
CHAPTER
SIX

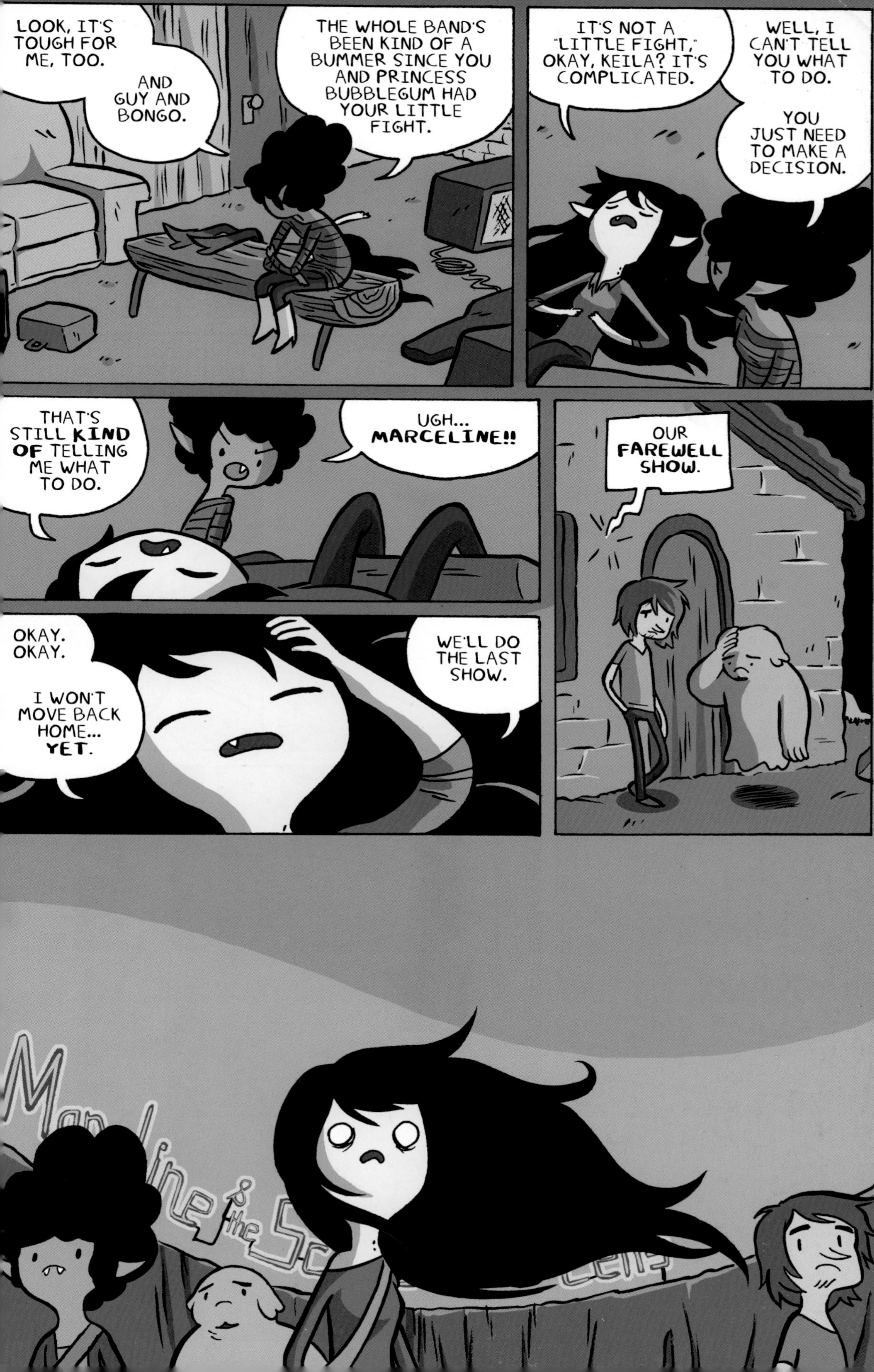

LOOK, IT'S TOUGH FOR ME, TOO.
AND GUY AND BONGO.
THE WHOLE BAND'S BEEN KIND OF A BUMMER SINCE YOU AND PRINCESS BUBBLEGUM HAD YOUR LITTLE FIGHT.
IT'S NOT A "LITTLE FIGHT," OKAY, KEILA? IT'S COMPLICATED.
WELL, I CAN'T TELL YOU WHAT TO DO.
YOU JUST NEED TO MAKE A DECISION.
THAT'S STILL **KIND OF** TELLING ME WHAT TO DO.
UGH... **MARCELINE!!**
OKAY. OKAY.
I WON'T MOVE BACK HOME... **YET**.
WE'LL DO THE LAST SHOW.
OUR **FAREWELL SHOW**.

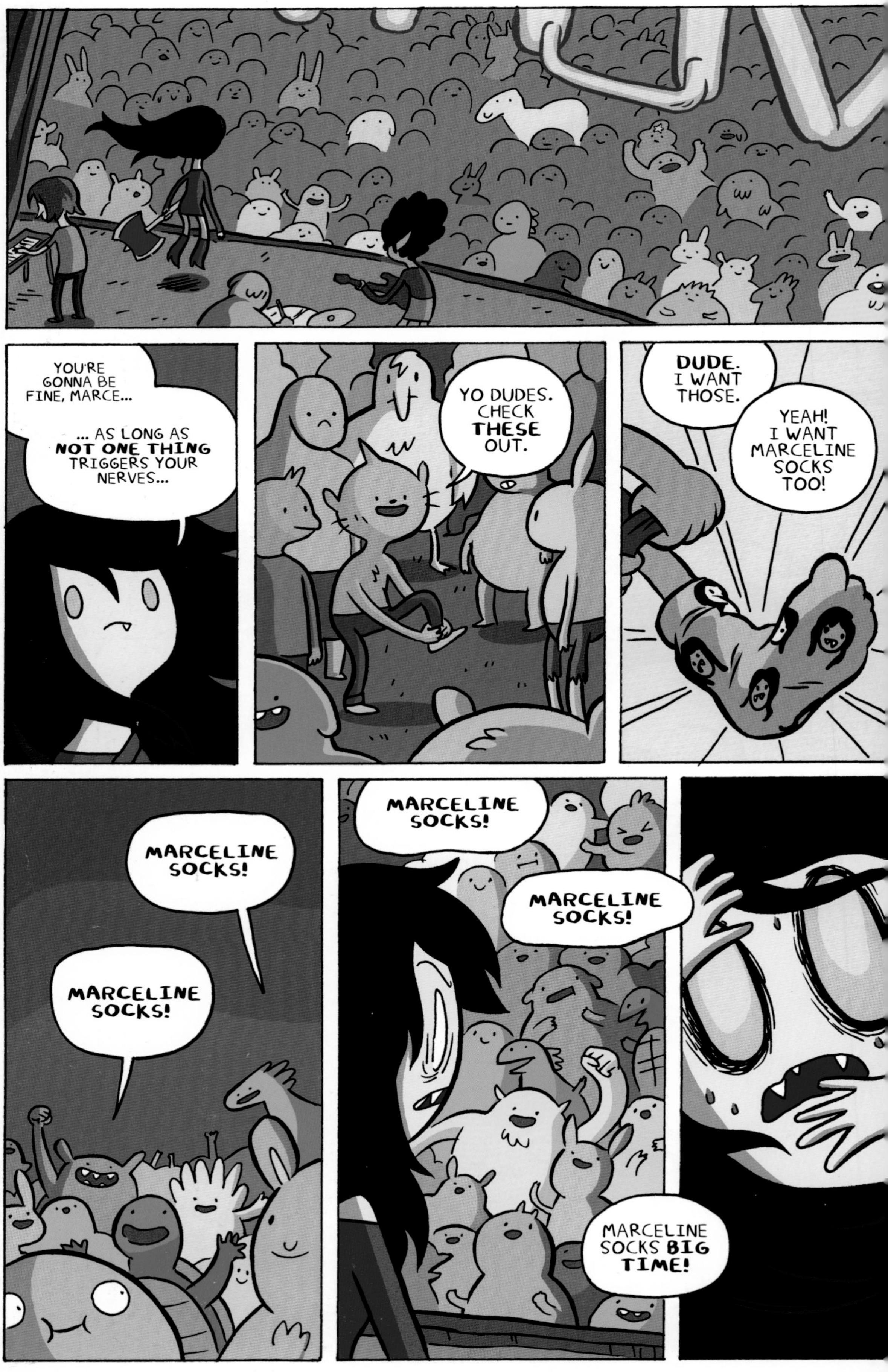
YOU'RE GONNA BE FINE, MARCE...
... AS LONG AS NOT ONE THING TRIGGERS YOUR NERVES...
YO DUDES. CHECK THESE OUT.
DUDE. I WANT THOSE.
YEAH! I WANT MARCELINE SOCKS TOO!
MARCELINE SOCKS!
MARCELINE SOCKS!
MARCELINE SOCKS!
MARCELINE SOCKS!
MARCELINE SOCKS BIG TIME!

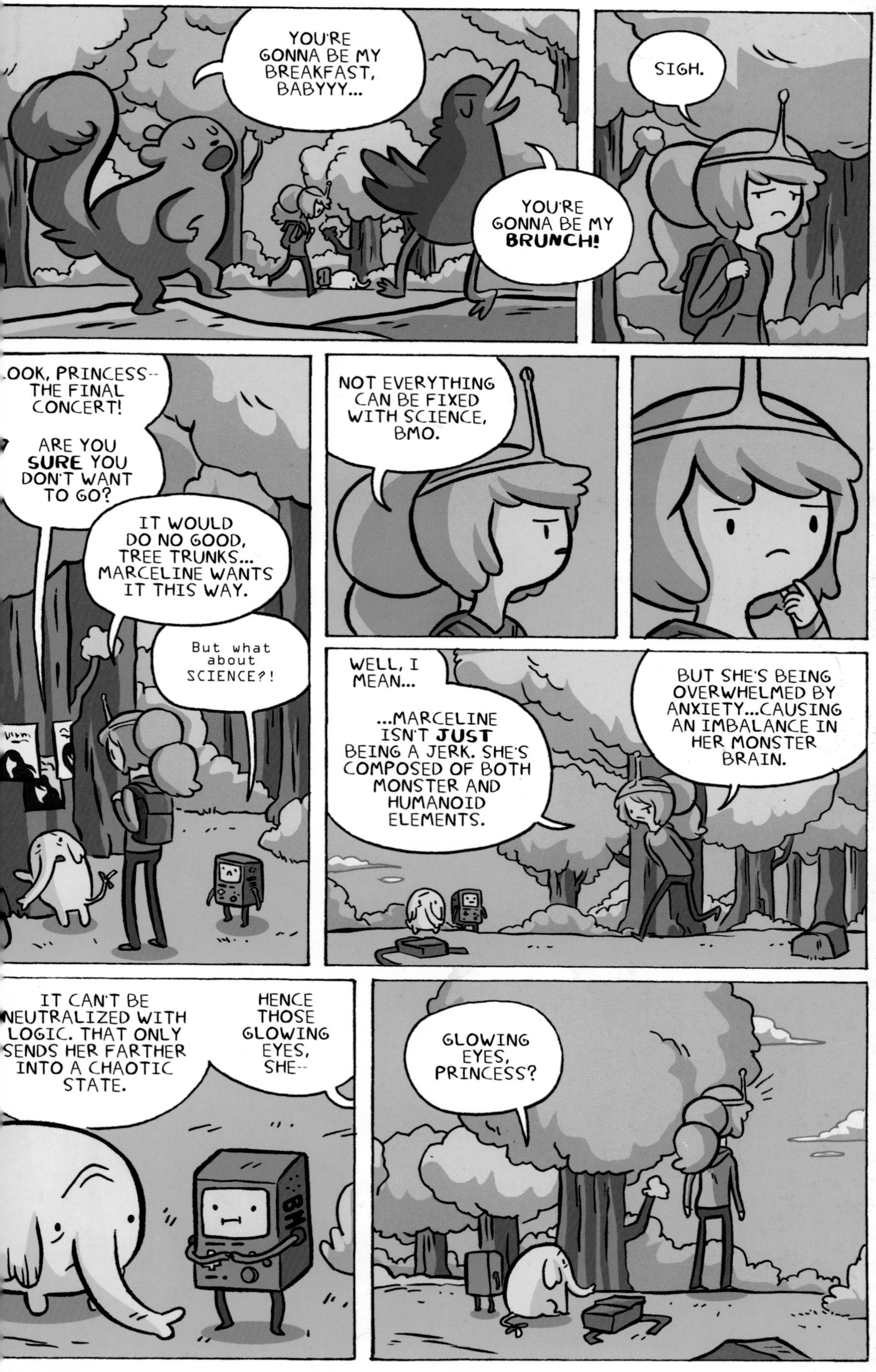
YOU'RE GONNA BE MY BREAKFAST, BABYYY...
YOU'RE GONNA BE MY **BRUNCH!**
SIGH.
LOOK, PRINCESS-- THE FINAL CONCERT!
ARE YOU **SURE** YOU DON'T WANT TO GO?
IT WOULD DO NO GOOD, TREE TRUNKS... MARCELINE WANTS IT THIS WAY.
But what about SCIENCE?!
NOT EVERYTHING CAN BE FIXED WITH SCIENCE, BMO.
WELL, I MEAN...
...MARCELINE ISN'T **JUST** BEING A JERK. SHE'S COMPOSED OF BOTH MONSTER AND HUMANOID ELEMENTS.
BUT SHE'S BEING OVERWHELMED BY ANXIETY...CAUSING AN IMBALANCE IN HER MONSTER BRAIN.
IT CAN'T BE NEUTRALIZED WITH LOGIC. THAT ONLY SENDS HER FARTHER INTO A CHAOTIC STATE.
HENCE THOSE GLOWING EYES, SHE--
GLOWING EYES, PRINCESS?

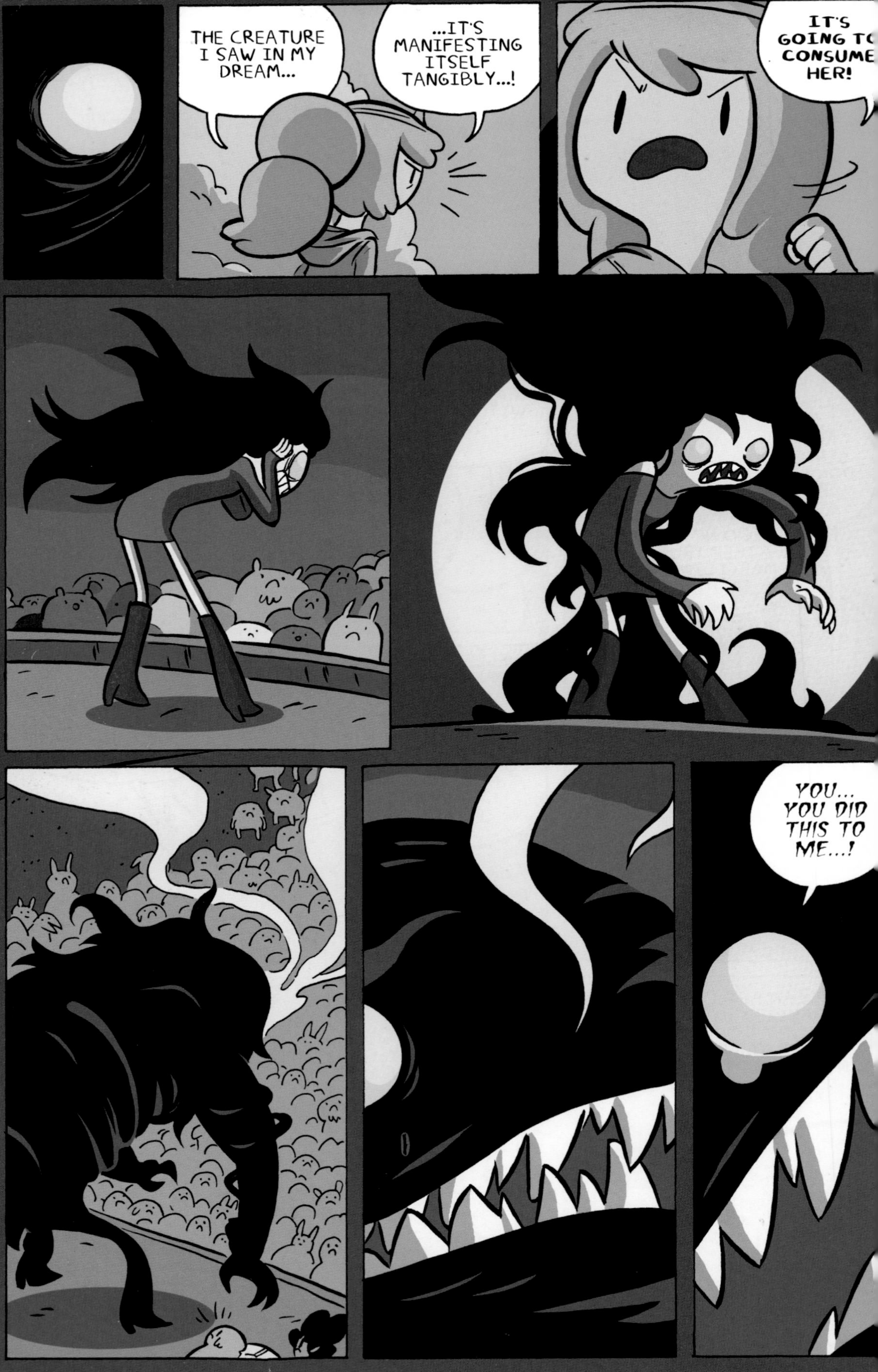
THE CREATURE I SAW IN MY DREAM...
...IT'S MANIFESTING ITSELF TANGIBLY...!
IT'S GOING TO CONSUME HER!
YOU... YOU DID THIS TO ME...!

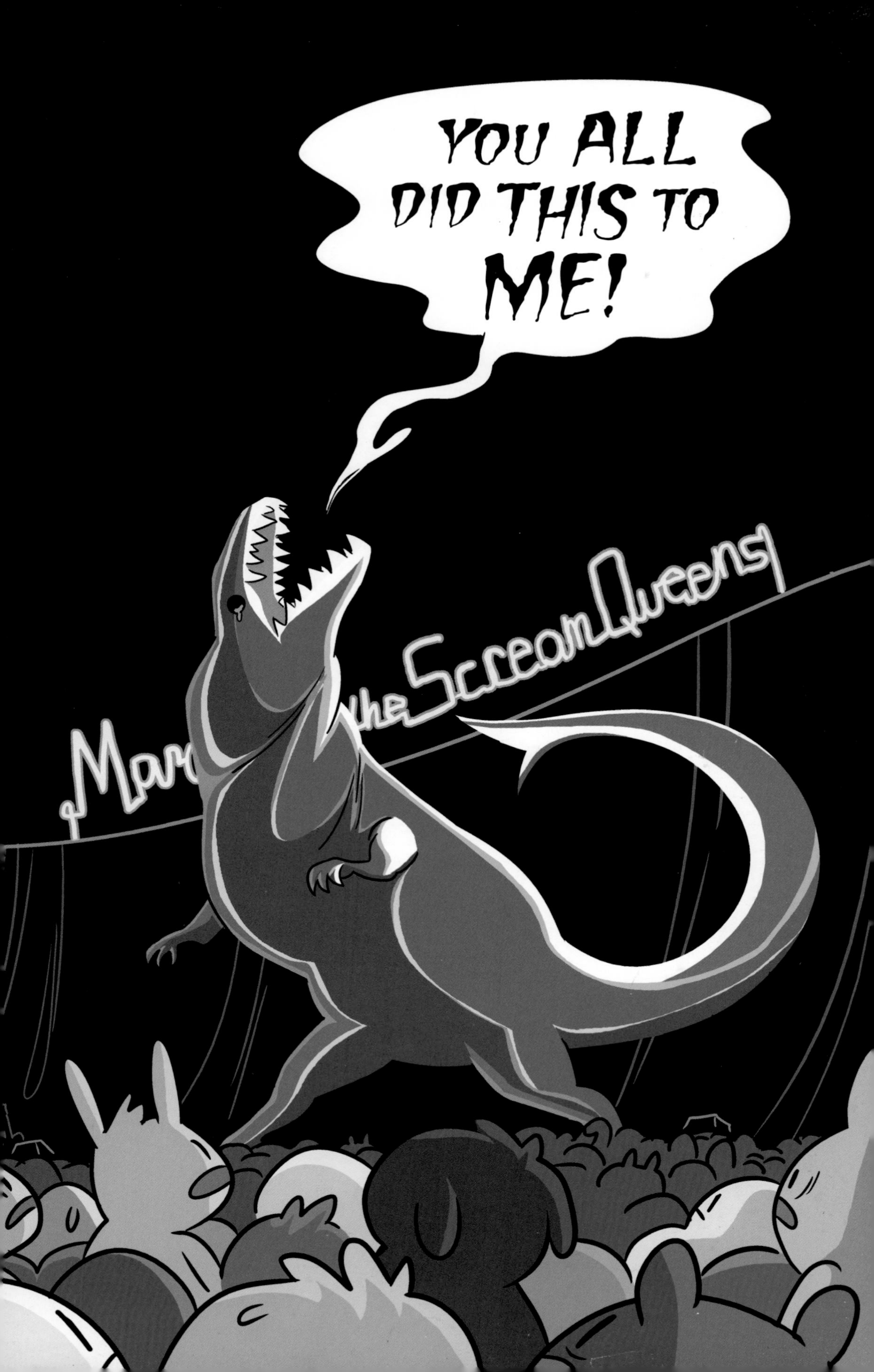
YOU ALL DID THIS TO ME!
the Scream Queens

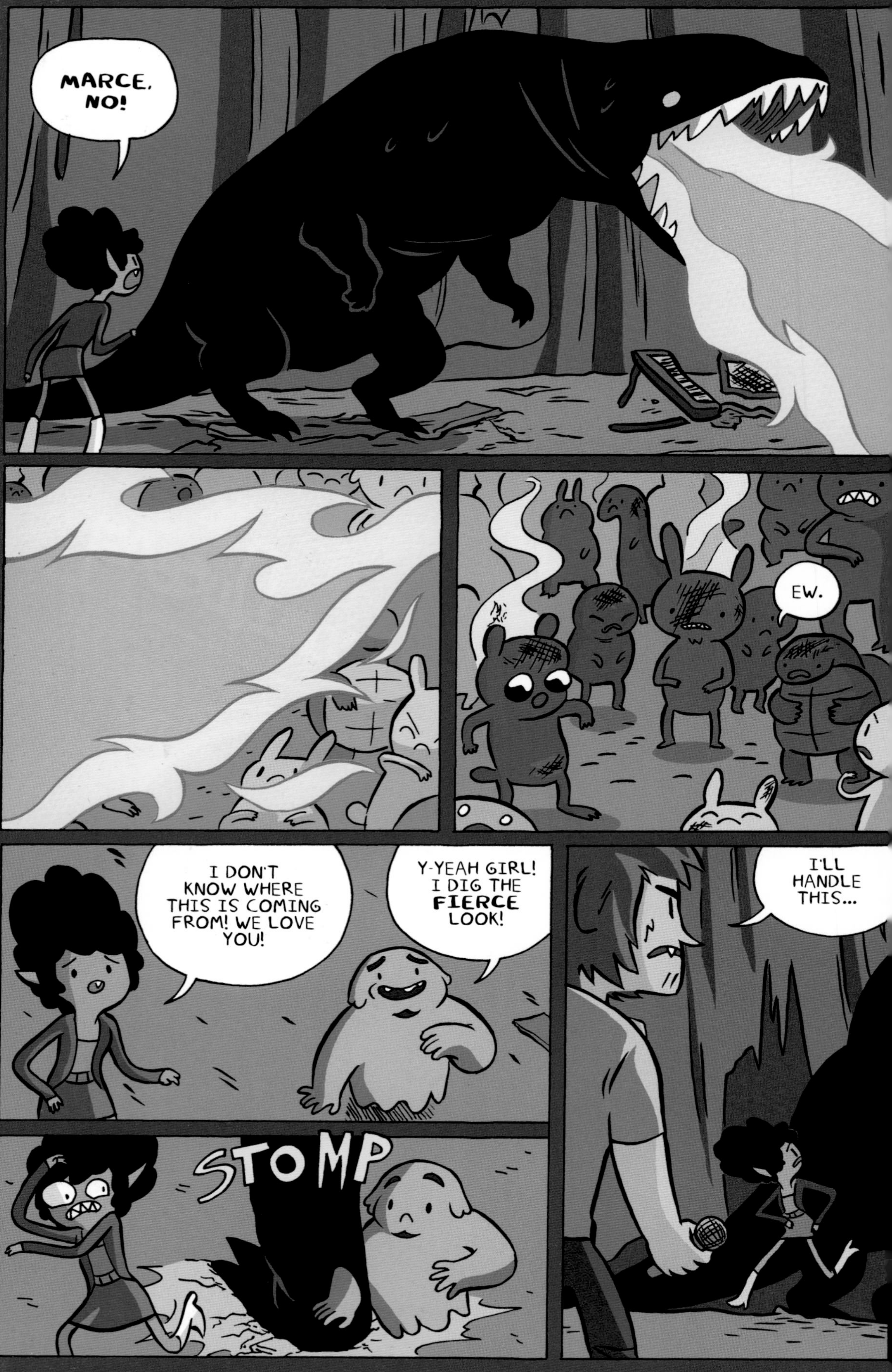
MARCE, NO!
EW.
I DON'T KNOW WHERE THIS IS COMING FROM! WE LOVE YOU!
Y-YEAH GIRL! I DIG THE **FIERCE** LOOK!
I'LL HANDLE THIS...
STOMP

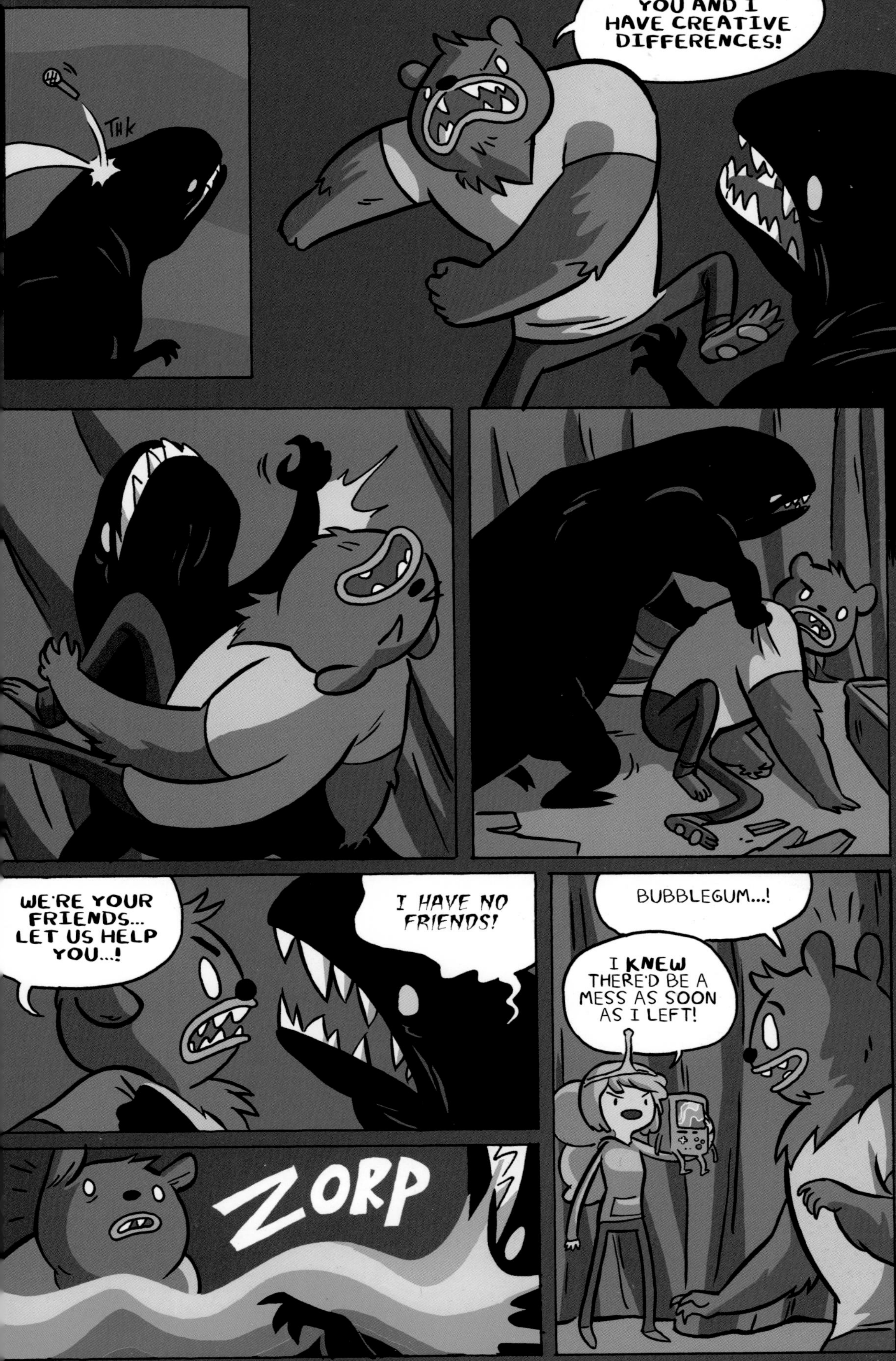
THK
YOU AND I HAVE CREATIVE DIFFERENCES!
WE'RE YOUR FRIENDS... LET US HELP YOU...!
I HAVE NO FRIENDS!
BUBBLEGUM...!
I KNEW THERE'D BE A MESS AS SOON AS I LEFT!
ZORP

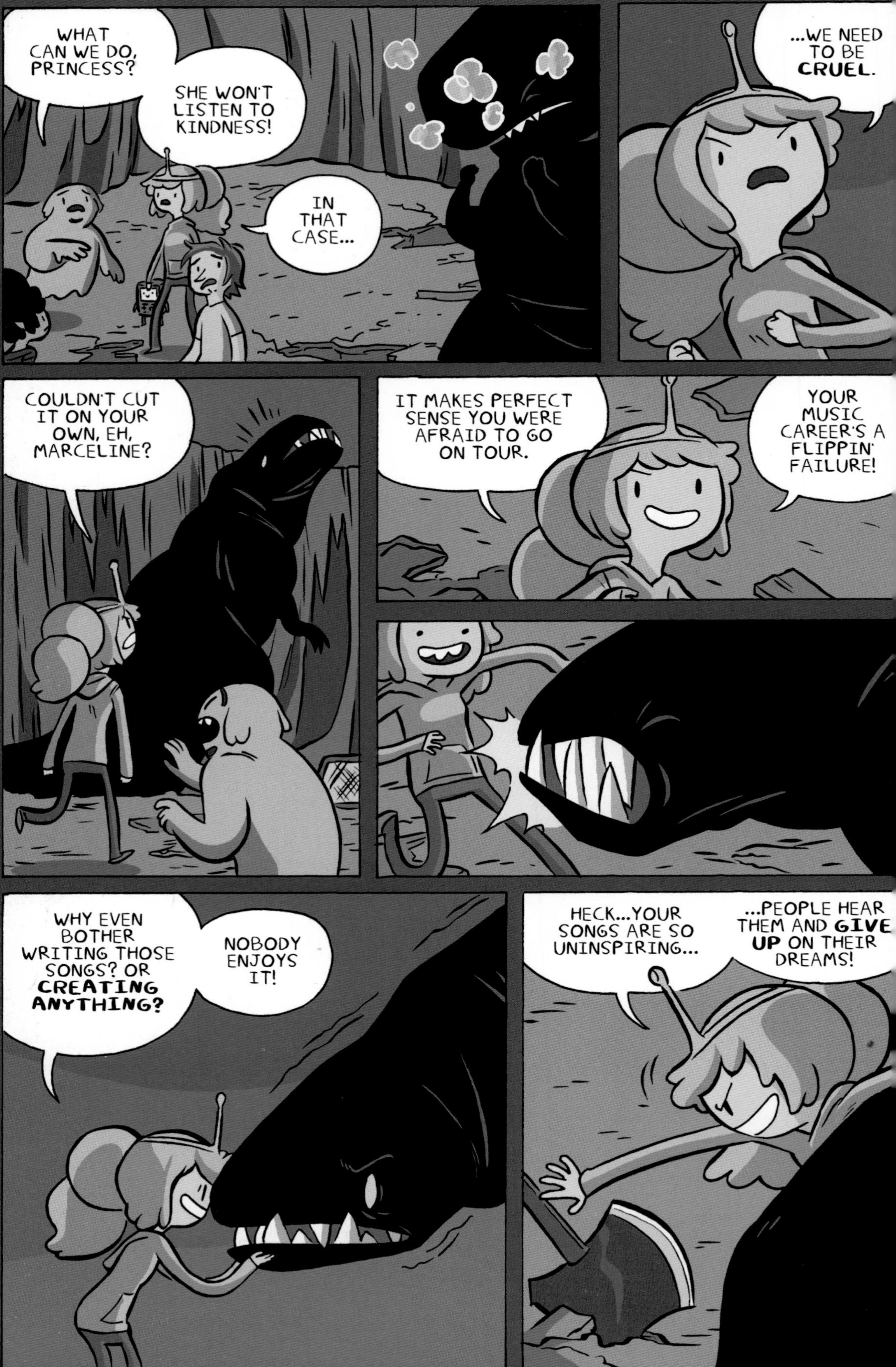
WHAT CAN WE DO, PRINCESS?
SHE WON'T LISTEN TO KINDNESS!
IN THAT CASE...
...WE NEED TO BE **CRUEL**.
COULDN'T CUT IT ON YOUR OWN, EH, MARCELINE?
IT MAKES PERFECT SENSE YOU WERE AFRAID TO GO ON TOUR.
YOUR MUSIC CAREER'S A FLIPPIN' FAILURE!
WHY EVEN BOTHER WRITING THOSE SONGS? OR **CREATING ANYTHING?**
NOBODY ENJOYS IT!
HECK...YOUR SONGS ARE SO UNINSPIRING...
...PEOPLE HEAR THEM AND **GIVE UP** ON THEIR DREAMS!

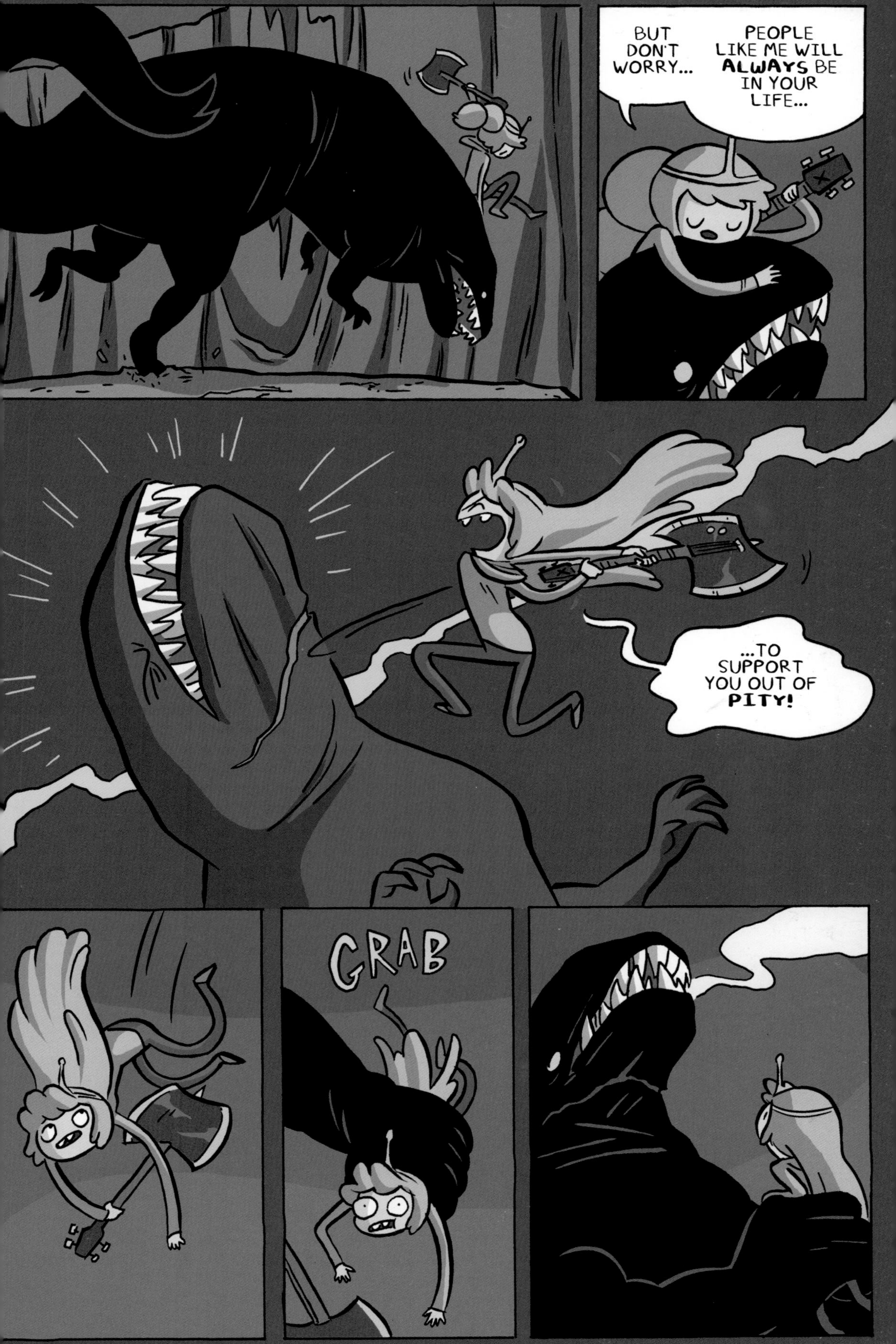
BUT DON'T WORRY...
PEOPLE LIKE ME WILL **ALWAYS** BE IN YOUR LIFE...
...TO SUPPORT YOU OUT OF **PITY!**
GRAB

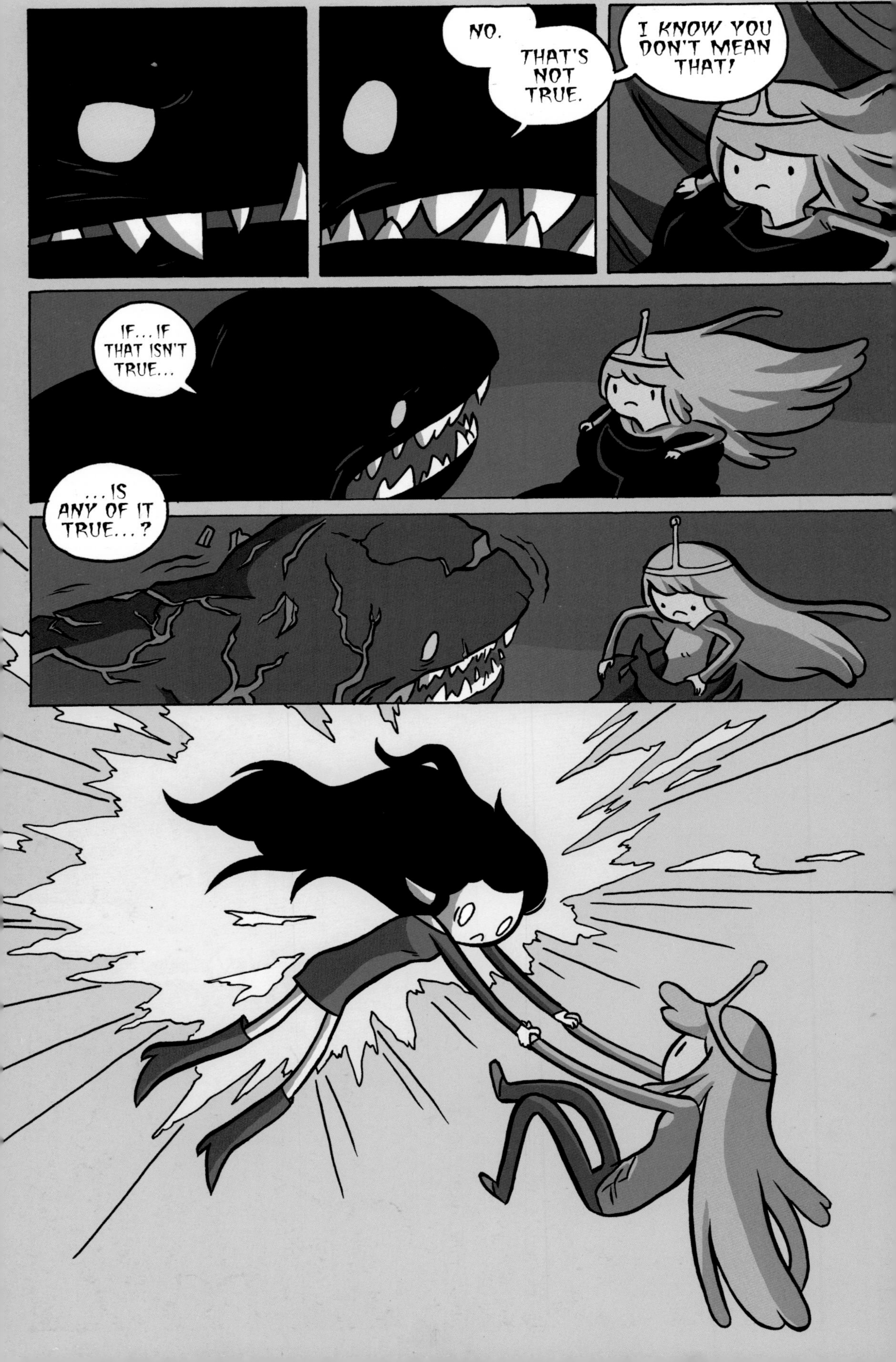
NO.
THAT'S NOT TRUE.
I KNOW YOU DON'T MEAN THAT!
IF... IF THAT ISN'T TRUE...
...IS ANY OF IT TRUE...?

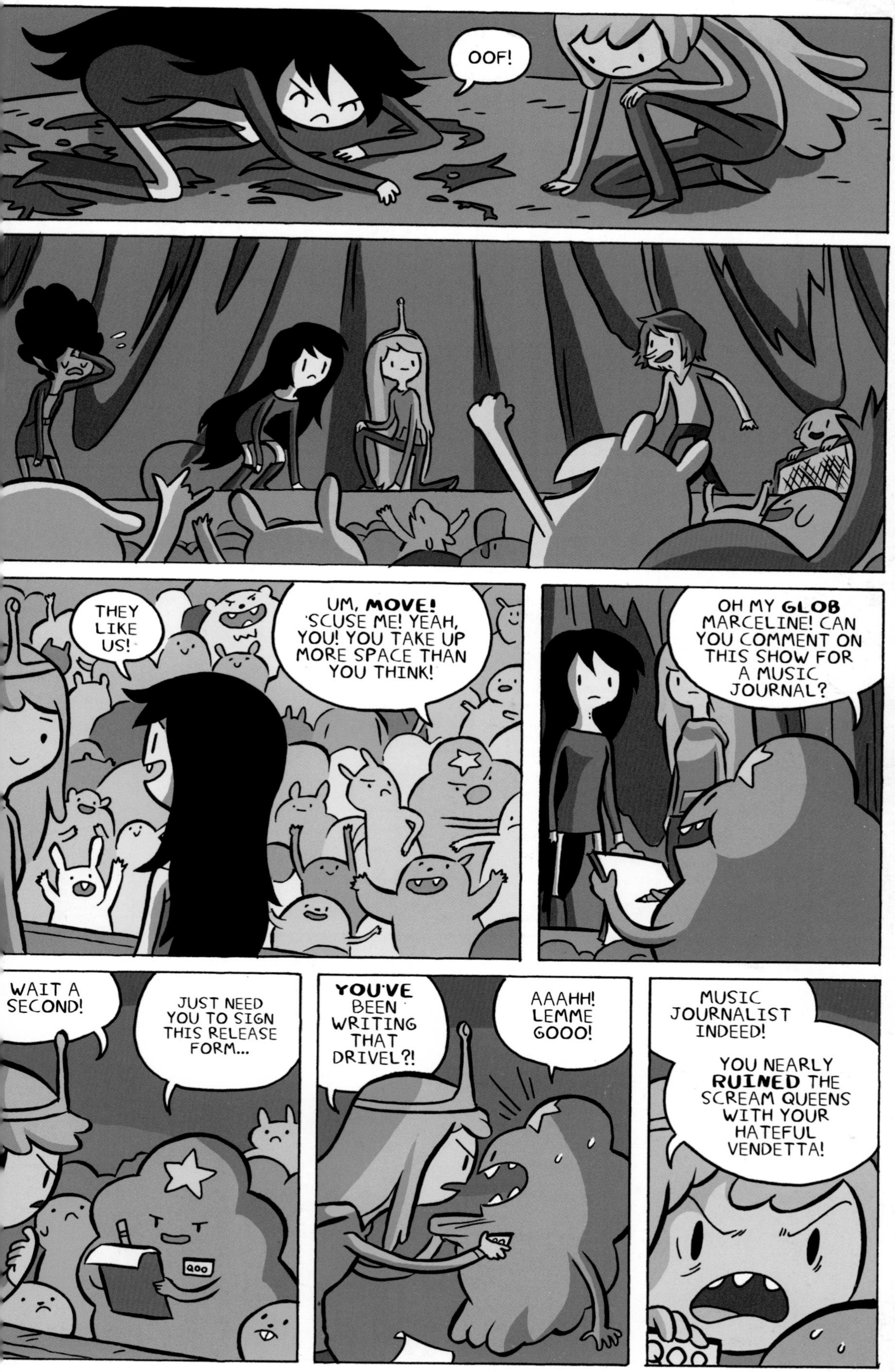
OOF!
THEY LIKE US!
UM, MOVE! 'SCUSE ME! YEAH, YOU! YOU TAKE UP MORE SPACE THAN YOU THINK!
OH MY GLOB MARCELINE! CAN YOU COMMENT ON THIS SHOW FOR A MUSIC JOURNAL?
WAIT A SECOND!
JUST NEED YOU TO SIGN THIS RELEASE FORM...
YOU'VE BEEN WRITING THAT DRIVEL?!
AAAHH! LEMME GOOO!
MUSIC JOURNALIST INDEED!
YOU NEARLY RUINED THE SCREAM QUEENS WITH YOUR HATEFUL VENDETTA!

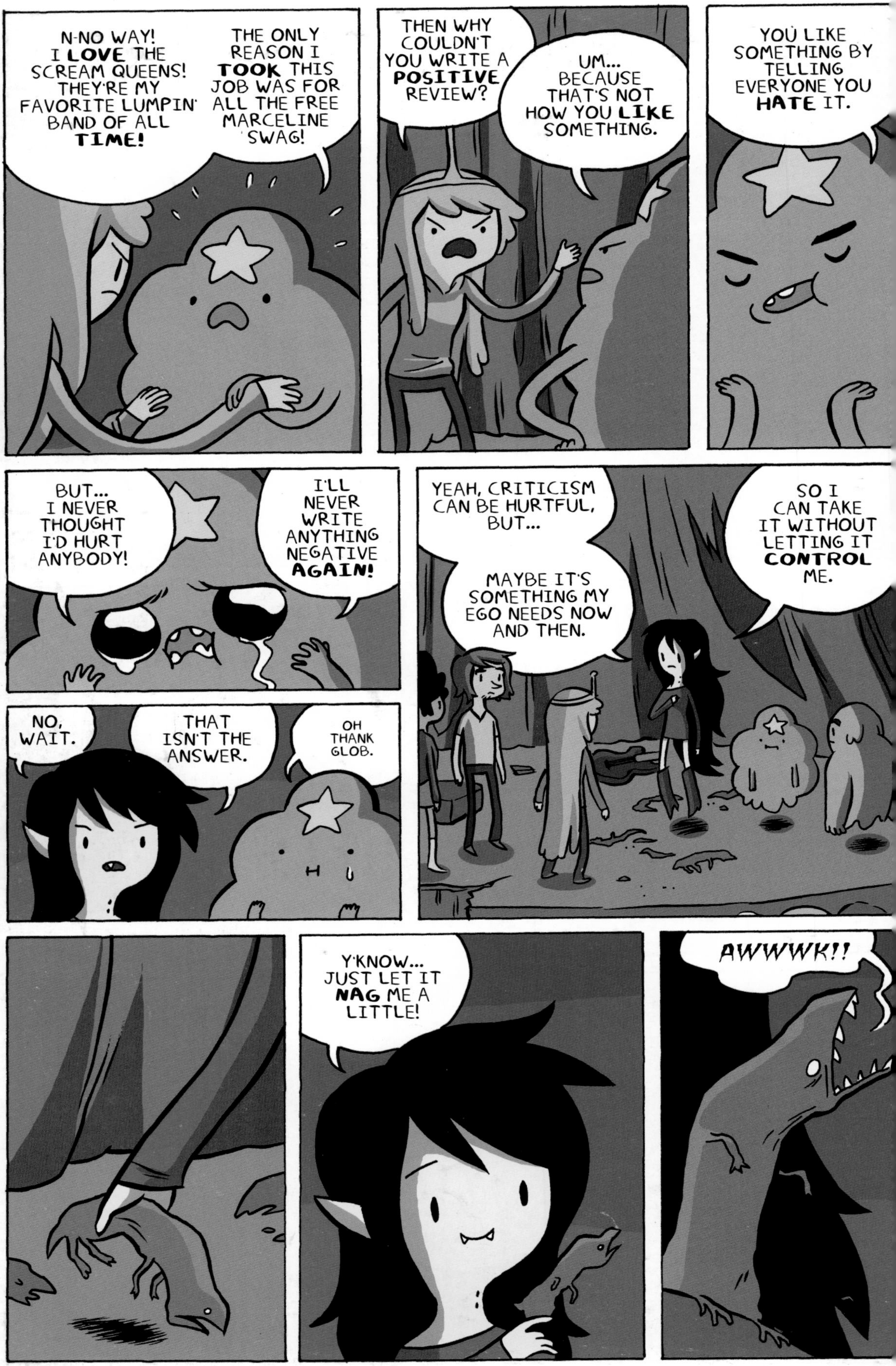
N-NO WAY! I LOVE THE SCREAM QUEENS! THEY'RE MY FAVORITE LUMPIN' BAND OF ALL TIME!
THE ONLY REASON I TOOK THIS JOB WAS FOR ALL THE FREE MARCELINE SWAG!
THEN WHY COULDN'T YOU WRITE A POSITIVE REVIEW?
UM... BECAUSE THAT'S NOT HOW YOU LIKE SOMETHING.
YOU LIKE SOMETHING BY TELLING EVERYONE YOU HATE IT.
BUT... I NEVER THOUGHT I'D HURT ANYBODY!
I'LL NEVER WRITE ANYTHING NEGATIVE AGAIN!
YEAH, CRITICISM CAN BE HURTFUL, BUT...
MAYBE IT'S SOMETHING MY EGO NEEDS NOW AND THEN.
SO I CAN TAKE IT WITHOUT LETTING IT CONTROL ME.
NO, WAIT.
THAT ISN'T THE ANSWER.
OH THANK GLOB.
Y'KNOW... JUST LET IT NAG ME A LITTLE!
AWWWK!!

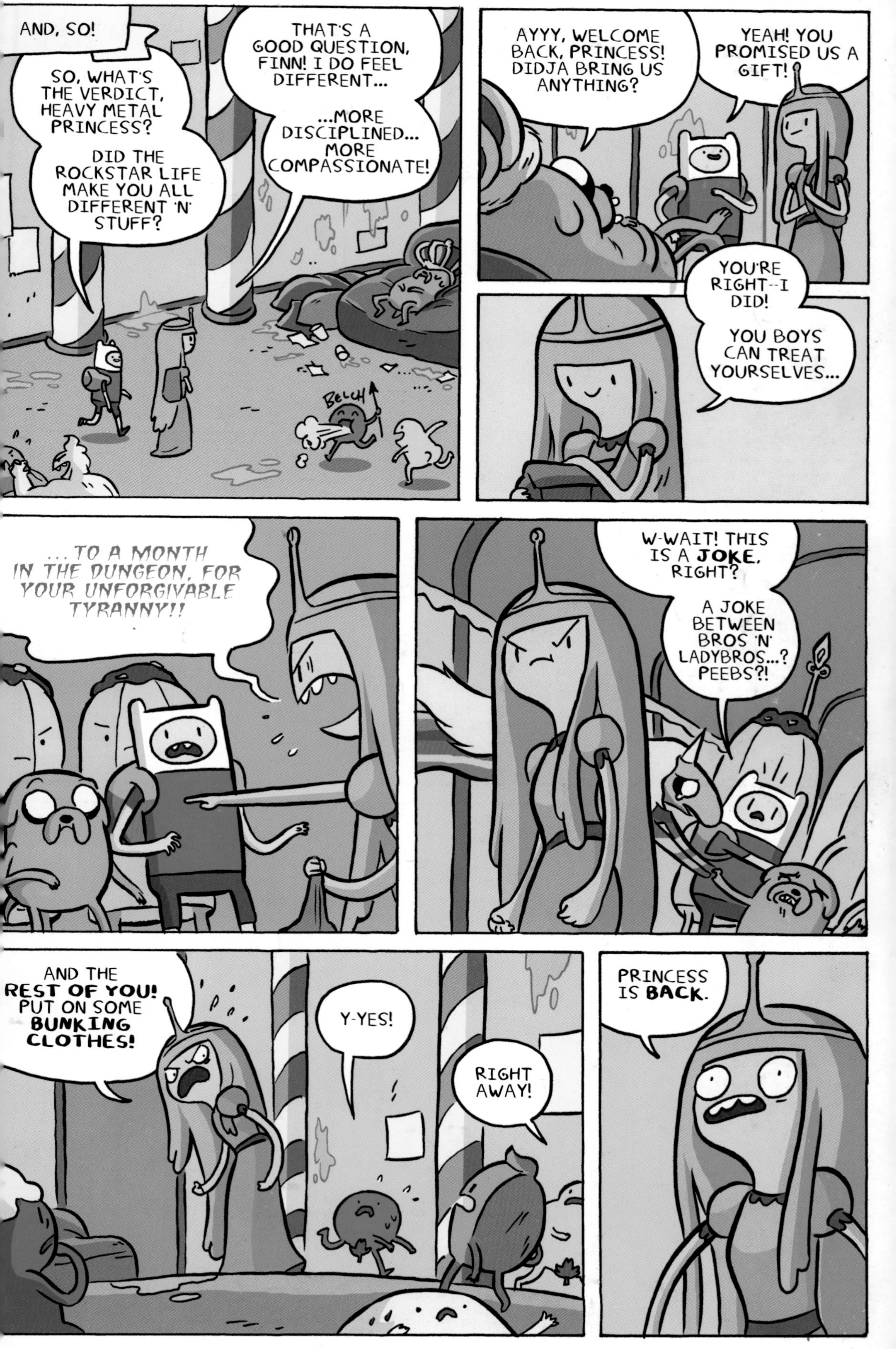

AND, SO!
SO, WHAT'S THE VERDICT, HEAVY METAL PRINCESS?
DID THE ROCKSTAR LIFE MAKE YOU ALL DIFFERENT 'N' STUFF?
THAT'S A GOOD QUESTION, FINN! I DO FEEL DIFFERENT...
...MORE DISCIPLINED... MORE COMPASSIONATE!
BELCH
AYYY, WELCOME BACK, PRINCESS! DIDJA BRING US ANYTHING?
YEAH! YOU PROMISED US A GIFT!
YOU'RE RIGHT--I DID!
YOU BOYS CAN TREAT YOURSELVES...
...TO A MONTH IN THE DUNGEON, FOR YOUR UNFORGIVABLE TYRANNY!!
W-WAIT! THIS IS A JOKE, RIGHT?
A JOKE BETWEEN BROS 'N' LADYBROS...? PEEBS?!
AND THE REST OF YOU! PUT ON SOME BUNKING CLOTHES!
Y-YES!
RIGHT AWAY!
PRINCESS IS BACK.

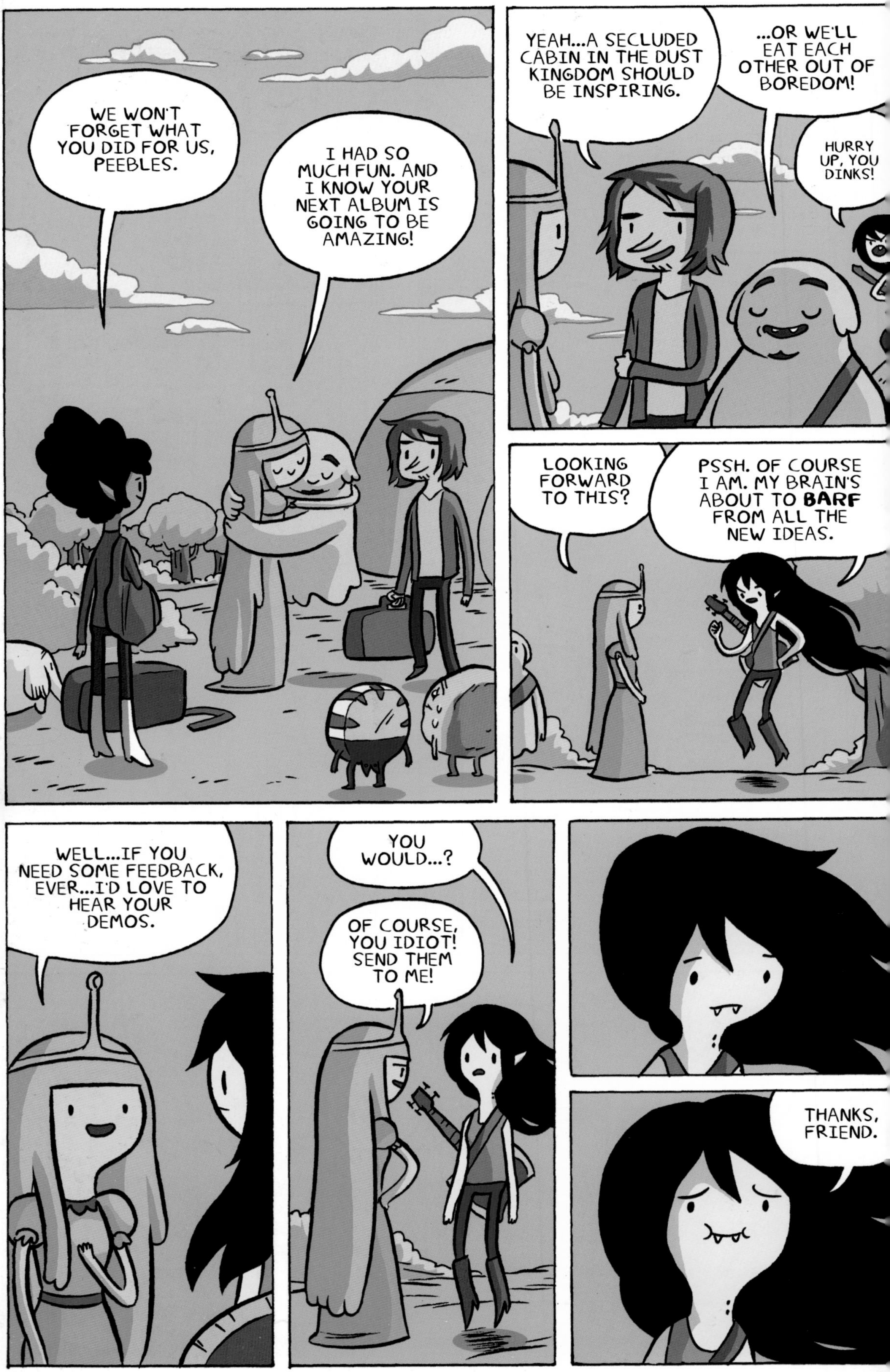
WE WON'T FORGET WHAT YOU DID FOR US, PEEBLES.
I HAD SO MUCH FUN. AND I KNOW YOUR NEXT ALBUM IS GOING TO BE AMAZING!
YEAH...A SECLUDED CABIN IN THE DUST KINGDOM SHOULD BE INSPIRING.
...OR WE'LL EAT EACH OTHER OUT OF BOREDOM!
HURRY UP, YOU DINKS!
LOOKING FORWARD TO THIS?
PSSH. OF COURSE I AM. MY BRAIN'S ABOUT TO **BARF** FROM ALL THE NEW IDEAS.
WELL...IF YOU NEED SOME FEEDBACK, EVER...I'D LOVE TO HEAR YOUR DEMOS.
YOU WOULD...?
OF COURSE, YOU IDIOT! SEND THEM TO ME!
THANKS, FRIEND.

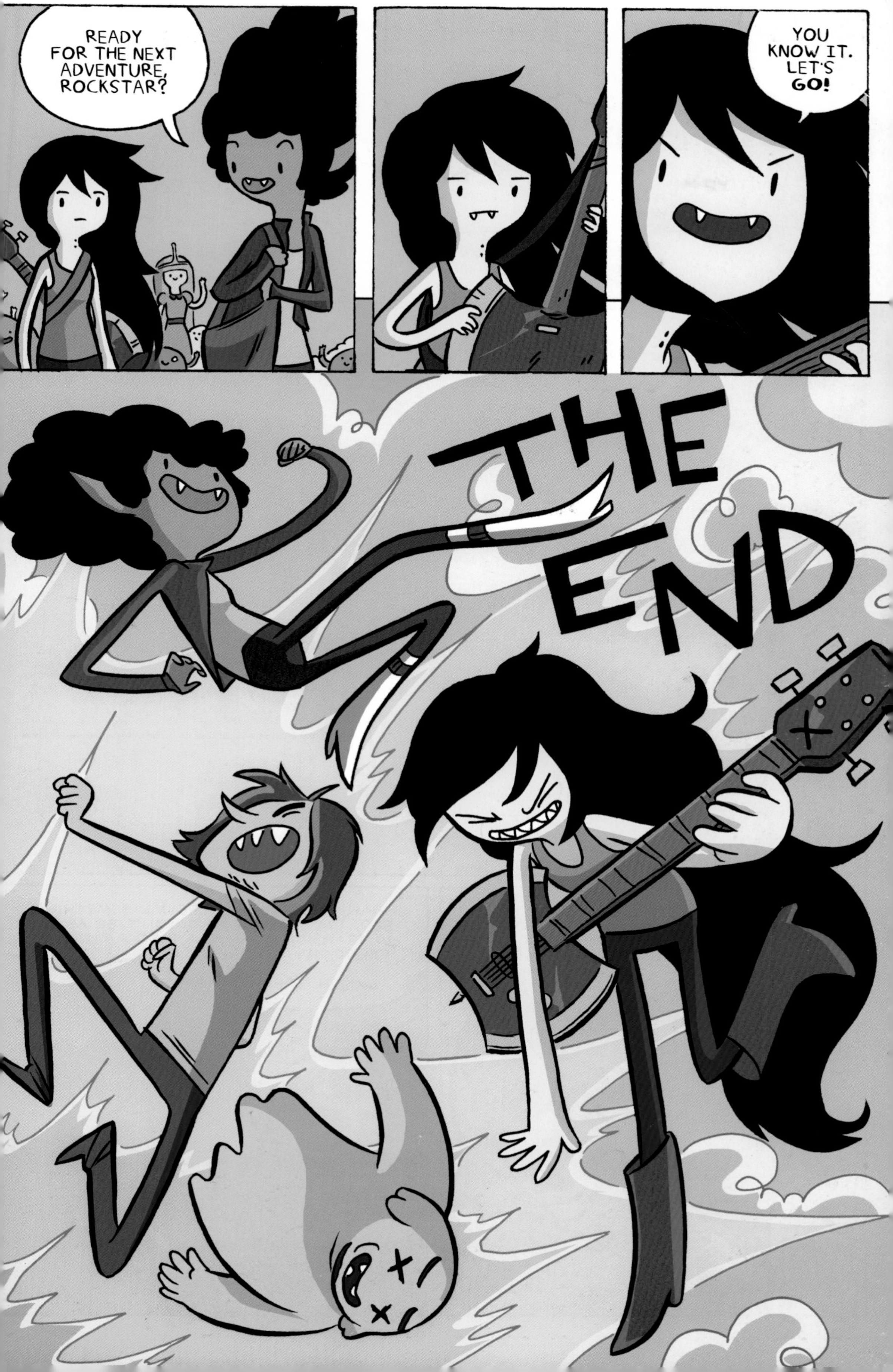
READY FOR THE NEXT ADVENTURE, ROCKSTAR?
YOU KNOW IT. LET'S **GO!**
THE END

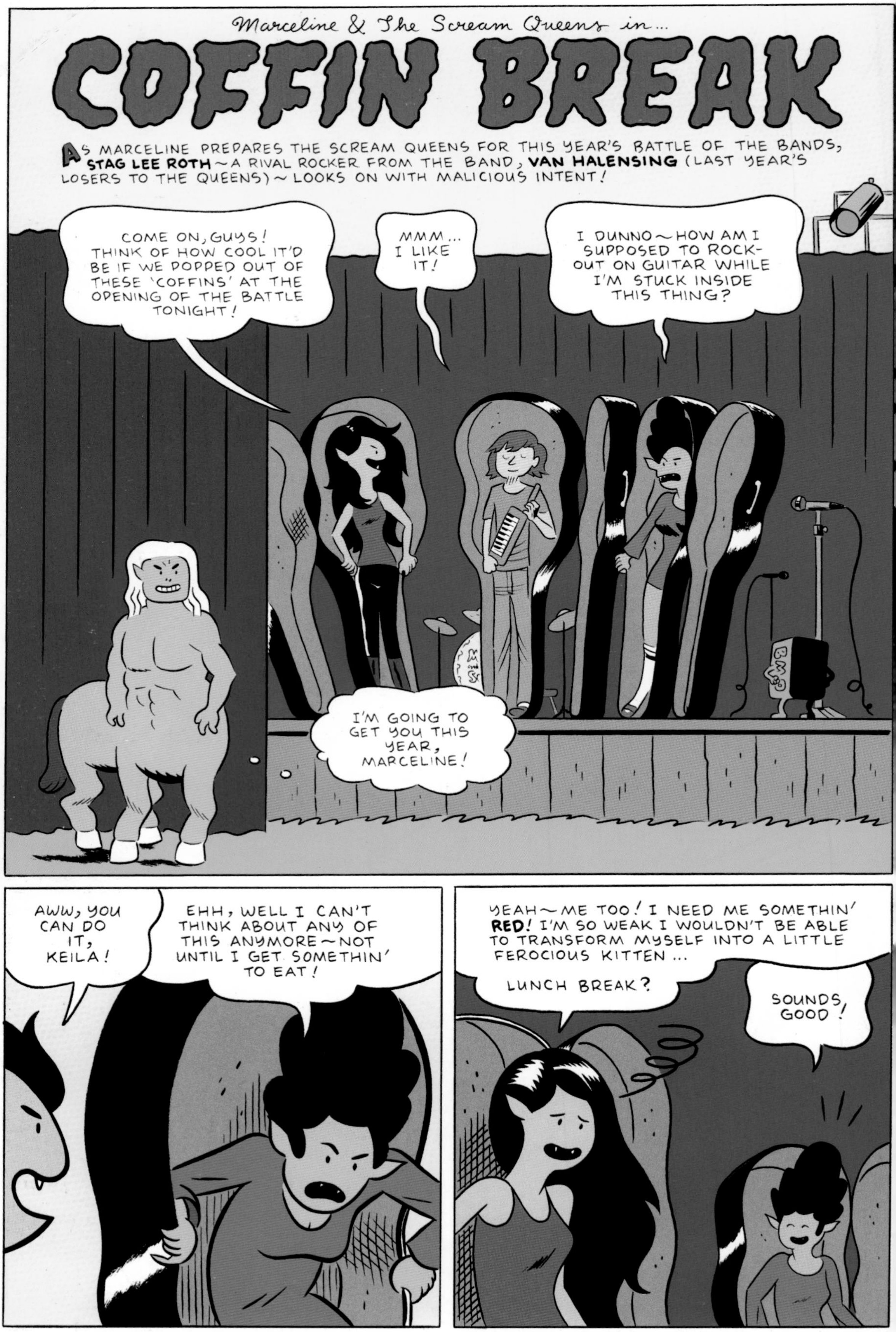
Marceline & The Scream Queens in...
COFFIN BREAK
AS MARCELINE PREPARES THE SCREAM QUEENS FOR THIS YEAR'S BATTLE OF THE BANDS, STAG LEE ROTH ~ A RIVAL ROCKER FROM THE BAND, VAN HALENSING (LAST YEAR'S LOSERS TO THE QUEENS) ~ LOOKS ON WITH MALICIOUS INTENT!
COME ON, GUYS! THINK OF HOW COOL IT'D BE IF WE POPPED OUT OF THESE 'COFFINS' AT THE OPENING OF THE BATTLE TONIGHT!
MMM... I LIKE IT!
I DUNNO ~ HOW AM I SUPPOSED TO ROCK-OUT ON GUITAR WHILE I'M STUCK INSIDE THIS THING?
I'M GOING TO GET YOU THIS YEAR, MARCELINE!
AWW, YOU CAN DO IT, KEILA!
EHH, WELL I CAN'T THINK ABOUT ANY OF THIS ANYMORE ~ NOT UNTIL I GET SOMETHIN' TO EAT!
YEAH ~ ME TOO! I NEED ME SOMETHIN' RED! I'M SO WEAK I WOULDN'T BE ABLE TO TRANSFORM MYSELF INTO A LITTLE FEROCIOUS KITTEN ...
LUNCH BREAK?
SOUNDS GOOD!

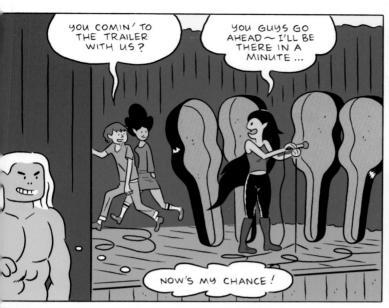

YOU COMIN' TO THE TRAILER WITH US?

YOU GUYS GO AHEAD ~ I'LL BE THERE IN A MINUTE...

NOW'S MY CHANCE!

5

WELL, WELL, WELL... IF IT ISN'T THE FAMOUS MARCELINE!

OH, HEY, STAG LEE! HOW'S IT GOIN'?

OH, IT'S GOING AWESOME! WE ARE GOING TO TEAR IT UP THIS YEAR!

WE GOT SOME GNARLY NEW SONGS TO ROCK OUT TONIGHT!

OH, YEAHHH?

WELL, WE'VE GOT SOME GREAT NEW STUFF TOO!

YEAH ~ STAGE LOOKS COOL... WHAT'S UP WITH ALL OF THE GIANT GUITAR CASES?

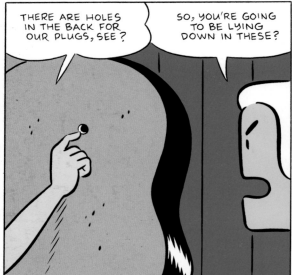

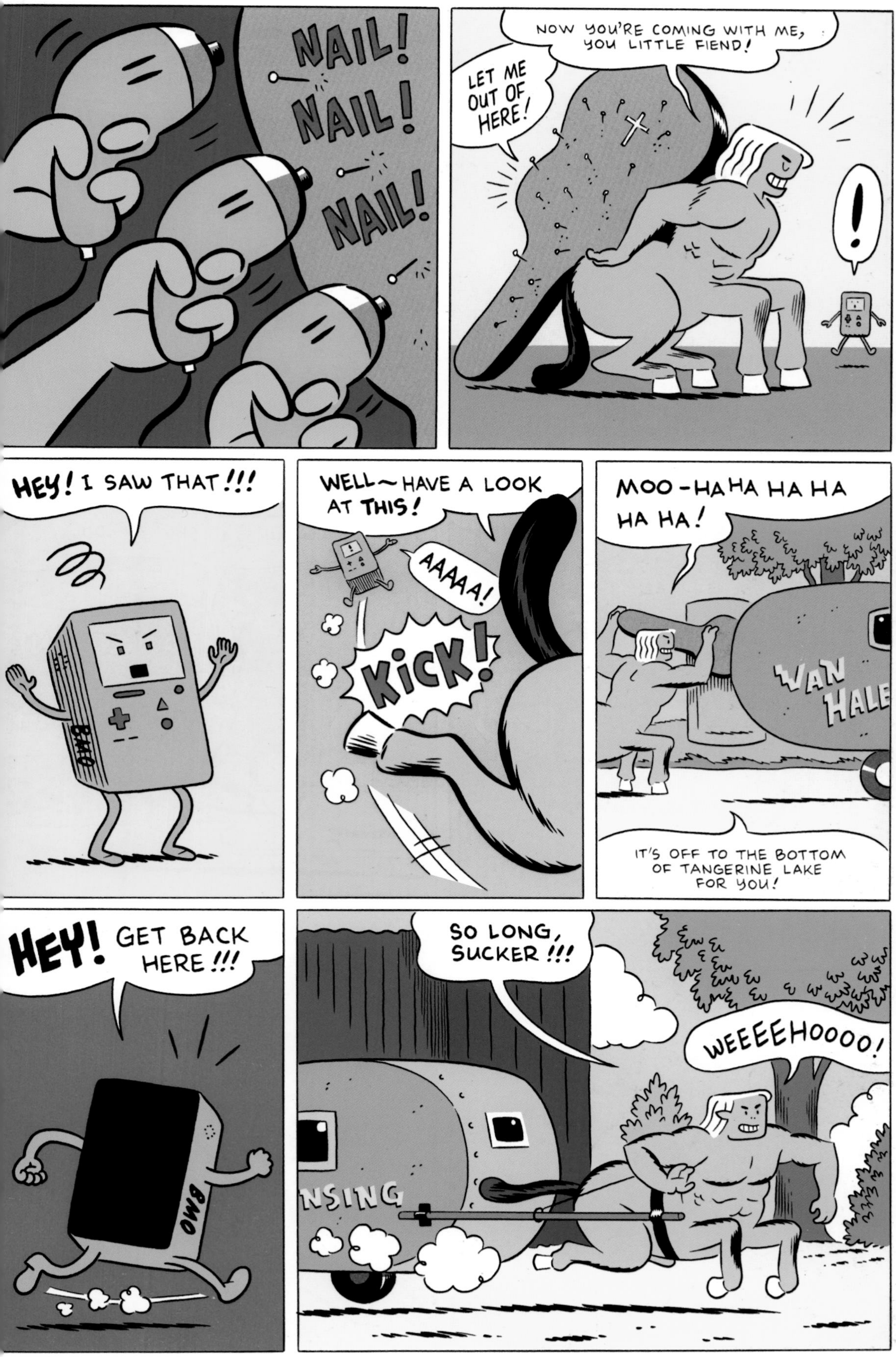
NAIL!
NAIL!
NAIL!
NOW YOU'RE COMING WITH ME, YOU LITTLE FIEND!
LET ME OUT OF HERE!
!
HEY! I SAW THAT!!!
WELL~HAVE A LOOK AT THIS!
AAAAA!
KICK!
MOO-HAHA HA HA HA HA HA!
VAN HALE
IT'S OFF TO THE BOTTOM OF TANGERINE LAKE FOR YOU!
HEY! GET BACK HERE!!!
BMO
SO LONG, SUCKER!!!
WEEEEHOOOO!
NSING

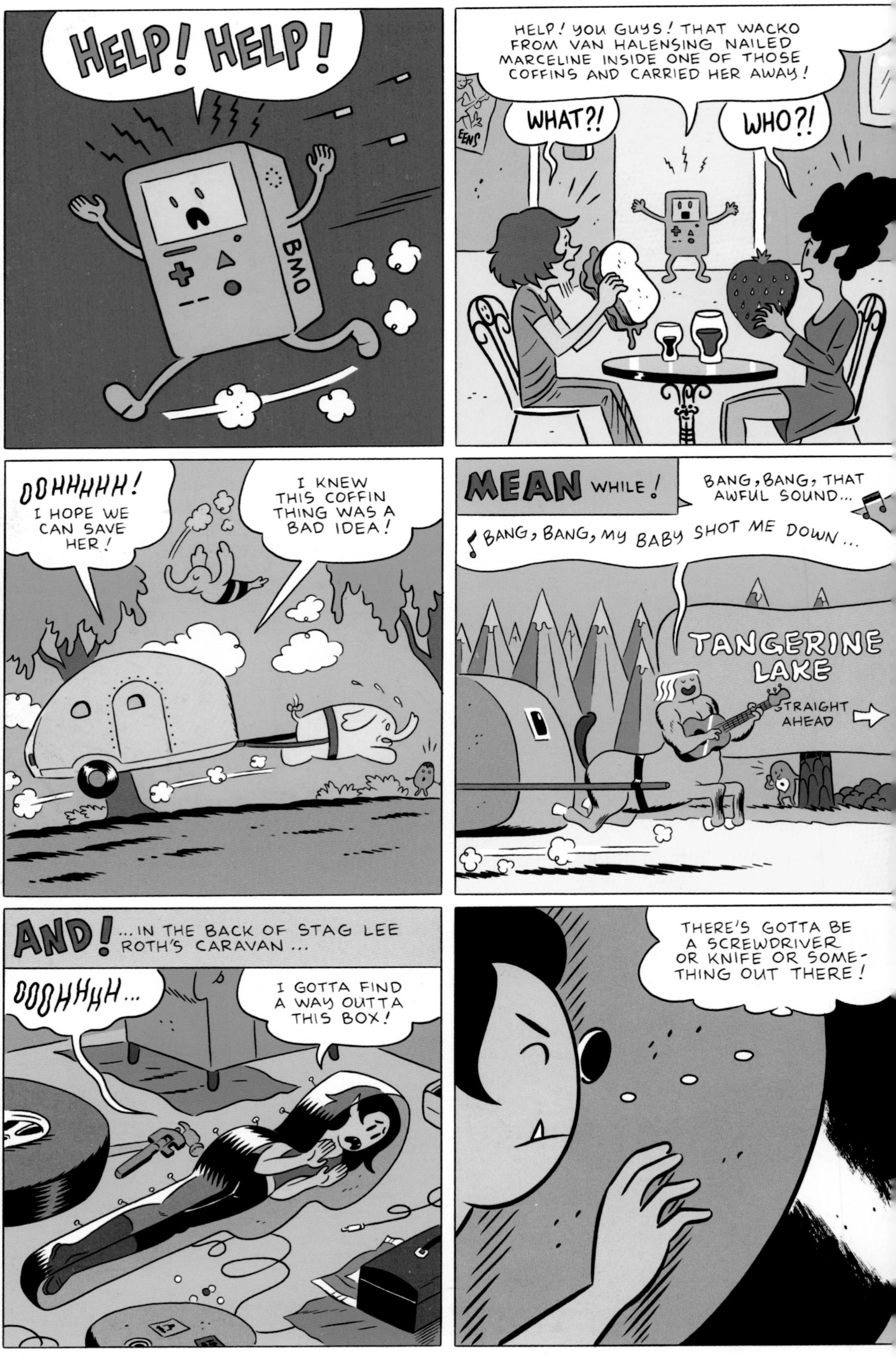
HELP! HELP!
BMO
HELP! YOU GUYS! THAT WACKO FROM VAN HALENSING NAILED MARCELINE INSIDE ONE OF THOSE COFFINS AND CARRIED HER AWAY!
WHAT?!
WHO?!
OOHHHHH! I HOPE WE CAN SAVE HER!
I KNEW THIS COFFIN THING WAS A BAD IDEA!
MEANWHILE!
BANG, BANG, THAT AWFUL SOUND...
BANG, BANG, MY BABY SHOT ME DOWN...
TANGERINE LAKE
STRAIGHT AHEAD
AND! ...IN THE BACK OF STAG LEE ROTH'S CARAVAN...
OOOHHHH...
I GOTTA FIND A WAY OUTTA THIS BOX!
THERE'S GOTTA BE A SCREWDRIVER OR KNIFE OR SOMETHING OUT THERE!

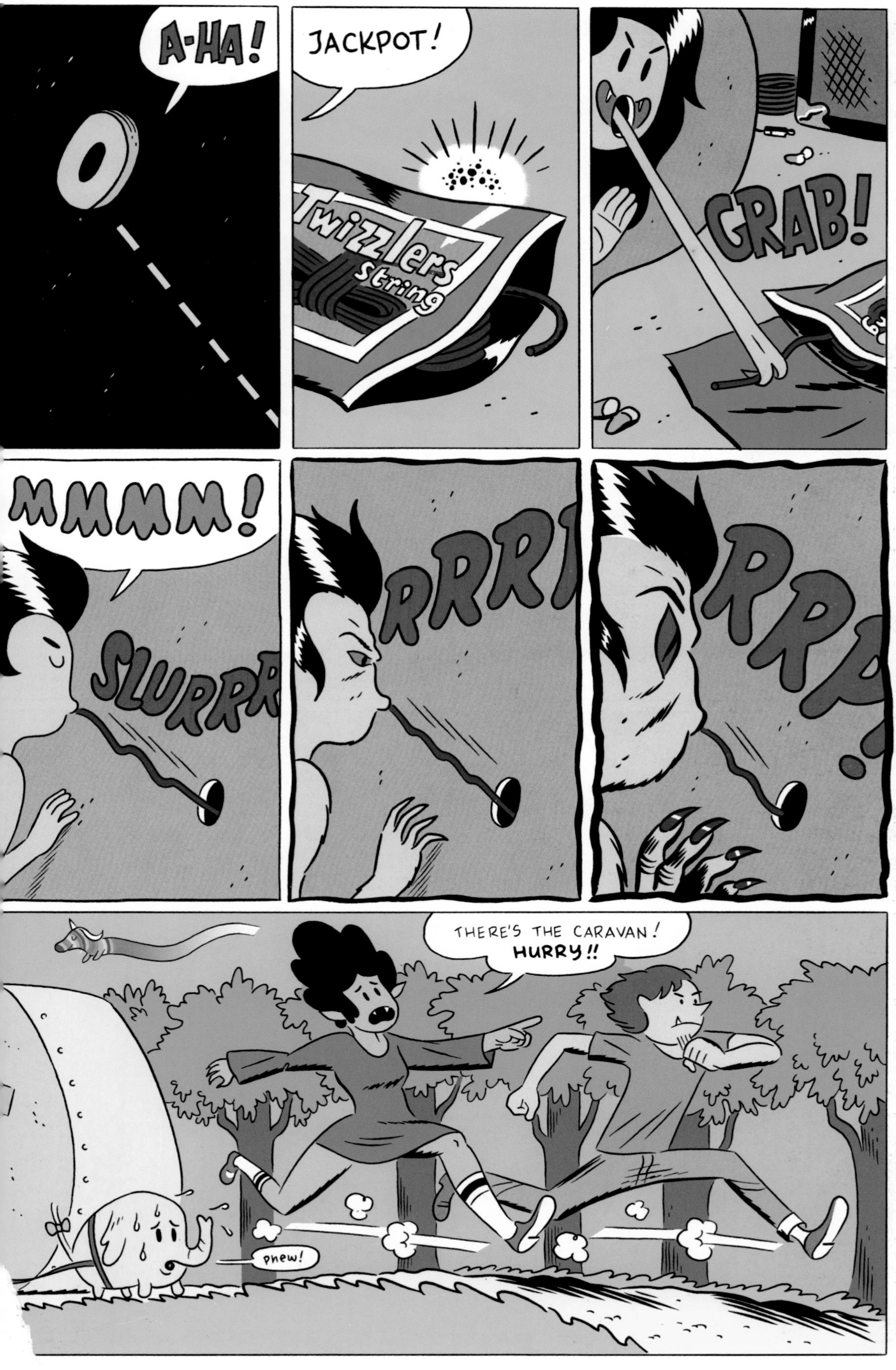

A-HA!
JACKPOT!
Twizzlers String
GRAB!
MMMM!
SLURRR
RRRR
RRRP!
THERE'S THE CARAVAN!
HURRY!!
phew!

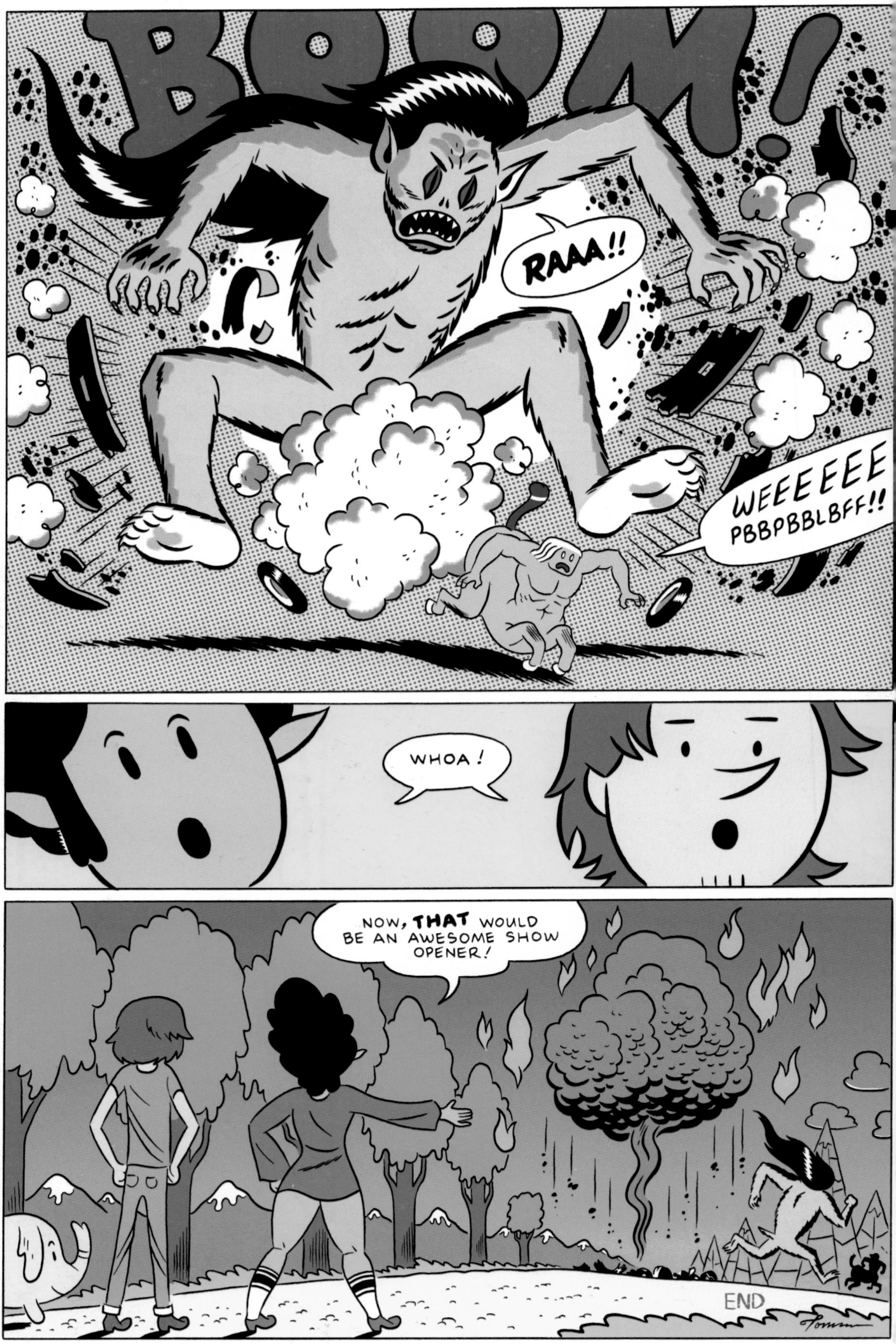
BOOM!
RAAA!!
WEEEEEEE PBBPBBLBFF!!
WHOA!
NOW, **THAT** WOULD BE AN AWESOME SHOW OPENER!
END

COVER GALLERY

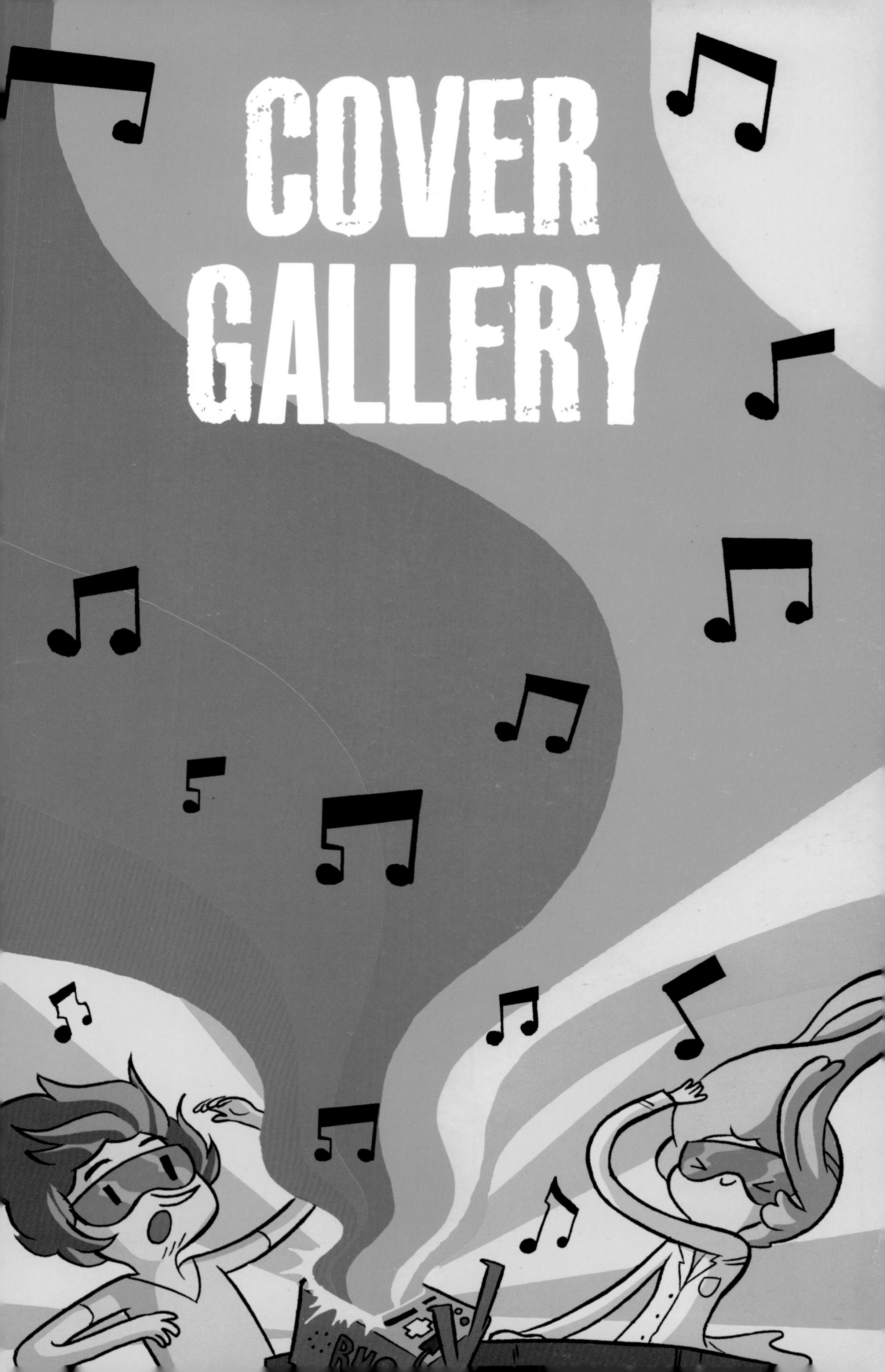

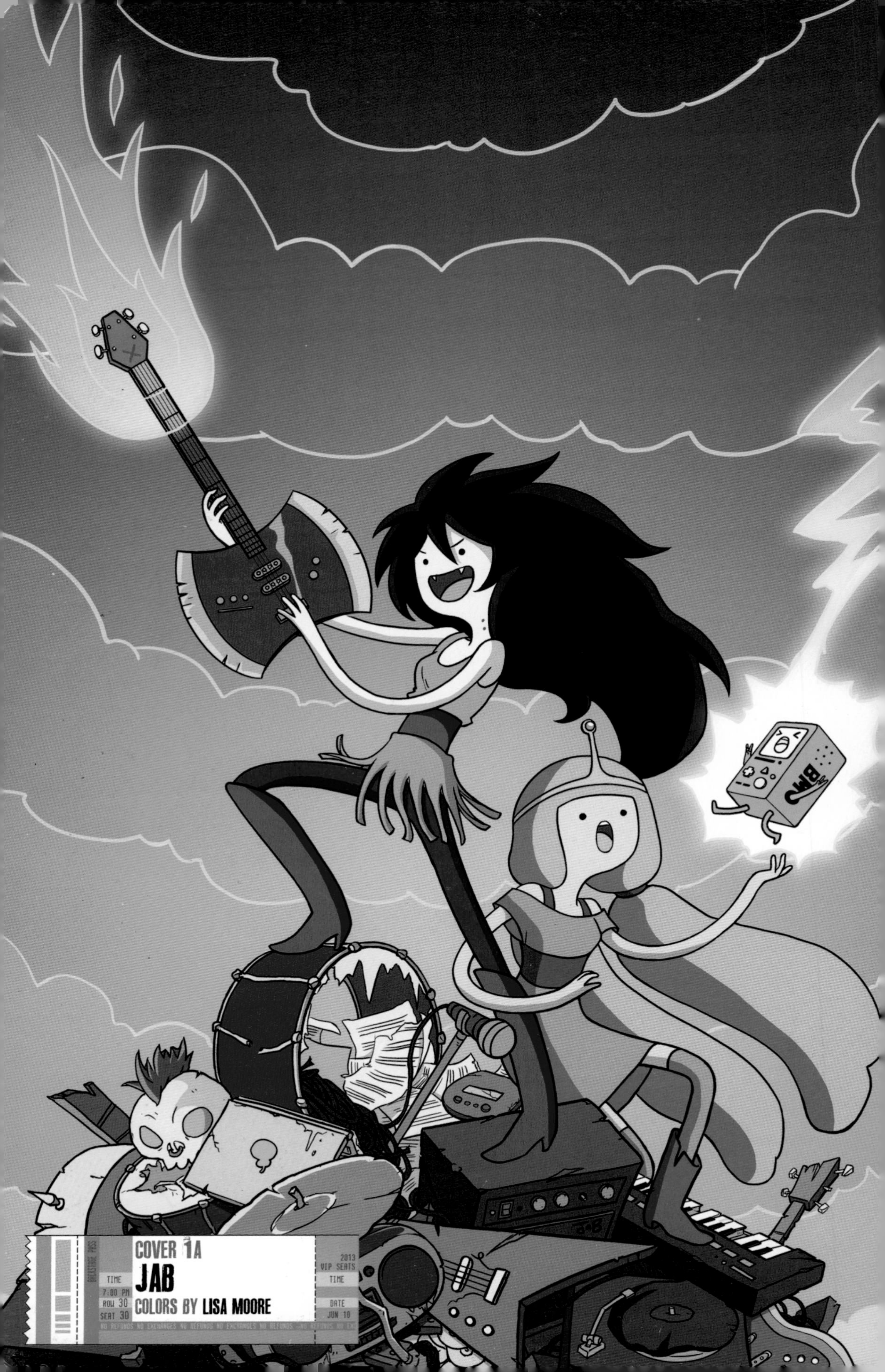
COVER 1A
JAB
COLORS BY LISA MOORE
BACKSTAGE PASS
TIME
7:00 PM
ROW 30
SEAT 30
2013
VIP SEATS
TIME
DATE
JUN 10
NO REFUNDS NO EXCHANGES NO REFUNDS NO EXCHANGES NO REFUNDS

BMO

2013
VIP SEATS
TIME
7:00 PM
ROW 30
SEAT 30

COVER 2A
JAB
COLORS BY LISA MOORE

TIME
7:00 PM
DATE
JUN 10

NO REFUNDS NO REFUNDS NO EXCHANGES NO REFUNDS NO EXCHANGES NO REFUNDS NO EXCHANG

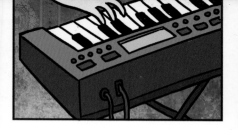

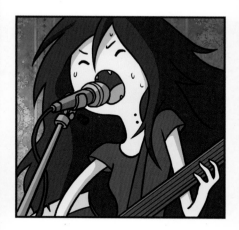

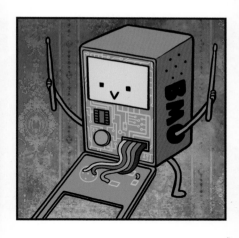

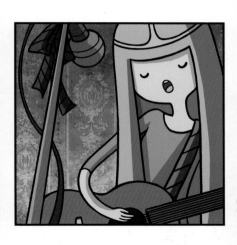

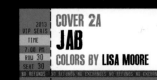

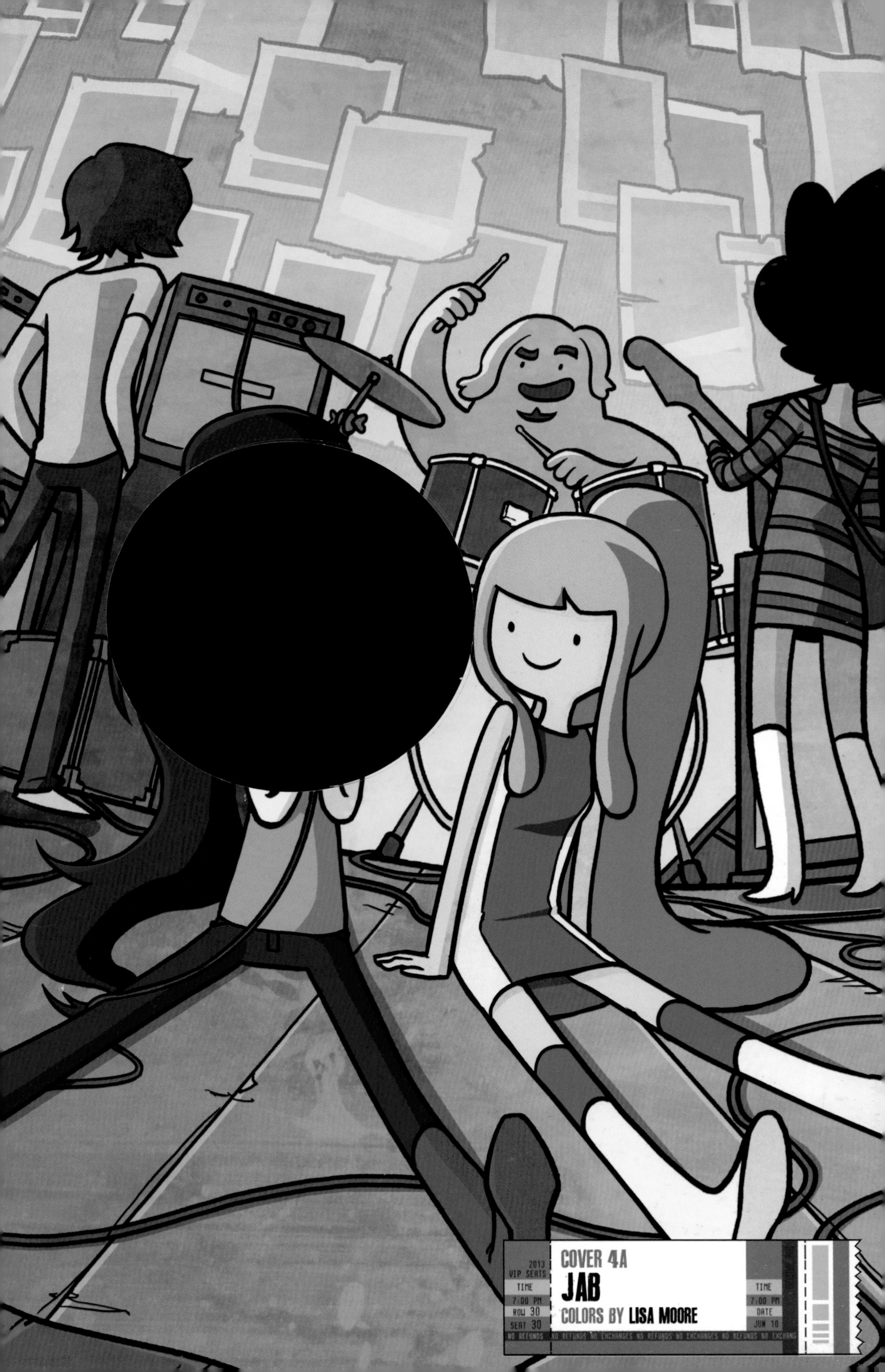
2013
VIP SEATS
TIME
7:00 PM
ROW 30
SEAT 30
COVER 4A
JAB
COLORS BY LISA MOORE
TIME
7:00 PM
DATE
JUN 10
NO REFUNDS NO REFUNDS NO EXCHANGES NO REFUNDS NO EXCHANGES NO REFUNDS NO EXCHANG

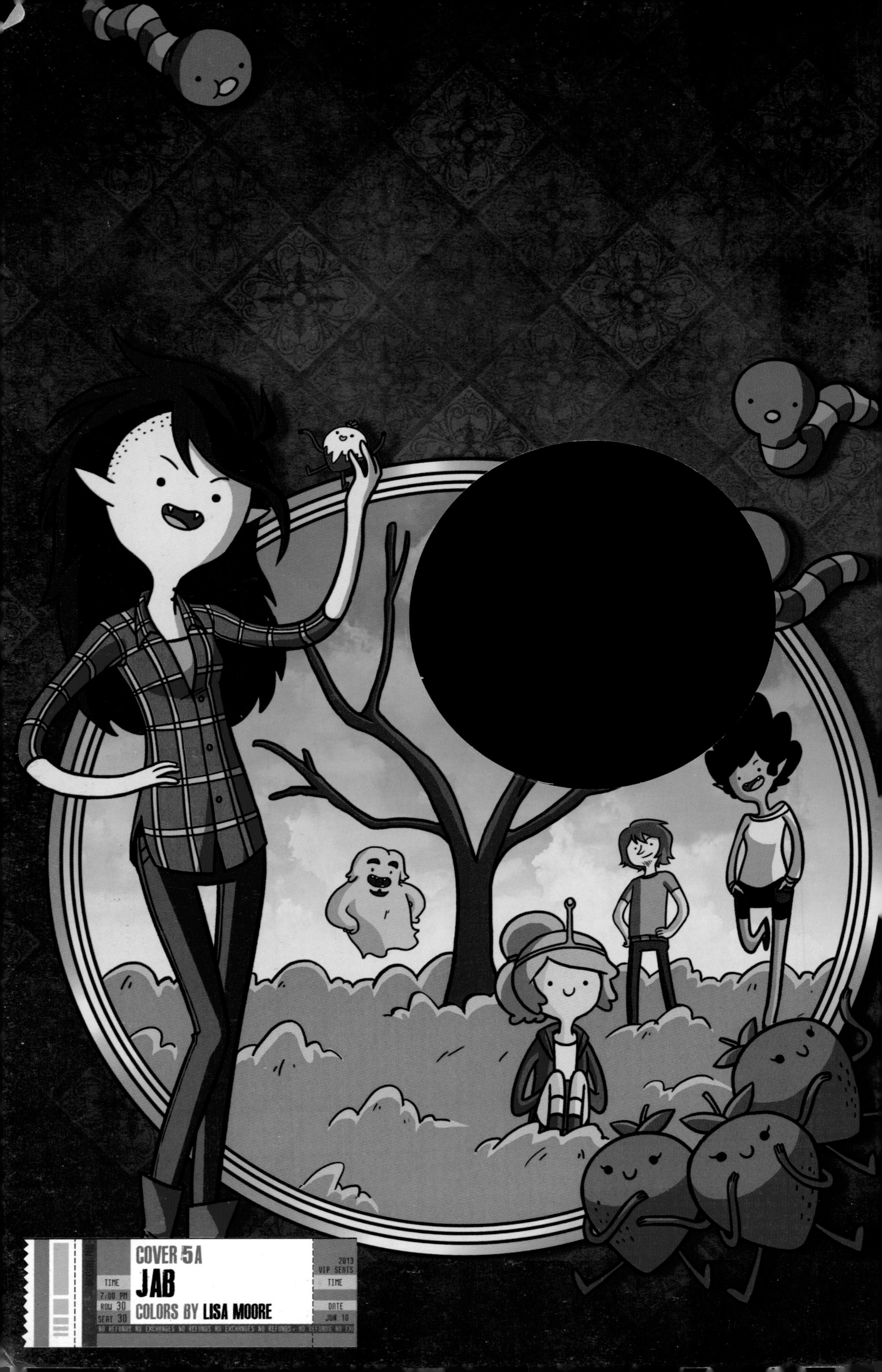
COVER 5A
JAB
COLORS BY LISA MOORE
TIME
7:00 PM
ROW 30
SEAT 30
2013
VIP SEATS
TIME
DATE
JUN 10
NO REFUNDS NO EXCHANGES NO REFUNDS NO EXCHANGES NO REFUNDS NO REFUNDS NO EX

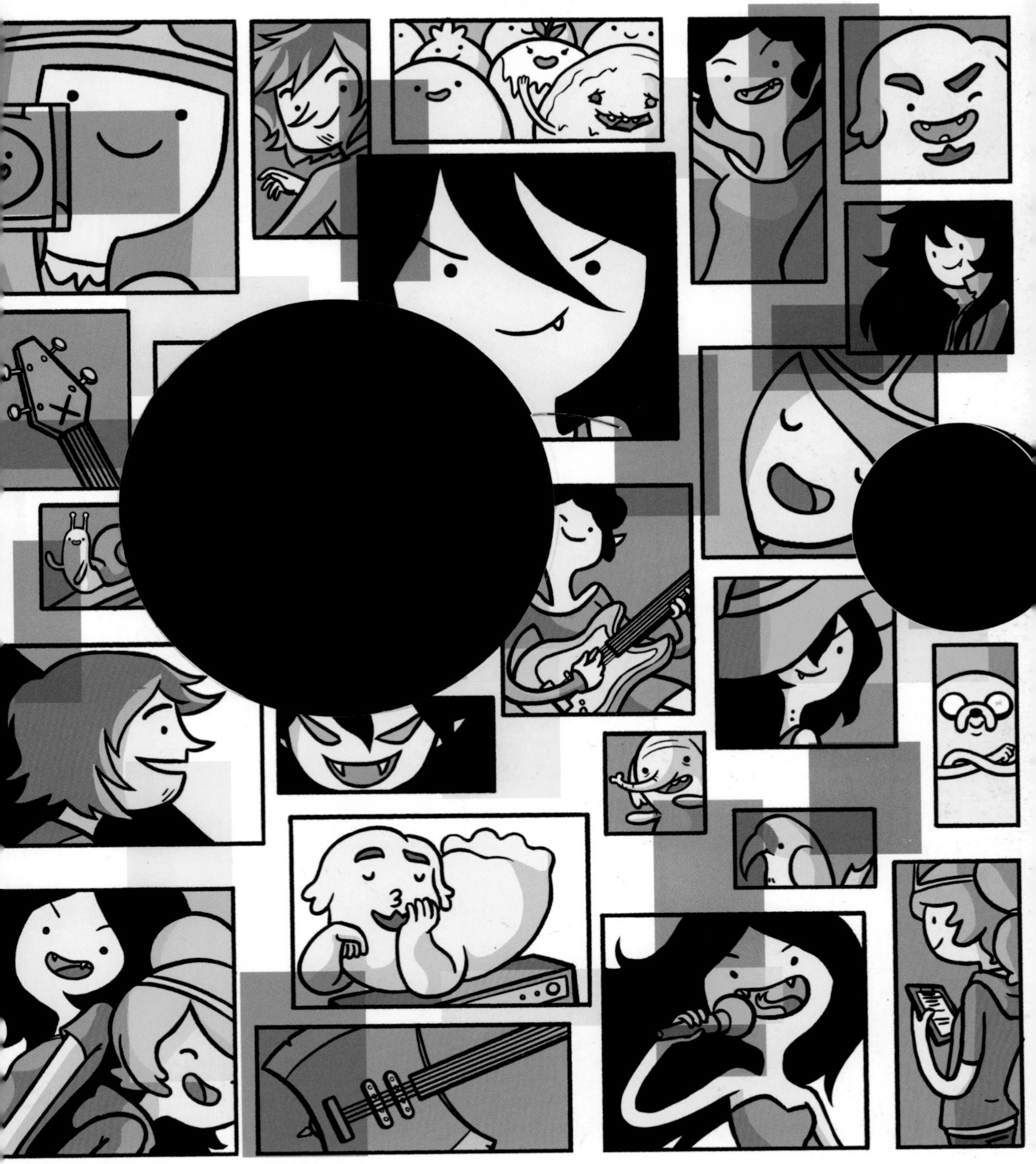

2013 VIP SEATS
TIME 7:00 PM
ROW 30
SEAT 30

COVER 6A

JAB

COLORS BY LISA MOORE

TIME 7:00 PM
DATE JUN 10

NO REFUNDS NO REFUNDS NO EXCHANGES NO REFUNDS NO EXCHANGES NO REFUNDS NO EXCHANG

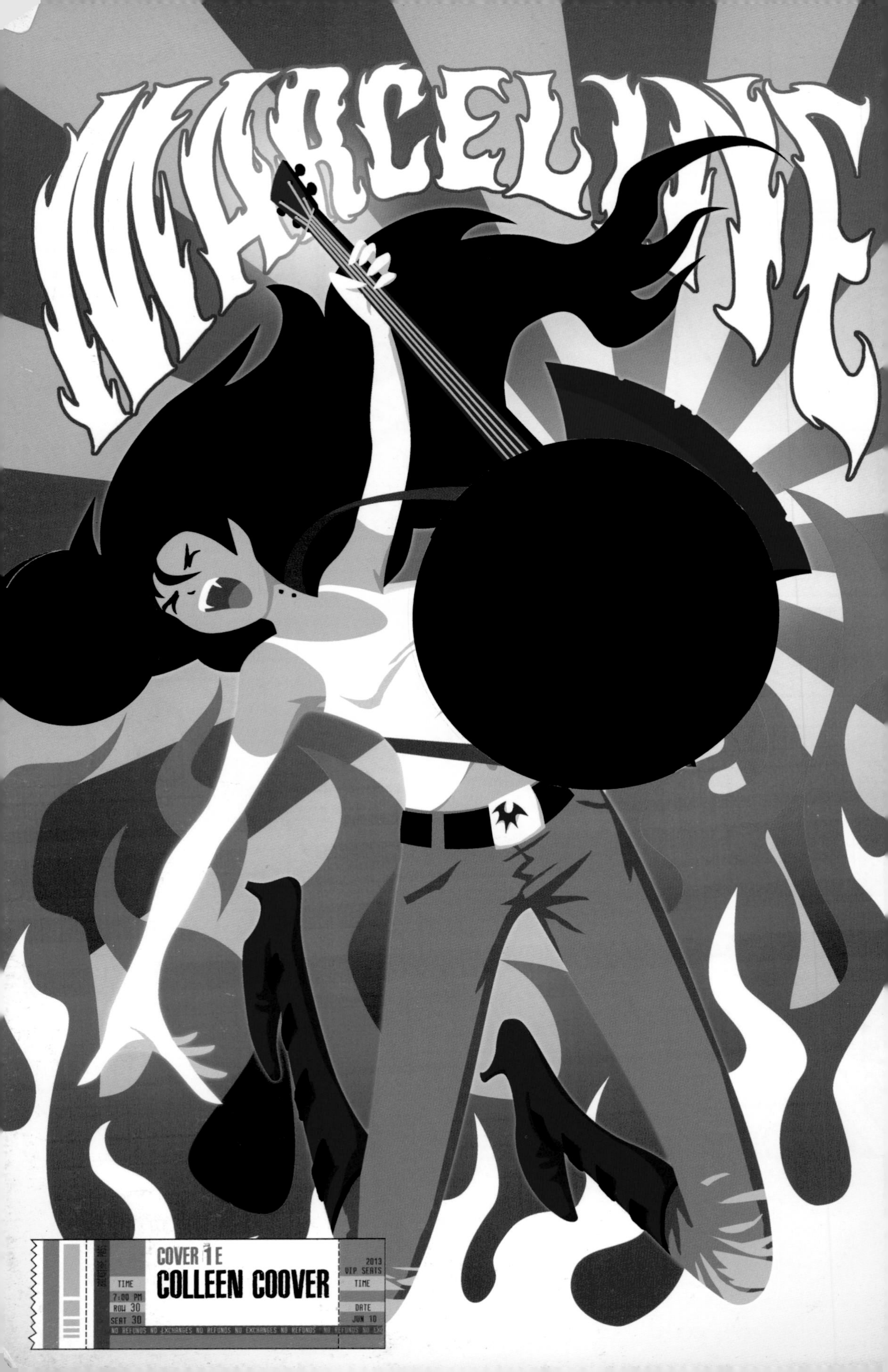
MARCELINE
COVER 1E
COLLEEN COOVER
TIME
7:00 PM
ROW 30
SEAT 30
2013
VIP SEATS
TIME
DATE
JUN 10
NO REFUNDS NO EXCHANGES NO REFUNDS NO EXCHANGES NO REFUNDS NO REFUNDS

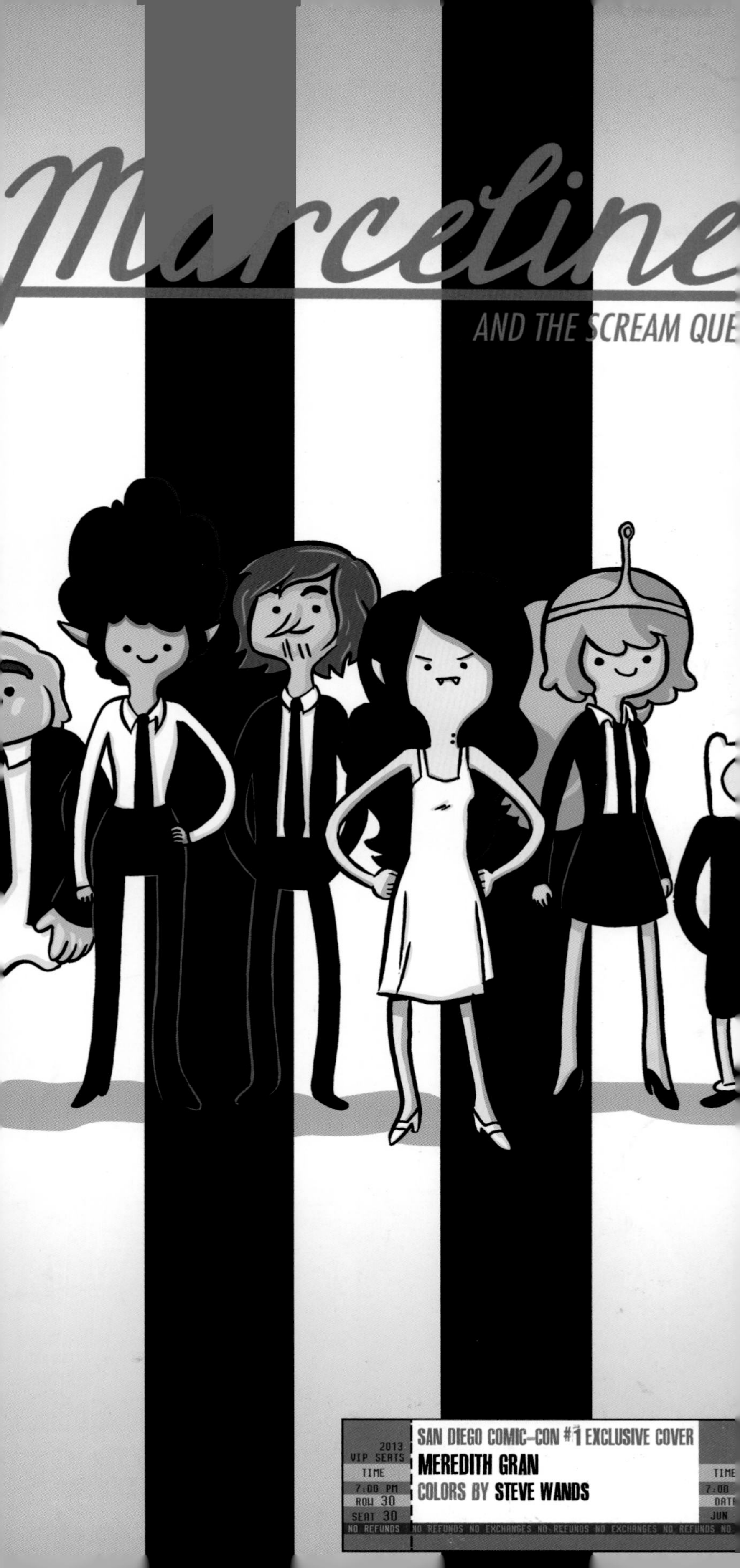
Marceline
AND THE SCREAM
2013
VIP SEATS
TIME
7:00 PM
ROW 30
SEAT 30
NO REFUNDS
SAN DIEGO COMIC-CON #1 EXCLUSIVE COVER
MEREDITH GRAN
COLORS BY STEVE WANDS
NO REFUNDS NO EXCHANGES NO REFUNDS NO EXCHANGES NO REFUNDS

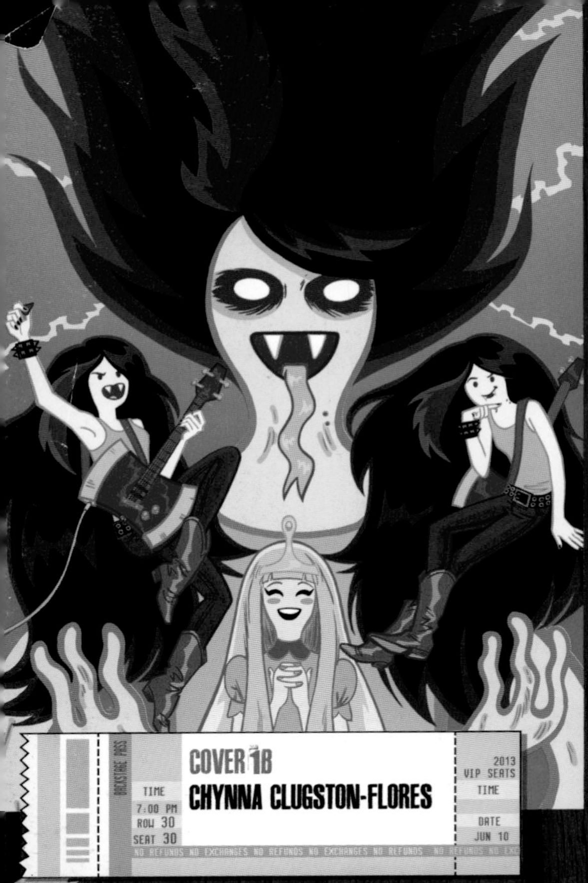
COVER 1B
CHYNNA CLUGSTON-FLORES
TIME 7:00 PM ROW 30 SEAT 30
2013 VIP SEATS TIME DATE JUN 10
NO REFUNDS NO EXCHANGES NO REFUNDS NO EXCHANGES NO REFUNDS

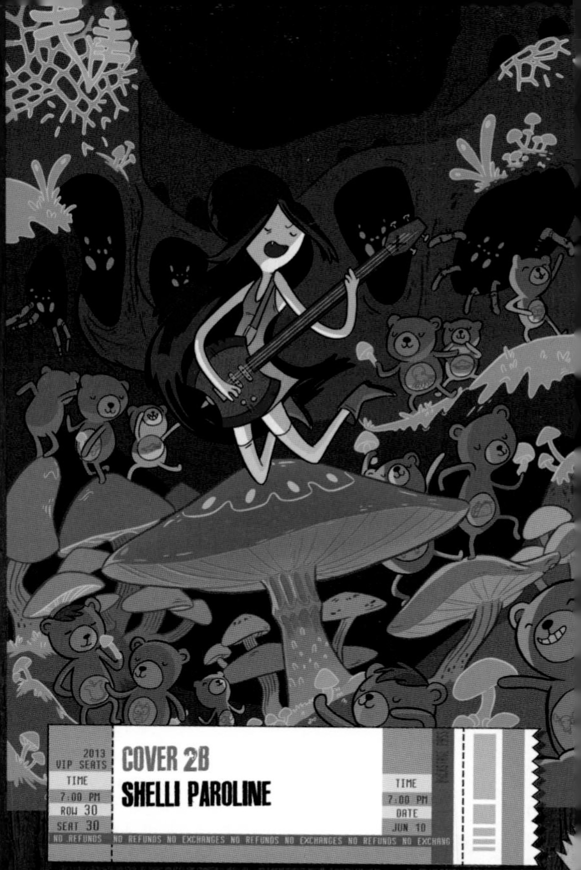
COVER 2B
SHELLI PAROLINE
2013 VIP SEATS TIME 7:00 PM ROW 30 SEAT 30
TIME 7:00 PM DATE JUN 10
NO REFUNDS NO REFUNDS NO EXCHANGES NO REFUNDS NO EXCHANGES NO REFUNDS NO EXCHANG

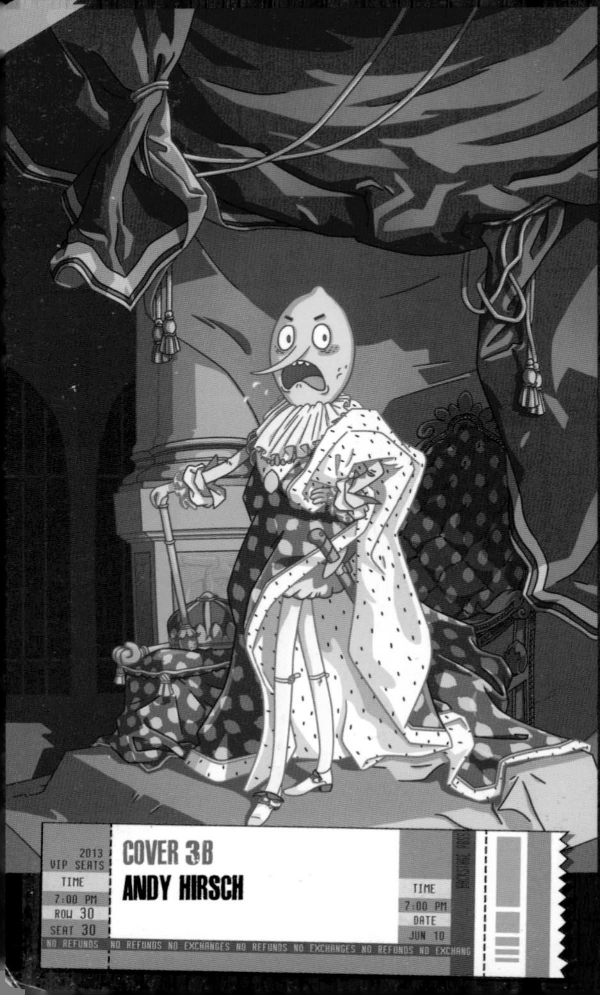
COVER 3B
ANDY HIRSCH
2013 VIP SEATS TIME 7:00 PM ROW 30 SEAT 30
TIME 7:00 PM DATE JUN 10
NO REFUNDS NO REFUNDS NO EXCHANGES NO REFUNDS NO EXCHANGES NO EXCHANG

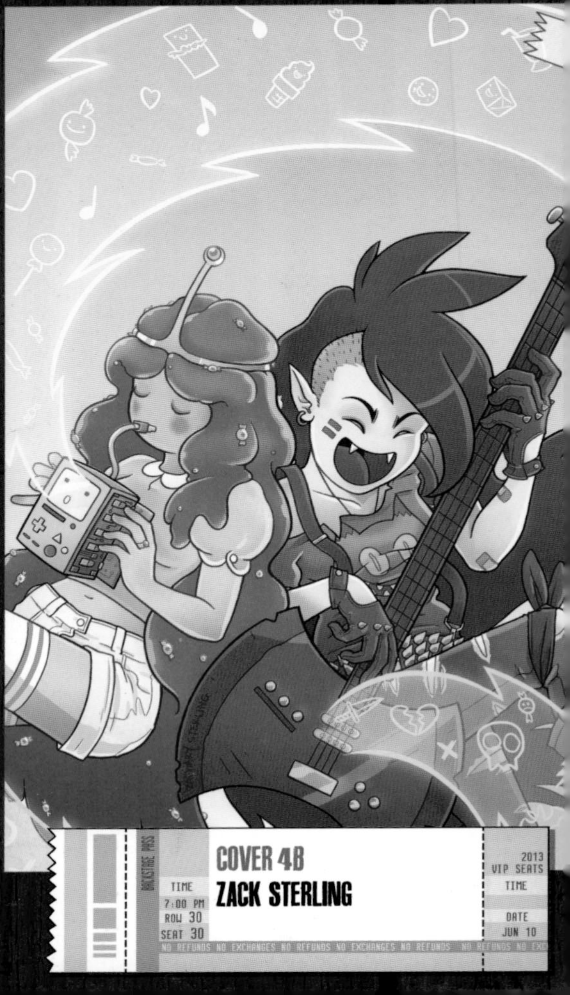
COVER 4B
ZACK STERLING
TIME 7:00 PM ROW 30 SEAT 30
2013 VIP SEATS TIME DATE JUN 10
NO REFUNDS NO EXCHANGES NO REFUNDS NO EXCHANGES NO REFUNDS NO EXCHANGES NO REFUNDS NO EX

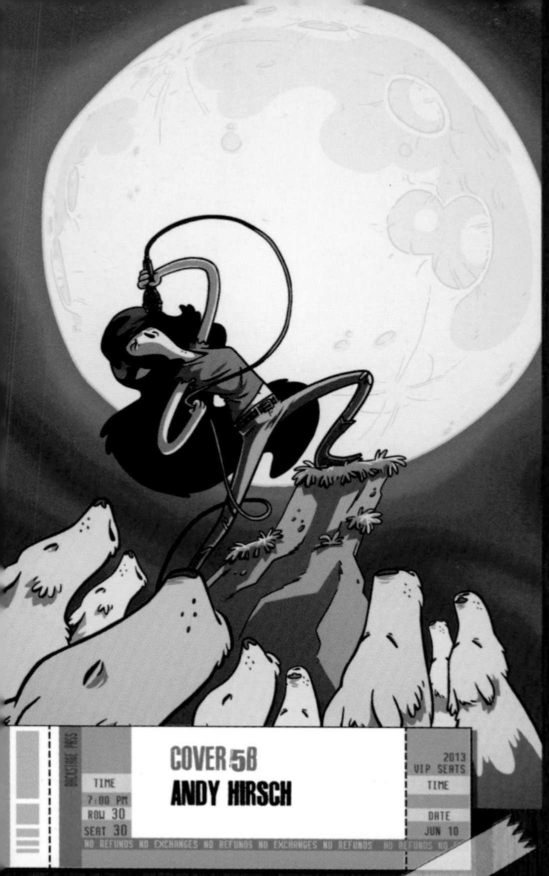
COVER 5B
ANDY HIRSCH
BACKSTAGE PASS
2013 VIP SEATS
TIME 7:00 PM
ROW 30
SEAT 30
DATE JUN 10
NO REFUNDS NO EXCHANGES NO REFUNDS NO EXCHANGES NO REFUNDS NO EXCHANGES

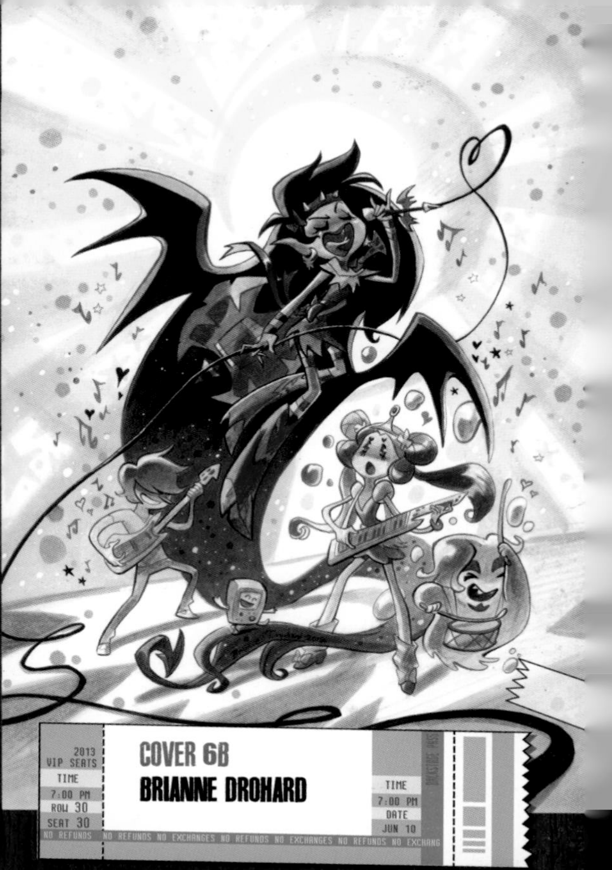
COVER 6B
BRIANNE DROHARD
2013 VIP SEATS
TIME 7:00 PM
ROW 30
SEAT 30
DATE JUN 10
BACKSTAGE PASS
NO REFUNDS NO REFUNDS NO EXCHANGES NO REFUNDS NO EXCHANGES NO REFUNDS NO EXCHANG

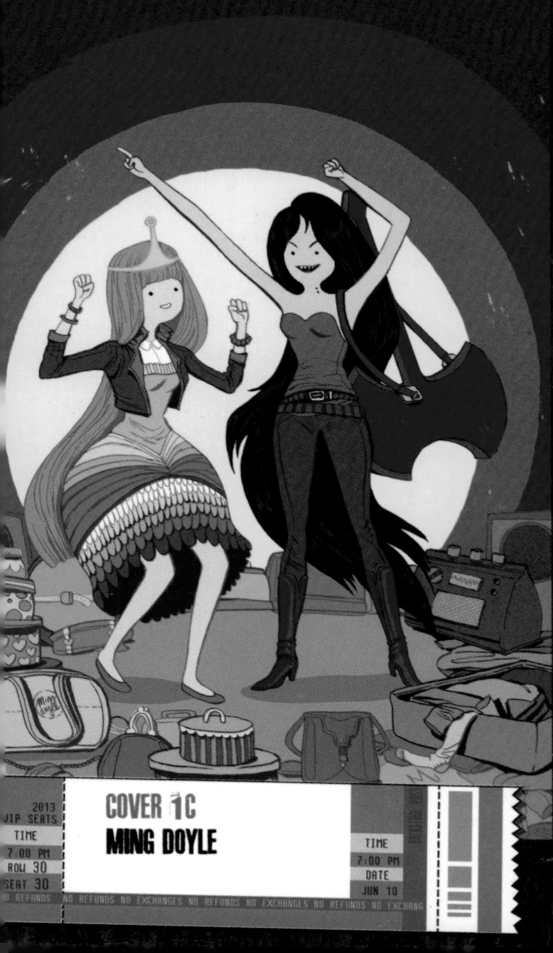
COVER 1C
MING DOYLE
2013 VIP SEATS
TIME 7:00 PM
ROW 30
SEAT 30
DATE JUN 10
BACKSTAGE PASS
NO REFUNDS NO REFUNDS NO EXCHANGES NO REFUNDS NO EXCHANGES NO REFUNDS NO EXCHANG

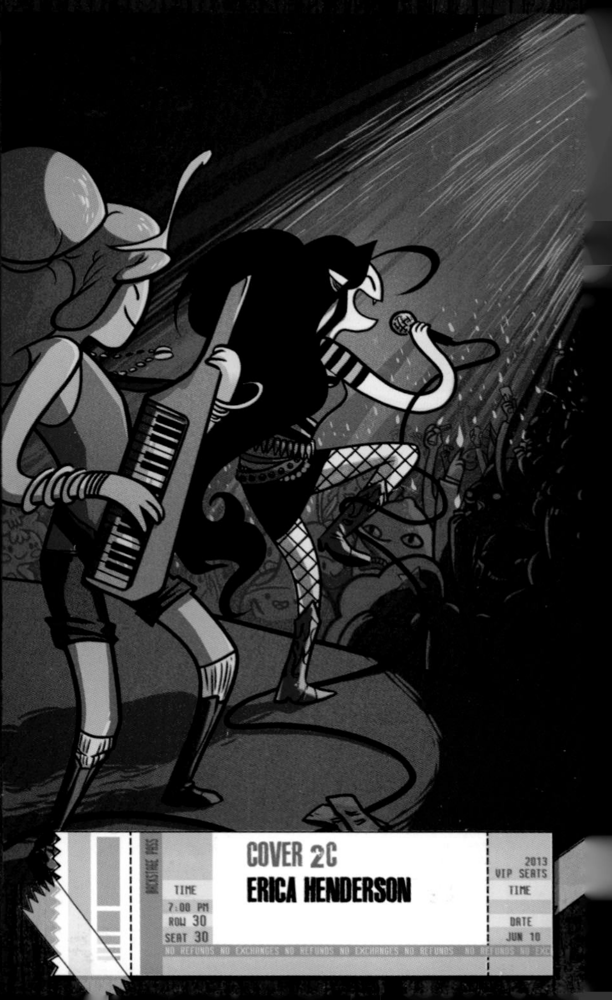
COVER 2C
ERICA HENDERSON
BACKSTAGE PASS
TIME 7:00 PM
ROW 30
SEAT 30
2013 VIP SEATS
DATE JUN 10
NO REFUNDS NO EXCHANGES NO REFUNDS NO EXCHANGES NO REFUNDS NO EXCHANGES NO REFUNDS NO EXS

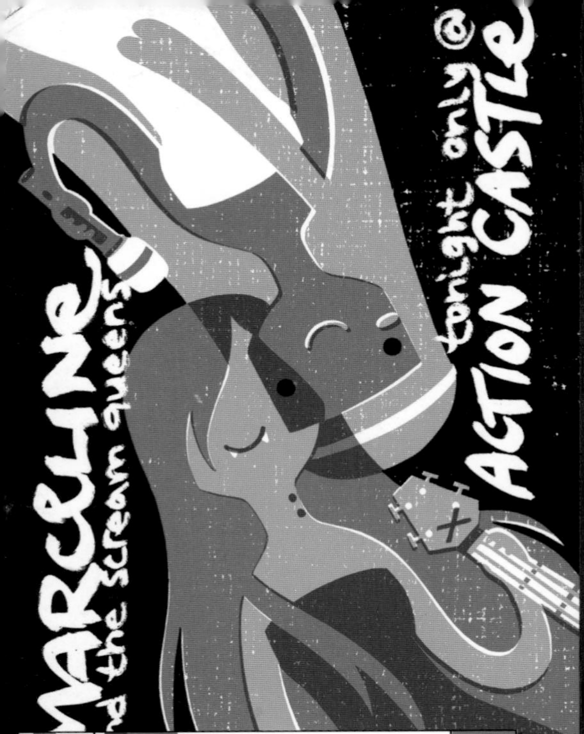
MARCELINE
nd the scream queens
tonight only @
ACTION CASTLE

BACKSTAGE PASS
COVER 3C
YUKO OTA
TIME 7:00 PM ROW 30 SEAT 30
2013 VIP SEATS TIME DATE JUN 10
NO REFUNDS NO EXCHANGES NO REFUNDS NO EXCHANGES NO REFUNDS

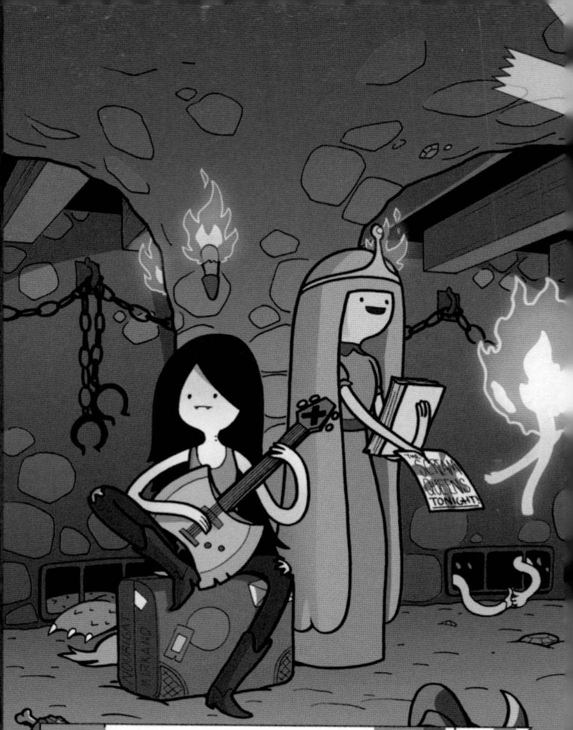
TONIGHT!

2013 VIP SEATS TIME 7:00 PM ROW 30 SEAT 30
COVER 4C
TALLY NOURIGAT
COLORS BY MIRKA ANDOLFO
TIME 7:00 PM DATE JUN 10
BACKSTAGE PASS
NO REFUNDS NO REFUNDS NO EXCHANGES NO REFUNDS NO EXCHANGES NO REFUNDS NO EXCHANGES NO REFUNDS NO EXCHANG

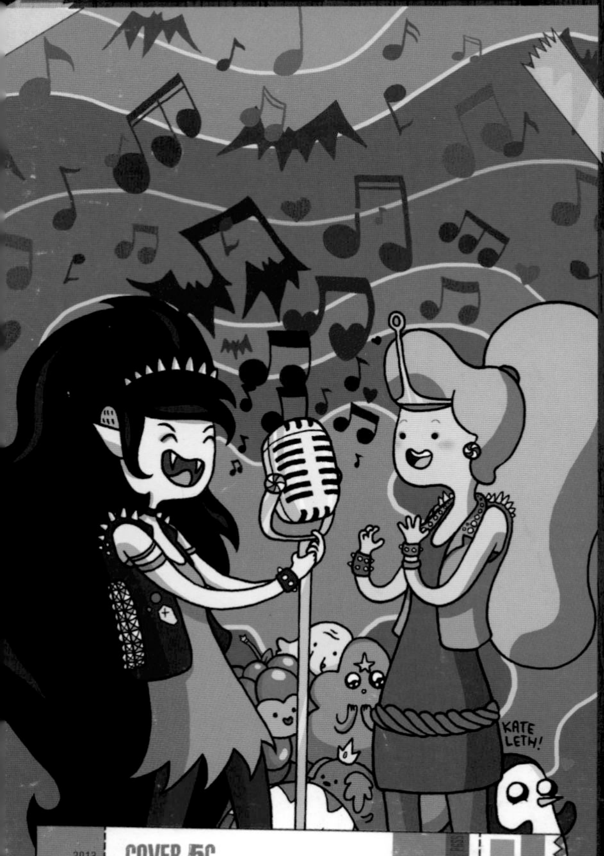
KATE LETH!

2013 VIP SEATS TIME 7:00 PM ROW 30 SEAT 30
COVER 5C
KATE LETH
TIME 7:00 PM DATE JUN 10
BACKSTAGE PASS
NO REFUNDS NO REFUNDS NO EXCHANGES NO REFUNDS NO EXCHANGES NO REFUNDS NO EXCHANG

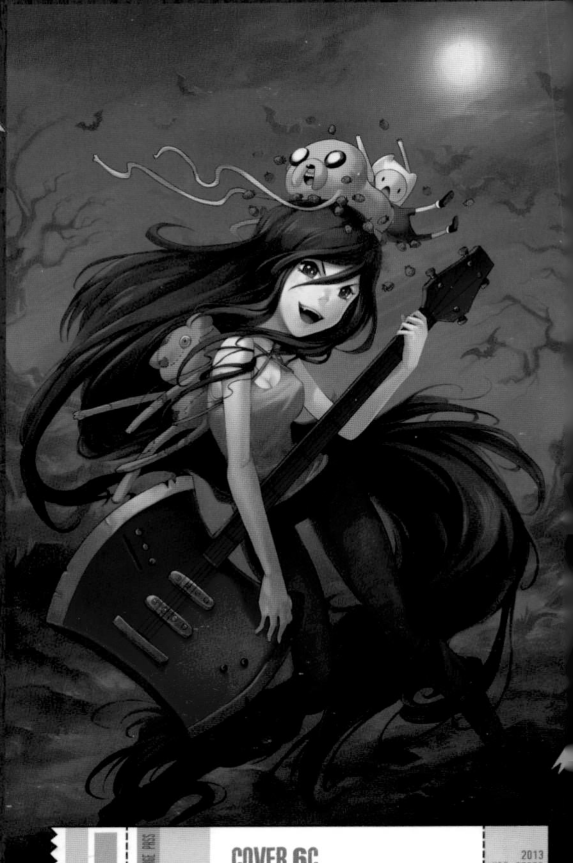

BACKSTAGE PASS
TIME 7:00 PM ROW 30 SEAT 30
COVER 6C
CAMILLA D'ERRICO
2013 VIP SEATS TIME DATE JUN 10
NO REFUNDS NO EXCHANGES NO REFUNDS NO EXCHANGES NO REFUNDS NO EXCHANGES NO REFUNDS

COVER 1D
LUCY KNISLEY

COVER 2D
JEN WANG

COVER 3D
VERA BROSGOL

COVER 4D
FAITH ERIN HICKS
WITH COLORS BY **NOREEN RANA**